T0194320

War of the Nations

The Caldwell Series

President-elect Wilson and cabinet during NIA briefing, December 1912.
American News Service wire photo

Dan Ryan

authorHOUSE®

AuthorHouse™
1663 Liberty Drive
Bloomington, IN 47403
www.authorhouse.com
Phone: 1-800-839-8640

First published by AuthorHouse   2/10/2011

ISBN: 978-1-4567-3340-7 (e)
ISBN: 978-1-4567-3341-4 (hc)
ISBN: 978-1-4567-3342-1 (sc)

Library of Congress Control Number: 2011901540

Printed in the United States of America

This book is printed on acid-free paper.

Author photo by Connie Ryan

ALSO BY DAN RYAN

Novels

Catywampus
Jigsaw
Admiral's Son General's Daughter
Admirals and Generals
Lull After the Storm
Death Before Dishonor
Calm Before the Storm

Reference

Lean Modeling for Engineers
Lean Office Practices for Architects
Robotic Simulation
CAD/CAE Descriptive Geometry
Modern Graphic Communication
Computer-aided Design
Computer-aided Architectural Graphics
Computer Programming for Graphical Displays
Principles of Automated Drafting
Technical Sketching and Computer Illustration
Computer-aided Kinetics for Machine Design
Graphical Displays for Engineering Documentation
Mini/Micro Computer Graphics
Computer-aided Graphics and Design
*Computer-aided Manufacturing (*Russian Language*)*
CAD for AutoCAD Users
Graphic Communication Manual
Computer Graphics Programming Manual
Computer Aided Graphics (Chinese Language)

Prelude

While my sons, James and Louis, were in the process of transferring from one US Navy assignment to the next, I was still at work in the White House. The Republication Party had been successful in electing its candidate, William Howard Taft. It convened to nominate a successor to my brother-in-law, Teddy Roosevelt. Teddy endorsed his secretary of war, Howard Taft. The Republican platform celebrated the Roosevelt administration's economic polices such as the keeping of the protective tariffs and establishment of a permanent currency system under the Federal Reserve. It championed enforcement of railroad rate laws, giving the Interstate Commerce Commission authority to investigate interstate railroads and reduction of work hours for railroad workers as well as general reduction in the work week.

In foreign policy, the platform supported a buildup of the armed forces, protection of American citizens abroad, extension of foreign commerce, vigorous arbitration, a revival of the US Merchant Marine, support of war veterans, self government for Cuba and the Philippines with citizenship for residents of Puerto Rico. In other areas, the platform advocated court reform, creation of a federal Bureau of Mines, creation of rural mail delivery, environmental conservation and greater efficiency in national public health agencies.

The Democrats met to celebrate their quadrennial nominating convention in Denver, Colorado, on July 7. The delegates nominated William Jennings Bryan for the third time in sixteen years. This was the first convention held in a western state. It was also the first time that women delegates attended. They were Mary Bradford of Colorado,

Elizabeth Hayward of Utah, Amanda Cook of Colorado, Harriet Hood of Wyoming and Sara Ventress of Utah. All these states allowed women to vote in state elections.

I did not attend the Democratic Nomination Convention. I thought that the special assistant to the out going president should stay close to his boss in case I was needed. When I heard that the Democrats nominated Bryan of Nebraska again, I just shook my head and looked for a landslide victory for my brother- in- law's pick, Howard Taft. Taft won in a landslide, 71% to 29%. The Republicans won 7,678,557 of the popular vote and 321 of the electoral vote, this amounted to 66 percent. The Democrats won 6,383,880 of the popular vote and 162 of the electoral vote, this amounted to 33 per cent. The remaining one per cent of the vote was shared by the Prohibition party, Socialist Party and the Independent party.

The United States Navy reported, in 1909, that it had an aeronautics division. I think the only reason that it was reported, was because England's war office had undertaken the aeroplane branch of aeronautics. Four Valkyrie bi-wing planes were added to the dirigibles housed at Barrow, England. These bi-wings were patterned after the German Valkyrie that Louis had flown out of Denmark.

We played catch-up again. We had an aviation school at Annapolis, with winter quarters in San Diego. The Curtis and Burgess-Wright hydro-planes had been flight tested on both sites. On February 17, 1909, Mr. Glen Curtis flew from North Island to the *USS Pennsylvania*, lying at anchor. He landed in the water, along side. His plane was hoisted out of the water and onto the deck of the Pennsylvania. The Pennsylvania put to sea and some time later she attempted to place the hydroplane back in the water. Mr. Curtis was supervising the operation from the deck of the Pennsylvania and survived the experiment because he was not inside the plane when it sank to the bottom.

The most common joke inside the Navy in 1909 was, "How do you sink a US Navy Hydro-plane? Answer, put it in the water!" In Glen Curtis' defense, he had merely applied the required floating apparatus to a wheeled plane. His engineers had not designed the attachments necessary to convert his machines into an effective hydro-areoplane. Within a few months, the Curtis hydro-plane was capable of alighting on and starting from either land or water. Additional modifications came within a year for a second pilot or navigator seat with dual controls which allowed the shifting of the steering tiller to either seat while in the air.

Tests were immediately begun with Burgess-Wright machines. The purpose of the tests were to see if a pilot could rise above the water from a stationary position, make a flight to and along side a ship, hoist the machine aboard, put to sea and launch again to continue a flight. Lt. John Rodgers was the first Navy flyer to accomplish this simple task. He stated that his experiments convinced him that it is impractical to launch a plane from a ship with a crane. The flight must be made directly from the deck of a vessel, either by the use of a monorail catapult or some other contrivance. When I read this report, to summarize for Teddy, I thought, my father predicted this from his college lecture during the last course that I took from him at Annapolis. How he would have loved to see Lt. Rodgers and his hydro-plane.

President Taft met with me March 4, 1909, and we agreed that the work of the Office of Naval Counter Intelligence should be expanded into a national agency so intelligence could be shared by all cabinet level secretaries in his administration. It took over a year to graduate enough agents from 'the farm' to form a world wide intelligence gathering organization. I became the first director of the National Intelligence Agency. My duties would be exactly what I had been doing for Teddy. I would keep my office in the White House and begin each working day with a security briefing for the president. My ability to read and remember data and then condense it would really be tested during the next few years.

President Taft had been Teddy's Secretary of War and his ability to organize and operate a world wide organization was legendary. He suggested, and I agreed, that the foreign capitols which had US Embassies would also serve as clearing houses for all NIA agents working within that country. Often the agent was assigned to a US Consul's office in a large city, because that city was the real 'hotspot.' NIA would operate in any hotspot within any country in the world, including the United States. Oddly enough, my first report to the President involved the city of Los Angles.

NIA's first assignment was in January to cover the first aviation meet to be held in the United States. We had agents at Dominguez Field near Los Angeles for the time it was in session. We took photographs of foreign manufactured aircraft for study of design modifications that might be used in our military aircraft.

"Good morning, Mr. President."

"Morning, James, what is on the burner today?"

"Photographs from Los Angles. I thought you might like to look at the French, German and Italian aircraft."

The first international crisis was February 20, 1910, when Boutros Ghali, the first native-born prime minister of Egypt, was assassinated. I sent additional agents to Cairo to assist our station chief in Egypt, James Caldwell, in his investigation and the arrest of the murderers.

"Good morning, Mr. President."

"Morning, James, anything from Cairo?"

"Yes, Mr. President."

On March 27, 1910, we sent covert agents into Albania to observe the uprising against the Ottoman rule.

"Good morning, Mr. President."

"Morning, James, where did we send agents?"

"Albania, Sir."

In April, the Comet Halley was close enough to see with the naked eye and many African provinces requested our assistance in the apparent invasion from space. We sent astronomers instead of agents and explained that if people lived long enough, they, or their children, might see the comet again. This seemed to help, until the earth passed through the tail of the comet on May 18th and many tiny provinces decided to band together for protection. On May 31, the Union of South Africa was created and the president sent for me.

"James, is the Union of South Africa a good thing?"

"Time will tell, Mr. President."

In June, we again had covert agents in Germany who purchased tickets to ride the Zeppelin, *Deustschland*, from Friedrichshafen to Dusseldorf, Germany. I worried that Louis' German would not hold up among the German population. He reported that he had several conversations with other passengers during the nine hour flight. The next month, July, NIA intercepted a wireless telegraph sent from the *SS Montrose*. This resulted in the identification and arrest of murderer, Dr. Hawley Crippen.

August was a busy month also, we investigated a fire at the World Exhibition in Brussels, arrests were made for arson. We sent covert agents into Korea to assist Emperor Sunjong to flee the country before Japan could arrest him. His whole family was brought back to the United States.

In October, we assisted King Manuel II of Portugal to flee to England after the overthrow of his government. During this daring escape, the first use of infrared photographs by Professor Robert Wood made NIA history. By the end of my first year as director of the NIA, it seemed the world was on a break neck pace of discovery and invention.

November: (7) first air mail flights in US, (20) Mexican Revolution,

(23) Sweden bans execution by guillotine after the death of Johan Alfred Ander that took two hours.

December: (4) first mono-wing airplane flight in Germany, (16) electric street cars in Austria-Hungary and Germany carried 6.7 million passengers, (30) Henry Ford reports 1910 sales of ten thousand model A's, (31) American Motors sells 1200 units, (31) the Wadai War continues with NIA agents in place.   By the end of 1911, it was apparent that conditions in Europe were ripe for a conflict between nations on that continent. In January the siege of Sidney Street in the east end of London was the first signal to me and I reported this to the president.

"My son, Louis, reports from London that Latvian anarchists and metropolitan police had a raging gun battle, Mr. President. London bobbies are not armed and they had to call for assistance from the Scot's Guard."

"The Guards made short work of it, of course."

"Not really, it took several days to kill all the Latvians. They fought to their deaths. No reason was ever found why the Latvians entered the country, what their demands were or why they fought to the last man."

"Why would Latvia sponsor such a thing, James?"

"My interpretation of events is that Latvia, with support from a larger nation, was encouraged to infiltrate the country in hopes of determining the reaction of England to a much larger crisis."

"Prussian influence again?"

"Since Prussia has joined the new federation of German States, their influence is clearly shown. The much larger crisis is the on going dispute over territory in the Balkans. Austria-Hungry is competing with Servia-Russia for territory and influence in the region, Mr. President."

"James, is Russia still a dominate power in the region since her defeat at the hands of Japan?"

"No, Sir. As you remember, Japan had offered to settle its interests in Manchuria and Korea at a conference with Russia and Russia refused. The Japanese launched a successful attack on Russian warships in Korea, at Inchon and in Port Arthur, China. This was followed by a land invasion of both disputed territories of Korea and Manchuria. Among other set-pieces, the Japanese astonished the European powers by destroying the entire Russian fleet at the Battle of Tsushima, a humiliating defeat for the Russians. Teddy mediated a peace agreement between Japan and Russia in the United States. But the damage to Russian 'invincibility' was noted in Berlin, Paris, London and Vienna. An attempted Russian revolt was put down by Czar Nicholas II and he began to rebuild the Russian military."

"That was five years ago, has he rebuilt?"

"Yes, NIA reports from Moscow indicate that the Czar is itching for revenge, Mr. President."

In January of 1912, I reported to the president that war had broken out over the Balkans. This time it was between Italy and Turkey. Turkey lost and was forced to hand over Libya, Rhodes and the Dodecanese islands to the Italians. Turkey's troubles were not over yet, peace with the Italians was followed by war, with no fewer than four small nations, over the possession of Balkan territories: Greece, Servia, Bulgaria and Montenegro. The intervention of the big three European powers, France, Germany, and Great Britain, brought about the end of the first Balkan War. Turkey was without the island of Crete and all of its African possessions.

Despite the re-establishment of peace in the Balkans, nothing had really been settled and tensions remained high. The numerous small nations that had found themselves under Turkish or Austro-Hungarian rule found themselves in nationalistic fervor. They united in identifying themselves as Slavic peoples, with the Slavic Russians as their ally. Russian Slavs were keen to encourage this belief that all Slavic people's protection came from Russia. What better way to rebuild and regain a degree of lost prestige? The big three powers were not without tensions of their own.

France was still smarting from the defeat by Prussia and the humiliating annexation by the newly unified Germany of the coal-rich territories of Alsace and Lorraine. The French government and military alike were united in thirsting for revenge. They looked at the aging Emperor Franz Joesf of Austria and his alliance with Kaiser Wilheim II of Germany. If they could split this alliance, then France would attack Germany using PLAN XVII. This was a war plan whose chief aim was the defeat of Germany and the restoration of Alsace and Lorraine. When a copy was stolen by NIA agents and sent to Washington, the plan was fatally flawed, it relied on an untenable extent upon the "elan" which was believed to form an integral part of the French army. The elan was an elite force that would sweep over its enemies in iron clad, mechanized troop carriers.

Germany, the second member of the big three was unsettled socially and militarily. The 1912 Reichstag elections had resulted in no less than 110 socialist deputies, making Chancellor Bethmann-Hollweg's task in liaising between the Reichstag and the autocratic Wilheim next to impossible. Bethmann-Hollweg became despondent and came to believe that Germany's only hope of avoiding civil unrest, lay in war. He wanted a short, sharp war, although he did not rule out a European-wide conflict if it resolved Germany's social and political woes.

NIA reports coming out of Berlin and Vienna confirmed that the Austro-Hungarian government was weighing its options with regard to Servia. Berlin had Austria, what has been commonly referred to as a blank check, an unconditional guarantee of support for Austria whatever she decided.

Germany's military unsettlement arose in the sense that Kaiser Wilheim II was finding himself largely frustrated in his desire to carve out a grand imperial role for Germany. While he desired 'a place in the sun', he found that all of the bright spots had already been snapped up by the other colonial powers, leaving him only with 'a place in the shade.' A report from Berlin indicated that the Kaiser was not keen on a grand war that involved all of Europe. "He fails to see the consequences of his military posturing. His determination to construct both land and naval forces equal to those of France and Britain will certainly bring an equal response from London and Paris."

His government and his military commanders did anticipate what was to come. A German plan to take on both France and Russia, on two fronts, had long been expected and taken into account. A copy of the *Schliefren Plan* arrived in Washington. Army chief of staff, Alfred Von Schliefren had carefully crafted a two-front war plan. The plan was to attack France first to knock her out of the war, on a western front, within five weeks before Russia could mobilize for war on the eastern front. The plan took no account of Britain's entry into the war, why would it? King George V of England was the German Kaiser's uncle and via his wife's sister, uncle of the Russian Czar as well.

In Britain, our NIA agents in London referred to the British policy as 'splendid isolation'. "It seems as though Britain was asleep until Kaiser Wilheim II took control of Germany. The dismissal of Bismark was a shock to the war office and coupled with Germany's colonial efforts in the Pacific and Africa, England began to awaken from its isolation policy. She agreed to a military alliance with Japan, aimed at limiting German colonial gains in the east."

Additional reports from my son, Louis, station chief in London, confirmed that the war office was beginning to respond to the German naval minister, Tirpitz', massive construction of a naval fleet the equal of Britain's. "England has begun a 14 month shipbuilding effort while her diplomatic core are signing alliances with France, Belgium and Russia. The stage is set."

By November, 1912, Russia, humiliated again by its inability to support Servia during the Bosnian crisis of 1908, or the first Balkan War, announced a major reconstruction of its military. In reaction to the Russian move, German Foreign Secretary Gottlieb Von Jagow told the Reichstag, that, "If Austria is forced, for whatever reason, to fight for its position as a European power, then we must stand by her." As a result, British Foreign Secretary Sir Edward Grey, responded by warning Prince Karl Lichnowsky, the German Ambassador in London, that if Germany offered Austria assistance in another Balkan War, then the consequences of such a policy would be incalculable."

With the recent Russian announcement and the British diplomatic communications, the possibility of war was a prime topic at the German Imperial War Council of December 8, 1912. The council met in Berlin on short notice by the Kaiser. Attending the Kaiser's council meeting were the following: Admiral Alfred Von Tirpitz (naval secretary), Admiral Georg Alexander Von Muller (chief of naval operations), General Von Moltke (army chief of staff), Admiral Von Heeringen (navy chief of staff), and General Moriz Von Lyncker (chief of Imperial Military cabinet). Oddly enough, Chancellor Theobald Von Bethmann-Hollweg was not invited.

After a long discussion, an agreement was made. Austria would be encouraged to attack Servia that December before the Russian buildup was completed. If Russia came to the aid of Servia, then Germany would declare war on Russia and end the military buildup, once and for all.

I was completing another year as director of the NIA when the Republicans held their nominating convention. This year the delegates to the convention could be elected in the presidential preference primaries to be held in some of the forty-eight states. Primary elections were advocated by the progressive faction in the Republican party, which wanted to break the control of political parties by bosses. Fourteen states held Republican primaries, Robert LaFollette, won two of the first four primaries (North Dakota and Wisconsin) and Taft won the other two. Teddy came in second in all four primaries. He came storming back, winning nine of the last ten primaries. As a sign of Teddy's popularity, he even won Taft's home state, Ohio.

The convention was held in Chicago from June 18 to June 22. The delegates began to assembly from across the country. Those elected in the primaries took their places and those from the party organizations were seated next. It was apparent that these delegates were solidly for a second term for President Taft. When Teddy saw this, he objected to those seated from southern states. These states had voted solidly for Democrats since the time of Jefferson and they would lose these states in the general election, unless he was the Republican candidate for president. He had carried these states in his election of 1904. Not since the 1872 election had there been such a major schism in the Republican party. Roosevelt asked his supporters to leave the convention and form the Progressive Party.

The Progressive Party held its own separate convention in Chicago. They nominated Teddy and Hiram Johnson of California as his running mate. When questioned by reporters, Teddy said he felt as strong as a "bull moose". The name stuck and everyone was talking about the "BULL MOOSE" party. Unfortunately, the two factions ran a bitter campaign against each other and ignored the Democrats. Teddy was quick to point out that Taft and Sherman were inexperienced in time of administration. Sherman was the first Vice President to be re-nominated since John C. Calhoun in 1828. He reminded voters that Republicans had also been progressive since the formation of the party and its first candidate, John Fremonte. He had posters made which showed the elections since Lincoln to his own in 1904. The election of Howard Taft was omitted from the bottom line, reminding voters that he was hand picked by Teddy as his replacement. The 1912 presidential campaign was among three strong candidates; Roosevelt, Taft and Wilson. Vice President Sherman died in office on October 30, 1912, leaving Taft without a running mate. With the Republican vote split, Woodrow Wilson captured the presidency handily on November 5th. Roosevelt was to the left of Wilson on many issues and had he not been in the race, Taft might have won. An assassination attempt was made on the life of Roosevelt during the campaign. On October 14th, while campaigning in Milwaukee, Wisconsin, a saloon keeper, named John Schrank, shot him with a pistol. The bullet barely penetrated his skin because it passed through his steel eyeglasses case and a 50-page double folded copy of the speech he was carrying in his breast pocket of his suit.

Teddy continued to conduct a vigorous national campaign for the Progressive Party, denouncing the way the Republican nomination had been stolen from him. He bundled together his reforms under the rubric of "The New Nationalism." He stumped the country for a strong federal role in regulating the economy, and especially watching and chastising bad corporations. Wilson happened to support a policy he called "The New Freedom." This policy was mostly based on individual and local government instead of a controlling federal government. Taft, knowing he would finish third or even fourth in the race behind the Socialist Party candidate, Eugene Debs, campaigned quietly and spoke of the need for judges to be more powerful than elected officials.

Teddy's strong second place finish in the race resulted in the only instance in the 20th century of a third party candidate receiving more votes than one of the major party candidates. Although he failed to become chief executive for a third time, he succeeded in his vendetta against Taft, who received just 23% of the popular vote. Taft won only 8 electoral votes, the worst showing ever made by a sitting president.

By December 5, 1912, I had decided not to serve another president, even if he was a democrat! I was fifty-seven years old and it was time to enjoy my life and my family. It was then that President-elect Wilson asked me to brief his incoming cabinet on the NIA activities under President Taft and to continue in that roll, after all, I was the lone democrat serving in the Taft Administration.

1

Inauguration Day

March 4, 1913

President Wilson and Vice-president Marshall were inaugurated on March 4, 1913. I estimated that over half a million people were gathered in Washington to witness the inauguration ceremonies. The inaugural parade included some 30,000 men and women, underlining the women's right to vote. Notable in the parade were the representatives from Princeton University and the State of New Jersey where Thomas Woodward Wilson had been governor.

I was in the Senate chamber, because Mr. Marshall had invited me and Emily to attend his inauguration. As is the custom, the Vice-president is sworn in before the President in front of both houses of congress, the Supreme Court members, and invited guests. The oath of office was administered by Senator Gallinger, president pro tempore of the Senate, and immediately the Sixty-second Congress adjourned and the Sixty-third assembled.

As president of the Senate, Mr. Marshall made a somewhat unusual address. It was earnest and original, here is what I remember of his address.

"Members of the Senate and House of Representatives you may be seated. It has been twelve years since the members of the President's cabinet have changed. President McKinley's original members were retained by President's Roosevelt and Taft. As I introduce the cabinet members that President Wilson

1

has asked to serve, and that you have approved, would they please rise and leave the chamber and take their places on the grandstand at the east wing of the capitol."

"Department of State. Secretary Bryan, Counselors Moore, and Folk, Assistants Osborne and Adee, Consular Hengstler, Chiefs Smith, Miller, Long and Putney. Department of the Treasury. Secretary McAdoo, Assistants Hamlin, Newton, Chiefs Flynn, Kimball, Parker, Burke, Osborn, and Roberts. Department of War. Secretary Garrison, Assistant Breckinridge and Generals Wood, Weaver, Mills, Andrews, Garlington, Crowder, Aleshire, Torney, Kingman, Crozier, Scriven, McIntyre and Black. Department of Justice. Attorney-General James Clark McReynolds and his assistants. Post Office. Post-master General Albert Sidney Burleson and his assistants. Department of the Navy. Secretary Josephus Daniels, under secretary Franklin Roosevelt, Admiral of the Navy George Dewey, and Chief of Naval Intelligence, Admiral Rodney Lowe. Department of the Interior. Secretary Franklin Lane. Department of Commerce. Secretary William Redfield. Department of Labor. Secretary William Wilson, and National Intelligence Agency. Director James Caldwell."

I did not stand. Emily elbowed me in the ribs and said, "Mister Director, I think your father's old job just got promoted to cabinet level. Stand up and walk to the east wing. I will meet you on the stand."

I reached over and raised Emily to her feet and we walked together towards the east wing where a grandstand to hold 10,000 persons had been built.

"The Vice-president introduced the undersecretary of the navy, Franklin Roosevelt. Is he related to Teddy?"

"Yes, the Roosevelts are an old money family, they intermarry."

"They what? Oh, James, you are kidding me, again."

"Not at all. Franklin's parents were distant cousins. James Roosevelt married Sara Delano Roosevelt to keep the money in the family. Franklin married his cousin Eleanor Roosevelt, the niece of Teddy."

"Do they have any children? Are they normal?"

"Franklin is thirty something, I think he was born in 1882. He attended Groton and then Harvard ('04), I think. He married his wife in '05 and they have four or five children. A girl named Anna Eleanor and the rest boys. They all seem normal."

"When did he begin his political career?"

"He was elected in 1910 to the New York State Senate. He worked in

Wilson's campaign and he was rewarded with his present position. We will see how he likes working at the federal level." We took a seat very near the back, being one of the last to leave the Senate Chamber.

We did not hear the rest of the Vice-president's address but shortly President Taft and President-elect Wilson appeared on the grandstand and were greeted with prolonged applause as the remainder of the Senate Chamber filed onto the grandstand. The oath was administered by Chief Justice White and Dr. Wilson's inaugural address began.

"There has been a change of government. It began two years ago. The House of Representatives and the Senate became Democratic by a decisive majority. The office of President has now been placed in my hands. What is the question that is uppermost in our minds today? That is the question I am going to try to answer, in order, if I may, to interpret the occasion."

"It means much more than the success of a party. The success of a party means little except when the Nation is using that party for a large and definite purpose. No one can mistake the purpose for which the Nation now seeks to use the Democratic party. It seeks to use it to interpret a change in its own plans and point of view. Some old things with which we had grown familiar and which had begun to creep into the very habit of our thought and of our lives have altered their aspect. We now look critically upon them with fresh, awakened eyes. They have dropped their disguises and shown themselves alien and sinister. Some new things, as we look frankly upon them, have come to assume the aspect of things long believed in and familiar. We have been refreshed by a new insight into our own life."

"We see in many ways that life is great. It is incomparably great in its material aspects. It is great in its body of wealth. It is great in the diversity and sweep of its energy. It is great in the industries which have been conceived and built up by the genius of individual men and the limitless enterprise of groups of men and women. It is great also, very great, in its moral force. Nowhere else in the world have noble men and women exhibited in more striking forms the beauty and the energy of sympathy, helpfulness and counsel in their efforts to rectify wrong. They excel in their efforts to alleviate suffering, and set the weak in the way of strength and hope. We have built up a great system of government. This system has stood through a long age as a model for those who seek to set liberty upon foundations that will endure against fortuitous change, against storm and accident. Our life contains every great thing and contains it in rich abundance."

"But evil has come with the good, and fine gold has been corroded.

With riches has come inexcusable waste. We have squandered a great part of what we might have used and have not stopped to conserve the exceeding bounty of nature, which our genius for enterprise would have been worthless and impotent, shamefully prodigal as well as admirably efficient. We have been proud of our industrial achievements, but we have not hitherto stopped thoughtfully enough to count the human costs. The cost of lives snuffed out, of energies overtaxed and broken, the fearful physical and spiritual cost to the men, women and children upon whom the dead weight and burden of it all has fallen pitilessly the years through. The groans and agony of it all had not yet reached our ears. The solemn moving undertone of our life is coming up out of the mines and factories and out of every home where the struggle had its intimate and familiar seat. With the great government went many deep secret things which we too long delayed to look into and scrutinize with candid, fearless eyes. The great government we loved has too often been made use of for private and selfish purposes and those who used it had forgotten the people."

"At last a vision has been vouchsafed us of our life as a whole. We see the bad with the good, the debased and decadent with the sound and vital. With this vision we approach new affairs. Our duty is to cleanse, to reconsider, to restore, to correct the evil without impairing the good. We seek to purify and humanize every process of our common life without weakening or sentimentalizing it. There has been something crude and heartless and unfeeling in our haste to succeed and be great. Our thought has been 'Let every man look out for himself, let every generation look out for itself,' while we reared giant machinery which made it impossible that any but those who stood at the levers of control should have a chance to look out for themselves. We had not forgotten our morals. We remembered well enough that we had set up a policy which was meant to serve the humblest as well as the most powerful. With an eye single to the standards of justice and fair play, we will remember it with pride. We were very heedless and in a hurry to be great."

"We have come now to the sober second thought. The scales of heedlessness have fallen from our eyes. We have made up our minds to spare every process of our national life again with the standards we so proudly set up at the beginning and have always carried in our hearts. Our work is a work of restoration."

"We have itemized with some degree of particularity the things that ought to be altered. Here are some of the chief items. One, a tariff cuts us off from our proper part in the commerce of the world, violates the just principles of taxation, and makes the government a facile instrument in the hands of private interests. Two, a banking and currency system that is based upon the necessity of the government to sell its bonds fifty years ago, and perfectly adapted to

concentration of cash and restricting of credits is wrong. Three, an industrial system which, take it on all its sides, financial as well as administrative, holds it capital in leading strings, restricts liberties and limits the opportunities of labor, and exploits without renewing or conserving the natural resources of the country. Four, a body of agricultural activities has not yet given the efficiency of great business undertakings or served as it should through the instrumentality of science taken directly to the farm or afforded the facilities of credit best suited to its practical needs. And five, water courses undeveloped, waste places unreclaimed, forests untended, fast disappearing without plan or prospect of renewal, unregarded waste heaps at every mine must be improved or eliminated."

"We have studied, as perhaps no other nation has, the most effective means of production; but we have not studied cost of economy as we should, either as organizers of industry, as a statesman, or as individuals. Nor have we studied and perfected the means by which government may be put at the services of humanity in safeguarding the health of the Nation. The health of its men, women and children, as well as their rights in the struggle for existence are paramount. This is no sentimental duty. The firm basis of government is justice. There can be no equality of opportunity, the first essential of justice in the body politic, if men and women be not shielded in their lives, their very vitality, from the consequences of great industrial and social processes which they cannot alter, control, or singly cope with. Society must see to it that it does not itself crush or weaken or damage its own constituent parts. The first duty of law is to keep sound the society it serves. Sanitary laws, pure food laws and laws determining conditions of labor which individuals are powerless to determine for themselves are intimate parts of the very business of justice and legal efficiency."

"These are some of the things we ought to do, and not leave the others undone, the old-fashioned, never-to-be-neglected, fundamental safe guarding of property and of individual rights. This is the high enterprise of the new day: to lift everything that concerns our life as a nation to the light that shines from the hearth-fire of every man's conscience and vision of the right. It is inconceivable we should do it in ignorance of the facts as they are or in blind haste. We shall restore, not destroy. We shall deal with our economic system as it is and as it may be modified, not as it might be if we had a clean sheet of paper to write upon. Step by step we shall make it what it should be, in the spirit of those who question their own wisdom and seek counsel and knowledge. The shallow, self-satisfaction or the excitement of excursions whither, they can not tell. Justice, and only justice, shall always be our motto."

5

"And yet it will be no cool process of mere science. The Nation has been deeply stirred. It has been stirred by a solemn passion, stirred by the knowledge of wrong, of ideals lost, of government too often debauched and made an instrument of evil. The feelings with which we face this new age of right and opportunity sweep across our heart-strings like some air out of God's own presence, where justice and mercy are reconciled and the judge and the brother are one. We know our task is to be no mere task of politics, but a task which shall search us through and through, whether we shall be able to understand our times and the need of our people, whether we be indeed their spokesmen and interpreters, whether we have the pure heart to comprehend and the rectified will to choose our high cost of action."

"This is not a day of triumph. It is a day of dedication. Here muster, not the forces of party, but the forces of humanity. Men's hearts wait upon us. Men's love hang in the balance. Men's hopes call upon us to say what we will do. Who shall live up to the great trust? Who dares fail to try? I summon all honest men and women, all patriotic and far looking men and women to my side. God helping me, I will not fail them, if they will but counsel and sustain me!"

2

Cabinet Meeting

March 5, 1913

President Wilson was in a good mood after his inauguration and he wanted to give his marching orders to his cabinet. We were all there sitting around a large table in the same room that I had made my presentation on December 12 of last year. The president sat at one end of a long table and William J. Bryan, his Secretary of State, sat at his right hand. I wondered if this was because Bryan had helped him write his speech that he gave yesterday and had coached him in its oral delivery. The best orator alive sat at the president's side. Next to Bryan sat William McAdoo, Secretary of the Treasury. He was from Georgia and the only other honest lawyer that Thomas Woodrow Wilson had ever met. McAdoo is best known as the successful builder and operator of the Hudson tunnels and railways which connect New York City with New Jersey under the Hudson River. Wilson knew him when he was governor of New Jersey and trusted him to perform his duties as outlined in the trustful manner laid out in the inaugural address.

The Secretary of War, Lindley Garrison is also a lawyer, native of New Jersey, where he had been Wilson's Vice-chancellor at Princeton since 1904 and therefore a trusted ally. Next to him sat the secretary of the Navy, Josephus Daniels, a native of North Carolina. He says he is a member of the bar but never practiced his profession, having devoted himself chiefly to journalism and politics. Rodney Lowe is going to have to teach him everything he needs to know about the Navy because he does not have clue, I thought. Next to him sat Franklin Lane, the secretary of Interior, he was born on Prince Edward Island, Canada, but has been a naturalized citizen and lived in California for over twenty years. His first job in California was in newspapers while he worked his way through law school and passed the bar in California. He held several political offices in California and became widely known to the public as a member of the Interstate Commerce Commission in 1905. He became chairman of the Commission in the fall of 1912. Next to him sat Albert Burleson, Postmaster-General, a native of Texas. For many years he was a member of the US House of Representatives and obtained a high reputation in that body for efficient and painstaking work.

On his right was the Secretary of Agriculture, David Houston, born in North Carolina, but for many years has been a resident of Missouri. He was widely known as an educator, and was at one time president of the Texas College of Agriculture. Next to him was James McReynolds, the Attorney-General. He was born in Kentucky. He was an assistant attorney-general under Mr. Wickersham, in President Taft's cabinet and I wondered how his appointment fit with the president's message yesterday to make a clean sweep of things. Continuing around the table was William Redfield, the Secretary of Commerce, he was born in New York State and is a manufacturer in Brooklyn. He has written and spoken much in favor of industrial peace and the treatment of laboring men and women on the human basis. He was a member of the US House of Representatives and made a high reputation for efficiency along with Albert Burleson. The last two members of the cabinet were the new Secretary of Labor, William Wilson, and myself. Wilson was born in Scotland and came to this country as a coal miner. He settled in Pennsylvania coal country and became an officer in the labor union. He was elected to congress but was defeated for re-election in November of 1912. He was a natural choice for Secretary of Labor as I was for the director of NIA.

I looked around the table one more time and I thought, *Good grief, I have become my father. I just gave a thumbnail sketch of the entire cabinet, just like he used to do for me in his letters where he would describe a newly elected president.* I began to remember some of those letters to me.

Caldwell International

June 26, 1889

Dear Son,

Well, I am another year older today. Thank you for the gift! Do you think a man of my age should be driving an automobile? It is beautiful, it is always something that I have wanted and your mother told me I did not need. Ha, ha. It has become a tradition that I write and tell you what I know about the new president. Here goes: Benjamin Harrison was born at North Bend, Ohio, August 20, 1833. He is the grandson of our ninth president. He was an excellent student in his youth and he attracted attention by his skill in debate. He attended Miami College in Oxford, Ohio. He became a law student at Cincinnati College and married Miss Lavinia Scott before his admission to the bar. When he became a lawyer he settled in Indianapolis, where he made his permanent home.

Harrison volunteered early in the war and was appointed colonel of the 7th Indiana. He was a brave and skillful officer. At the recommendation of General Hooker, he was made a brigadier general. He was very ill for a time, but recovered to render excellent service. He joined Sherman at Goldsborough to command a brigade to the close of the war. He was elected to the Senate in 1880 and served a full term.

Grover underestimated him in the election campaign and he will not do that again! I talked to Grover and he plans on running again in four years. If elected, he will be the first president to serve four, relax four and serve again. More power to him. I am glad I am out of it, it is time to get to know my grandchildren. Did you know Ruth had another girl!?

Well, I digress, old age does funny things to your mind.

Your Loving Father

JE Caldwell

Dear Son,

Dan Ryan

James Abram Garfield was born in Orange, Ohio, November 19, 1831. While he was an infant his father died, and he was left to the care of his mother. Brought up in the back woods, he became rugged, strong and active. While still a boy, Garfield exhibited remarkable mechanical ability, and his services were in demand among his neighbors. When a young man he was a driver for a canal-boat, and at the age of seventeen attended high school in Chester, Ohio. He entered Hiram College in 1851. He then graduated in only two years having completed the four year curriculum. He sought a graduate degree at Williams College. He was then made President of Hiram College. He was elected to the Ohio Senate when the Civil War broke out. He was the colonel of the 42nd Regiment of Ohio Volunteers. He was promoted to brigadier-general and became General Rosecran's chief of staff. He was awarded another promotion for gallantry at Chickamauga. After the war, he was elected to the US House of Representatives and served for seventeen years before being nominated for President.

Hope this is helpful,
Your Loving Father

His vice-president, Chester Arthur, became President on September 20, 1881. A week later, a second letter arrived from my father.

Chester Alan Arthur was born in Franklin County, Vermont, October 5, 1830. He graduated from Union College in 1849, taught school for a while and then moved to New York City and became a lawyer. He was very successful in his profession and during the war he was quartermaster-general of the State of New York. He was made Collector of Customs for the Port of New York in 1871 and held that office for seven years, when he was removed by President Hayes. This put him squarely in the camp of those who did not want to see Hayes nominated for a second term. I heard that all of the cabinet members handed in their resignations and he asked all of them to remain in office, saying he had no wish to change the policy of the administration.

10

Hope this also helps,
Your Loving Father

My thoughts were interrupted when the president began speaking.

"This is the first of many meetings to be held in this room, gentlemen. It is my intent to be proactive and try to accomplish as many of the five points that I outlined in my address yesterday. In order to bring your focus upon these points, it will be necessary to keep abreast of events, both nationally and internationally, so that we are never in a position to react to crisis. This administration is not a fire department that puts out fires once they have started. Thanks to our NIA briefing in December, we can expect war in Europe before the end of this year. Mr. Garrison, I would like to hear from you first this morning. Please tell us the status of our military."

Lindley Garrison began his comments. "Mr. President I have the following information from the last administration. On June 30, 1912, the actual strength of the regular army was 4,470 officers and 77,835 enlisted men. This was a yearly increase of 189 officers and 7,834 enlisted men. There were, in addition to, Philippine scouts numbering 180 officers and 5,480 enlisted men. The geographical distribution of the army is as follows: within the US 61,584; Alaska, 1232; Philippines, 10,970 and 5,660 scouts; China, 1256; Puerto Rico, 614; Hawaii, 3969; Panama, 821; and foreign stations including NIA, 1859."

"Excuse me, Mr. Garrison, I have a question about the foreign stations."

"Yes, Mr. President."

"Why do we have troops on foreign soil?"

"According to the information left for me, the 1859 of these are all officers, not troops. We have eleven foreign embassies around the world that require protection: Austria, Brazil, France, Germany, Great Britain, Italy, Japan, Mexico, Russia, Spain and Turkey. I believe these troops are usually marines, Mr. President. Each of these embassies have army and navy officers assigned to them in various assignments."

"I understand that. That would mean we have 169 officers in our embassies."

"No, Mr. President. We also have Ministers Plenipotentiary offices world wide. These account for an additional thirty-one locations:

Argentina, Belgium, Bolivia, Chiles, China, Colombia, Costa Rica, Cuba, Denmark, Dominican Republic, Ecuador, Greece, Guatemala, Haiti, Honduras, Netherlands, Nicaragua, Norway, Panama, Persia, Peru, Portugal, Rumania, Salvador, Siam, Sweden, Switzerland, Uruguay and Venezuela."

"So, what is the normal military level of assignment to each of these? Is it 45 officers for each foreign office?"

"No. It varies depending upon the foreign office, foreign military assignment to friendly nations, members in transit between home and foreign locations and many other factors. Let me give you an example, you are in the process of changing ambassadors to all countries other than France, while at the same time replacing 21 of the 31 foreign ministers. The amount of military in transit for these changes is higher than it has ever been in our history. It does correspond to Point 1 of your address, *'a tariff cuts us off from our proper part in the commerce of the world, violates the just principles of taxation, and makes the government a facile instrument in the hands of private interests.'* You have stopped the practice of awarding ambassadorships based on private interests and demanded that world commerce be the number one consideration for those countries who maintain embassies here in this country."

"Thank you Mr. Garrison, you may continue." Lindley had lost his place in his pile of notes and he scrambled to find it.

"During the last year, 395 second lieutenants were appointed in the army. Of these 177 were graduates from USMA, West Point, 29 were from within the enlisted men in the army, and 189 were from civil life. There are still 134 vacancies in the regular office corps and 20 vacancies in the corps of engineers. The total strength of the army is 4.5 % below its authorized strength. Last year there were 158,917 applicants for enlistment and re-enlistment and only 25 % were accepted. In light of the briefing by Director Caldwell in December, I recommend that we accept all those qualified to service. We need to build our strength to that of the German Empire.

The army reorganization plan that I submitted to this cabinet two months ago should be studied and adopted or rejected as soon as possible. I recommend its adoption, it was perfected by the war college division of my general staff.

The legislation affecting the war department is usually the appropriation bill. The last one was October 21, 1912, and this year we will ask for an increase to meet the new level of enlistments and the addition of military hardware. On February 16, of this year, the House of Representatives adopted an amendment to the army bill providing for the consolidation of the office of army-general and inspector-general with that of chief of staff. I agree with that amendment and have already made the necessary assignments. The House also adopted a measure abolishing five of the fifteen cavalry regiments and indorsed the action which it had taken on the previous day in advancing the terms of enlistment from three to five years. This proposal was strongly opposed by General Wood, by Secretary Stimson and President Taft. My position is this; these two items should be separated. I support the enlistment beyond three years, it should be four or five years. The entire fifteen regiments of cavalry should be brought into the twentieth century. There is no place in a modern army for horse and buggy methods. We should instead, pay close attention to what Admiral Caldwell described in his briefing to us about what is going on in Europe. Poland is the only army on the continent with horses. All the rest move troops by armored carriers of one type or another. There is still a place for cavalry units in our army, mechanized cavalry pulling field artillery by trucks and tanks. If we submit our cavalry against any in Europe it would be a death knoll to all serving in the United States units.

There were many other pieces of legislation passed last year, but the most important, in my judgement, was the act which involved the National Guard. The purpose of the National Guard has been to support the execution of the laws of the union, suppressing insurrection and repelling invasion. The new law provides for the direct control by the government when war is threatened or declared. The word *threatened* is important, because you do not have to wait for the congress to declare war, Mr. President, you may call them in the event of any national emergency, such as the outbreak of the revolution in Mexico last year. This act was not passed when President Taft sent the Second Cavalry from Fort Bliss, El Paso and the Fourteenth Cavalry to Forts Clark and McIntosh. On September 7, 1912, owing to border raids by Mexicans, formerly part of Orozco's rebel army, the Ninth Cavalry was ordered from Fort Russell to Douglas, Arizona and the Thirteenth Cavalry was ordered to El Paso, Texas from Fort Riley."

"Excuse me again, Mr. Secretary, all of these units were horse mounted cavalry?"

"Yes, these troops assisted the State of Texas in the suppression of General Reyes' attempt to instigate an insurrection against Madero's government. Horse mounted troops were necessary in these remote areas without roads."

"And, I take it the State of Texas already has a mounted National Guard system in place."

"That is correct, Mr. President, federal troops will not be necessary in the future. Most of my information from the War Department involves naval forces and I will let Secretary Daniels brief you on those events."

S ecretary of the Navy, Joe Daniels, began his remarks. "Thank you, Lindley. The Navy was busy last year on the erection of coast fortifications. The work at Pearl Harbor, Honolulu during 1912 is now about 90% complete. The fortifications at Subic Bay, Philippines are now complete. The Manila Bay construction is 75% complete. At Guantanamo, Cuba, some emplacements were provided for medium and rapid fire guns. About $250,000 was expended for that purpose and for the erection of structures for the mining system.

I have appointed four assistant secretaries, they will function as aides for (1) operations of the fleet, (2) personnel, (3) materials, and (4) naval inspections. Because I have no military or Navy experience, I will depend heavily on these individuals. I have also asked Admirals Caldwell and Lowe to take charge of all naval intelligence and counter intelligence from this date forward."

"Excellent, excellent. Secretary Garrison, what about army intelligence? Can this be placed under Admiral Caldwell as well?"

"Not at this time, Mr. President. We plan to ask the NIA to provide us with all foreign intelligence. In fact, the army intelligence for overseas should all be moved to NIA. All domestic army intelligence should remain with the War Department. Domestic includes all the states and territories of the United States. The NIA should stay out of Cuba, the Philippines, Hawaii, Alaska and all other territories."

"So ordered. Admiral Caldwell, you will be given those overseas War Department personnel, starting today." I was taking some serious notes, this would nearly double the size of NIA.

"Mr. President, the fleets were busy last year. As you know The Atlantic fleet, under the command of Admiral Hugo Osterhaus, was responsible for maneuvers and the visit by the German fleet to Hampton Roads and New York. The Pacific fleet, under the command of Admiral Southerland, consists of two divisions, one in Hawaii and the other in the Philippines. Part of the Philippine division is stationed in China and part of the Hawaiian division was sent to Nicaragua during the revolution under General Mena and through their efforts order was established in that country.

The Atlantic torpedo fleet of destroyers and submarines continued their valuable and instructive exercises in developing the offensive and defensive tactics of torpedo boats. This fleet ceased to exist as a separate organization under the last administration. I plan to separate them from the Atlantic fleet and place them under the command of commodore James Caldwell."

My head snapped up from my note taking. My son had just been promoted to commodore under the new administration. I would lose him as the station chief of NIA in Cairo, Egypt. I made a note to find a replacement as soon as possible, it would not be easy to find someone who spoke Arabic on short notice. Secretary Daniels completed his remarks by introducing two new battleships, the Wyoming and the Arkansas. Each of these had a displacement of 26,000 tons and were the largest of any navy in the world. He declared it necessary that navy continue its plans for construction of other new vessels to include a total of 41 battleships. This would place the US on a safe basis in its relationship with the other world powers.

S ecretary Houston was the next person seated at the conference table and President Wilson nodded for him to begin his report.

"Mr. President, in keeping with point four of your address yesterday; *'a body of agricultural activities has not yet given the efficiency of great business undertakings or served as it should through the instrumentality of science taken directly to the farm or afforded the facilities of credit best suited to its practical needs.'* The Department of Agriculture will be consumed by the provision of credit facilities for farmers. The last administration turned a deaf ear to the lobbying of former Governor Herrick and Mr. David Lubin, organizer of the International Institute of Agriculture. My department will be begin various investigations of this subject during the next year. We will send a small body of representatives to study the subject in Europe. I will form a committee consisting of two members from each State of the Union to study this problem and suggest I credit bill for introduction to Congress. This committee will attend the meeting of the International Institute of Agriculture in Rome in May of this year. The American Banker's Association in 1911 directed that an inquiry on this subject be made. At the same time the Department of State was interested and cooperated with the banker's committee. I would welcome Secretary Bryan's input on this at this time."

William Jennings Bryan, cleared his throat and began speaking. "Mr. Secretary, it my understanding that under the direction of former Governor Herrick a thoroughgoing investigation of systems of agricultural credit in various European countries was made and the results submitted to the government at Washington. So general became the interest in the subject, that all three major political parties in the last election embodied a plank in their platforms recommending the establishment of some system of agricultural credit suitable to American conditions. The Bull Moose party pressured President Taft to take the first step in the direction of establishing such credit facilities in a letter to the governors. He urged that this be made a subject of consideration at the Congress of Governors in December of last year. This was done. President Taft expressed his belief that the cooperative credit societies of Germany, known as Raiffeisen banks, might be adapted to American conditions. He pointed out that the 12,000,000 farmers of this country pay interest charges estimated at $510,000,000 per year. They are charged at the rate of 8.5 per cent, as compared with 3.5 to 4.5 per cent paid by German farmers. He thought it possible that such cooperative farmer's banks having been instituted, Congress might be induced to create national land credit banks similar to the land credit banks of Germany and France. Secretary McAdoo can give us the details of that."

Willam McAdoo, Secretary of the Treasury stood and began his talking point. "In keeping with point two of the presidents address, *'a banking and currency system that is based upon the necessity of the government to sell its bonds fifty years ago, and perfectly adapted to concentration of cash and restricting of credits.'* I have proposed the following:

1. Extend the scope of national banking privileges by permitting banks to make loans on real estate and develop the interest of State banks in farmer's business.

2. Establish governmental agricultural banks.

3. Provide for the organization of cooperative credit societies after the German model."

"I am also working with Secretary of Commerce Redfield and Secretary of Labor Wilson to implement points three, *'an industrial system which, take it on all its sides, financial as well as administrative, holds it capital in leading strings, restricts liberties and limits the opportunities of labor, and exploits without renewing or conserving the natural resources of the country.'* With reference to point three, I would like to point out that more than 2000 national banks are now located in towns of less than 6000 population and are therefore accessible to farmers. Similarly, several thousand State banks which are not hampered by loan restrictions are available. The rapid development of manufacturing and commerce, together with the prosperity and individual character of our agriculture, has turned the attention of bankers to the development of facilities for trade and industry."

The president had not spoken for several minutes until he said, "What about our point five? *'water courses undeveloped, waste places unreclaimed, forests untended, fast disappearing without plan or prospect of renewal, unregarded waste heaps at every mine.'"*

The next person to speak at this first cabinet meeting was Secretary of the Interior, Franklin Lane.

"Mr. President, I am from Canada, and I have seen first hand your concerns with point five of your address. I pledge to work closely with your Attorney General, Mr. McReynolds to write a series of laws that will protect our wild life and natural resources. I will present these laws at our next cabinet meeting."

The last item given to the president was by postmaster-general. It was in the form of a summary.

"The total revenues of the Post Office Department from all sources for last year were $248,525,450. The expenditures amounted to $246,744,015, whereby $1,781,434 was returned to the US Treasury. The chief source of revenue was the sale of stamps, stamped envelopes, newspaper wrappers and postal cards. The largest expenditure was for transportation of mails on railroads, rural delivery, and office employees."

3

NIA Presidential Briefing

March 6, 1913

I began my third day of the Wilson Administration in a closed meeting with the president. My last meeting had been in December of 1912 as President Taft's director of the NIA. President Wilson needed to know what had happened in Europe during the last two months of the Taft Administration.

I began with the last statement that I gave the president-elect in December.

"Mr. Wilson, if there is a war in Europe the underlying causes will be several. Among the several causes of the war, first importance must be assigned to the development of national militarism, based on a sentiment of national patriotism."

I had based this comment on the many NIA station reports from all over Europe; Austria, Belgium, England, France, Germany, Italy, Russia and Turkey. From these reports, I gleaned that in the first twelve years of the twentieth century, it was commonplace that a compact people speaking the same language and sharing the same historical traditions and social customs should be politically united as a free and independent nation.

A hundred years ago, nationalism was a revolutionary doctrine. At the beginning of the nineteenth century there was no such thing as a German nation, no such Italian nation. Goethe (1749-1832) was proud to be "a citizen of the world." But the all conquering armies of the French Revolution brought to the disunited nations of Europe a new gospel of

Fraternity, that men of the same nation should be brothers-in -arms to defend their liberties against the tyrant and their homes against the foreign foe. Poetry from Europe, glorified the idea of national patriotism, religion sanctioned it, and political theory invested it with all the finality of a scientific dogma. In the course of the nineteenth century, the spirit of nationalism produced an independent Greece, a Servia, a Rumania, a Bulgaria, a Norway, an Italy and a Germany. Each nation was proud of its national language, its national customs, its frequently fictitious but always glorious national history and, above all, of its national political unification and freedom. Not all nations were successful in achieving unity and independence. Ireland was still governed from Westminster; Poland was still divided among Hapsburg, Hohenzollern and Romanov; Servia lacked Bosnia: Rumania longed for Transylvania and Bessarabia. According to the principle of nationalism, the Hapsburg Empire should have been partitioned and given to Germany, Italy, Servia and Rumania. Because the integrity of the Hapsburg Empire was thus menaced by nationalism, and because the Russian Orthodox Slavs favored the nationalist aspirations of the Servian Slavs, the Austro-Hungarian government felt fear. Fear makes the conditions for war possible and those who do not learn the lessons of fear, taught by history are doomed to repeat those lessons.

Thus far I had briefed the president-elect on the nationalist half of the national militarism. Most often, during the nineteenth century, the growth of nationalist sentiment was combined with tendencies toward democracy, and foremost patriots were abundant. Such was the case in Hungary, Italy and France. Such, too, was the case in Germany as the democratically-minded Frankfort Assembly tried in 1848, but this first attempt failed. The second attempt to unify Germany was by Bismarck and his "iron and blood" approach was successful. Bismarck had Germany fight three wars; 1864, 1866 and 1871, which built the German Empire by use of the Prussian army. Thereafter, German national patriotism was to be inseparably associated with large armies. Because the empire was born of the Franco-Prussian War of 1870 and 1871, the German military writer Friedrich Bernhardi said, "War is the father of all things."

It was now time to brief President, not president-elect, Wilson. He began with this comment. "Admiral Caldwell, I very much appreciate your decision to remain as director of NIA. What you said in our briefing in December impressed me. 'Long before Darwin recognized it, the struggle for existence is, in the nature of life, the basis of all healthy development.' I would like to add that it is not only a biological law, but a moral obligation, and as such, an indispensable factor in civilization."

"Yes, Mr. President, that is how I see it."

"According to this new pseudo-biological political theory of yours, international politics will become the struggle for existence, in which the fit survive."

"It will, Mr. President. Using the spirit of the famous German historian Treitschke, General Bernhardi declared Germany the fittest to survive, for, 'From their first appearance in history the Germans have proved themselves to be a civilized nation of the first rank.' What did you perceive when you were Ambassador to Germany, Mr. President?"

"Exactly the same thing, the Germans believe the most important task of a modern State consists in making its armed force as powerful as possible."

"You met my son, Louis, in Berlin, Mr. President. Would it surprise you to know that he thinks, since war is fought in the interest of biological, social, and moral progress, it is Germany's admonition to prepare for war."

"Yes, Louis, is very bright and we have had a number of interesting conversations. I agree with some of his observations, in particular, his warning that huge standing armies and universal compulsory military service has become the general rule. This fact alone will lead to war on the continent of Europe. The role of the NIA is to keep me informed on the growing tensions upon the continent. I would like a monthly report on each nation likely to be dragged into this European conflict."

"I can prepare eight reports on the most likely nations involved, Mr. President."

"I do not want to you start with Germany. We have a good handle on what is likely to occur there. Last month, Germany put all of Europe in a panic by preparing an Army Bill whose terms became known. Their army has added 117,000 men and 19,000 officers, bringing the total strength to 870,000. If American forces were required to take the field against them, we would be badly out numbered in every category. The only hope is to build our forces during the next few months and enter the war only if England and France can not control the situation."

"I agree, Mr. President, the Superior Council of War in France has replied to the German challenge by proposing, March 4, that the term of military service be increased from 2 to 3 years, in order to augment the strength and improve the organization of the French army."

"I would assume that this will mean that Russia, the ally of France, and Austria-Hungary, the ally of Germany will do likewise."

"I would think so. My son reports from London, that England seems to be asleep and unaware of what is happening on the continent, but they are bound by treaties with both France and Russia."

"Then you see a conflict between the allies of France and the allies of Germany sometime in the next year?"

"By midyear 1914, yes, Mr. President."

"See you tomorrow morning, Admiral. Bring me a report on Austria one month from today."

"Yes, Mr. President."

War of the Nations

Part II

GERMANY

TURKEY

BELGIUM

ENGLAND

FRANCE

ITALY

RUSSIA

AUSTRIA

4

Reports From Austria

April 6, 1913

I returned to my office after my briefing on March 6 with President Wilson and immediately cabled the NIA station chiefs in Vienna and Budapest. I needed current troop strengths and other military information for a report that was due in a month. I reread the past several reports from NIA stations in Vienna and Budapest. I could probably write the introduction or background introduction from these reports. I sat at my desk and took my pen and paper to write the first part of the report to the president.

Introduction

The Austro-Hungarian monarchy was formed in 1867. It consists of the Austrian empire, the Hungarian kingdom and the territory of Bosnia and Herzegovina. Vienna is the capitol of Austria and Budapest is the capitol of Hungary. In these cities, the common legislature convenes alternately. The permanent residence of the sovereign, Emperor Franz Joseph I, is in Vienna. The area of the monarchy is stated at 261,241 square miles, an area slightly smaller than our State of Texas. This monarchy is conspicuous among the countries of Europe for its diversity of race and language. The 1910 censuses reported that there were several languages spoken. In millions, the censuses reported German (10), Magyar (10), Bohemian (8), Polish (5.5), Ruthenian (3.9), Servian (5), Croatian (5), Rumanian (3.2), Slovene (1.2), Italian (1) and others at 1.1 million. This resulted in 28.5 million people living in Austria and 18.5 million people living in Hungary.

Under the constitutional compromise of 1867, the administration of the monarchy as a whole is directed by the emperor, acting through three ministries (foreign affairs, finance and war), who are responsible to the delegations. These bodies consist of sixty members each. They are deliberately separate, communicating only in writing; but if they reach no agreement after three exchanges, they meet as one body and vote without debate. Their duties are to examine the requirements of the common services of the monarchy and to advise the parliament as to necessary appropriations. The parliament deals with finance relating to the monarchy as a whole, foreign affairs, the diplomatic , postal and telegraphic services, army, navy and certain state monopolies. The officials that report to Franz Joseph are:

Premier; Count Leopold Berchtold, appointed 2/1912
Minister of finance; Dr. Leon von Bilinski, also 2/1912
Minister of war; Gen. Ritter von Krobatin 12/1912
Admiral of the navy; Count Rudolf Montecuccoli 2/1913
Minister foreign affairs; Count Karl Sturgkh 11/1911
Minister interior; Baron Karl Heinold 11/1911
Minister education; Max von Hussarek 11/1911
Minister commerce; Rudolf von Bonnott 11/1911
Minister agriculture; Franz Zenker 11/1911

I put away my pen and papers and decided to call it a day. One thing I had learned as director of the NIA under President Taft was to pace myself and focus on the big picture. The big picture was Europe, not Austria or Hungary. The defeat and spoliation of Turkey from Europe, and the subsequent quarrels of the victorious Balkan allies were of vital concern to the monarch. His dreams of influence, if not of expansion in the Balkan peninsula, were violently disarranged. Russia was posing as the "big brother" of the Slavs and was thwarting Austria-Hungary at every turn; the Balkan states might be so strengthened and united as to defy Austria-Hungary penetration. Italy might at any moment prove to be an embarrassing rival, and Germany might not always be willing to support Austro-Hungarian demands upon its neighbors. The financial resources of the monarchy were being sadly over-burdened by the expenses of mobilization and maintaining an army and a navy ready for instant intervention in the Balkans or even in Russia.

I pushed my head through my office door and asked my secretary if he could locate my driver, I was ready to go home and talk to Emily and read the latest letter from our son, James, who was just promoted to commodore. The navy driver knocked a few minutes later and asked, "Ready for the home and hearth, Admiral?"

"Today is only the third day of the Wilson administration and it seems like three years, Kenny. Let's get this show on the road." I handed him a large box of manilla folders and we walked to the basement garage. We were headed to Forest Heights, the southern suburb of Washington, D.C. Emily and I had found a small acreage there. I had left the Navy in retirement just before the Spanish American War and I was called back to service. We lived in Beaufort while I was in command of the Marine Training Depot in Port Royal. After the war we moved back to Seneca Hill for a short time and Vice President Roosevelt, my brother-in-law Teddy, found us this place in Forest Heights.

The navy grey model A Ford turned off the highway and started down the lane toward the estate known as "Bellawoods". It was not always an estate, we bought a broken down dairy farm. I had always liked this place ever since my brother-in-law found it right after the last war in 1899. There was no sign at the beginning of the lane as it merged into the highway, nor was there a locked gate. The idea was to make it look normal, like any other medium priced property south of the nation's capital. There was an old milk can, like dairy farms used, about 3 feet high and two feet around, it was filled with concrete and painted flat black. A mail box was mounted to the redwood 4 x 4 which extended through the milk can cap. The lane ran for two or three hundred yards and then took a sharp turn to the right. A set of stone pillars were built on either side of the lane and a small, stone, gate keeper's cottage connected all three with a heavy iron chain similar to the harbor chains used a century ago. My father had liked that nautical touch. A gate keeper with a shotgun slung over his shoulder came out and unfastened the chain between the pillars and let the Ford drive across it, it was too heavy to drag out of the way.

When Emily and I first saw the place that Teddy Roosevelt had said had possibilities, it was a working dairy farm in financial distress. It had many acres of woods and open fields in which to plant grass for hay and field corn for the dairy barns, which at one time held scores of milk cows. As we looked at the giant farm house with four brick chimneys, two at each end, we knew we were looking at something built between the Revolutionary and Civil Wars. It reminded us of our Beaufort home. We walked around the house and decided that would be the center of a much larger house to be completed whenever we might have the time and energy to undertake such a large endeavor. We decided to offer cash on the barrel head, as my father described it, so much an acre, forget about the barns and house. The owners took the offer and the farm land was immediately rented out, on shares, to local farmers. Each year the income was plowed back into the construction of the main house. The purchase was made in 1899 and six years later "Bellawoods" was a masterpiece. It was three or four times as large as the original Virginia farmhouse, with the additions now complete. The center retained its four massive brick chimneys and the eight fireplaces on two floors. A large front porch, two stories high, was added to the center. It had exact copies of the columns that supported the portico at the White House. The left wing was a single story, white clap board, framed structure built to match the west wing of the White House, only smaller. The east wing was made of brick, painted white to match the east wing of the White House. The White House had 135 rooms, we settled for 29 rooms, four inside bathrooms, one outside bathroom attached to the swimming pool and patio, which ran along the back of the house. The main barn was converted to a very large garage where I kept my collection of antique steam automobiles and my modern automobile. There was even a trap range and small office where a small barn had once stood. It over looked a small valley. I had said, "Now that Seneca Hill is a woman's college, we need a family gathering place."

The Ford stopped in front of the house and Emily came walking out the front door to meet us. A butler and a maid followed along in her wake.

"Reginald, get the box of manilla folders from the trunk. The Admiral always brings work home with him. Maria, help my husband into the house and help him get settled in his study."

My wife had taken command. "James, I want the property guards doubled, see to it today. All our children will be home for Easter and I want the safety of everyone protected."

Emily had never gotten over the attempts on our lives here at Bellawoods after the failed assassination attempt of our son, Louis, at the Navy Yards in Washington. German agents had been assigned to try again after Louis was released from the hospital and he was recovering at our home.

"If the German agents followed me to Bellawoods, Dad, they will know where I am."

I looked at him and said, "Your Uncle Teddy has a detachment of marines on their way as we speak, I hope the dumb sons-of-bitches try to break in here, they will all be dead. Their orders are to take no prisoners, even if they surrender."

Louis had never heard me say more than damn or shit in my whole life, he knew I must be really angry. And, more importantly he probably hoped that all the agents assigned to the German Embassy would converge on Bellawoods and the matter could be settled once and for all.

The next day a moving van arrived with the household belongings of my son. It was admitted to the estate after twelve marines inspected the undercarriage, motor compartment and crawled into the rear storage areas. Louis and I were lying next to the swimming pool soaking up the sun rays. Within a few minutes of the moving van, a model T Ford came as far down the lane as the stone guard house and stopped at the harbor chain blocking their entrance. The same guard, with the shot gun, came to see what they wanted. They claimed they were lost and asked directions to the main road into Washington, D.C. The driver had a local accent that sounded normal, but the three others did not speak. The guard reported this to Captain Merfield of the United States Marines on special assignment, Bellawoods. He trotted up to the house, found me and said, "Contact with four suspects at the front gate, Sir."

"Good hunting, Captain. You understand your orders from the President?"

"Yes, Sir. No prisoners, no survivors. Remains to St. Elizabeth Hospital for processing. You can sleep safely in your beds tonight."

The woods around the house were salted with anti-personnel mines by the marines. They would be impossible to see at night and a single detonation would sound the alarm that an assault on Bellawoods was underway. The family was on edge, we ate a somewhat normal meal and went to bed around midnight. At 1:30 in the morning, the first mine exploded under the foot fall of an intruder. We heard small arms fire for about ten minutes and then nothing. Captain Merfield ordered his men to stay clear of the mined area and check for bodies. In two minutes the small arms fire began again. At sunrise, four bodies were recovered and identified as the four men in the model T Ford. The automobile was found parked on a side road adjacent to the property. They had walked from the automobile directly into a mine field and a cross fire from Captain Merfield's marines.

"Are any of these men the five agents that you were looking for, Louis?" I was hopeful.

"Yes, I believe this man is Gunther Hesse from the German Embassy, NIA had him under surveillance, he must have slipped away. I do not recognize any of the other three."

"There is no identification on any of these men, Sir." Captain Merfield's men had checked each of the bodies.

"Check the clothing labels, sometimes they forget to remove them." I said. I reached down and looked for labels on Hesse. He was a pro, nothing at all.

"Here is one, Sir." A marine had found a German language label.

"Let's get these bodies to the morgue, Captain." Louis walked away towards the house.

"Are all the mines clearly marked for daytime safety?" I asked Captain Merfield.

"Yes, Sir, Admiral, you can walk in the woods, but I would not suggest that until this is over."

"You think this is not over?"

"No, sir. It has just started. It will continue until they run out of agents in Germany, not the embassy. The embassy is just a stopping off place, until they come to this site and meet their deaths. Spies are not equipped to mess with troops, the troops will win every time, Admiral." He was smiling, he liked this.

They came back the next three nights, the first group contained five men who met their deaths from mines, small arms fire, and rifle fire. The second group contained ten men who met their deaths from mines, grenades, rifle fire and machine guns. The final group contained fifteen men, ten were killed and five had surrendered to Captain Merfield. He placed them in handcuffs and sent them off to St. Elizabeth Hospital for processing. It was a suicide mission on the part of the intruders, but the emotional damage inside the house had taken its toll. I had not been to work in the last four days and I left early the morning of the fifth day and headed to the White House. A marine patrol went ahead of my automobile and behind it and returned to the house.

The President, my brother-in-law, was waiting for me, I handed him a piece of paper with the body count and the names of those who we knew were dead or captured. The president picked up his phone and asked to speak with Admiral Lowe. He hung up. He picked up a second phone and asked to speak to the German Ambassador to the United States. He waited a few minutes and the President spoke very slowly, he did not wait for any responses.

"Mr. Ambassador, this is the President of the United States. You may inform your government that I have issued the following orders to my military police. Your embassy is considered German soil and I will not send someone onto that soil. I have instead, asked the police to stop all persons from leaving or entering the German Embassy until further notice. I have also closed the American Embassy in Berlin and have asked that all consul offices be closed throughout the German Empire and for those officials to return home. We have broken all diplomatic ties with your government. If you, or anyone else, leaves the embassy you will be arrested. Do you understand everything that I have told you? Good!" He hung up.

His first phone buzzed. He picked it up. "Hello Rodney, do you have any names for me? You do, bully for you old man. I will give you to James and he can write the names down on our list. I have some more calls to make. Good talking to you again too." He handed the phone to me. He picked up a second telephone and called the Washington Post.

"Hello, I assume my secretary has given you the proper code words and you know that this is the President of the United States speaking. I have an interesting story for you." He visited for about twenty minutes and hung up. He placed another call to the New York Times.

"Hello, I assume that my secretary has given you the proper code words......" He spent the rest of the entire day speaking with newspapers across the country. He wanted to let them know that he had recalled all US diplomats from the German Empire. This total recall, a defacto declaration of war, was in response to the terrorist actions coming directly from the German Embassy in Washington, D.C. A total of thirty-four murder attempts had occurred in the last four days. He had given the Governor of Virginia and his state police permission to fire upon any vehicle carrying German diplomatic plates. He hoped the German Government in Berlin would come to their senses and make contact with their Embassy in Washington. He had also said that he would welcome the closing of all German Embassies and consul offices and the recall of all diplomats within a 48 hour time limit. After that time, all diplomats trying to enter the US would be arrested and deported. All diplomats within the United States would be placed under arrest to face charges of murder and attempted murder of American citizens. The German Empire is a rouge nation without honor of any kind whatsoever and as President of the United States, he considered it an insult to see his name appear upon an assassination list taken from one of the those already involved. He was taking this method of informing the people of the United States of the actions already taken. And, those actions that might be needed in the near future, that was why he was now ordering the Secretary of War to place the country upon a war time footing and to begin calling officers that had served in 1899 to return to active service. He was sorry that he had to take this action, but unless changes were made in Berlin, war was certain to follow.

It took a day to print and distribute over 65 million newspapers across the country. Twenty-fours after that, things began to happen. The Ambassador of the Austro-Hungarian Embassy asked for an emergency meeting with the President. He came to the White House with a telegram from Emperor Franz Josef and Kaiser Wilhelm II informing him that OttoVon Bulow was no longer the Chancellor of the German Empire, he was replaced by Bethmann Hollweg. The entire diplomatic staff from Germany, now serving in the United States has been recalled and would be replaced as soon as the Americans return to their embassy in Berlin. The Kaiser had also included a personal hand written letter to Theodore Roosevelt that included an apology for the actions of his late Chancellor. He wrote that it is not the policy of his Empire to engage in terrorism of any kind, we meet our enemies upon the battlefield with respect and honor. My respect for you and the United States has not changed and my offer to exchange college professors is hereby reaffirmed.

My brother-in-law finished reading the letter and picked up his telephone and placed a call to the president of Princeton in New Jersey.

"President Wilson, this is Theodore Roosevelt...... do you remember our last conversation? .... Good, I am glad that the board of trustees will release you from your contract to accept the Ambassadorship to Berlin...... Yes, the situation is volatile........ Your publications are much admired by the Kaiser and he will listen to you, Woodrow..... You have my full support, when you have the situation defused, come home and run for Governor of New Jersey, I will endorse you from the rose garden so that the newspapers will have a field day seeing a Republican in support of a Democrat.....Yes, I know politics does make strange bed fellows, best of luck, Woodrow, I will not forget this kindness, goodbye."

B y the end of March, I had gathered enough information to complete the report for President Wilson. The station chiefs in Vienna and Budapest had done such a complete job with my request, I simply attached them to the introduction that I had written.

Army

The dual monarchy maintains a common army which derives its composition from both kingdoms, though with a single organization. The second line armies, however, which are fully organized in time of peace, are distinct and are on a national basis, known as the Landwehr in Austria and the Honved in Hungary. In addition, certain parts of the empire maintain special recruiting services and enlist independent troops under their own regulations, as, for instance, in Bosnia-Herzegovina. The laws of July 1, 1912, tending to the reorganization and increase of the army, and increasing the period from two to three years, came into effect this year. There are 16 army corps, which include 8 cavalry divisions and 33 infantry divisions of the active army, with a Landwehr or Honved division attached to it. The common army, on a peace basis, is organized into 58 brigades of infantry, including 102 regiments of the line of four battalions of four companies each, 55 of which are from the Austria and 47 from Hungary. The technical troops of the Austrian army are undergoing considerable reorganization. The peace strength of the army is 339,366 in the common army, Landwehr 50,544, Honved 38,529, and Bosina 6618. On a war basis the law provides for 1,360,000 common army, 240,000 Landwehr, 220,000 Honved, and Bosina-Horzegovina responsible for bringing the total number to 1,820,000 troops.

This year the military command proposed to bring the annual recruit contingent up to 270,000 to produce a standing army of 3,000,000 by July of 1914. The military budget for this year is 1,000,000,000 Kronen. A portion of this is to be spent over a five year period to modernize the cavalry into mechanized units including machine gun and mobile artillery batteries. There was no provision for horses in the army after 1910. The number of these new cavalry units has increased from 1900 to 3000 from 1910 to 1912, bringing them to the strength of the other continental powers in Europe. The Austrian army (339,366) has more men under arms and more modern military units than the entire military in the United States (82,413).

Navy

The seacoast of the monarchy begins at the Italian border and runs south for over 400 miles to the border with Turkey. The largest seaport in the north is Trieste, located in the Gulf of Venice. Over 300 islands are scattered along the coast line and are considered part of Kustenland, Croatia and Dalmatia provinces. The warships of the navy are scattered at naval bases through these islands. This report will deal only with those warships of 1500 tons or more and torpedo boats of 50 or more tons. The Austrian navy has a number of battleships, including the dreadnought class (battleships having a main battery of all big guns of 11 inches or more). Four dreadnoughts of 40,000 tons exist and they are building others, six smaller battleships (10,000 tons) exist and they are building others. The navy also has coast-defense vessels to include; small battleships, heavy cruisers, monitors, light cruisers, destroyers, torpedo boats and submarines whose total tonnage exceeds a half a million tons. Austria-Hungary is eighth among the nations largest navies ranked just behind Italy. This ranking does, however, exclude any vessels over twenty years old. The world's navies retire most ships after 25 years. Austria does not, they reconstruct and rearm them for service. Austria can therefore match any navy other than Great Britain ship for ship. They also have more old transports, colliers, repair ships, torpedo depot ships and other auxiliaries vessels than any world navy this year.

Officers and men on active duty are 20,574, including 1 admiral of the fleet, 3 full admirals, 10 vice-admirals, 67 rear-admirals, 614 captains and 180 other line officers. These men are serving on the most modern vessels in the fleet, the *Viribus Unitis* was commissioned in October, 1912, and is the largest dreadnought in the world. The Kaiser Franz Joseph is still in the ship yard and is due to be christened on July 1, of this year. Montecuccoli is due to retire as marine commandant no information is available on his successor. Count Rudolf has retired as fleet admiral and has been replaced by Admiral Anton Haus.

Respectfully submitted to the President of the United States, April 6, 1913

Admiral James Jason Caldwell, Director NIA

5

Reports From Belgium

May 6, 1913

B elgium is a constitutional monarchy just north of France and bordering
on the North Sea. Is one of the many neutral and smaller European
states. I contacted our NIA office in Brussels and asked for military
information to include in the president's report. My reply was short and
to the point, Belgium does not have a military. It has no treaties of alliance
with any other nations in the world. The total population as of December
31, 1910, was 7,423,784. Roughly half of these are male (3,611,892) and
have or will participate in national service. National service consists of
army training or naval service of two years. If Belgium is attacked by one
of its neighbors, the army of 1,100,000 can be called to local centers and
put into the field within twenty-four hours. The navy is another matter.
No information is presently available for number of vessels or types at this
time.

This report might be short and not very useful to the president. I took
my pen in hand and wrote the introduction anyway.

Introduction

Belgium, like Austro-Hungary, is composed of many different
spoken languages. French (2,833,334), Flemish (3,220,662),
German (31,415), and English are major languages with almost
everyone speaking more than one language. The monarchy is

presently hereditary in the male line. This was the procedure in the case of the late Leopold II, who died without male heirs, December 17, 1909. He was succeeded by his nephew, Albert Leopold who has a son, Leopold Philippe, born November 12, 1912. The legislative power rests in the king and a legislative body composed of a senate and a chamber of deputies. A responsible ministry is appointed by the king. As constituted November 12, 1912, the ministry is as follows:

C. de Broqueville, premier and minister of military law
H. C. de Viart, minister of justice
J. Davignon, minister of foreign affairs
P. Berryer, minister of interior
P. Poullet, minister of arts and sciences
M. Levie, minister of finance
G. Helleputte, minister of agriculture and public works
A. Hubert, minister of industry and labor
A. van de Vyvere, minister of railways
P. Segers, minister of marine posts and telegraphs
J. Renkein, minister of colonies in Africa

I put away my pen and papers and decided to call it a day. One thing I had learned as director of the NIA was to pace myself and focus on the big picture. The big picture was Europe, not Belgium. I doubted Belgium would be attacked by any of its neighbors, it would be like kicking open a hornet's nest. I tried to remember the last time I was in Brussels. It must have been in May, 1899, when ninety-eight delegates met at The Hague to form the greatest conference of the century, and I was chosen to represent the United States. World leaders were very concerned about the global scale of the recent conflict between the United States and Spain. In fact, for the last quarter of a century the nations of the world had been devoting all their ingenuity to the invention and perfection of means of destruction, with the result that a point at last was reached, which meant that the next great war must terminate in the ruin of one combatant and annihilation of the other.

The signatures on the peace agreement in Washington, between the United States and Spain, were hardly dry when this question was asked by the world powers. How will the next war between belligerent nations end? The answer came from the least expected quarter. The foreign ambassadors to the Court of St. Petersburg were handed a printed document from

Count Muravieff, the Russian Minister for foreign affairs. This document has since become famous as the Czar's Rescript. It contained an invitation to all the world powers who were represented in the Russian capital, to hold a conference to discuss the possibility of putting "some limit to the increasing armaments, and to find a means of averting the calamities which threaten the whole world."

At the same time the Czar's circular pointed out that, "The ever increasing financial burdens attack public prosperity at its very roots. The physical and intellectual strength of the people, labor and capital are diverted for the greater part from their natural application and wasted unproductively. Hundreds of millions are spent to obtain frightful weapons of destruction, which, while being regarded today as the latest inventions of science, are in fact, destined tomorrow to be rendered obsolete by some new discovery. National culture, economical progress and the production of wealth are either paralyzed or turned into false channels of development. Therefore, the more the armaments of each world power increase, the less they answer to the purposes and intentions of the people. Economic disturbances are caused in great measure by this system of extraordinary armaments."

The Czar went on to say, "It should be a happy augury for the closing of the nineteenth century. It will powerfully concentrate the efforts of all countries which sincerely wish to see the triumph of the grand idea of universal peace over the elements of trouble and discord."

His comments were printed in the London Times and an editorial comment is worth noting: "The documents which Count Muravieff has presented to the representatives of the Court at St. Petersburg, are remarkable and most unexpected. On the eve of inaugurating a memorial to his grandfather, Czar Liberator, the present autocrat of Russia seizes the opportunity to appeal to the civilized world in the still more lofty capacity of the Czar Peacemaker."

All of the countries which received the Czar Rescript, agreed to the conference with the following agenda.

1. An agreement not to increase military and naval forces for a fixed period; also not to increase the corresponding war budgets; to endeavor to find means for reducing these forces and their budgets in the future.

2. To interdict the use of any kind of new weapon or explosive, or any new powder more powerful than which is at present in use for rifles and cannons.

3. To restrict the use in war of existing explosives of terrible force, and

also to forbid the throwing of any kind of explosives from balloons or by any analogous means.

4. To forbid the use of submarine torpedo boats or plungers and any other similar engines of destruction, in navel warfare; to undertake not to construct vessels with rams.

5. To apply to naval warfare the stipulations of the Geneva Convention of 1864.

6. The neutralization of ships and boats for saving those shipwrecked during and after naval battles.

7. The revision of the declaration concerning the laws and customs of war elaborated in 1874 by the Conference of Brussels.

8. To accept in principle the employment of good offices in mediation and optional arbitration in cases which lend themselves to such means in order to prevent armed conflict between nations; an understanding on the subject of their mode of application and the establishment of some uniform practice in making use of them.

With the agenda in place, the ninety-eight delegates met at The Hague, where they were welcomed by the Queen of the Netherlands. That night I wrote to my son, James. Slowly, but surely, things began to take shape. It was seen that the Czar's proposal, far being confined to disarmament, was based on three distinct ideas, which might be roughly classed as the Means to War, the Horrors of War, and the Prevention of War. Strange to say, only one of the eight points on the agenda concerns itself with the prevention of war. As soon as this fact was pointed out, we began to see our way. Our work was then divided into three sections. To the first section was given the discussion of points 1 - 4 (Armaments for armies and navies). The second section will undertake points 3 - 7 (Rules of War, Geneva and Brussels accords). The third section, of which I am the chairman, will consider the possibilities of arbitration.

The section chairmen report to the conference presidents for each section. One, M. Beernaert, the Belgian Minister of Finance; two, M. Marten, a Russian linguist and three, M. Bourgeous, Prime Minister of France. The super president of the whole conference is M. De Staal, the Russian Ambassador to the Court of St. James.

The final act was drawn up and presented to the delegates. Each section was voted on separately, the results:

Section one; signed by 88 countries, those who abstained were, Germany, Austria-Hungary, China, Great Britain, Italy, Japan, Luxemburg,

Servia, Switzerland and Turkey. What this tells me is that these countries are in the process of building their armies and navies for a future war.

Section two; signed by 87 countries with those abstaining being the same as section one, plus Portugal. Why any country would object to the Geneva Convention is beyond my understanding.

Section three; signed by the same 87 countries that signed section two. Why anyone would object to arbitration is also beyond my understanding. I am in the process of sending my recommendations to the President of the United States. I will recommend that those nations not signing the agreement to be placed on a "watch list". I predicted that these nations will be at war with each other or some other nation within the next few months.

The delegates parted with mutual expressions of encouragement and goodwill, M. De Staal, as President of the conference gave the farewell address with these closing words, "For myself, who has arrived at the term of my career and decline of my life, I consider it as a supreme consolation to have been able to witness the advent of new prospects for the welfare of humanity, and to have been able to cast a glance into the brightness of the future."

Within a few months the Boer War was raging in South Africa. And Great Britain, one of the abstainers, was at war with the Dutch settlers in Northern Natal at a location called Elandslaagte on October 11, 1899. Three months later the civil war in China broke out and foreign troops entered the capital to protect their embassies. By the end of 1900, there were over a million deaths in China. Japan prepared for war with Russia, Servia and Turkey prepared for war on the Balkan Peninsula.

B y the end of April, I had gathered enough information to complete the report for President Wilson. The station chief in Brussels had done such a complete job with my request, I simply attached it to the introduction that I had written.

Military Law

The Military law of June 19, 1912, contains various amendments from the military law passed under King Leopold II. The first was a reduction in the time of national service from two years to one year. The second was a provision for regional defense army recruitment (which would allow the creation of separate Flemish and Walloon regiments to form a permanent standing defense army) this was defeated in the Ministry Chamber, but when it was presented to the full Chamber, it passed 104 to 63. It was ratified by the senate. The new law, put in affect in December, 1912, provided for general compulsory service of one year, instead of a two year national service requirement contained in the military law of December 14, 1909. The annual contingent of recruits remained nearly the same, except a standing army of 350,000 active and highly trained soldiers replaced the 1 million citizen army that needed to be called to regional depots.

By many Europeans, this attempt of Belgium to keep pace with the military expansion of larger states was regarded as a piece of costly and senseless jingoism. When asked why Belgium should attempt to compete in military preparation with the larger states of Europe, the president of the Chamber replied, "We do no doubt the sincerity and loyalty of the great nations who are the guarantors of our neutrality. But we have seen by numerous declarations that in case of war, Belgium would be called upon again to offer Europe a battlefield. We can not permit our national dignity to be lowered, nor can we allow our national self-respect to be impaired."

Respectfully submitted to the President of the United States, May 6, 1913

Admiral James Jason Caldwell, Director NIA

6

Reports From England

June 6, 1913

When I wrote the station chief in London to request information for the president's report, I was also writing my son, Louis. Louis was in the midst of an interesting career. Louis has a twin sister Louise, named after my mother, Louise Buchanan Caldwell. The twins were inseparable as children, they loved to play with puzzle boards, maps and charts. They would make up their own games about traveling the world together. They were accepted to William and Mary College and attended a summer session in Paris before they graduated. Louise began her teaching career and Louis entered law school at Georgetown. When he graduated he wanted to do something meaningful with his law career and he joined the navy, took basic training in San Diego, went to language school in Monterey and returned to work in the Washington, D.C. Judge Advocate General's Office. I remember reading his official navy autobiographical when it came across my desk.

I am Lieutenant LJ Caldwell. I am a lawyer and I work, officially, out of the Judge Advocate's Office. Unofficially, my time is spent 'on loan' to the Office of Naval Counter Intelligence, ONCI. I have been with JAG for a year, joining right after law school. My father and brother were over-joyed with my decision to join the US Navy. I come from a long line of Naval Officers, beginning with my grandfather, five star Admiral Jason Caldwell. My father is three star Admiral James Caldwell and my brother is Captain

J. Jason Caldwell, commander of the submarine fleet stationed in Norfolk, Virginia. I am the black sheep of the family, because I did not go to Annapolis like both of them. I was valedictorian of William and Mary and first in my law school class at Georgetown. My office was wherever I was sent to work on the most difficult cases. My rank went up and down like a yo-yo. I was undisciplined and unaware of most of the requirements for climbing the ladder of advancement within the US Navy. Because I was a lawyer, I was given a commission to join the investigation division of JAG. Rank meant nothing to me, I thought it was a cumbersome system to start with, an ensign and shift to lieutenant, and what was all this junior grade and lower division crap? Either you could do the job assigned to you or you can't.

The whole family was home for Grandma Caldwell's birthday party at Seneca Hill. Louis wanted to see his grandmother, she always understood him, they were two of a kind. When she asked him how he was doing with his appointment at JAG, he told her that he was a brand new LT(LG) or something close to that. He knew he had been given a deduction in rank, but he did not want his brother, James, to know it. His brother overheard their conversation and asked, "What happened Louis? Why were you busted?"

"No one hit me. They were upset at how I solved the case given to me, but that has become almost routine lately. I get results which turn into convictions and that is why I love my job."

"It is not a job, Louis. You have a career and you come from a long line of US Naval Officers."

"No, I did not graduate from Annapolis, therefore, the Navy is not my career. The law is my profession. I can practice it anywhere. Whenever the Navy wants me to quit and get a real job with a much higher salary, they will tell me." I knew my jab about a real job would get to James.

"Why do you think naval rules and regulations don't apply to you, Louis?"

"What? Of course, naval regs apply to me, I am in the US Navy."

"Then why don't you follow them?"

"I follow them to the letter, otherwise, no convictions!"

"That is not what I am talking about. You use the regs against the criminal actions of others in order to prosecute, but you think they don't apply to you."

"Yes, they do. If I committed a crime, then the regs would be used to punish me."

"Do you see a demotion as a form of punishment?"

"No, I see it as a warning to be more careful in pursuit of the bad guys."

"Don't you care what rank you are?"

"I am not impressed by titles. My income does not come from the Navy. I sign my check over to the naval widows and orphans fund every month. My income comes from my seat on CI, just like yours does, brother."

Louis would have liked to continue his discussion with his brother, I was sure, but he was on his way to see his other grandparents who lived in Georgetown. When his Grandpa Schneider heard that he had joined the Navy right out of law school, he said, "Louis, my son, I am so proud of you. The men on both sides of your family have served their time in the Navy. Come down to the basement and change clothes and I will teach you what you need to know to get through the eight weeks of basic training."

They spent several hours that day and Louis returned the next day with a few questions.

"I now know how to stop a man's fist or knife coming near me. How do I take that knife or weapon away from him and kill him with it?"

"Louis, Louis. That is not self defense! You are just beginning to learn how to defend yourself, it will take days more with me before you are ready to start your basic training."

It was then that he told him what he wanted to do with his career.

Louis' bio was written in 1904, in June of 1913, it would look very different. In the last eight and one-half years, Louis' life has taken many turns, some for the worse - some for the better. The worst time of his career was probably the botched assassination attempt on his life in the Washington Naval Yards. I remember it like it was yesterday. It is not often that you think one of your children is certainly going to die a horrible death. It was the spring of 1906 and Louis and his partner, Tim Jacobson, had returned to Washington from an overseas assignment in Germany. They returned aboard a transatlantic steamer from South Hampton and reported for their debriefing at The Farm, the ONCI training facility at Lancaster, Virginia. I had invited myself to the debriefing so that I could report to President Roosevelt. Louis read the after action reports forwarded from Hans Becker, the station chief in Berlin. Admiral Lowe, Louis' boss, indicated that all activity from the Spanish Embassy had ceased and the Jigsaw murders were now solved. The German Embassy was another matter. Agents were seen coming and going. Three were followed to New York where they met two more who came off the French ocean liner, *Enceintes des Philbus.*

Admiral Lowe began the debriefing by saying,"It will not take the Germans long to figure out what happened and they will come after you two and your families. I will alert the White House about the added risk level. The world is ready to explode because of what Otto Von Bulow considers manifest destiny. The German Empire began in Prussia and he envisions an empire that has seaports which stretch from the Gulf of Danzig in the north to the port of Cherbourg in the south. This would include all of the coast line of what is now northern France, Belgium, Holland, and Denmark."

"Prussia is already half way up the peninsula of Denmark and they have taken the Frisian Islands which used to belong to Holland. How much of Europe does Von Bulow want?" I asked.

"All of it, piece by piece. Austria and Hungary are giving way in the south, France has given Lorraine in the west, Poland has given territory in the east and the Baltic Sea is now a German Sea." Admiral Lowe was foreseeing the great war of Europe that he was sure to come.

Louis and Tim needed to get back to the safe house and get some clean clothes, they stunk. Louise was teaching in Alexandria and they had the house to themselves.

"Did the Admiral say that we needed to report to RLSO, Louis?"

"Yes, today, when do you want to drive over to the Navy Yard?"

"Let's get it over with, Morton is a pain in the ass." They were dressed in civilian suits and ties. They each had a shoulder holster and their hand guns, extra clips in their suit jacket pockets. They were not expecting any sort of trouble this soon after landing back in the United States. They got in the navy gray model T Ford and backed out into the street and left The Farm. It took them less than forty minutes to drive and find a place to park outside the RLSO building inside the Navy Yard.

They entered the JAG office and headed for a desk in the corner. Commander Morton's door was closed and his office light was off. They both breathed easier until they saw the pile of case files stacked on his desk.

"It never ends, Tim. Look at all these sailors who have managed to get their ass's caught in some sort of legal crack. I am not going to sit here and read all of these, let's take them back to the safe house and we can go through them with Louise. She always has good ideas."

Louis scooped them up into his arms and they headed back to their gray colored Ford. Tim opened the back door and Louis crawled into the seat still holding a hundred or so files. They could not have been inside the RLSO more than ten or fifteen minutes. They were not very diligent about their surroundings and they had jumped into the Ford without thinking. Tim pushed the starter with his foot. The motor did not turn over, the entire front of the Ford exploded in an giant orange ball of flames. The last thing Louis remembered seeing was a cloud of paper ascending all around him and then total blackness.

The best time of his life was probably when he met his future wife on assignment in Germany. She was a British field agent working in Germany and she describes their meeting this way.

M y partner, Fiona McBride and I were assigned to Berlin to try and steal the plans for the guidance system from the German Zeppelins presently being mass produced for possible war purposes. I had managed to get hired as a stewardess on the Count Zeppelin, a commercial vessel making flights inside the German Empire. When I reported for my first flight, after a month long training session, I had never seen an airship before. It is hard to describe a set of buildings and a site large enough to hold a 480 foot long and 60 foot diameter dirigible. The repair hanger, next to the airship terminal must be longer than 500 feet, contain the necessary equipment to deflate and inflate the hydrogen cells, do the necessary repairs on the crew and passenger compartments, and resupply the zeppelin after each long flight across Germany. The height of the hanger must provide for the 60 feet of the dirigible plus the height of the two compartments below the dirigible. The Berlin Aerodrome was a showplace for visitors to Germany, the Kaiser wanted to show the world how advanced the Empire had become in such a short time. I was impressed and scared to death, how was I ever going to get the plans and operational manuals off the dirigible? I began praying for God to help me. My prayers were answered as I sat in the main lobby and waited to be shown to the crew's departure lounge by the ticket master. In walked two men dressed in civilian clothes but were obviously military from their bearing. I tried to observe and overhear what they were saying.

They showed their tickets and a letter of invitation to visit the Kaiser at the ticket window and the man inside fell all over himself when he looked at the letter. In the month long training, I had already completed, we were shown photographs of VIP's who would be traveling on this flight. The two persons were Professor Becker and a Mr. Caldwell, a relative of the President of the United States. I continued to listen.

"Welcome to Berlin Aerodrome, Professor Becker and Mr. Caldwell, we have been expecting you. Come with me to the VIP lounge." His high German was perfect and Mr. Caldwell must have had trouble understanding him, but Professor Becker babbled on and on to him as all three of us followed him down a hallway and around a corner to the lounge areas. One wall was entirely windows and there was the Count Zeppelin III tied to its mast awaiting the boarding of passengers. We stopped dead in our tracks and gazed at the giant, silver cigar before us. Our ticket master smiled and said, "When someone sees the Count for the first time, it is awesome, yes?"

"Yes, it is! Dirigibles in the United States are 100 feet long and twenty feet in diameter. That is a monster." the professor said.

"Yours are experimental, carrying two or three people, the Count is more comparable to a small ocean liner, while yours is like a row boat."

"That is a very good comparison, Sir. Can I use that when I see my Uncle Teddy?" The ticket master looked confused and turned to the professor. He repeated the statement in high German and the ticket master smiled and said, "I think the President of the United States would like you to say exactly that, young man."

The ticket master never left us and I wondered who was at the ticket window. They were given a small meal of bread, cheese, sausages, Rhine wine and a dessert, as I left the lounge to help load suitcases into the crew compartment, I saw theirs among them. The ticket master must have told them that the luggage was placed above the crew's compartment because after the Count was in flight the president's nephew asked me to help locate his brief case.

This was my first commercial flight for the company and everything was new to me. I listened and tried to learn as much as I could.

"Good Morning, welcome aboard the Count Zeppelin. I am Captain Nedimeyer speaking to you from the flight deck directly above you. Our flight to Kaiserslautern is about 4 hours and ten minutes. You will need to find a comfortable seat and remain seated until I announce that we have reached our flight altitude. Matches, lighters and open flames are not permitted while you are aboard. This is a non-smoking flight."

I was serving drinks to the passengers and standing beside them when I heard, "Four hours? That can not be right, Hans, it is 298 miles to Kaiserslautern."

"Kilometers, not miles, Louis." He had just gotten that out of his mouth when the cable was released from the mooring mast and we floated twenty feet above the ground. I could hear the sound of the propellers turning and I felt the tail sink slightly and we moved forward along the ground. We picked up speed as we traveled parallel to the ground, I heard a hissing sound and the Count slowly began to rise vertically at a steady rate.

"That must be the full inflation of the hydrogen cells, Louis." The professor was enjoying this. The hissing stopped the tail dipped nearly ten degrees and the Count roared into the air at a high rate of speed. I nearly spilled my tray of drinks, but recovered in time to hear the handsome partner ask me, "How fast are we going?"

"You must be one of the Americans on board, I can tell by your German accent. We are traveling about 30 kilometers per hour during the assent. When we reach our flight altitude, the captain will level the Count and increase speed to 80 or 90 kilometers per hour."

"90, I had no idea!"

"Kilometers, not miles, Louis." The professor wrote 54 mph on his note pad. In a few minutes, the voice through the grill spoke again.

"Good morning again. This is your captain speaking. We have reached our flight altitude of 650 meters and we have increased our forward thrust to 90 kilometers per hour. We have increased our flight speed today because we will have a military escort. In a few minutes you will be able to see a flight of four Valkyrie, German made, aeroplanes. Two will be on our port side and two will be on our starboard side. These new German fighters are in honor of our two guests who are representing the President of the United States. Professor Becker, please raise your hand so the rest of the passengers can meet you. Professor Becker is a language professor and he is fluent in German, his mother tongue, English and Spanish. Please feel free to visit with him in your native language. Accompanying Professor Becker is President Roosevelt's nephew, Louis Caldwell. These two representatives will be attending the same conference that you ladies and gentlemen will be attending. Please feel free to get acquainted before the conference begins. If you have any questions about the Count or the newest German fighter aeroplanes, please ask the steward who has just entered the compartment. He will take your dinner orders shortly and we will be changing the compartment from opera seating to tables and chairs. Please take a seat on one of the couches provided on each side of the compartment. Thank you."

"So much for keeping a low profile." The professor was smiling.

"It is better to hide in plain sight, Hans. You are the expert, I am just the retarded nephew of the war like Roosevelt." I looked at him in surprise, he had a sense of humor.

The flight of German Valkyries appeared outside our windows. I had seen the English Valkyrie in my training as a Royal Naval Officer, a small, one seat aeroplane about twenty five feet long with a wing span of about the same length. We called them "mosquitoes." These valkyries were much larger, two seats, one forward and one facing rear. The pilot, of course, faced forward to fly the aeroplane and to operate two machine guns forward. The rear seat was manned by a gunner who had a single machine gun mounted on a swivel. No more sneaking up on the pilot's rear, I thought.

They obviously had radio communication with the Count. The pilot's voice came through the grill work.

"Good morning, passengers on board the Count. I am Captain Ludwig Schmitz of the hundred and first fighter wing out of Leipzip. You are about a fourth of the way to Kaiserslautern and it is my honor to escort you for the next hour. You will then be met by another group who are stationed at Frankfort. That flight is made up of our newest single seat Valkyrie model, they will be with you for about an hour and a half and then they will leave and you will be accompanied by the final escort from Kaiserslautern. If you have any questions about our Valkyrie aeroplane, please ask the stewards in your cabin and they will forward your request to Captain Nedimeyer who will radio your question to me or one of the other pilots in my group. Have a good flight."

"Are you impressed, Louis?"

"Not until I see the toilets on this monster, I am going to ask the stewardess where they are."

He turned to me and smiled and my heart melted. What was wrong with me, this was just a man from a foreign country on a holiday to visit the Kaiser of German and hand him a letter from his uncle, the President of the United States. That was what was wrong, I was in over my head. I was a commoner from the lake district of England, I had always wanted a career in the Royal Navy and when I managed to put myself through London University, I signed on. During my orientation and examination of my university records, it was discovered that I had minored in Romance Languages. I was pulled out of basic training and sent to language school in Leads, England. Here I had met Fiona McBride, a fiery Irish lass who could kick the butt of any Englishman she met, or so she said.

After months of intensive training we were given our ranks as Ensigns and assigned to MI 5. MI 5 had wanted all the operation manuals on the guidance system for the Count Zeppelin III, that was why I was on this flight, not to go weak kneed over so handsome Yank.

"Ja, while you are gone, I am going to ask the steward why a fighter is called a Valkyrie."

I left with Louis Caldwell (what a strong English name, he must have ancestors somewhere in Great Britain.) The professor took the opportunity to expand his understanding of other cultures and peoples. What he learned from the steward, was that a Valkyrie was a mythology maiden of the God Odin. She was adorned with golden ornaments and she rode through the sky in brilliant armor. She delivered death according to Odin's commands. Death was by light streams from the points of her lance and a flickering brightness announces her arrival in battle. Valkyries travel in threes, sometimes nine and are said to represent storm clouds. The folk-lore of Valkyries says that whoever gains possession of their feather robes, has them in his power. Valkyries were made famous in Richard and later Siegfried Wagner's Der Ring des Nibelungen, second act "Die Walkure".

He also learned that there were two Wagners. Richard the father and Siegfried the son, the father was the famous German composer (1813-83), while his son is the famous conductor. Hans learned that Siegfried wrote several comic-romantic operas. His present opera is Bruder Lustig (1905) and is presently playing in Berlin. Hans made a note of attending upon his return to Berlin. Others still in production are Der Kobold (1904), Herzog Wildfang (1901-1903) and Der Barenhauter (1899-1901).

Louis told me later that it was really nice that your partner can get a cultural education while you are looking for the toilet on an airship 650 meters in the air and traveling at the speed of 90 kilometers per hour. When we returned, the professor was surrounded by most of the college professors who were on their way to the conference at Kaiserslautern. He was trying his best, but he was obviously not a college professor and it would be apparent soon to the others, also. Louis decided to rescue him.

"I am sorry, I was looking for the toilet. You have to ask the stewardess for directions. Did you know that this floor covering is not carpet? It is a rubberized covering to reduce static electricity. If you leave this compartment, you have to take your shoes off. Less chance of a spark, you see, the hydrogen cells, you know."

No one was impressed with Louis' German except the two professors from Munich, they understood every word, while those from Hamburg looked at us like we were a couple of idiots.

"My uncle, the President of the United States, has accepted the Kaiser's proposal for a university professor exchange. I was sent here to interview candidates for positions at William and Mary, Harvard, Yale, Princeton, Dartmouth and Cambridge. The applications are in my luggage, otherwise you could begin filling them out. I will ask the same stewardess if a crew member could locate my luggage."

He found me across the cabin and asked me if I could escort him to the flight deck, up the ladder into the hold of the Count, across the cat walk and into the luggage compartment. I looked at him and said, "Is your handbag clearly marked, Mr. Caldwell?"

"It is."

"I will ask if I can be excused for a few minutes to look for it, otherwise it will brought to you after lunch is served, you and the passengers can begin your paper work then."

I found my immediate supervisor and asked him what Louis had asked me. I turned and pointed to him among the college professors eating lunch. Louis nodded his head at us and my supervisor said I could go and get his brief case. This may be the only time I would be alone on the short flight.

I left the cabin and left my shoes inside the locked door, put on special shoe like socks and climbed up past the flight deck and into the hold above the flight deck. No one on the flight deck paid any attention to me. I was on a cat walk. It was about 18 inches wide, made out of a grid-like metal, I guessed it was aluminum. The hold of the Count was over 400 feet long and it was a mass of crisscrossing metal strips and cables that made up the shape of the zeppelin. I walked nearly 200 feet and was in a storage area above the crew's compartment. I spotted his brief case at the same time as I noticed a locked cabinet, labeled, flight manuals. Germans are so efficient and organized, why not hang a sign on the cabinet which says "spies look in here." I picked up Louis' brief case and made a mental note to return to the cabinet and get the guidance manuals later. I retraced my steps and went back outside the locked door and I put on my shoes to enter the passenger compartment. I handed him his briefcase and smiled, "Will there be anything else I can do for you, Mr. Louis Caldwell?" The use of

English threw him at first because I had spoken only German during the flight.

"Your English is very good. Where did you learn it?"

"Most of the employees for the Zeppelin Company are from foreign countries. I am Danish. In Denmark we learn English from the first grade."

"How did you know my name?"

"All the stewards were shown a photograph of you and Professor Becker before we left Berlin. This is a common thing for all VIP passengers. In fact, every person on this flight was interviewed a week before the scheduled flight. University Professors and their wives were invited to Berlin to be screened and selected for the conference. Only those likely to be selected by you and Professor Becker were put on the Count. The rest left four days ago by train."

"So, the couple from Munich traveled all the way to Berlin where they were selected for this flight. Munich is a short distance to the conference site, Kaiserslautern. That does not seem like a very efficient, German-like system of selection." Louis smiled at me again and I had that melting feeling.

"You must have some German ancestry. I am Danish, I do not pretend to understand the German mind set."

"My mother was German, a Schneider."

"Ah, the German name for 'Cutter', you must come from a long line of small boat builders."

"No, mine were butchers." He was feeling uncomfortable, the hair was standing up on the back of his neck. I asked him what was bothering him.

"My brief case has been opened and searched." Now the hair on my head was tingling. When you are in the spy business, you become paranoid. You never leave a personal item outside of your immediate eyesight, if you do, make sure that the procedure for opening and closing that personal item is rigidly followed. At Leads, we were trained to check for trip wires to make sure that someone had not put an explosive device inside. This was a sloppy job. There were no trip wires, but someone might as well have written a note and placed it inside the brief case saying, "Thank you, your luggage has been searched and no items hazardous to a flight in a hydrogen filled death trap have been found. Have a nice day!"

I was smiling at my memory of my daughter-in-law's description of her meeting my son when my driver stuck his head into my office and asked, "You want to get home before the capitol rush, Admiral?"

"Yes, Phillip, I do. Grab that box of manilla folders and let's get the car out of the garage."

The box of files would produce the report to be sent to the president before June 6, 1913.

7

Reports From France
July 6, 1913

France has been a steadfast ally since the American revolution and has always been eager to share military information with us. During 1912 there were few changes in the general organization of the French military, but it was realized that the new German army act was likely to result in an increase in German troops. This fear was passed on to the NIA field agents working in France and it was communicated to me. French general Joffre was designated as the officer in command of the military in case of war with Germany. The French army is recruited by compulsory service for two years and eleven years in the reserve. The total number in active service is 214,449 as of July 6, 1913. In case of war, the French would call upon the reserves and this would provide a first line effective strength of 2,500.000. Another 2,000,000 had been trained before 1901 and were classified as inactive reserves and could be called to active service from Lille, Amiens, Rouen, Le Mans, Orleans, Rennes, Nantes, Limoges, Clermont-Ferrand, Lyrons, Marseilles, Montpelier, Toulouse, Bordeaux, Algiers, Tunis and Nancy. The famous French Foreign Legion, composed of colonial troops would provide another 31,367 officers and 606,000 men.

The beginning of the new year, six month ago, witnessed a revival of the animosities which had embittered the famous Dreyfus case. The affair was again brought to the attention of the public by the announcement that Colonel Paty du Clam, notorious for his part in the prosecution of Captain Dreyfus, was about to be reinstated in the army by order of the minister of war, Millerand. A great public hue and cry was raised; with vehement denunciations the opponents of the government attacked what seemed to be an attempt to rehabilitate the now discredited colonel. Millerand explained that his act was without political significance, that the placement had been promised to Colonel Paty du Clam by a previous minister of war. The blunder cost him his portfolio; the Poincare ministry, however, was not unseated. It allowed Millerand to shoulder all the blame. On January 11, Millerand sent in his resignation, assuring Poincare, " It has been pleasant to have been closely associated in the national republican endeavors of his cabinet." Minister Lebrum, minister of colonies, was transferred to war, and Minister Besnard filled the post vacated by Lebrum.

On January 14, the chambers met again. After the election of Minister Deschanel as president of the deputies and of Minister Antonin Dubost as president of the senate. The first important business was the election of a president of the republic for the term 1913 - 1920, to succeed Armand Fallieres. The preliminary caucus was of more than ordinary interest and excitement. The rivalry was indeed not between parties, as here in the US, but between personalities. True, the revolutionary Socialist, Vaillant, represented a partisan issue, but he was hopelessly out of the race, the two leading candidates were both members of the previous cabinet, Poincare and Pams. Pams was minister of agriculture, the other aspirants to the presidency were; Ribot, Dubost, Deschanel and Dupuy. Pams led with 323 votes to 309 for Poincare. The strength of Pams was surprising, Pams was strongly supported by a group of radicals; Clemenceau, Combes, Monis, Cailaux and Clementel. On the following day, the elections were held, in accordance with the constitutional provision that the president shall be elected for seven years by a majority of the chamber and senate sitting in joint session at Versailles. On the first ballot a majority was not obtained, but on the second ballot the results were; Poincare 438 and Pams 296. President-elect Poincare immediately resigned his post as president of the council, which was taken by Minister Briand.

The election of Raymond Poincare was heralded throughout the country and the continent as a victory of nationalism, for Poincare has always been a firm patriot and a supporter of the Triple Entente. Russia especially was pleased and Czar Nicholas II sent a telegram to Poincare stating, " The bonds which unite France and Russia will draw still closer for the greatest good of the two allied and friendly nations."

In England and Spain, there was jubilation also, but in Italy unpleasant comments were passed. In France, there was a premonition that the new president, a politician in his prime, would not readily consent to abandon the role of statesman for that of dignitary. The confirmation came speedily, even in the presidential address. For the first subject dealt with in that document, after the customary promise of loyalty to the constitution, was the scope of the powers of the presidency.

"The prerogative of parliament will easily be reconciled with the rights and duties of the government, the lessening of the executive power is desired by neither chambers nor the country. Without a firm and clear-sighted executive, the welfare of the administration would soon be endangered, at times the public peace might even be menaced."

The president of the republic should become a more trusted and a more important magistrate of the people and a close friend to the US. Proof of that is apparent when Poincare asked Briand to form a new cabinet. This cabinet lasted until March 18, when Briand resigned as president of the council. Minister of Justice, Barthou, assumed the president of the council. Here are the cabinet members that the Wilson administration will be working with:

President of the Council and Public Instruction - Louis Barthou
Justice - Ratier
War - Etienne
Interior - Klotz
Marine - Baudin
Foreign Affairs - Pichon
Finance - Dumont
Colonies - Morel
Agriculture - Clementel
Commerce - Masse
Public Works - Thierry
Labor - Cheron

8

Reports From Germany

August 6, 1913

Our station chief in Berlin, Hans Becker, reported that when the Reichstag resumed its labors on May 27, after almost a month's vacation, the center of interest had shifted from clerical politics to the government's proposals for increasing the size of the army. An army bill, together with five bills to provide new funds for military expenditure, had been passed by the Bundesrat on March 28 and introduced in the Reichstag on April 7. Considered from the point of view of the increased burdens placed upon the German people, or from the point of view of the pacifist, this new addition to the burden of taxation and the new impetus to militarism might indeed be inexcusable, but excuses could hardly be lacking when Austria-Hungary was threatening to involve the continent in war, when France was cherishing the memory of Alsace-Lorraine, when England was boasting of naval supremacy and when the Triple Entente was winning the friendship of Spain.

To be sure, in his public statement, Chancellor Bethmann Hollweg commented on the effective work of Sir Edward Grey in preserving peace, affirmed that relations with Russia were friendly and with France, they were good and he rejoiced at the solidarity of the Triple Alliance. In secret, however, the international situation was assumed to be so grave that no real patriot could doubt that Germany might at any moment be called upon to fight for its existence. Since a majority of the deputies in the Reichstag were unwilling to be other than patriots, the army bill encountered little opposition, except from the Social Democrats.

When the bill was reported to the Reichstag, there was little discussion; even the Social Democrats were thinking more about the financial than the military measures. On June 30, the bill was passed. It is easy to decide on a larger army; it is quite a different thing to pay for it. The cost of carrying the new law into effect is estimated at almost a billion marks. This must be added to the annual cost of the army which is 54,000,000 marks.

The most effective antidote to Germany's militarism was the sensational allegation made on April 18, by Dr. Liebknecht, the Social Democrat orator. The great German armament firms, notably, the Krupp family, so often praised as patriotic and public-minded manufacturers of the arms for Germany, were now accused of misinforming the French Press in order to stimulate militarism. The Krupps were accused of obtaining military secrets by bribery and underhand methods and conspiring with other firms to force up the price of munitions of war. On the following day, the political centrist, Dr. Pfeiffer, demanded explanations and reminded the minister of war that some years ago the Centrist Party had proved that the, supposedly patriotic, Krupp firm was selling its wares cheaper abroad than to the fatherland. He waved a copy of a bill of sale for a Valkyrie aeroplane to one Louis Caldwell, a foreign national from Copenhagen, Denmark.

So unsatisfactory were the explanations offered by the ministry, that on April 21, the Centrist's brought in a bill requesting Chancellor Hollweg to appoint a commission of experts and of Reichstag deputies to investigate the foundations of Dr. Liebknecht's charges. The commission was constituted accordingly and met, but Dr. Liebknecht was not allowed to testify and the Social Democrats refused to have anything to do with the commission. In the meantime, the military court at Berlin tried seven military officials suspected of complicity in the malpractice of the Krupp firm. They were found guilty and received short prison terms ranging from three weeks to six months. The most interesting phase of the Krupp case began with the trial of Maximilian Brandt, a former agent of the firm and Otto Eccius, a director. Damaging evidence was brought to light, but no such sensational revelations were forthcoming as had been anticipated. Herr Eccius, as the man higher up, was dismissed with a fine of 1200 marks, while Brandt was sentenced to four months in jail.

H ans Becker had included a rather interesting observation about the international entanglement which grew out of the Balkan wars.

Germany was supposed to be a loyal ally of Austro-Hungary, but the German ambassador at London worked with Sir Edward Grey in the interests of European peace - at least that was the report to Chancellor Hollweg. During the war, German influence seemed to be exerted in favor of Turkey, many comments were made upon the fact that the Turkish army had been trained by German officers. The opposing armies to Turkey were trained by the French. King Constantine gave an impression to the contrary when he also thanked Germany for their assistance, a clear case of Germany backing both sides in the war. The Triple Alliance, formed by Austria, Germany and Italy in 1882, seemed to be stronger, if anything, after the Balkan wars than before. The interests of Austria had almost involved the Triple Alliance in war with the Triple Entente, England, Russia and France. A difference of opinion had arisen after the Treaty of Bucharest, when, instead of seconding Austria, the Kaiser had exchanged congratulatory telegrams with King Charles of Rumania. One reason for the vigor of the Triple Alliance was the fact that Herr von Jagow, who, as ambassador to Rome, helped to renew the alliance a year ago. Jagow was now German foreign minister, having succeeded Kiderlen-Waechter, who died last December.

My sources in Berlin inform me that Anglo-German relations are characterized throughout the past year by mutual endeavor to eliminate any misunderstanding between the two countries. In discussing foreign affairs in the Reichstag, von Bethmann-Hollweg voiced his approval of the British policy in Turkey, and especially in Asia Minor. The improvement in Anglo-German relations is marked by reduced naval competition. On February 7 of this year, Admiral von Terpitz, after consulting with Herr von Jagow, announced that the 16 to 10 relation of ships of the line, was quite acceptable. About a month later Mr. Churchill, speaking before the House of Commons, suggested that Germany and England might agree to a year's interruption of their naval construction programs. This would lessen their rivalry, provided a ratio of 16 to 10 could be maintained. In commenting on the idea, the German Press was inclined to look to England to take the initiative in bringing about the "naval holiday".

I finished reading Hans report and remembered when Woodrow Wilson was the President of Princeton University and President Roosevelt asked him to take a temporary leave of absence from his office and travel to Berlin. The tensions between the two countries were at the boiling point. The Kaiser was a champion of higher education within the German Empire and Theodore Roosevelt wanted to insure him that the United States was not seeking a war with Germany. He persuaded the foremost educator at the time, Woodrow Wilson, to pour oil upon the troubled waters in Berlin.

Wilson was born in Staunton, Virginia. He graduated from Princeton in 1879, then studied law at the University of Virginia, and for two years, in 1882-83, he practiced law in Atlanta, Georgia. In1884, he entered the newly opened John Hopkins University where he was awarded the degree of PhD, presenting as his thesis, *A study of Congressional Government* which won him a reputation as a scholar and a clear, original thinker. He was an associate professor of history at Bryn Mawr, 1885-88. He moved to Wesleyan University as department chair until 1890, when he returned to Princeton as professor of law. In 1902, when President Patton left Princeton, he was elected president as his replacement where he was serving until 1905, and the visit from the President of the United States.

The total number of letters, diagrams, maps, and other documents sent with Wilson totaled 37 in number. If he used all of them, it would take him more than a year to send NIA agents in Berlin to the surrounding estates, airfields and military installations. In his orders from the president he was very particular to point out that he was to go and see everything that the Kaiser suggested and everything that the Kaiser was particularly proud to show him. He was, after all, the close personal friend of Theodore Roosevelt. He began his quest by asking Hans Becker to tell him what he knew about Count Zeppelin's airships.

"Ja, but I am not the vone ya should ask about dis, Mr. Ambassador. Der are military experts assigned to da embassy besides me, one of dem can bring ya up to speed on the Zeppelins in service."

"What about the history of airships?"

"Ja, dat, I can help ya width, Zeppelins or all airships?"

"I have to write report about the effectiveness of Zeppelins in support of ground troops, so I suppose you better brief me on the Zeppelin and all others that might be used in a military conflict."

"Da Zeppelin is da notable airship, both for da size and da design. In 1900, Count Zeppelin made several voyages to London, Madrid and Paris. Da 1900 model consisted of a row of seventeen balloons, confined like a row of lozenges in der package. Da package vas placed in a cylindrical shell 420 feet long and 39 feet in diameter, width pointed ends. Dese balloons vere filled width hydrogen to lift da structure in da air, vere it vas driven forvard or backvard via means of large screw propellers operated via benzine motors. A pair of rudders, vone forvard and vone aft, serve da steer da airship. Da crew and da passengers occupy two aluminum cars suspended forvard and aft, below da body of da shell."

"Commander Becker, you are to report on how the Germans manufacture their metal you just called aluminum. Can I interrupt you long enough to take a side trip into aluminum?"

"Ja, ya are referring to Zeolites, a family of minerals including hydrated alkalies or alkaline earths, usually containing aluminum and sometimes magnesium. Magnesium is highly flammable and combined width hydrogen, it would be a death trap for anyone inside da Zeppelin. Derefore da refinement of aluminum from da Zeolite ore must be as pure as dey can make it. Zeolites are all secondary minerals and are found largely in cavities and fissures in da basic igneous rocks such as Basalt, Diabase, and da others."

"Thank you, Commander. You can tell Washington to forget about aluminum frames."

"Or stay away from hydrogen, use helium instead, da vestern United States is full of da helium. Dat is one of da items that da Kaiser, or vone of his aides, will ask ya to make a commitment about."

"I don't understand."

"Germany has been trying to buy liquid helium from the United States since 1900. Ve have feared that it vould be used in da Kaiser's war efforts and not for commercial travel."

"I see, I will inform the Kaiser that I will pass his request on to Washington. I may not even get an appointment to see the Kaiser."

"Ja, I have a feeling ve vill be lucky if one of mine agents can travel from Berlin to Kaiserslautern vithin a few days of receipt of da letter to him."

"I am sorry, Commander, continue about the history of the Zeppelin."

"Da cars vhich are hung from the aluminum frame of da Zeppelin have a speaking tube dat runs between dem. From da crew's car a ladder runs up into da Zeppelin vere the machinery is located. A crew member can move a large veight along a cable. Vhen the Zeppelin is in level flight, da veight is in the center of da ship. Vhen da veight is moved forvard, da nose starts to tip down. Vhen da veight is moved backvards, the tail tips down. The rudders cause right and left movements during da flight. Da Daimler benzine engines, vone below each car, are 16 horsepower and veight 700 pounds each. Da propellers, two for each engine had four blades on da 1900, model."

"What was the ground speed of the older models, Commander?"

"It vas not wery good, depending upon head vinds or tail vinds, it averaged 12 to 13 miles in da hour. None of da 1900 models are in service."

"Tell me about the later models used for commercial travel. Why would anyone take a Zeppelin when a train is so much faster?"

"Because, da Zeppelin ve vill ride in dis week vill not need a set of tracks and its ground speed is 45 mph from da start to da finish. A train can not average 45 mph because of all the stops necessary on a crowed railroad and the need to pick up additional passengers at every railroad station. Have ya ever ridden in da dirigible, Mr. Ambassador?"

"No, why do you ask?"

"Ya are in for da treat. Da ride is smoother than da train or da ship at sea. The furnishings are wery luxurious, indeed!"

"What changes were made to make the speed so much faster?"

"Da 16 horsepower engines vere replaced width 170 horsepower and da propellor design changed to be similar to da aeroplane. Do ya have any more questions, Mr. Wilson?"

"No, Sir. There are 37 pages inside that brief case and we have looked at the first three. Hans, flip through the rest of the pages, are they in code?"

"Ja, dese all have to go down to crypto in order for us to read dem."

"Then I will leave you to get at the decoding and I will retire to my office to write a letter to the Kaiser, informing him that two representatives from President Roosevelt have arrived in Berlin with a reply to his request for university professor exchanges beginning next year. I would carry your letter from Fairfield with you on our visit, Hans."

"Ja, Sir, Mr. Ambassador I vill."

The next day, Hans Becker and Ambassador Wilson had a decoded version of the next 34 pages contained in his delivery from Washington, D.C.

Data sheets for observations of Zeppelin airship passage from Berlin to Kaiserslautern:

A. Description of airfield in Berlin used by commercial zeppelins,

B. Photograph of zeppelin loading passengers if possible,

C. Interview with crew members on board if possible,

D. Tour of zeppelin if possible, and the

E. Weight and amounts of luggage allowed on flight.

Data sheets for observation of Kaiserslautern:

A. Photograph of zeppelin airfield at Kaiserslautern if allowed,

B. Description of Kaiser's compound and working offices,

C. Description of troops stationed at Kaiserslautern,

D. Photograph or description of aeroplanes and/or airfield at Kaiserslautern or nearby locations, and an

E. Interview with Kaiser and aides at Kaiserslautern.

Report format for visit to Valkyrie aeroplane factory:

A. Photographs of processes if possible,

B. Description of assembly process,

C. Description of wing design,

D. Gun mounts and number placement, and a

E. Part inventory if possible

Report format for inspection of armored tracked vehicle factory:

A. Photographs of processes if possible,

B. Description of armored vehicles,

C. Description and/or photograph of MAV,

D. Photograph of steel tracked vehicle, and

E. Part inventories if possible.

Report format for summary of professor exchange conference:

A. Names of certified professors and universities,

B. Names of persons who might be possible agents,

C. Speech by the Kaiser,

D. Speeches of interest by German University Professors, and a

E. List of names who might want to immigrate to the US.

Report format for visits to Lorraine, Wurtemberg and Baden:

A. Description of the extensive arsenal built in Strassburg,

B. List of manufacturing facilities and those toured,

C. Tonnage produced in a normal production run,

D. Division of rounds into army, navy, and other

E. Estimate of numbers of workers employed.

Berlin to London courier instructions:

A. Contacts within the embassy, Berlin,

B. Contacts within the embassy, London,

C. Contacts within the British War Department,

D. British reaction to the massive buildup of war materials within the German Empire, and

E. Diplomatic passports for agents returning to US with you.

9

Reports From Italy

September 6, 1913

The third member of the Triple Alliance is a constitutional monarchy of southern Europe, hereditary in the male line of the house of Savoy. It includes the Apennine Peninsula and the islands of Sicily and Sardinia. From the capitol of Rome, the NIA station chief submitted this report.

The militaristic and imperialistic enthusiasm which made the war with Turkey possible, subsided rapidly after the conclusion of the Treaty of Lausanne in October of last year. The high cost of living in Italy, coupled with the prevalence of unemployment, was an active agency in stimulating resistance to the increased financial and military burdens. The occupation of Libya might be gratifying to Italian patriotism, but it is costing $200,000 a day to maintain. Then, in addition, the enormous military expenditure, millions must be spent on harbors, docks, railways and improvements. If the newly acquired province is to be worth anything, over and above the cost of garrisoning Libya, millions more would be demanded to make Italy's navy and army impressive enough to compete with her new dignity and strong enough to defend the new position.

The Social Democrats have set themselves squarely against all further expenditure on the conquest of Libya. On June 1 of this year, Premier Giolitti said, "If it becomes necessary an appeal to the country will be made in the interest of national defense. It is the firm intention of the government to demand nothing from the lower classes, but to levy new taxes on the wealthy."

My interpretation of this statement is that Italy will defend itself but will no longer promise troops to the Triple Alliance unless one of the members is attacked by its neighbor. I base this interpretation on the Social Democrat's position, which is that in order to fund the Libyan expedition, the ministry had resorted to disguised loans and appropriated the anticipated excess of the income tax receipts as far in advance as 1930. Vice admiral Pasuale Leonardi Cottolica, has been subjected to criticism on account of the proposed naval increases, he has resigned and is succeeded by Admiral Enrico Millo, the leader of the famous raid on the Dardanelles of July 1912.

A "no confidence" vote has been given by the Chamber and a new general election will be held in October of this year. Premier Giolitti is already on the campaign trail, giving out a statement of policy which emphasizes the benefits of colonial expansion and the need for military occupation of the interior of Libya. He has declared that the armament of Italy is to be strengthened, he urged that measures be taken for the regulation of labor disputes, the provision for accident insurance and the need for educational reforms.

His opponent, Signor Sonnino, the leader of the Constitution Opposition, is declaring the same issues in his statements. I will forward the results of the election in October and you can add that information to this report. The Italian army will probably not be called upon in the last quarter of 1913, and probably not in 1914, the budget is just not there. The present army is organized in 12 corps, each of two divisions, the first line is estimated to consist of 310,000 men. In addition, there is maintained a considerable active reserve and a mobile militia. Military service in Italy is compulsory and extends from the twentieth to the thirty-ninth year. This compulsory service consists of two years in the active army for those actually called to the colors, while the second class spend a shorter time, practically but a few months, while the third class are allowed to go on unlimited leave. These third class are enrolled in the mobile militia and are called from time to time for instruction.

Italy has the seventh largest navy in the world, just ahead of Austria. Because Italy is an ally of Austria, the two nations often hold joint exercises in the Adriatic Sea. In case of a naval engagement in the Adriatic, the joint forces would sweep away the Triple Entente navies with little difficulty. The British navy tends to concentrate its naval forces in the Mediterranean from Gibraltar east as far as the Tyrrhene Sea. The Italian navy controls the Tyrrhene, while Austria controls the Adriatic. In the case of global conflict, the Triple Alliance will control the Mediterranean.

10

Reports From Russia/Servia

October 6, 1913

R ussia is an empire of eastern Europe and northern Asia, extending from the Baltic Sea to the Bering and Black Seas. My station chief reports from St. Petersburg the population of 169,500,000 is spread out over area of 8.5 million square miles. As I was writing the introduction for the president's report, I remembered the last time I was in Russia. It was my senior year cruise from Annapolis. The purpose of the cruise was, of course, to give experience to the cadets at Annapolis but it also allowed the *USS Castor, Monongahela* and *Nispsic* to complete their crews and make port of calls in Europe. Both the English and American navies were perennially short of men, but with this difference, American war ships lacking crews stayed in port, while English ships had to go to sea. The safety of Britain depended on it.

The three ships partaking of the US Naval Academy summer cruise that year were:

USS Nispsic, a 1375-ton Adams class gunboat, was the last vessel built at the Potomac Dock Yards prior to the Civil War. At the close of the war she was rebuilt one and one half her original size and was now ready for sea trials. I was assigned as her gunnery officer.

USS Monongahela, a 2078-ton steam sloop built at the Philadelphia Navy Yard in January 1863. She participated in the Gulf of Mexico fleet under Farragut, was in the battles of New Orleans and Mobile Bay. She had just returned from assignment in the western and southern Atlantic.

USS Castor, a 2100 ton Canonicus class monitor built in Jersey City Ship Yards in 1864. She was famous for her two battles at Fort Fisher in North Carolina. The first destroyed the fort and the second sealed off the port of Wilmington. She was involved in the capture of Richmond in 1865. She remained out of commission until 1869 when she was recommissioned as the *USS Mahopac.*

I was not familiar with any of these ships, I went to the Naval Institute and located the detailed descriptions and pulled the photographs. The first was photo #:NH 2151 of the Nispic. I would be the gunnery officer on this ship and I wanted to get a list of her ordnance. The new Nispic would not be recommissioned until she completed her sea trials. She was steam powered with a single smoke stack between two masts which carried six yard arms which were steam powered. She looked like an ironclad typical of the Civil War. I pulled the photo #: NH 45205 next and was looking at another steam powered ship roughly twice the size of the ship I would be serving upon. She was a famous Civil War ship of the line. She would stop at Annapolis for Major Sam Mason, while I would go on board the Nispic. I pulled the final photo # NH 59428 and was looking at the largest monitor I had ever seen, a completely iron and steel ship four times the size of The Monitor that fought at the battle of Hampton Roads. She looked dark and lethal.

The US Navy had decided to send these three vessels on a transatlantic cruise to the European ports of : South Hampton, England; Copenhagen, Denmark; Oslo, Norway; Stockholm, Sweden; Helsinki, Finland; St. Petersburg and Tallin, Russia; Danzig, Prussia and then back to South Hampton. In order to get to South Hampton, the three ships needed to complete their crews. The three ships arrived in Annapolis on June 7, 1876. All officers and hands were given 24 hours shore leave and on the morning of June 9, 1876, we left Annapolis and sailed south back down the Chesapeake and into the Atlantic Ocean. I had spent many hours aboard ships inside the Chesapeake and across the middle Atlantic to Bermuda and back to Annapolis. I was fairly comfortable with the Nispic, she was, after all, classified as a 'gun boat' and I was the ordnance officer in charge of every gun on board.

We had smooth sailing to Philadelphia, two short days, then left for Yarmouth, Nova Scotia. The temperatures dropped fifteen degrees during the five day sail. We were given 24 hours leave again, but I was assigned to ship duty because during the rougher water of the North Atlantic some gun mounts needed adjustment and realignment. June 17th was the day we were to begin heading across the North Atlantic to England in one giant leap, but the Castor began to slow in the heavy seas. She was a monitor and designed for calmer seas. Her decks were awash most of the time and the constant pounding of the bow into the sea was beginning to take its affect. Her captain signaled the Mongongela and Admiral Hagood that she needed to head for Halifax, Nova Scotia to check for repairs. All three vessels headed back to Halifax. We found the damage was slight and soon repaired. Admiral Hagood made the decision to make the crossing in short hops rather than one giant leap. We headed for St. John's, the last stop in Newfoundland. The Castor fared better in calmer seas and we headed across the Baffin Bay to Sydproven, Greenland. Summer in Greenland was winter to most of the American crews.

"Why do they call it, Greenland? It is white!" I asked my crew chief.

From there it was a day to Reykjavik, Iceland. Here we found bright green fields, steaming hot water pools alongside the roads and summer like temperatures.

"Iceland is really Greenland!" I said to another midshipman as we hiked the hills outside Reykjavik.

Each short hop was appreciated by the crew of the Castor. It was a long day and a short night to Scotland. We docked in Orkney. Because they were so far north on the short hop route, Admiral Hagood decided to skip the courtesy call in South Hampton and sail directly into the Baltic. He indicated that the South Hampton port of call would be made on the return leg of the cruise.

Three days later we docked in Tallin, Russia. There were no English speaking natives and no Americans with Estonian language skills. The German speaking naval cadets sought out those Estonians who also spoke German and in this manner we toured Katherine the Great's summer palace and the city of Tallin. The city of Tallin rises dramatically above its port, proud of being the best preserved medieval city in Northern Europe. The city was also founded by Teutonic Knights, that is why the town center looked like a town of German origin. The oldest parts visible to me were the corner towers, including the one nicknamed Pikk Herman.

"That looks a little bit like 'Herman the German' who works for my father." I said to a shipmate.

The upper town was the preserve of the Bishop and the Knights, but the lower town was the heart of the commercial district and the town's wealth. We visited St. Nicholas, St. Olav and Holy Ghost Churches. These were built by each foreign ruler of Tallin; Prussia, Sweden and Russia.

Two days later we docked in St. Petersburg as the midnight sun was just beginning to catch the gold on the spires and domes throughout the city. By design, it was to be the world's most beautiful city, and the capital of its largest empire. Peter the Great, Czar of all Russia, had commanded that a "window to the west" be built to replace the old capital, Moscow. He hired the best Italian, French and German architects to design palaces and buildings in the baroque style. My friends and I admired the Admiralty building which Czar Peter had placed in the geographic center of the city. The soaring gold spire was a symbol of his new navy and merchant marine fleets. Lost American sailors used the spire as a landmark to travel around the city. His wife, Katherine I, succeeded him and continued the construction of the city. She was succeeded by her two daughters Czarina Elizabeth and Katherine II. The city gained its most beautiful buildings after Peter's death.

Since I was including Servia in this report, I remembered that my son, James, had served in the Balkans. A small task force was sent to the Balkan Peninsula by President McKinley in August before the national election. The presidential election of 1900 was unique in that it was the first of the twentieth century and it would be the first election where he could vote. I had sent him a letter describing the Democratic Convention of 1900.

My son finished reading the description of the democratic convention in my letter and asked the captain of the USS *Delaware* how much longer until he would launch his portable submarine, the USS *Swordfish*.

"One hour until sunset, Ensign Caldwell, you better go find the rest of your crew and get on board."

"Aye, aye, Sir." Our mission that night was to begin the mapping of the opening of the Bay of Cattaro in southern Herzegovina. The Department of the Navy was convinced that a war on the Balkan Peninsula was only a matter of time. This peninsula is the eastern most of the three great southern peninsulas of Europe, bounded by the Adriatic Sea, where we were located, on the west and the Black and Aegean seas on the east. Its northern boundary is generally considered to be the Danube, with its tributary, the Save. Thus defined, the peninsula comprises, within an area of 175,000 square miles, the countries of Turkey, Bulgaria, Rumelia, Servia, Montenegro, Bosina and Herzegovina, Novibazar and Greece. Servia, Rumelia and Novibazar had no coast line, thank God. Greece alone contained over 300 separate islands, all with sea ports of some kind or another. The Captain of the Delaware estimated that if the Department of the Navy wanted all the sea ports from the Adriatic to the Black Sea mapped, it would take us about 10,000 man years of effort. He was then told to limit his efforts to one year with the ships and submarines at his disposal. He decided to start with all the major harbors and bays which might see action during a war between these countries. The captain hoisted the Swordfish off his deck and lowered it into the Adriatic.

"See you in the morning, Captain Caldwell." I liked being called a captain, even though the surveying party was only four men and a mass of equipment.

"Aye, aye, Sir." I clamped the hatch on the conning tower, stepped off the ladder and slid to the deck of the Swordfish. "Get us underway, Mr. Fisher. The Delaware and the others will be launching immediately after us." I was speaking through a tube to the engine hold at the rear of the sub. I put the tube to my ear and heard, "Aye, aye, Captain, engine turning over, engine started, drive engaged, moving forward."

"Keep us on the surface tonight, Mr. Jamison, there will be no moon." I did not need a speaking tube, the navigator was at my elbow.

"Aye, aye, Captain, bearing to mapping point is N13oW."

"Which sector are we assigned, Mr. Jamison?"

" Northwestern area 10-3, Sir."

"Increase your speed to 17 knots and keep us on the surface. Ensign Godwin, what do you see through the periscope? The conning tower windows are blurred now."

"Surface is clear all the way ahead, Sir." My exec was a year older than me but had less time in rank. The periscope on our portable submarine was a form of camera obscura, consisting of a long vertical tube with a prism or inclined mirror at the upper and a reflecting surface or prism, below. The upper end is designed to project several feet above water when the boat is entirely submerged. The periscope is, however, practically useless at night or in rough weather. For these and other reasons, the conning towers of portable submarines are built very high, so that direct vision through the glass windows of the conning tower may be obtained without exposing the body of the boat to the observation or attack of the enemy. That is why I was in the conning tower and my exec was at the periscope. Thanks to my year of transfer to Goat Island, I had considerable experience in a small submarine used for mapping. It was almost like second nature to me now to deal with the conditions affecting the stability of an entirely submerged boat, compared with those while on the surface.

Since the sectional area of the immersed body remains unchanged at all angles of heel, the position of the center of buoyancy is constant; the righting moment, therefore, grows more slowly as the boat heels. By suitable ballasting or arrangement of weights, adequate transverse stability is not very difficult to attain. But longitudinal stability is quite another matter. Any possible assistance from ballasting or the arrangement of permanent weights is insignificant, and the change of trim due to the using of fuel and shifting of weights is a very serious matter. This tendency to "heel upwards" is counteracted by the use of horizontal rudders, or shape of the hull, vertical screws, or quickly shifting water ballast. If the boat has a slight surplus buoyancy, the tendency to rise to the surface can be counteracted by vanes or a shape of the head of the boat, which tends to make the boat descend so long as it is moving forward. But as the effect of hull shape or permanent vanes changes with the speed, while the buoyance effort is constant, horizontal rudders are a necessity. From this description, it follows that short, deep and broad boats are the most stable, but such a shape is incompatible with a portable sub designed to be carried on a surface vessel, so I was constantly giving orders to my crew.

Until I had many more years of experience as a captain of a submarine, I would remain with the portable submarine or surface torpedo boat. The Holland Class and the newer, larger submarines had sea-going capacity and a wide radius of action. The scope of usefulness of the portable submarine seemed confined to harbor defense or mapping assignments like we were on tonight. The qualities of the new submarines made it possible for them to accompany a battle fleet. The tactics for these new submarines were yet to be developed and I was confined to this "death trap" as my instructor, WH Hornsby, used to call them. Only fools and Englishmen ever volunteer to get in a portable submarine, the life expectancy is 92 days of service. His statement was burned into my memory as we approached the opening to the Bay of Cattaro.

We never saw the torpedo boat net that stopped our forward motion and sent us all sprawling on the deck.

"Stop all engines." I screamed, I forgot that a portable only has one engine. "Radio, send a message to the Delaware. Torpedo boat nets in place, warn all others. Keep repeating it until you hear back from them."

"Aye, aye, Sir." Came through the speaking tube and from the cross-trained seaman near me. I needed to find out what type of net was in place. Most nets are made of heavy wire rings connected with one another by smaller steel rings, once ensnared, it was almost impossible to free oneself in a few hours. We had until sunrise. I needed to forget about mapping and get my divers in the water with lights to examine the damage. They were already in their gear and I explained to them that the typical net was made up in sections about 15 by 20 feet in size, and those sections join to make the total defense, which is divided into three parts called the "main defense", "bow defense" and "stern defense". Most harbor nets omit the bow and stern defense and use only a main defense. We had to find out what system we were facing. If I restarted my engine to back away and a stern defense was there, it would wrap around our propeller and we would be captured by the coast defenses in the morning.

I sent the divers out through the conning tower and into the water.

"In coming from the Delaware, Sir."

"Read it to me, Radio."

"Maintain radio silence and return to us. It was sent to all boats in the survey parties, Sir." My mind was reeling. If we are ensnared and we can not free ourselves then we are captured, by the order to maintain radio silence, the Delaware has written us off as the 92 day makers. It seemed like hours but it was only minutes and the divers were back.

"It's a Bullivant net, Sir. Attached to two long booms, we must be directly under the ship which has deployed it, Sir."

"Then they heard our messages to the Delaware. They know we are here and will be closing the booms and trapping us like rats. I picked up the speaking tube and screamed, "Start engines." Again, a portable only has one engine, but you get the picture of how frightened I was. "Full speed astern, load torpedo tubes."

"Sir, we don't have any torpedoes on board."

"Throw what ever trash, including the survey equipment, you can find to fill them and close inner doors and crank open the outer doors, I want the captain of that ship above us to hear the sound of the outer doors opening, they make a racket."

"Aye, aye, Sir. Are we going to dump our garbage on them if they don't surrender?" Everyone around me began to laugh. Sometimes a lot of pressure does funny things to men trapped in a tin can called a submarine.

"Edwards, remind me to put you in for a promotion to boat comedian, if we are alive tomorrow morning and standing on the deck of the Delaware." The USS *Swordfish* began to pull away from the torpedo boat net as the booms began to slowly close. I wished I was a diver and in the water to see what the closure rate was and how narrow our escape might be. "Navigator, put us on the bottom. The ball is in his court now. Will he drop charges on an unknown submarine? Will he radio for assistance? Let's see what he will do. Silence in the boat!"

We sat there, waiting. I whispered to my radioman, "Any sound of a message?" He shook his head no. An explosion rocked us and I screamed, "Fire all tubes!" I picked up my speaking tube and said, "Engine stop, switch to battery power."

"Aye, aye, Sir."

"Navigator, get us off the bottom and head for the last location of the Delaware, I assume that it has moved since we launched but I have no idea where it is now. We will start with its last known location and begin a search pattern. Let's hope that all that garbage will make the captain above us think we are hit and he will stop dropping charges."

"Aye, aye, Sir." We all watched the clock face inside our boat. We knew that the next explosion would be soon. The surface garbage would not contain seaman's bodies and an oil slick. It was two minutes and we felt the second explosion. It rocked us just slightly as we pulled out of the charge's circle of death. We had cheated death this time, I need to get out of these portable boats or I may not be as lucky next time.

Servia is one of the Balkan states, a constitutional European monarchy, hereditary in the male line of the house of Karageorgevich. Until 1878 it was an autonomous Turkish dependency, once a part of the great Ottoman Empire. It's capitol is located at Belgrade. Servia recovered Uskub, the ancient capitol, from Turkey in November,1912. By terms of the Treaty of Bucharest, Servia gained as the result of the wars in the Balkans, the eastern part of Novibazar, Kossovo and central Macedonia. This increased the size of Servia by 3 million people and 48 thousand square miles.

The success of Servia's army in the war against Turkey was obvious. A small state with a population of 3 million, just prior to the war, was able to put 12 complete divisions of no less than 400 thousand men into the field within three months of the declaration of war. An additional 200 thousand volunteered in three weeks. Servia has one of the few remaining horse mounted cavalries in Europe, each of the 200 thousand volunteers provided his own horse. In Servia, not only men, but carts and horses are registered with the government and those citizens not possessed of horses are required to pay a heavy tax which is used for the purchase of artillery horses from Austria and Russia. For military service the kingdom is divided into five districts, each of which furnishes a complete division; the first is the Morava, second is the Drina, third is Shumadda, fourth is Timok and the fifth is the headquarters division located at Zayechar. While Servia has military advisors from Austria and Austrian students registered in its university, it maintains a treaty of friendship with Russia. Servia is not part of the Triple Alliance, but it is without doubt that Russia would come to the aid of Servia if attacked by one of its neighbors. Nicholas II, the reigning czar, is of the house of Romanoff-Gottorp-Karrageorgevich, he therefore considers his cousins to be living in Servia.

The unsettled condition of the Balkan nations made the year a trying one for the Russian foreign office. Russian interests in the Black Sea basin, the possibility that Bulgaria might obtain a foothold on the Sea of Marmosa, the weakening of Turkey, its effect on Russian interests in Asia Minor, the promotion of pan-Slavic interests, the diplomatic duel with the Triple Alliance and the preservation of the Triple Entente was of paramount importance. In a general, way it may be said that Russia wished to have her Balkan allies successful against Turkey, to have them look to Russia as their patron and protector, to prevent Austria from intervening and to secure such a settlement as would not readily allow future Austrian expansion southwards. It was quite natural that relations with Austria should have been strained, the remarkable thing was that peace was maintained. The mission of Prince Hobenlohe, who brought the czar an autographed letter from Emperor Franz Joseph I in February, was undoubtedly of great importance, coming as it did when misunderstandings and conflicting policies had almost brought the two nations to the point of war. The situation again became critical in March. Just before the fall of Adrianople, General Radko Dimitryev visited St. Petersburg with the objective, well-informed newspapers affirmed, of obtaining Russian support for the contemplated attack on Constantinople. While General Dimitrev was at the Russian capital, news of the fall of Adrinaople inspired the pan-Slavists with wild enthusiasm. A thanksgiving service was held in the Church of the Resurrection, the Bulgarian national anthem was sung in the streets, the demonstration became so vigorous that the mounted police had difficulty in clearing the streets. The Duma, always enthusiastic over Slavic victories, resented the depression of the demonstration and interpellated the home minister on the subject. Minister Maklakov shifted the responsibility to the police. On the following Sunday a procession was held in the Nevsky Prospekt and banners were displayed with the motto, "Scutari to Montenegro." The prefects of St. Petersburg and Moscow thereupon forbade demonstrations. In spite of the prohibition, a demonstration was held in St. Petersburg on April 24 to celebrate the capture of Scutari. Subsequently the excitement subsided as the situation in the Balkans grew less threatening.

11

Reports From Turkey
November 6, 1913

The most important events of 1913 in Turkey were connected with two more or less distinct wars: (1) that began in October, 1912, and concluded in May, 1913, between Turkey and the Balkan allies (Albania, Bulgaria, Greece, Montenegro and Servia); and (2) July, 1913, between Bulgaria and Turkey allied with Rumania. These two conflicts can be conveniently treated together for this report to the president. Negotiations for peace opened in London on December 16, 1912. The two sides were deadlocked by absolutely contrary views on three weighty matters. The first, both Bulgaria and Turkey maintained that Adrianople was essential to their national safety. The second, Greece demanded the cession by Turkey of all the Aegean Islands, which are populated almost exclusively by Greeks, while Turkey insisted that the retention of some of them (Imbros, Tenedos and Lemnos) was necessary to her for the protection of the Dardanelles. Finally, the allies not only opposed the assumption of any share fo the Ottoman debt, but also urged the payment by Turkey of a war indemnity. This would totally destroy Turkish credit. The Turkish diplomats, therefore, rejected the victor's terms of peace, on January 6, 1913, the allies suspended the conference. Ten days later, the great powers, (Britain, France, Germany, Austria, Italy and Russia) were fearful of a resumption of hostilities in the Balkans, advised in a collective note, to yield on the question of the surrender and cession of Adrianople and to leave the other unsettled problems to the powers for adjudication. For a few days it was believed that the adjudication would hold. On January 22, a coup d'etat in the Turkish capital overthrew the conciliatory ministry of Kiamil Pasha and put in its place a "no surrender" delegation headed by Mahmud Pasha. The only concession which the new government would propose was one for the division of Adrianople and grant of autonomy to the Aegean Islands. This was, of course, unacceptable to the Balkan allies and the first conference in London came to an end.

The war began again on February 3, 1913. During the peace talks, the Bulgarians had dug trenches along the line of cease fire in December. They succeeded in combating every effort of the Turks to advance. The Bulgarian entrenchments forced Enver Bey to try and turn the Bulgarian right flank by means of an advance from the Gallipoli peninsula toward Rodosto. This effort was thwarted after several weeks of rather desultory fighting. Meanwhile the sieges of Adrianople, Janina and Scutari were vigorously persuaded by the allies. On March 6, Janina surrendered to the Greeks. The Bulgarians and Serbs captured Adrianople on March 9, and on the 26th of March the whole eastern line of defenses was carried and Shurki Pasha was compelled to surrender with some 30,000 defenders. The Greek navy then began to capture each of the Aegean Islands and the hostilities finally ended in May, 1913.

The second peace conference now began in London. The capture of Scutari by the Montenegrins on April 26, made the truce general, as soon as King Nicholas had submitted to the powers and surrendered Scutari on May 14, to the international naval force, delegates of all the Balkan allies and Turkey again set out for London. On May 21, they opened the second peace conference for the discussion of the terms of peace. Headed by Sir Edward Grey, the British secretary for foreign affairs, he warned that the great powers would not tolerate protracted deliberations that wrecked the first conference. The diplomats signed the Treaty of London on May 30. Its principal provisions were as follows: (1) The boundary between Turkey and the allies is a line from Midia to Enos to be demilitarized by an international peace keeping force; (2) The borders of Albania to be determined by a committee composed of the great powers; (3) Turkey to cede Crete to Greece; (4) The powers committee will decide the status of the Aegean Islands; and (5) The settlement of all the financial questions arising out of the war to be left to an international commission to meet in Paris.

12

Reports From Balkan States
December 6, 1913

The Treaty of London was a solemn witness to the fact that within eight months, the Ottoman Empire had been shorn of all her European possessions except Constantinople and a small tract of adjacent land east of the Maritza River. That this had been done was due mainly to the union and harmony that had characterized the Balkan allies. But the surprising rapidity and ease with which the result had been achieved only served in the long run to whet the ambition of each of the Balkan states to secure the bulk of the spoils. Even before the conclusion of the Treaty of London, evidence was not lacking of a bitter rivalry and lamentable disunion among the victorious Balkan allies which was to lead, as the event proved, straight to another armed conflict in the region. To understand the genesis of the second Balkan war, it is necessary to consider the validity of the claims advanced by the various states.

When the secret treaty of alliance between Bulgaria and Servia against Turkey was signed in March, 1912, a division of the territory that might possibly fall to them in ease of war was agreed upon. Neither Bulgaria nor Servia ever officially published the treaty, but from the version printed in the Paris newspaper, Le Matin, we know that the division was to be made. A line running from a point just east of Kumanova to the head of Lake Ochrida was to divide the conquered territory between Bulgaria and Servia. This would give Monastir, Koprili, Ochrida, Prilip and Istib to the Bulgarians. Any disputed cities near this dividing line would be left to the arbitration by the czar of Russia. The chief aim of this division was that Servia should obtain a seaboard upon the Adriatic and Bulgaria upon the Aegean. By this division, Bulgaria would obtain western Thrace and the greater part of Macedonia, while Servia would secure the greater part of Albania. These schemes had been entirely upset by the course of events. Bulgaria's share had been considerably increased by the unexpected conquest of eastern Thrace, including Adrainople, whereas Servia's portion had been greatly reduced by the creation of an independent Albania. Prime Minister Pashitch of Servia pointed out that the treaty of alliance required Bulgaria to send detachments to assist the Servian armies operating in the Vardar valley, the reverse had been found necessary and Adrianople had been taken only with the help of 60,000 Serivans and by the means of the Servian siege guns which destroyed the Turkish trenches. Equity demanded that the new conditions, which had arisen and which had entirely altered the situation, should be given consideration and that Bulgaria should not expect the preliminary engagements to be carried out. The answer of Dr. Daneff, the Bulgarian foreign minister, was that Bulgaria bore the brunt of the entrenchment fighting and that had Bulgaria not kept the main Turkish force pinned down, Servia and Greece would have been defeated. He claimed that a treaty is a treaty and that the additional gain of eastern Thrace in no way invalidated the old alliance between the two nations.

The recriminations between Greece and Bulgaria were similar. The treaty of alliance between them, signed in September, 1912, contained no provision for any division of conquered territory, this fact enabled each to indulge in the most extravagant claims. The main bone of contention was the possession of the port of Salonika. At the very beginning of the first Balkan war, both sides pushed forward troops to occupy the port. The Greeks arrived first, their garrison was still much stronger numerically. They maintained that, except for a few merchant Jews, the population was Greek. The Prime Minister of Greece, Venezelos, insisted that the erection of an independent Albania deprived Greece of the port and a large part of northern Epirus. Servia countered this claim by saying Albania was part of Old Servia and belonged to them. Venezelos continued with his objections. He asserted Bulgaria alone would retain everything she hoped for, securing nearly three-fifths of the conquered territory and leaving only two-fifths to be divided by among her three allies. This was despite the fact that but for the activities of the Greek navy in preventing the convoy of Turkey's best troops from Asia; Bulgaria would never have her rapid success at the beginning of the second war. Finally, Venezelos, strenuously objected to the whole seaboard of Macedonia going to Bulgaria where the population was Greek. The answer of Dr. Daneff to the Greek contention was to the effect that Greece already had several good sea ports on the Mediterranean, while Bulgaria had none. Besides, he contended that Greece would get Crete, at least part of the Aegean Islands and a part of the mainland. Greece had suffered least in the wars and was really overpaid for her services.

Behind all these formal apologies and statements of fact, were the conflicting ambitions and the racial hatreds which had existed from time immemorial and which no discussion could effectually resolve. It had been a source of surprise in Vienna that the Christian peoples of the Balkans were able to unite in 1912 on any terms; it was a greater surprise that they had remained united long enough to wage an eight-months' war against Turkey. It surprised no one that Emperor Franz Joseph I, saw this as an opportunity to expand the Hapsburg sphere of influence. The sixty-five year old emperor called upon Francis Ferdinand, the Archduke of Austria, to send intelligence agents into the Balkans to encourage and incite unrest where ever they could find it. It soon became apparent that the sending of over 300 agents into the Balkans was producing results. Even before the surrender of Adrinaople by the Turks, on March 26, military conflicts had taken place between Bulgaria and Servia and Greece. On March 12, a pitched battle occurred between Bulgaria and Greece at Nigrita. A war commission drew up a code of regulations for use in towns occupied by joint armies, both sides ignored the code. The Servians shortly afterwards expelled the manager of the branch of the National Bulgarian Bank at Monastir, a step which elicited emphatic protests from Sofia against the policy of Serbizing districts in anticipation of a final peace. On April 17, Minister Pashitch informed the Servian Skupschtina that his government would refuse to be bound by the terms of the treaty of alliance of March, 1912. From that date until the signing of the Treaty of London on May 30, the recent allies carried on an unofficial war, oftlinewhich consisted of combats of extermination marked by inhuman cruelty. Each of the combatants strained to press forward to occupy new territories, while each continued to accuse the other of violating every principle of international law. The ambassadors of the powers at the capitals of the Balkan states made urgent representations to the respective governments to restrain their armies, but without effect. On June 10, 1913, the Servian government dispatched a note to Sofia demanding a categorical answer to the Servian request for a revision of the Treaty of London. On June 11, the czar telegraphed to King Peter and King Ferdinand appealing to them to avoid a fratricidal war, reminding them of his position as arbitrator under the treaty. The czar warned them that he would hold responsible whichever state used force.

"The state which begins war will be responsible before the Slav cause."

This well-meant action had an effect the opposite of that hoped for. In Vienna it was looked upon as an indirect assertion of moral guardianship of Russia over the Slav world. The Austrian press insisted that the Balkan states were of age and could take care of themselves, if not, it was for the great powers of Europe, not for Russia, to control them. The political horizon grew still darker when one week later Dr. Daneff answered the Servian note in the negative. This resulted in the Servian minister withdrawing from Sofia, the Bulgarian capital, on June 22.

Bulgarian troops had already been set in motion westward from their entrenched positions at Tehataldja and Adrianople. The general plan of the war office in Sofia was to send one force to operate against the Greeks along the line of the Salonika-Seres railway and to surprise the Servians by dispatching masses of Bulgarian troops into the home country of Servia by way of the passes leading directly from Sofia through the western mountains. Such a plan would separate the Greek and Servian forces, at the same time would cut off the Servian armies operating in Macedonia from their base of supplies and require their immediate recall for the defense of the home territory. Against combined Servia, Greece and Montenegro, Bulgaria could oppose, with the aid of Austrian advisors, at least equal forces. The Archduke Francis Ferdinand had sent an unlimited number of military advisors to Bulgaria. If this was the only alignment in the extension of the war, Bulgaria and Austria stood an excellent chance of appropriating the lion's share of Macedonia. But just at this juncture diplomatic relations between Bulgaria and Rumania reached a breaking point. Rumania was the decisive factor in the extension of the war.

As I read the reports from the NIA field agents in the Balkan states, I was amazed when I read Rumania's reaction. They must have had Russian backing, I thought. Rumania had maintained a strict neutrality ever since the Russo-Turkish War of 1877. Rumania had won her independence but lost her province of Bessarabia to Russia, maybe Russia has dangled Bessarabia before the Rumanians, I thought. Since 1877, Rumania had directed her foreign policy in harmony with that of Austria and had, therefore, been considered a true friend of the Triple Alliance. In the past,

Austria had repeatedly used Rumania as a counterpoise to Servia, thus when the Macedonia question was particularly acute and it seemed that action would be taken by Bulgaria, Rumania declared that she would not tolerate an alteration of the status quo, with this declaration, Austria yielded.

Quite aside from Austria's conduct, however, there had long been three important reasons why Rumania would be interested in any projected change in the Balkan situation. In the first place, scattered throughout the Balkans were colonies of Rumanians, the so called Kutzo-Vlachs, their national customs and institutions, long recognized and respected under the old regime, must be guaranteed and maintained under the new. Rumania would hardly allow people of her nationality to be Bulgarized, Servized or Hellenized.

Secondly, Rumania viewed with jealousy and fear the steady growth of her neighbor, Bulgaria, in power and strength. Crowded in between the military empires of Russia and Austria, she naturally looked upon the development of her southern border of another military state, as a menace to her national existence.

Thirdly, against her southern neighbor, Rumania had the weakest kind of frontier known as the Silistria Heights. Rumania lost this district to Bulgaria in 1877, at the same time she lost Bessarabia to Russia. The rectification of her southern boundary had, therefore, always been one of Rumania's chief aims.

War of the Nations

Part III

Archduke Francis Ferdinand inspecting forts at Przemysl, January 1914.
American News Service Wire Photo

13

Chronic Unrest and Nationalism

January 6 - June 27, 1914

The first six months of 1914, was remarkable for attempts made to conciliate the various minority groups whose nationalist sentiments were responsible for the chronic unrest prevalent within the Hapsburg empire and Balkan states. To settle the racial questions throughout the empire, a conference of Czechs and German Bohemians was held. Owing to the serious illness of the aged Emperor, Archduke Francis Ferdinand represented the Crown at the opening sessions. One of the topics was the feud between the Poles and the Ruthenes in Galicia, This was at least modified as the result of a conciliatory efforts by the Archduke. In Croatia the restoration of constitutional government was completed by aid from the Archduke in the spring of 1914. The Archduke was seen in public along with his wife, the Duchess of Hohenburg. The American News Service reports and photographs followed them throughout the empire and Balkan states.

The Archduke was successful everywhere he went, except the dealings of the Hungarian government with the 3,000,000 Rumanians who inhabited eastern Hungary, the Bukovina and Transylvania. The announcement that the Archduke and his aide, Count Tesza, were negotiating for the support of the Rumanians was met with angry protests from the Magyars, and their Count Czernin. The rejection of Count Tesza's kindly overtures by Rumania did not improve the situation. The American News Service reported that the Rumanian League of Culture, decried Hungary's treatment of the Rumanians in Transylvania. The League also indicated that they could see the day when Russia would aid Rumania to take Transylvania, while Servia would annex Bosnia-Herzegovina. Apprehension grew in Vienna as Russia was poised to add the Ruthenian districts of Hungary and Austrian Galicia. Count Vladimir Brobrinsky was arrested for treason because he was the president of the Russo-Galician Association.

At his treason trial, Count Bobrinsky described the proselytizing activities of the association and acknowledged its endeavors to spread the Russian Orthodox religion. He denied that his efforts were directed against the Hapsburg monarchy. In the course of the trial, another 189 members of the association were arrested for alleged Russophil propaganda among the Ruthenes. The trial ended March 3, 1914, when 32 were found guilty of incitement against religion and state and were sentenced to terms of imprisonment varying from six months to four years. Two of those sentenced were Edwardo Princip, the father of Garvrilo Princip a student studying in Sarajevo, Bosina and Nedeljko Cagrinovic.

A second trial was begun in April, of an American News Service journalist, two Orthodox priests and a law student, on the charge of having conducted an agitation for annexation of Galicia to Russia. The four were acquitted and set free in June.

American News Service was created as an independently owned company of Caldwell International. My father, Admiral Jason Edwin Caldwell, had founded CI in the mid 1800's and I had reorganized it under his direction two years before his death. After his death, I decided to form a separate company for commercial photography attached to, but separate from, the New Yorker Magazine in New York City. I rented office space in the building owned by Teddy and Ruth Roosevelt and hired a staff of dedicated workers screened by my sister, Ruth. I met with them in order to indicate what I hoped to accomplish by this new research effort. My idea for this research was simple. The improvements in the mode of production of light for common use are sufficiently new and remarkable to distinguish this century from all the ages that preceded it.

But they sink into insignificance when compared with the discoveries which have been made as to the nature of light itself, its effect on various kinds of matter leading to the art of photography and the complex nature of the Solar Spectrum leading to Spectrum Analysis. This group of investigators, employed by CI and supervised by my sister, would make remarkable breakthroughs beyond what Thomas Young had managed to do. I explained it this way.

"Although Huygens put forward the wave theory of light more than two hundred years ago, it was not accepted, or seriously studied, until the beginning of the 1900's, when Thomas Young and others began to explain all the phenomena of refraction, double-refraction, polarization, diffraction and interference, some of which were inexplicable on the Newtonian theory of the emission of material particles. I am an engineer and before I put you all to sleep, let me give you an example of what I am talking about. Before commercial photograph, newspapers and magazines printed their sheet stock from solid blocks of metal type. If they wanted to print a cartoon or a map or a diagram to place in the paper, they had to hire an engraver to etch or scribe lines into a block of material that would be set along with the type. If you picked up a paper during the Civil War, there were no photographs in the paper, only these engraved images.

I want you folks to devise a system that takes a photograph and breaks it into a series of dots. ATT sends dots and dashes across great distances. These are then printed as words on a piece of paper. By the end of this calendar year, I want to send a series of dots to San Francisco and let the Herald Offices there put the dots together as a picture suitable to publish in the next day's newspaper."

I stopped and looked around the room. I continued, "How can we do this? The same way the alchemists in the Sixteenth Century did it, granted, we have a few more tools than they did, like Hertz wave transmission. In 1802, Wedgewood described a mode of copying paintings on glass by exposure to light, but neither he nor Sir Humphry Davy could find any means of rendering copies from the glass plates. This was done by M Niepce of Chalons, France, and perfected by Daguerre in 1839, known as the Daguerrotype. Permanent portraits were taken by him on silvered plates, and they were so delicate and beautiful that probably nothing we will do can surpass them. By 1850, the far superior collodion-film on glass was perfected and negatives were taken in a camera-obscura, which, when placed on black velvet, or when coated with a black composition, produced pictures almost as beautiful as the Daguerrotype. As everyone in this rooms knows, positives were printed from the transparent negatives which is the process you use here for the New Yorker. It is extremely costly to print a photograph in a magazine – so we see very few today, in a little more than a year the dot process I have proposed will make photographs cheap to print in any newspaper or magazine. The process we shall keep a secret, we will not even apply for a patent. The wealth of this idea is the transmission of the photograph to OTHER newspapers and magazines. I want to create an *American News Service* which will sell the images ready to print. That means that we will need photographers employed by us, to capture these images for us. For the near future, almost all of our new employees will be women. If you have girl friends who want a job, ask them to apply, we will train them."

I looked around the room which contained some women but mostly men. I now focused the discussion upon them.

"I still have not told you how we are going to send a photograph over a telephone. The principle is the same for the light waves of photography as it is for sound waves. The voice sets up vibrations in the transmitting diaphragm, which, by means of an electric current, are so exactly reproduced in the receiving diaphragm as to give out the same succession of sounds. This is even more apparent when we consider the phonograph, where the vibrations of the diaphragm are permanently registered on a wax cylinder, which, at any future time, can be made to reproduce the sound recorded. Therefore, the wire photo is assembled at the receiving end the same way a phonograph plays the wax recording."

"Mr. Caldwell, how is the wire photo produced at the sending end?" One of the men was on the same page as me.

"The method is as follows: A sensitive film, of some of the usual salts of silver in albumen or gelatin, is used, but with much less silver than usual, so as to leave the film quite transparent. It must also be perfectly homogeneous, since any granular structure would interfere with the number and types of dots produced. Remember, these dots are going to be sent over a telephone line as electric pulses, the louder the pulse, the darker the dot. A solid line in a regular photograph is not a solid line when sent over the telephone, it is series of dots placed close together."

"Yes, I understand that, but how are the dots created?"

"This film is placed on a glass sheet built into a frame that you will construct here in the office shops. The back of this frame has a shallow cell that can be filled with mercury which is in contact with the film. It is then exposed in the usual way, but much longer than for an ordinary photograph, so that the light waves have time to produce the series of dots. The light of each dot's darkness, being reflected by the mercury bath, meets the incoming light and produces a set of standing waves – that is, of waves surging up and down, each in a fixed plane. When these standing waves are passed through a magnetic field, the electric pulses are produced, some strong, some weaker. The result is that the metallic particles in the film become sorted and stratified by this continued wave action to form a dot pattern to be sent over the telephone."

"How does the quality of this wire photo compare with our continuous tone, black and white photos that we produce for the New Yorker?"

"From the naked eye you can not tell the difference. If you drop a jeweler's loop over the wire photo, however, the dots appear. To increase the quality of the wire photo we shoot negatives at a much larger scale than we normally would. For example, an 11 x 14 inch negative on the sending end will result in a 5.5 x 7 inch wire photo at the receiving end."

"Oh, I see, the smaller the photo received and the larger the photo sent, the better."

"You got it, brother. Now for the good part. The receiving end does not bother to make a photo. The image is sent over the telephone as sound pulses, so why not burn those directly onto a metal plate designed to run on a newspaper press?"

"You can do that?"

"That is what this research department is going to be doing in the next several months. My father, Jason Caldwell, had a few good men working for him, the first was Professor Samuel Morse from MIT and the second was Alexander Bell from Boston University. My father provided the encouragement and financial backing for both of these men and look what they produced. Someone in this room will experiment long enough with mercury and magnetic fields to give us the results we are looking for. As you know, I am an Admiral in the United States Navy and special assistant to the President. He keeps me busy. I don't have a lot of time for research, I wish I did. I am the financial backing that this venture needs to succeed and my sister and son here today are my eyes and ears for this project. James Jason Caldwell II is taking early retirement from the US Navy and he will be managing this development project. I will now turn the meeting over to him."

He was not used to public speaking, it did not come up much in a crowded submarine. But then he remembered that there can only be one captain on a ship of war, it was not a place where the crew voted on what they wanted to do. They followed their captains, even to their deaths.

"My father has given you his plan for the research that will be conducted in this office for the next year. I am still a Commander in the United States Navy and I will be until sometime in future, when the navy decides what they will do with me, either promote me or release me. My Aunt Ruth is likewise engaged here at the New Yorker with her husband until he decides if he would like to run for another term. I have no idea what her plans will be at that time, she might return to the New Yorker or she might not. The point is, there is a managing editor for the New Yorker and he is in constant touch with my sister. So if your questions and concerns are related to the magazine, please contact him. If, however, your question involves the *American News Service* that my father mentioned, you will be working under the leadership of Charlie Reuter. Would you stand so that everyone can see you, Charlie? Thank you, you may sit down." He saw the look of surprise on some of the people in the front row of our meeting hall, he shifted gears.

"I may seem a little abrupt or military in my speech and mannerisms. I am not from the business world, neither is my father, we were trained by the military as leaders. We will not apologize for that, I think you will appreciate our direct and honest approach to business problems and the solutions suggested for those problems. My father has trust in my leadership of this and several other CI divisions that he is in the process of forming this year. He is the idea man and I am your worst nightmare if you do not decide to give us your total commitment and effort on the task before us.

The task, as I see it, is an opportunity to work on one of the most revolutionary technologies of our times. Photography is this beautiful and wonderful art, which already plays an important part in the daily life and enjoyment of all civilized people. Commercial photography, as described by my father, will extend the bounds of human knowledge into the remotest regions of this country. His idea is not an improvement of, or development from, anything that went before it, but is a totally new departure.

Think for a moment what photography did for mankind. Cave man drew on the walls of his cave with a charcoal stick, he wanted to capture the mammoth that he just killed, or the beauty of his surrounds outside the cave. He became the painters and sculptors of our society. It is true that the greatest Greek or Roman art can not be equaled by the productions of the photographic camera; but great artists are few and far between, and the ordinary, or even the talented, draftsman can give us only the suggestion of what he envisions, so modified by his peculiar mannerism as often to result in a mere caricature of reality. From such wanderings as these, we shall be saved by commercial photography, and our descendants in the middle of the century will be able to see how much and what kind of change really does occur from decade to decade and century to century.

That such a new and important concept as commercial photography for newsmen should have had its birth this day, and have come to maturity, so closely coincident with the other great discoveries of the century already mentioned by my father, is surely a very marvelous fact. One which will seem more extraordinary to the future newsmen and women, than it does to those of you who will discover, develop, and perfect the process. That is often the case, those who have witnessed the whole process of its growth and development are not awed by it. My father and I will be the ones awed by your work, by your discoveries, by our perfection of the wire photo. It is yours to take credit for, to be proud of and your children and grandchildren who you will tell how you took the old man's ideas and made them blossom."

14

Revenge in Sarajevo
June 28, 1914

The first event of the war of the nations covered by American News Service was the assassination, June 28, of Archduke Francis Ferdinand, nephew of Emperor Franz Joseph and heir to the Hapsburg throne. This was the Archduke's first official visit to the capital of Bosina and he traveled with his wife, as usual. Their entry into the city had been interrupted by the explosion of a bomb, thrown by a Nedeljko Cabrinovic and fortunately enough, the Archduke warded off the flying package with his arm. The bomb exploded under the following automobile, wounding the Archduke's aide for the day, Colonel Merizzi. With admirable coolness the Archduke stopped his car and gave orders to have the colonel and other injured persons attended to. He then ordered the procession to the town hall, where he was greeted by the Mayor of Sarajevo. After the welcoming ceremony, the Archduke set out for the hospital to inquire about the condition of the injured parties. As the royal car rounded the corner of Rudolph street, Gavrilo Princip fired several revolver shots from the sidewalk, wounding the Duchess in the side and the Archduke in the neck. Both lost consciousness and died before reaching the hospital. Princip and Carrinovic were arrested and held for trial. The bodies of the unfortunate couple were taken back to Vienna, where they lay in state in the chapel of the imperial palace on the morning of July 3 and were viewed by thousands. After the funeral rites were observed in the chapel, the remains were ferried across the Danube to Arstetten on a boat lighted by torches, they were interred there.

A merican News Wire Service: Dateline London, July 5, 1914. Requiem masses were said here in London and in other foreign capital cities for the repose of the souls of the Archduke and his wife. As the children of the murdered Archduke have been excluded from the succession by their father's oath, the new heir to the Austrian throne is Archduke Charles Joseph, the eldest son of Archduke Ferdinand's younger brother, Otto. The news that the Archduke had fallen victim to an assassin caused a tremendous outburst of indignation, manifested by popular anti-Serb demonstrations throughout the empire. Many hopes for the future had been pinned on the murdered Archduke Ferdinand. His piety had made him a favorite with Pope Benedict, his vigorous patriotism and his conscientious fulfillment of his administrative duties promised him a future greatness as the Dual Monarch. Most significant of all, he was a conspicuous friend of the Slavs. He was known to favor the reorganization of the empire so as to place the Slavs on an equal footing with the Germans and the Magyars. For the very reason that he aspired to conciliate the discontented racial elements in Austria-Hungary, he was most dangerous to the Pan-Serbian cause........

A merican News Wire Service: Dateline Vienna, July 6, 1914. What has caused the fiercest indignation here is the widespread belief that the Sarajevo crime is part of the Pan-Serb agitation for the incorporation of Bosina into a larger Servia. Bosina and Herzegovina, taken together, form a triangular block of territory, less than half the size of New York State, wedged in between Servia and Montenegro on the east.........

A merican News Wire Service: Dateline Belgrade, July 7, 1914. The shock of the murder of Archduke Ferdinand has spread through the capital of Servia like a wild fire. The claims from Vienna that the two persons arrested for the crime are Serbs is ridiculous. Nedeljko Cabrinovic is a convicted felon from the courts in Hungary. He was convicted and served three months in prison because he was found guilty of incitement against religion and state. Edwardo Princip, the father of Garvrilo Princip, a student studying in Sarajevo, Bosina, is still serving his sentence for the same crime. The Sarajevo affair is not the first blood deed for which Austria has blamed us, but the high rank of the victims and the manufactured evidence that the plot has been hatched here in Belgrade, will give Vienna reason to believe that the time has come to stamp out Pan-Serbianism once and for all ....

Amerikan News Wire Service: Dateline Sarajevo, July 19, 1914. The news of a third arrest in the murder investigation of Archduke Ferdinand has the population buzzing. Trifko Grabez is being held along with Gavrilo Princip and Nedeljko Cabrinovic, all citizens of Bosina. The three are being charged with murder and attempted murder. A fourth man, Milan Ciganovic, is wanted for questioning. In statements given to the judicial investigators, Ciganovic, a Servian State employee, is accused of importation of bombs and arms from the Servian army depot at Kragujevac. Grabez has confessed that he was trained by Ciganovic in the use of the bombs and the pistols, that the arms were smuggled across the Bosnian frontier by a secret system of transport under Ciganovic's direction and with the connivance of Servian frontier officials.......

American News Wire Service: Dateline Vienna, July 23, 1914. The Austro-Hungarian government has presented an ultimatum to Belgrade. A copy of this extraordinary document was given to American News. It is couched, in the most peremptory terms, its spirit is that of an outraged government, exasperated beyond endurance and determined to stop Pan-Serb criminal actions. Quoting from the document - "the crimes culminating in the Sarajevo tragedy has compelled this government to abandon its attitude of benevolent and patient forbearance, to put an end to the intrigues which form a perpetual menace to the tranquillity of this nation and to demand effective guarantees from the Servian government. The Servian government must publish on the front page of its Official Gazette and in the Official Bulletin of the army, a declaration condemning the propaganda against Austria, regretting the participation of Servian officers and functionaries of the propaganda and warning its population that henceforward such machinations will be vigorously suppressed and punished. The Servian government is further called upon to:

1. Suppress anti-Austrian publications,
2. 2. Dissolve the anti-Austrian society Narodna Obrana,
3. Eliminate anti-Austrian textbooks from its schools,
4. Discharge any Servian government employee who is a member of Narodna Obrana or other similar anti-Austrian society,
5. Accept Austria collaboration and investigation of all Servian government employees,

6. Take judicial proceedings of all Servian government employees found to have taken place in the plot of June 28,
7. To locate and arrest Milan Ciganovic and his accomplice Tankosic,
8. Stop the illicit traffic in arms and explosives across Servian borders,
9. Retraction of all anti-Austrian utterances by Servian officials,
10. Signify acceptance of the demands within 48 hours." ....

American News Wire Service: Dateline London, July 24, 1914. The Austro-Hungarian Note, was communicated to the other members of the European Powers today. It was delivered in English, French, German and Russian so that few translations would have to be made. Most diplomats have agreed that it is a formidable document, to which Servia could hardly yield without a humiliating surrender of her sovereign rights. The Political Director of the Powers Committee has advised Servia to invite arbitration and to act with all caution; Sir Edward Grey urged compliance with as many points as possible, but he stated that complete acceptance by Servia seems out of the question ....

American News Wire Service: Dateline Belgrade, July 25, 1914. Under support of Russia, Belgrade has asked for an extension of time to begin an investigation of the charges. Whether a refusal for a time extension would cause Austria to declare war immediately, is not clear here. If Austria attacks Servia, Russia will immediately declare war upon Austria. By strong ties of racial kinship and religion, Russia is treaty bound to protect us, in the meantime, the Servia government is prepared to concede to all demands except the Austrian participation in the investigation......

American News Wire Service: Dateline London, July 27, 1914. Sir Edward Grey proposes joint committee of Germany, France, Italy and England to investigate the claims of Austria against Servia. The German ambassador in London declared, "The German government desires urgently the localization of the dispute, because every interference of another European power would, owing to natural play of alliances, be followed by incalculable consequences." This has been interpreted by the war department here, that if Russia intervened, Germany would once again stand at the side of her ally.....

American News Wire Service: Dateline Berlin, July 28, 1914. The German government has declined the invitation from Sir Edward Grey to attend the solution committee that he proposed. Austria has declared that a state of war now exits between Austria and Servia. Austria has begun seizing Servian vessels on the Danube. The Triple Entente countries have sent a message to Vienna, encouraging Austria to extend the deadline. The Russian foreign minister here has demanded a prolongation of the terms of the ultimatum, England and France have decided to support the Russian demand. German minister, Herr von Jagow, replied that he had doubts as to the wisdom of Austria yielding at the last moment and was inclined to think that such a step might increase the assurance of Servia. Herr von Jagow fears that the plea would have no result. Meanwhile, the Russian charge d'affaires in Vienna was not allowed to present his communication from St. Petersburg to his counterpart in Vienna ....

15

Declarations of War
July 28 - December 1914

Owing to a difference of thirteen days between the calendar used in Orthodox countries and the calendar used in Western Europe, the Austro-Hungarian note of July 23 was received in Servia on July 10. When the deadline for response to the note of July 25 arrived in Vienna, Austria did not at once declare war on Servia. They waited until the deadline arrived on the Orthodox calendar and began the mobilization of the their army and moved the standing army to the Servian border just north of Belgrade. Expecting an invasion, the Servians moved their capital from Belgrade to Nish and began the mobilization of their army and sent a request for aid to Petrograd (St. Petersburg).

This written request was notification of the possibility of a formal declaration of war between Austria-Hungary and Servia . Servia renewed its request for a delay in responding to Vienna and a pledge to the czar that Servia would not declare war on Austria or cross its border to the north. The reaction in St. Petersburg was certainty that Russia and other powers would be drawn into the conflict. It became of prime importance to prevent or at least delay the Austrian declaration of war. With this in view, the Russian minister of foreign affairs, Sazonov, interviewed the Austrian ambassador to Russia, Count Szapary and asked him to obtain the permission of his government for a private exchange of views in order to redraft certain articles of the Austrian Note. Such direct conversations between Vienna and St. Petersburg might lead to an amicable understanding and would surely remove the unfortunate impression created by Vienna's failure to explain her intentions frankly to St. Petersburg.

While these Russian overtures were awaiting Austrian approval, a parallel effort to preserve the peace was being made in the United States and England. Sir Edward Grey had already proposed that the conflict between Servia and Austria be settled by a committee of European nations, when this was met with a curt refusal from Vienna, he wrote President Wilson. The president called his cabinet together and read the note from Sir Edward.

"President Wilson, the situation in eastern Europe has come to a head between Servia and Austria. It is my fear that the entire continent will be drawn into the conflict. I am requesting that all the heads of state in the free world send messages of concern to Vienna. The American News Service has American citizens in both Vienna and Belgrade, it is time to advise all Americans in eastern Europe that conflict is within days of commencing."

The shock on some of the cabinet members faces was proof that the president was not sharing my daily briefings with the entire cabinet. It was time to speak or hold my tongue.

"Mr. President, may I respond first?"

"Yes, Admiral, what is it?" It was clear that Mr. Wilson was irritated with my interruption.

"I propose that you send identical notes of concern to the Emperors of Austria-Hungary, Germany and Russia, the King of Great Britain and the President of the French Republic."

"Nothing to Belgrade?"

"No, Mr. President, Servia is doomed in my opinion. The best outcome that I can see is annexation as a Russian Provence."

"What about the rest of the Balkan states?"

"Again, the best outcome will be annexation into the neighboring empires to avoid a world at war."

"You mean, a war in Europe."

"No, Mr. President, the war will be a worldwide. It will begin in Europe and spread into western Asia, northern Africa and into the Atlantic Ocean. Germany has a very large navy and they will carry the war to the eastern seaboard of the United States in order to starve England into submission."

"You see England in the conflict and you see us protecting England." The Secretary of State had spoken for the first time.

"Yes, Mr. Secretary, we should prepare to assist England in the next few weeks."

"You are not the Secretary of War, Admiral, the president makes those decisions." The Secretary of War had spoken for the first time. Before long the entire cabinet had expressed their opinions.

"All right, all right. We have had a good and frank discussion. It is now time to respond to Sir Edward." The president was still irritated with me.

"Mr. Byran, what would you say in a note to Sir Edward?" The president asked.

"I would not reply to Sir Edward, Admiral Caldwell is correct. You should only communicate with heads of state."

"What would you say to the King of England, George V isn't it?"

"Yes Mr. President. This is what I would send, "As official head of one of the powers signatory to The Hague Convention, I feel it to be my privilege and my duty, under Article 3 of that convention, to say to you in a spirit of most earnest friendship that I should welcome an opportunity to act in the interest of European peace, either now or in the future, as an occasion to serve you and all concerned in a way that would afford me lasting cause for gratitude and happiness."

The cabinet meeting was abruptly ended and the President asked me to see him in one hour in the Oval Office, not his working office. This probably meant that he was about to ask for my resignation from his cabinet. The meeting began this way.

"James, you surprise me every time we meet in public. Why didn't you bring those concerns to me in our daily briefings?"

"Mr. President, have you shared the materials from my briefings with all of the cabinet members?"

"Some, but not all, why do you ask?"

"The look of shock on some of the faces, prompted me to speak my mind. I apologize if I was out of line, Sir."

"You were not out of line, out of place, is all. I want your thoughts during our daily briefings, understood."

"Yes, Mr. President."

"Now tell me what you hear from your sons, Louis is in London and James is in the middle of the Atlantic, probably."

"Louis is station chief in London, Mr. President, James is in command of the Atlantic submarine fleet and happy to be out of the NIA, he really was not a very good spy, Sir." We both chuckled.

"What did you think of Bill Bryan's note to the kings?"

"I would send it, Sir."

"I have already written the telegram as stated by Bill and had the communications center in the basement send it out. I will share with you the responses, oh and by the way, I want you to name your successor as Director of NIA, you are going to be promoted to Presidential Advisor for Foreign Affairs."

"I recommend, Admiral Lowe. Why the promotion, Mr. President, this sounds like something that the Secretary of State or the Secretary of War should be doing."

"That's just it, it falls between the two, right down the proverbial crack. You are aware that Bill has a golden tongue, but has no clue about what is really going on below the surface in eastern Europe. He can handle situations after they arise. I need you to tell me your best guess of what might happen, not what has already happened."

"Yes, Mr. President, I hate guessing, but I will try. We are headed for war, I am certain of that."

"So am I, James. I will delay our entry into it as long as I can. I do not want American's killed in Europe for a centuries old conflict that will never be resolved."

The responses came back to the White House within a week. England, France and Italy welcomed the president's interest and concern and gave their consent to a private meeting with the presidential advisor for foreign affairs, newly appointed Admiral Caldwell. I would be traveling again. The German Chancellor declined the president's offer of assistance and refused to meet with his advisor in Berlin. He preferred to rely on the direct exchange of views between Vienna and Petrograd. At the same time Germany refused to urge her ally, Austria, to accept the president's statement "to abstain from all action which might aggravate the existing situation." The German Chancellor insisted that the quarrel with Servia was a purely Austrian concern with which Russia had no right to meddle. The French president in Paris declared that France desired to work for the maintenance of peace, but would no longer insist on joining a British sponsored arbitration. The Kaiser, in Berlin declared that "We can not encourage Austria, in her dispute with Servia to come before a European tribunal."

I kissed Emily goodbye and boarded a ship for South Hampton. I would not get any American News Service newspaper reports for five days. Things were happening so fast, that five days seemed like a lifetime before

Louis, Cathleen and their seven year old son, Spencer, met me in South Hampton. The first thing I asked Louis was, "What has happened in the last week while I was at sea?"

"Didn't you get wireless telegrams on board?"

"Yes, of course, but that was what was happening in response to the president's telegrams to European heads of state. What has Austria done?"

"July 29th they began the bombardment of Belgrade. Russia called her reservists to service. July 31st Germany demanded that Russia cease mobilization within twelve hours. Germany and Belgium begin mobilization."

"What have you heard from Washington, Dad?" Cathleen and Spencer looked neglected.

"Not before I kiss your beautiful wife and son, Louis." I placed a juicy one on Cathleen's cheek and started to hug Spencer and give him a kiss. He pulled away and offered his hand to shake.

"Grandfather, really, I am seven years old and in my second year at White Book school for the gifted."

"And how do the gifted greet their Grandfathers from America?" He relented and let me hug him. "Jolly good, lad. Now let me see your muscles." He laughed and gave me the mister atlas look with both arms showing his biceps. It was something we had always done since he could walk.

Louis found us a cab and we found my luggage and loaded it for the trip to their London apartment. The topic of conversation continued.

"The president received a telegram on July 27th, in reply to his telegram to Czar Nicholas. He stated that he has sent a note to the Prince Regent of Servia saying, *Neglect no step which might lead to a settlement. If in spite of our pacific endeavors, war breaks out, your highness may rest assured that Russia will in no case disinterest itself in the fate of Servia.* He then went on to indicate that the order for mobilization against Austria would be issued on the day that Austria crosses the Servia frontier."

"Has Germany responded to the president?"

"Yes, several telegrams have been exchanged. The latest, July 28th, stated, *Russia is throughly in earnest, a general war can not be averted if Servia is attacked by Austria.*"

"Well, that has already happened, Dad."

"So it is an official declaration of war by Austria?"

"Yes, dated July 28th, the official deadline in the Austrian Note. I have many bits and pieces of information from my sources in London and from Hans in Berlin and Vlady in Petrograd. Valdy got his hands on the German ambassador's note to the Russians, it stated, *Preparatory military measures by Russia have forced us to counter-measures which must consist in mobilizing the army and navy.*"

"But mobilization means war, Louis."

"Yes it does. As we know, the obligations of France towards Russia, this German mobilization will be directed against both Russia and France."

"We can not assume that Russia desires to unchain a European war, Louis."

"Hans reports that apparently official circles in Berlin believe that the Russian government is only bluffing and could be easily intimidated by Germany, for both the German Secretary of State and the Austro-Hungarian ambassador at Berlin expressed the opinion that Russia was neither desirous nor prepared for war. Only such a conviction - or else a deliberate intention to provoke a European conflict - could explain the action coming from Vienna in declaring war on Servia. The declaration of war has made mediation impossible and your trip here was wasted."

"Why is it wasted?"

"Because while you on the ocean, the Russian government decreed the mobilization against Austria of 13 army corps in the four southwestern military districts of Kiev, Kazan, Odessa and Moscow. Since Vienna has declined direct conversations with Russia, declared war on Servia, mobilized its entire army corps and has sent troops to the Russian borders, a state of war exists now between Austria and Russia."

"Has Servia declared war on Austria?"

"No need, they severed relations with Austria on July 26th."

"Has Austria declared war on Russia?"

"The NIA station in Vienna says it was be sent on August 6th. It came as a surprise because Vlady had reported that Russia was still willing to carry on direct conversations with Vienna, or to accept the new British proposal for a Four Power conference (Italy, England, France and Germany), or better yet, to combine both methods."

"That is exactly what the wireless telegrams from Washington said, I have some of the them here in my brief case, would you like them, Cathleen? You can take them to the war office and copy them of you like."

"Thank you, Admiral. Austria and Germany have both rejected our offer of a peace conference and the Russian proposal. France, Italy and

Russia signaled their willingness to accept any kind of diplomatic action which Sir Edward might think most effective for the preservation of peace. Sir Edward had communicated with the Germans and asked them to suggest any method by which the influence of the four powers could be used together to prevent war between Austria and Russia."

"So where does England stand, Cathleen?"

"Sir Edward is 'keeping score', so to speak. The declarations of war to date are: Austria against Russia on the 6th, Montenegro on the 8th and of course Servia on July 28th; France against Germany on the 3rd and Austria the 10th; Germany against Russia on the 1st, France on the 3rd, Belgium on the 4th; England against Germany on the 4th and Austria on the 12th; Montenegro against Austria on the 12th and Germany on the 9th; Russia against Austria and Germany, Serbia against Austria and Germany, and the month of August is not even over."

"I know, Cathleen, this has just started, President Wilson has told me that we will be in it up to our eyebrows because we have begun to send war materials to France and England. When Germany realizes this, they will extend the war into the Atlantic as far as our shipping ports along the eastern seaboard. I would like to see the war contained to Austria and Servia, but Turkey is the wild card, if they join Austria and Germany, England and France will be required to protect their holdings in north Africa and Asia minor."

Reporting from London, I sent the following messages to the White House.

Germany and France: at 7pm on July 31, five hours before the German ultimatum was delivered at Petrograd, Russia, another ultimatum was presented in Paris. This demanded, within 18 hours, a declaration whether France would remain neutral in a Russo-German conflict. The French President gave a noncommittal reply on August 1, and ordered the mobilization of the French army. Germany did not declare war on France until August 3rd.

Germany and Russia: in declaring war on Russia, Germany alleged that Russia had begun the conflict by moving troops into German territory. This can not be verified, but I assume it is the same propaganda used against France when Germany claimed the French army air corps flew into Germany and dropped bombs on Wessel and Nuremburg. It is true that the Germany army entered France on August 2nd at the village of Joncherey.

Luxemburg and Belgium: these buffer states are in the path of the German armies approaching France and on the morning of August 2, Germany invaded Luxemburg to protect the use of railways which had been leased to Germany by Luxemburg. Luxemburg protested against this violation of its neutrality and Germany paid a $250,000 indemnity to Luxemburg. This was followed by an ultimatum to Belgium. The ultimatum was really a note of Germany intentions, "reliable information regarding the contemplated march of French forces on the line of the Meuse by Givet and Namur....." In self-defense, Germany is sending forces to repel the French invasion through Belgium. If Belgium would maintain its neutrality, like Luxemburg, Germany would pay an indemnity similar to what it paid Luxemburg. Twelve hours were allowed for the Belgium reply. Immediately, the Belgium foreign minister notified Berlin that France in August, had notified Berlin that France would honor Belgian neutrality and that the proposed German action would be a flagrant violation of international law. King Albert of Belgium sent a telegram to King Edward of England and asked for assistance if Germany attacked a neutral nation. German forces entered Belgium at Gemmenich on the morning of August 4. Belgium telegraphed London, Paris and Petrograd to assist in opposing the German invasion by force of arms. On August 10, the Belgian government received a second German communication, forwarded through the Netherlands, regretting that bloody encounters should have resulted from the Belgian's resistance. It urged the Belgian government to "spare Belgium the further horrors of war by forming a compact with Germany." The invitation was returned unopened, attached was the declaration of war by Belgium upon Germany.

Great Britain and Germany: The violation of Belgium neutrality is the official reason for England's entry into the war against Germany. German Chancellor Herr von Bethmann-Hollweg contacted Sir Edward Grey and offered the same thing he had offered to Luxemburg and Belgium, if Great Britain would remain neutral, he promised to not annex any Belgium or French territory and add it to the German Empire. If, however, England tried to protect Belgium and France, any conquered territory in Belgium and France would be added to the German Empire.

The reply by Sir Edward was a masterpiece. He went to the House of Commons and I was in the visitor's gallery, he presented this speech, "Whilst Great Britain is under no treaty obligations to assist Belgium or France, I have, this day, assured the King of Belgium and the President of France that the British Fleet will prevent the German fleet from leaving the

Baltic Sea. Any German vessel, of any type will be sunk, so help me God." After a rousing demonstration by the members of the house, he went on to explain that as a guarantor of Belgium neutrality and independence, Great Britain was vitally concerned in preventing the conquest of Belgium as part of the German Empire. The war office was forming an expeditionary force to be sent to Belgium in the next few days.

Three separate war fronts: the war began by the invasion of Servia by Austria against the "Slavic Peril" (Russia, Servia and Montenegro). But from the early days of August and September, defense against Russia was of minor interest as compared with the attacks on Luxemburg, Belgium and France. The reason was simple, Austria was to sweep down and conquer Servia in a few days and keep the Russian hordes off the German army while they quickly subdued the low countries and entered France all the way to Paris. Having crushed France, the German army would be transferred to the east to turn back the tide of Russia's slow-mobilizing multitudes. For Russia, with all her 171 million inhabitants in Europe and Asia, was spread over so vast an area it was impossible for troops to arrive in less than a month. Germany left 5 of her army corps to cooperate with 12 Austria corps in dealing with the "southern front" against Servia and Balkan troops.

The attack on Belgium and France, however, was met with such fierce resistance that although 13 reserve corps were sent into France on the heels of the active 21 corps, in October, the German army had to fall back after their first swift stroke and could then do little more than hold a long intrenched battle line against the enemy. The "western front" was still active when the dreaded "Russian hordes" attacked from the east. The "eastern front" ran from East Prussia thorough Poland and into the corner of Alsace. Austria and Germany were forced to fight on all three fronts. The Austrian army began to show alarming weakness and were unable to either conquer the Serbs in the south or to hold back the Russians from entering the Hapsburg Empire.

I was in the process to sending another report when the President of the United States called me home. He had read the following American News Service item. Dateline London, December 1, 1914. Although in America the tremendous armed conflict which began July 28th has been frequently referred to as the "War in Europe" or the "European War," a less appropriate name could hardly have been invented for a war on whose battlefields, in three continents, soldiers are fighting and dying. The title employed by this wire service is preferred, not only because it may be used in Europe, but in Asia and Africa as well. This conflict suggests the fact that national sentiment, more than especially, characterizes the belligerent peoples in this war. It is truly a War of the Nations: Austria-Hungary vs Servia, Russia vs Austria-Hungary, Germany vs Russia, Great Britain vs Germany, France vs Germany, Belgium vs Germany, Turkey vs Russia, and Japan vs Germany; in which the whole fighting strength of each country goes forth to battle inspired by a passionate devotion to the "national honor" or the "national existence" of the "Fatherland" or "la Patrie."

This war is unparalleled in the development of national consciousness. When combined with militarism and imperialism, by the diplomatic grouping of the powers in two mutually hostile coalitions, and by the conflict of economic interests, the stage was set. The great nations of Europe have placed themselves in so perilous a position that a comparatively trivial occurrence was sufficient to precipitate an almost universal war. On June 28, the Austrian heir-apparent, the Archduke Francis Ferdinand and his wife were assassinated in Sarajevo. Austria accused Servia of complicity in the Sarajevo crime. Austria also alleged that the anti-Austrian followers of Servian patriots menaced the Hapsburg Empire. Austria-Hungary on July 23, delivered an ultimatum containing demands with which Servia would only partially comply, and on July 28, Austria declares war on Servia. Russia mobiles for war and Germany declares war on Russia to protect Austria on August 1. War between Germany and France begins on August 3. Preparatory to the invasion of France, Germany gobbles up neutral Luxemburg on August 2, and begins the invasion of Belgium, also a neutral nation, but Belgium troops stand and fight. The German violation of neutral Luxemburg and Belgium brings England into the war on August 4th. Montenegro joins Servia against Austria on August 8th. Germany refuses to surrender Kiaochow and Japan declares war on Germany on August 23. Turkey, allied with Germany, declares war on Russia on October 29. Great Britain returns the favor by declaring war on Turkey November 5. Further declarations complete the alignment of Servia, Russia, France, Belgium, England, Montenegro and Japan against Germany, Austria, Hungary and Turkey.

Beginning in late July until this date, the following actions have occurred world wide:

1) The Austrian invasion of Servia, stalls in the second month of fighting and a counter-invasion of Austria from Russia is underway.

2) In the Franco-Belgian theater, the gallant Belgian defense of Liege

and a French invasion of Alsace, failed to stop the onward march of German armies through Belgium, Luxemburg and Lorraine toward Paris. After the battle of the Marne, September 6-10, the German right wing falls back to the Aisne River, where a tremendous, but protracted battle was fought on September 15-28. The Belgian stronghold of Antwerp succumbed to German siege guns on October 9. As of this date, the Franco-Belgian, British armies face the German invaders along an intrenched battle line extending from Flanders to Alsace.

3) In the east, Russian armies invaded Austrian Galicia and German East Prussia, while German and Austrian forces occupy a portion of Poland and Russia.

4) The Turks wage war on Russia in the Black Sea and against Great Britain along the Suez Canal.

5) The Japanese capture the German fortress of Tsingtao in China on November 6th.

6) The German island possessions in the Pacific were easily taken by British and Japanese forces.

7) In Africa, German Togoland and Kamerun are occupied by Anglo-French troops, and German Southwest Africa is invaded by British South Africa, but German East Africa defeats British attacks.

Meanwhile in the United States, the congress was prompt to the emergency brought about by the war. On August 3, the House adopted a bill made to assist American trade interests in Europe by liberalizing existing laws so as to permit the immediate registry of foreign built ships. The United States is a neutral nation in the conflict and wishes to trade with all European partners on an equal basis. The registry of all foreign built ships and owned by American companies was critical to our neutral status. On August 21, the Senate adopted an emergency measure appropriating 5 million dollars to insure American vessels and their cargoes against loss by war. On September 4, both Houses assembled to hear an address by Woodrow Wilson on the necessity of providing additional revenue to meet the deficit which would be created by the falling off of imports from the countries affected by the war. During the next two months a number of revenue bills were passed until today, December 1, 1914, the United States' sixty-third Congress had been in continuous session for 1 year, 6 months and 17 days, this being the longest continuous session since the beginning of the government, with a record number of measures passed:

1) War Revenue,

2) War Risk Insurance Bureau,

3) Federal Construction of Railroads in Alaska,
4) Hetch Valley Water Bill,
5) Cotton exchange,
6) Coal lease in Alaska,
7) The 8 hour labor bill,
8) Tax on opium,
9) Rivers and Harbors bill,
10) Seaman's bill,
11) Nicaraguan and Colombian Treaty,
12) Modification of the Immigration laws (literacy test),
13) Philippine Government Act,
14) Farm Banking Bill and Mining Act, and
15) Federal regulation of the Stock Exchange Act.

In addition to the laws enacted, there was considerable debate over the surprise and indignation that ten nations should be involved in a terrific combat, simply because an Austrian archduke and his wife were shot in Sarajevo. These debates missed the reality. The Sarajevo incident was not the cause, but merely the immediate occasion to go to war.

By December 7, 1917 the following declarations of war were made:
Austria against Belgium, Japan, Montenegro, Russia Aug. 28, 1914
Austria against Servia, July 28, 1914
Brazil against Germany, Oct. 26, 1917
Bulgaria against Servia, Oct. 14, 1915
China against Austria, Germany, Aug. 14, 1917
Cuba against Germany, April 7, 1917
France against Austria, Bulgaria, Germany, Turkey, Nov. 5, 1914
Germany against Belgium, France, Rumania, Russia, Aug. 1, 1914
England against Austria, Bulgaria, Germany, Turkey, Nov. 5, 1914
Greece against Bulgaria, Germany, July 2, 1917
Italy against Austria, Bulgaria, Germany, Turkey, Aug. 15, 1915
Japan against Germany, Aug. 23, 1914
Liberia against Germany, Aug. 4, 1917
Montenegro against Austria, Germany, Aug. 9, 1914
Panama against Germany, April 7, 1917
Portugal against Austria, Germany, May 19, 1915
Rumania against Austria, Aug. 27, 1916
Russia against Bulgaria, Turkey, Nov. 3, 1914
San Marino against Austria, May 24, 1915

Servia against Bulgaria, Germany, Turkey, Dec. 2, 1914
Siam against Austria, Germany, July 29, 1917
Turkey against Rumania, Russia, Nov. 23, 1914
United States against Austria, Germany, April 6, 1917

War of the Nations

Part IV

William Jennings Bryan and Robert Lansing June 8, 1915
American News Service Wire Photo

16

American Neutrality

The Oval Office, 1915

From the beginning of hostilities, Pope Benedict XV exerted all of his great personal influence with the belligerents to induce them to ameliorate the common conditions of warfare and the extraordinary ones that the war had developed, he submitted to each member a number of identical proposals having in view the conclusion of a speedy and lasting peace. On June 1, 1915, he sent another to each belligerent, stronger and more detailed than the previous ones.

Various conditions were placed on this appeal by the recipients. The Teutonic Allies (Germany, Austria, Hungary, Bulgaria and Turkey) made respectful but non-committal replies, on behalf of the Entente Allies (England, France, Russia, Servia and the rest of the Balkan states), it was generally conceded that they had chosen President Wilson as their common spokesman.

President Wilson had Secretary of State, Byran, draft a reply to His Holiness using his prepared notes.

To His Holiness, Benedictus XV

    In acknowledgment of the communication of your Holiness to the belligerent peoples, dated June 1, 1915, the President of the United States requests me to transmit the following reply:

    Every heart that has not been blinded and hardened by

this terrible war must be touched by this moving appeal of his Holiness. As a neutral party in this conflict, we must feel the dignity and force of the humane and generous motives which prompted it and we must fervently wish that we might take the path of peace he so persuasively points out. (Bill, insert some pertinent facts and close with) The United States will continue to work for peace in the three continents involved in the conflict, we will continue to ship food and other human necessities to all nations involved in the conflict. We will send hospital ships to any nation that requests them, regardless of which side they represent. The people of the United States came from Europe and are shocked at the senseless loss of life, we urgently urge the nations at war to heed the Pope's warning and begin a process of peace making communications.

Thomas Woodrow Wilson, President

William Jennings Byran was shocked at the handwritten note from the president. He drafted his own reply for the president's signature.

To his Holiness, Benedict XV

In acknowledgment of the communication of your Holiness to all nations, dated June 1, 1915. Every heart that has not been blinded and hardened by this terrible war must be touched by your moving appeal and must feel the dignity and force of the humane and generous motives which prompted it. But it would be folly to take it if it does not, in fact, lead to the goal you propose. Our response must be placed upon the stern facts and upon nothing else. It is not a mere cessation of arms we desire, it is a stable and enduring peace. This agony must be stopped and it must be a matter of very sober judgement that will insure us against it again.

His Holiness, in substance, proposes that we return to the status quo. The status quo will not bring back the innocent murdered victims in the Balkan States, Belgium, France, Russia and Japan. How can we establish freedom of the seas if we return to the status quo? The object of this war is to deliver the free peoples of the world from the menace and the actual power of vast military establishments, controlled by irresponsible governments, which, having secretly planned to dominate the world, proceeded to carry the plan out without regard either to the scared obligations of treaty or the long established practices and long-cherished principles of international action and honor, which chose its own time for the war, delivered its blow fiercely and suddenly, stopped at no barrier, either of law or of mercy; swept a whole continent within the tide of blood – not the blood of soldiers only, but the blood of innocent women and children and to the helpless poor. Germany now stands balked, but not defeated, the enemy of four-fifths of the world.

This power is not the German people. It is the ruthless master of the people. It is no business of ours how that great people came under its control or submitted with temporary zest to the domination of its purpose; but it is our business to see to it that the history of the rest of the world is no longer left to its handling.

To deal with such a power by way of peace upon the plan proposed by his Holiness the Pope would, so far as we can see, involve a recuperation of its strength and a renewal of its policy; would make it necessary to create a permanent hostile combination of nations against the German people, who are its instruments. Can peace be based upon a restriction of its power or upon any word of honor it could pledge in a treaty of settlement and accommodation?

Responsible statesman must now everywhere see, if they never saw before, that no peace can rest securely upon political or economic restrictions meant to benefit some nations and cripple or embarrass others, upon vindictive action of any sort, or any kind of revenge or deliberate injury. The American people have already gone on record as follows:

December 26, 1914, we protest the detention of American shipping en route to neutral ports.

January 10, 1915, Germany concedes the principles stated in the protest, but is unable to discern a clear way of applying them.

January 20th, we protest the use of the American flag used on the Greenbrier moved from Bremen, Germany to Kirkwall, England.

January 21st, in reply to this we are informed that all American shipping captured on the high seas will be taken to a prize court and sold.

January 28 th, German armed cruiser *Prinz Eitel Friedrich* attacks and sinks the unarmed American Merchant Marine *William Frye.*

February 2nd, we are notified that British warships will seize all cargo inbound to Germany. A German agent is arrested for trying to dynamite the international railroad bridge over the St. Croix river between the United State and Canada.

February 5th, Germany, in a "Berlin Decree," declares that all the waters around the British Isles will be considered a war zone and all ships will be sunk by U-boat attacks.

February 8th, Great Britain rejects American protest to the use of the American flag, flown from the Cunard Ocean Liner *Lusitania,* stating that English merchantmen have a right to use neutral flags and to arm passenger ships.

February 10th, US warns Germany against sinking American shipping and calls on Great Britain to show respect towards the American flag.

February 13th, Germany warns the US to leave the waters surrounding the British Isles and the North Sea before the 18th.

February 15th, replying to the US note, Germany suggests naval convoys for American shipping, states willingness to undertake further deliberation in aid of neutral shipping to Germany; declares her U-boat warfare was forced upon her by Great Britain; claims the right to maintain it.

February 19th, England answers the US note of 2/10/1915, insisting that she will continue to use the American flag and to arm her vessels to protect her shipping to England.

February 20th, US sends an identical note to Germany and England urging upon them mutual concessions to insure the safety of unarmed neutral shipping and to protect neutral rights; asks Germany to abandon her U-boat warfare. US asks England to permit foodstuffs to reach the civilian population of Germany.

February 28th, Germany accepts US suggestions.

March 5th, US sends identical notes to England and France, asking a statement of their intended measures to cut off all commerce with Germany and questions the legality of such action.

March 15th, England sends US copy of "Orders in Council,"

prohibiting trade of any kind with German ports, including foodstuffs.

March 28ᵗʰ, an American life is lost by the sinking of the *Falaba* by German U-boat.

April 18ᵗʰ, American oil tanker *Cushing* bound from Philadelphia for Rotterdam is sunk in the North sea.

April 23ʳᵈ, Imperial German Embassy in Washington publishes the following "Notice" as an advertisement in a New York newspaper: "Travelers intending to embark on the Atlantic voyage are reminded that a state of war exists between Germany and her allies and England and her allies. The zone of war includes the waters adjacent to the British Isles and in accordance with formal notice given by the Imperial German Government, vessels flying the flag of Great Britain, or any of her allies, are liable to destruction in those waters and that travelers sailing in the war zone on ships of Great Britain or her allies do so at their own risk."

May 1ˢᵗ, German U-boats sink American oil tanker *Gulflight* off the Scilly Islands.

May 7ᵗʰ, Cunard liner *Lusitania*, bound from New York to Liverpool, when on the high seas is sunk by German U-boat while flying the American flag. An SOS is heard in Old Head, Ireland. Rescue ships reach the *Lusitania*, survivors are still in the water and aboard life boats, 708 out of the 1,906 passengers survive including the American diplomat Louis Caldwell and his wife..

May 11ᵗʰ, Germany responds to the US note of protest by stating that neutral shipping will be safe in the war zone around the British Isles under specified conditions. They promise that if a neutral vessel is harmed by mistake, she will allow the question of responsibility to be decided according to the Hague Convention rules.

May 13ᵗʰ, US sends final note to Germany on the *Lusitania* sinking, demanding reparation of the loss of American lives and property. US demands end to U-boat operations against merchantmen.

May 17ᵗʰ, US Bureau of Navigation reports that 68 Teutonic passenger and cargo ships have been interned in various US ports for the duration of the war. Estimated gross tonnage is 527,298, estimated value is $100,000,000, largest number in Hoboken, New

Jersey, German vessels = 54, Austrian vessels = 14. Two German cruisers, *Prinz Eitel Friedrich* and *Kronprinz Wilhelm*, pursued by British warships, sought refuge at Norfolk, Virginia, and were interned there, a like fate befell a German gunboat at Honolulu.

May 20th, On US protest, Great Britain promises to pay for 18 seized American cargo shipments, as soon as ownership of the cargoes is established.

May 28th, Germany replies to American note of May 13, "It is far from the German Government to have any intention of ordering attacks by U-boats on neutral vessels in the zone, which have not been guilty of any hostile act .... instructions have been repeatedly given to German U-boats to avoid attacking such vessels."

Referring to the cases of the American steamers *Cushing* and *Gulflight*, "In all cases where a neutral vessel, through no fault of its own, has come to grief through German U-boat attacks and according to the facts as ascertained by the German Government, this government has expressed its regret at the unfortunate occurrence and promises indemnification where the facts justify it."

Regarding the sinking of the *Lusitania*, the reply states, "The US proceeds to assume that this vessel is an unarmed merchant vessel. The Imperial German Government begs in this connection to point out that the *Lusitania* was one of the largest and fastest English commerce steamers, constructed with British Government funds as an auxiliary cruiser troop transport and is expressly included in the navy list published by the Lord First Admiral, Sir Winston Spencer Churchill. It was reported by our field agents that this vessel left New York with its holds filled with small arms and ammunition. According to reports from the U-boat commander concerned, which is confirmed by other reports, there can be no doubt that the rapid sinking of the *Lusitania* was due to the explosions of the cargo holds and gun mounts and ammunition stored on the main and second decks where lifeboats are usually located. Otherwise, in all human probability, the entire list of passengers of the *Lusitania* would have been saved."

Secretary Bryan finished his reply to the Pope with these comments, "The test, therefore, of every plan of peace is this: is it based upon the faith of all the peoples involved, or merely upon the word of an ambitious and intriguing Imperial Government, on the one hand, or of a group of free peoples, on the other? This is a test which goes to the root of the matter and it is the test which must be applied."

"The purpose of the United States in this war is known to the whole world – to every people to whom the truth has been permitted to come. They do not need to be stated again in this missive. We seek no material advantage of any kind. We believe that the intolerable wrongs done in this war by the furious and brutal power of the Imperial German Government ought to be repaired, but not at the expense of the sovereignty of any people – rather a vindication of the sovereignty both of those that are weak and of those that are strong. Punitive damages, the dismemberment of empires, the establishment of selfish and exclusive economic leagues, we deem inexpedient and in the end worse than futile, no proper basis for a peace of any kind, least of all for an enduring peace. That must be based upon justice and the common rights of mankind.

We can not take the word of the present rulers of Germany as a guarantee of anything that is to endure, unless explicitly supported by such conclusive evidence of the will and purposes of the German people themselves as the other peoples of the world would be justified in accepting. Without guarantees, treaties of settlement, agreements for disarmament, covenants to set up arbitration in the place of force, territorial adjustments, reconstitutions of small nations, if made with the German Government, no man, no nation, could now depend on.

We must await some new evidence of the purposes of the great peoples of the Central Powers. God grant it may be given soon and in a way to restore the confidence of all peoples everywhere in the faith of nations and the possibility of a covenanted peace.

When this reply was placed on President Wilson's desk for his approval before typing and his signature, he called for his Secretary of State, his Counselor of the State Department, Mr. Robert Lansing and his presidential advisor for foreign affairs. The three of us sat in the Oval Office waiting for President Wilson.

"James, how has your son, Louis, adjusted to his rescue from the sinking of the *Lusitania?*" Counselor Lansing seemed concerned.

"I have received only one letter from him and his wife since May 9th when they were finally back on terra firma. He jokingly says he never wants to take a liner across the ocean, he will wait for commercial aircraft to fly."

We all had a chuckle over the impossibility of flying across the Atlantic. The concealed door to the Oval Office opened and the president walked to his desk.

"Gentlemen, I am ready to make this note to his holiness an agreement among all of us. So far, Bill has managed to put his twist on things, I would like you, Admiral and Counselor, to add or subtract anything that you would like." Robert you can go first.

"I must confess, I have not read it, Mr. President."

"Bill, you wrote this without input from the Admiral or your own State Department Counselor?"

"Yes, Mr. President, I did not have to consult them, I knew what I felt and what needed to be said."

"You did? Is this written from the viewpoint of your present position as the Secretary of State or is it what you would have said if you were the sitting president?" I could not tell where President Wilson was going with this.

"In this case, I tried to do both." He quickly added, Mr. President.

"Bill, you ran for president three times, you are not the president or even the vice-president or anything close to the president. I would like you to take a few days off and decide what you want to do in the next two years of this administration. You are dismissed from this meeting." William Jennings Bryan looked like a kicked dog as he left the Oval Office.

"Counselor Lansing, Admiral Caldwell, here are copies of what Mr. Bryan proposes to send to his holiness." He handed them across his desk to us, we sat quietly and read. Robert Lansing finished first and said, "Mr. President, this is clear and to the point, a bit long, I would have used fewer words to say the same thing."

"Admiral, what do you think?"

"I think you are angry or disappointed with your Secretary of State, Mr. President, but I have no idea why."

"Very astute, as usual, James. Here is a copy of the note that I gave Mr. Bryan to complete." He handed a copy to each of us. We read it. I handed my copy back to President Wilson and went out on a limb.

"It says, please add the pertinent facts and close with your remarks."

"Yes, it does, James. This is supposed to be a short note to the sitting Pope in Rome, not the diplomatic position of the United States in the current war."

"Mr. President, why not take out the list of dates and complaints and use your closing and get this sent?" Robert Lansing had cut through all the golden tongue of William Jennings Bryan.

"Robert, I need you to standby as acting Secretary of State while Mr. Bryan is thinking over his decision, I will give him until the 28th of June to resign his portfolio – then we are looking at the new Secretary of State. Do you accept?"

"I do, Mr. President, thank you for your confidence."

"James, how soon can your son, Louis, get to Washington?"

"He is not due to rotate until next year, Mr. President."

"I am not talking about naval rotation, I want him to take Robert's place." I was dumb founded.

"As commander-in-chief, you can recall and reassign any member of the military, Sir. I would not do that in this case, Mr. President. Louis has just had a ship blown out from under him. If you order him back on one this soon, he will probably resign his commission and stay in London and offer his services to MI 5."

"He would abandon his citizenship and responsibilities?"

"No, Sir. He is a crime fighter at heart, he understands the German mind set and wants to see them defeated, he believes that we should be in this fight. He will not wait long to offer his services to the British, he has a British wife and son."

"I see. Do you feel the same way, Admiral?"

"I do, Mr. President, I am a dual national. I am also known as, Sir James Caldwell, protector of Bermuda. If the German's attack Bermuda, I have no choice but to offer my services in their defense. The longer we wait to clean up this mess, the harder it will be. It is a stalemate, we can tip the balance."

"Why is it a stalemate?"

"Because this is a European war fought out of trenches, Mr. President. The Spanish used the same thing in Cuba and the Philippines. Teddy Roosevelt thought the trenches were death traps and had his troops swarm them from the front and both ends simultaneously. He never stopped to have tea or lunch and discuss what to do next. He told his troops to kill everyone in the trenches, no survivors. When this was spread by the fleeing Spanish troops, fear spread among the next line of trenches and the Spanish would not stand and fight, they fled in fear. 1200 rough riders defeated 7,000 troops in the trenches in Cuba, Mr. President. We need another Teddy Roosevelt to land in France as soon as possible."

"Why don't the allies use this technique in France?"

"I don't think they believe it will work. They have never studied the Spanish American War in the Philippines, Mr. President. General MacArthur used a different technique for the trenches."

"What was it?"

"When he saw that the Spanish had dug their trenches and piled the earth in front of the trenches to form a raised fortification, he sent two groups of machine gun emplacements at each end of the trenches. While they fired over the heads of the Spanish, General MacArthur had his army engineers bring bulldozers along the front and push the piled earth into the trenches. When the Spanish tried to escape their deaths in the trenches and tried to flee they were killed by machine gun fire."

"Admiral, will you go and cable your son in London and get his response to my offer to become my new Counselor of the State Department?"

"I will, Mr. President, when would you like his response?"

"June 8th or before."

I left the Oval Office and headed to the basement communications center that my father had installed in the White House for James Buchanan and sent the following telegram.

LOUIS CALDWELL
AMERICAN EMBASSY
LONDON, ENGLAND
JUNE 6, 1915
THE PRESIDENT OF THE UNITED STATES REQUESTS YOUR SERVICES AS COUNSEL TO THE DEPARTMENT OF STATE. APPOINTMENT DATE SHALL BE JUNE 28, 1915, UNTIL THE END OF THE PRESENT ADMINISTRATION ON MARCH 4, 1917. PLEASE CABLE THE WHITE HOUSE WITH YOUR ACCEPTANCE NO LATER THAN JUNE 8, 1915.

ADMIRAL JAMES CALDWELL
PRESIDENTIAL ADVISOR FOR FOREIGN AFFAIRS

I sent it off and wondered what the reaction would be in the Caldwell household in London.

When the cable arrived in London at the American Embassy it was decoded and brought to the desk of Louis Caldwell. He read it and said, "Alright, who is the joker that typed this to look like a telegram?"

"I brought it directly from the com center, Commander, it is for real. Who do you know in the White House?"

"Thomas Woodrow Wilson. I worked for him when he was the American Ambassador at Berlin. I am going home to talk with my wife, Lieutenant, I will be on a long lunch hour."

Before rushing out of the office, I told my assistant, Lieutenant David Walker, to lock everything I was working on in the safe. I stuffed some papers into the burn bag and put on my trench coat. It was June 8ᵗʰ in London and it had rained every day so far. I waved down a cabbie and gave him my address. Cathleen and I had moved from her tiny, cold water flat before Spencer was born into a much larger apartment close to the embassy row in London. Cathleen thought we could not afford such a place until I explained the Caldwell International Trust for the entire family. She accepted the fact that I was not poor and hired a nurse for Spencer after he was born, then a nanny and then private school when he was six years old. I had been very happy living where we did, until January of this year. That was when the first Zeppelin bombings of London began.

Airships had originally been produced in Germany for civilian transport by Count Ferdinand Zeppelin and were named after him. Cathleen and I met on a Zeppelin from Berlin to the Kaiser's summer palace. She was a field agent then assigned to steal some operational manuals. Had it been eight years ago? Was I the father of a seven year old son? It had all seemed like a dream until the first incendiary bomb exploded not far from Embassy Row in London. The bombing raids were supposed to be directed against industrial, military and naval targets, but poor visibility and navigational errors meant that many bombs fell on civilian areas. The Zeppelin raids on London brought the war home to Cathleen and me. It seemed incredible that a woman standing on her doorstep in this luxurious neighborhood could be killed by a bomb brought from Germany. But in January alone, 38 people in this neighborhood were killed and 124 wounded. It was time to offer Cathleen and Spencer another location in which to observe the 'war of the nations,' as my father called it.

The cabbie stopped and let me out. I handed him a pound note and told him to keep the change. "Thanks, yank. When are you colonialists going to get into this fight?"

"Who are you calling a colonialist, I am the son of Sir James Caldwell, protector of Bermuda."

"Does everyone in Bermuda talk like you. I thought you were a yank, sorry, mate." I tipped my hat and shook the rain from my coat and headed for the steps of the apartment. Cathleen must have been watching from the front bay window, because she met me at the door.

"What is wrong, Louis, you are never home at this hour."

"I just got a telegram from the White House."

"Quit your kidding, what has happened? Has the US declared war?"

"Nothing as earth shaking as that, my dear. President Wilson must have fired his Secretary of State because the lawyer who is the State Department's Counsel is the acting Secretary." I handed her the telegram from my father.

"What does this mean? Are we moving to Washington? Oh, can we, Louis, I am so frightened for Spencer and the next one." Cathleen had announced that she would begin to show "around her middle" as she called it.

"I thought I would have a hard sale."

"I am ready to leave London, Louis, it is not safe here. We will be safe in the United States, won't we? The telegram says you have to answer by the 8th and report on the 28th. How are we going to get there? I am not stepping foot on a Cunard Liner again, Louis. Find us another way, I am going to fix you some lunch." She left the room while I still had my mouth open to speak. I followed her into the kitchen and found her crying.

"Would you like to take your parents with us, Cathleen?"

"Oh, could we, Louis?"

"Of course, I will make all the arrangements after I cable the White House this afternoon."

We sat and ate and I told her how my father came across the Atlantic when he was a cadet at the naval academy. She said she did not understand and I got up and went into the study and picked up my globe and returned to the kitchen. I sat it down in front of her. I put my finger on England and said, "Here we are. We purchase train tickets to Kirkwall, Scotland. From there we take the ferry boat to the Faroe Islands, you know the one your Royal Danish family owns, Elska Van Mauker." She elbowed me in the ribs, I never let her forget that was her cover name when we met.

"We are out of Great Britain and into a Danish territory, how does that help us?"

"We can purchase tickets to the next Danish territory, Iceland."

"Iceland? Are you out of your mind?"

"It's June, honey, you will love Iceland, we can spend a few days there soaking in the hot springs. Then we need to keep moving through Danish territories. It is a short way to Cape Farewell, we stay there a few days and move on into Canada, see, this is St. John's. Once we get this far we can get on a train or take the ferries down the coast to New York."

"How long have you been planning this, Louis?"

"Ever since I heard the explosion on board the *Lusitania* and I thought I had lost you and we had left Spencer an orphan."

"So it was not the constant bombing this year, that made you want to take us to safety?"

"No, I realized on board the *Lusitania*, the bombings are random, the attack on an ocean liner was deliberate. We have to stay off the liners, we will never get there."

"How will we tell Spencer that he is moving to America, Louis?"

"Our son is a very mature little boy for his age. He talks about honor and family to me all the time. It is time to tell him that his father is a very rich man who enjoys being a lawyer and the best job a lawyer can have has just been offered to him. We also tell him that is time that this family starts doing everything they can to end the war as soon as possible. The best way to do this is to encourage the United States to enter the war."

"You can do that?"

"No, the President of the United States can do that with a speech to the Congress. I know my father has already told the president that we should enter in support of Great Britain. It is obvious that is why Thomas has asked me to come into the State Department."

"Who is Thomas?"

"Thomas Woodrow Wilson, the Ambassador to Germany when you stole the Zeppelin plans, Elska."

"Stop that, I am not Danish!"

"You are my little Danish muffin. How about some butter on that muffin?"

"Not now, we have too many things to do. You have to get Spencer from White Book and I have to pack."

"One suitcase each, Cathleen. We will continue to lease the flat, leave everything including clothes in the closet. Take only traveling items we will need on the railroad and the water for days. We will buy things along the way. No steamer trunks like last time. Do you understand?"

"Yes, when are we leaving?"

"Tonight."

"Tonight! I can not be ready by tonight. What about my parents?"

"They will come in few days if they want to. We will leave money and train tickets to Kirkwall with them, they can follow."

17

Flight to America

June, 1915

I left the apartment without buttering the muffin and headed back to my office in the embassy. I had the cab drop me off at our bank and I told them I was transferred back to Washington and would they do a wire transfer rather than have me carry that much cash on my person. We filled out the papers and I transferred some of the balance to my account in Washington and put the rest in my wallet. I decided not to get another cab, the rain had stopped and I walked the rest of the way to the embassy. I went directly to the com center and sent a telegram to the President of the United States, thanking him for his confidence in me and that my family and I would try very hard to meet the June 28th start date. I sent a telegram to Admiral Lowe and informed him of my opportunity and recommended that Hans be pulled out of Berlin and brought to London to replace me.

I cleaned out my desk, boxed it and marked it for shipment to the State Department, Washington, D. C. I left the office and headed for the small private school called White Book. Spencer and I met with the headmaster and explained the sudden development in Washington. He congratulated me and shook hands with Spencer.

"Spencer, when this war is over, you and your family return to London and a place will be waiting for you here at White Book."

"Thank you, Sir. My father has been restless since this war began, you are aware that he is a dual national. He is torn between serving the Crown and his duties in the United States Navy. My mother will be so glad that he has decided to serve his birthplace and resist the German effort to expand their empire." We both looked at this little boy with amazement.

"Spencer do you have everything from your cubby?"

"Yes, Sir. Hopefully the war will not last forever and I can get back on the cricket fields next year!"

"Commander Caldwell, your son is amazing, we will miss him here this year. Take good care of him and his mother on your journey home."

Spencer and I rode home with his knapsack and his cricket bat in the back of a black London cab.

"Father, would it be alright if I use my first initial and middle name when I enroll in an American school?"

"You don't like, Spencer?"

"Yes, but it is English sounding. My middle name is Carson, that sounds American. S. Carson Caldwell, that sounds American doesn't it?"

"Your Mum is not going to like the sudden change of name, Spencer. When it is just you and I, I will call you Carson. We will use Spencer until we get safely to Washington D.C., alright?"

"Right you are, it will be important that we don't show how afraid we are to Mum. Is she really frightened, father?"

"Not as much as I am, Carson. Your Mum is really a lot braver than I am."

"She is? You are afraid?"

"I am afraid for England first, my family second and myself last. The sinking of the Cunard Liner *Lusitania* was a wake up call for me."

"Why are we going to America then, we have to cross the Atlantic on a liner, don't we?"

"No, Carson. You remember that I have told you that your Mum and I spent some time in Denmark before you born."

"Yes, how does Denmark fit into this?"

"We still have our false Danish Passports and we may be able to use them to catch a ferry from Scotland to the Danish Islands between Scotland and Iceland."

"The Islands of Faroe, I remember studying that in geography class, which one are we going to?."

"The southern most, it is called Suduroy and the seaport village is called Tveroyri. The Faroe Islands and Iceland are both Danish. Once we get to Iceland, we can book passage on a mail steamer to Greenland, also

Danish, and then on to Canada. Once we get to Canada, we can take the railways into Washington or use the coastal ferries."

"When are we leaving?"

"I have train tickets to Kirkwall, we leave before dark here and arrive in Scotland the next morning in time to catch the ferry to Tveroyri."

"Can I take my cricket bat?" Now he sounded like a little boy.

"If you want to, yes. Danish children play cricket, but you are aware that no children in America play cricket, they play baseball."

"Can I use my bat to play baseball?"

"I don't see why not, but when you start hitting homers they will probably want to make your bat illegal."

"What's a 'homer'?" The rest of the short ride was consumed in explaining the difference between baseball and cricket.

The cab stopped in front of our apartment and Cathleen was standing in the front windows. She waved to us and wiped a tear from her cheek. I knew she had talked to her parents and that they wanted to remain in England. Spencer bounded up the steps and hugged his mother and went to his room to pack his suitcase. I talked to Cathleen and confirmed that her parents might come to America, but not now. The Royal Navy was beginning to destroy the Zeppelins before they could drop their bombs on London, many were shot down over the channel. I knew that the Zeppelins would be replaced by larger bi-wing aeroplanes from Belgium, designed to drop heavy loads of incendiary bombs. Every wooden building in London would be ablaze before this world war was over.

We arrived in Kirkwall about mid morning and left the train station in the middle of town. Cathleen and I had not slept much. We watched Spencer peacefully slumber in a coach seat that I had laid flat for him. I told her what Spencer and I talked about on the way home from the school.

"He wants to be called, Carson?"

"Yes, isn't that a hoot? He probably thinks every other person in western America still rides a horse to work."

"Can we take him to Virginia City, Nevada, to see some of the Caldwell property there? Your family still have horses to ride there, don't they?"

"Cathleen, you and I have a house in Beaufort, South Carolina, a ranch in Nevada, a cottage in Bermuda and an apartment in Washington. Spencer should not only see them, he should spend some time in each one, so should you."

The cabbie stopped at the ferry station and we bought tickets to Tveroyri and carried our suitcases on board and found our cabin. A cabin on a coastal ferry is really a misnomer, it is more like a narrow walk-in closet. The door from the outside swung out onto the deck, there was not room inside the cabin for it to swing inside. The room was 6 feet wide and 10 feet long. Four bunks were folded into the walls, a single pie-shaped sink was just inside the doorway, bolted to the corner of the cabin. If all four bunks were folded down, you could not walk between them easily. I folded down the top bunk from one wall and placed all three suitcases up on it. A common bathroom was at each end of the row of cabins and Cathleen left to wash up. Spencer and I stood and looked around the cabin.

"Father, would it be alright if I call you, Dad, when we get to America?"

"Carson, you can call me whatever you like. I called my father, Dad and my grandfather, Papa Caldwell."

"You did? Did he like that?"

"Grandfathers love their grandsons, Carson. Your Great Grandfather Schneider spent a great deal of time with me when I was your age. He would have loved spending time with you, Carson."

"How far is it to Tveroyri, Dad?"

"Not very far miles wise, probably less than 300 miles. But remember a ferry is not very fast, suppose we average 20 miles an hour, how long will it take us to get there?"

"Wow, more than 15 hours, probably. We are not even underway yet."

"That is correct, Carson. You slept most of the way here. Your Mum and I did not get very much sleep on the way. We have to take extra special care of your Mum, Carson, she is going to have another baby."

"She is, I am going to be a brother?"

"Yes, she is. It will be late this year or early next, she just found out."

"Why don't I already have brothers and sisters?"

"Your Mum lost two babies in the last four years, Carson. You were too little to understand why your Mum was sick for a few days in bed and then fine again. That was why."

"Are we ever going to come back home, Dad?"

"Carson, the most important thing in the world is make your Mum happy. If she decided to move to India, you and I better think of India as home. We are all British citizens, Carson. You think of home as London, while I think of St. George's, Bermuda as home. Both are part of Great

Britain, it does not matter where we live, Carson. The three of us are family bound to each other, the roof over our heads, the city we live in, or the country where that city is located is no concern of mine. Your Mum is my whole universe, do you understand?"

"I think so. Will I ever meet someone and feel like that about them?"

"For seven years old, you are a deep thinker, Carson. Now open up your suitcase, get out your PJ's and hop onto that top bunk. Make believe you are asleep and I will put your Mum into the bunk below you so she can get some rest."

I heard the door to the cabin swing open and Cathleen was back from her face washing. I found her night gown and helped her into the bunk below her son.

"He must be really tired, he is asleep already."

"We all need some rest, honey, see you in a few hours." I laid down on the third open bunk beside her and was asleep in few minutes.

We did not wake up in a few hours. All three of us awoke when the ferry thumbed into the wharf side at Tveroyri on the island of Suduroy. We washed our hands and face in the cabin corner sink and put on a fresh change of clothes. We would spend a couple of days here and we needed lodging and a good meal. I had picked up a travel guide to the Faroe Islands at the London train station and we sat in a small dockside café awaiting our meal. I read some of it to Cathleen and Spencer.

Suduroy and Litla Dimun. *Suduroy is the southernmost island in the Faroes and it is this distance from the rest of the country, which partly explains its uniqueness, not only geographically but also in terms of language and cultures. It is said, that the people of Suduroy are more moderate, open and easier to approach than the people throughout the rest of the country.*

Its landscape is magnificent and idyllic, green and welcoming with spellbinding steep bird cliffs to the west. A perfect balance with the east coast, the island can conjure up an almost surreal beauty, both by day and night. Instead of rushing around by automobile in one day, stay two days and you will more than double the experience.

As with most of the other islands in the Faroes, the back of Suduroy faces west towards the mighty Atlantic Ocean whilst its fjords and coves open towards the morning sun. The entire west coast is made up of sheer bird cliffs, broken only by four fjords at Hvalba, Lopra and Vagur. You can easily reach everywhere by automobile giving you the opportunity to enjoy the magnificent and unique scenery that can be idyllic or frighteningly violent, depending upon the weather ....

Our food had arrived and I stopped reading. We had ordered breakfast even though it was not much before noon. The café we were sitting in was built in 1836 according to the back of the menu we had ordered from. It was originally a store located on the northern side of the natural harbor. The store was called Trongisvasfjordur's and a hotel was added. That is where we had checked in earlier. The village that grew up around the store became Tveroyri and quickly grew to be the most important trading place in the Faroe islands. The old store, warehouses and sail loft had been lovingly restored and are now in use as the café, hotel and museum. When I registered in the hotel for two days, the man behind the desk asked if we would like an automobile added to the room. It was waiting for us behind the café. We finished our meal and found the automobile. It did not look like the ones we were used to seeing in London. It was open with a canvas top and had a back seat. I told Spencer to get in the back and I helped Cathleen get in the front with me. There was no starter. A man walking by said, "Vagur das automobile kas da vindin?"

I had no idea what he said, "I do not speak Danish very well." I replied.

"That was not Danish, it is Norwegian."

"You speak wonderful English, Sir."

"Are you looking for the starter? These cars have cranks. You will find it in the boot." He continued on his way.

"I will look in the boot, Cathleen slide over here and sit behind the wheel. Do you see this lever on the steering wheel left hand side?"

"Yes, what is it?"

"It will allow me to start the car without breaking my arm. You push it down while I crank and then you push it up as soon as the motor catches."

"Got it!" She slid over and I rummaged around in the boot. I found the crank and walked around to the front of the machine. Spencer was enjoying this. Starters were push buttons on the floor of the autos in London. I turned the crank and pulled it out when the motor caught, coughed a couple of times and came to life as soon as Cathleen pushed the lever up. I had not even checked to see if the beast was in neutral – but my intelligent wife had pushed in the clutch pedal and moved the shifting bar to the middle of the H. I grinned sheepishly and returned the crank to the boot. She slid over and we were off to explore the villages near Tveroyri, they were Trongisvagur and Frodba, where there were some unusual basalt column formations worth seeing.

"Frodba is where the famous Viking Brandan stepped ashore, father."

Spencer was reading from the travel guide I had handed to him. We headed north on a dirt path and in less than an hour we came to Hvannhagi with its beautiful lake.

"What does the guide say we will find here, Spencer?"

"It says we are close to the farming village of Oravik. Nearby is the islands ancient meeting place known as 'Uppi Milum Stovur,' similar to Stone Henge back home. A five minute drive south of here will bring us to the village of Hov. According to the Faroese Sagas and local stories, it is here that the Viking Havgrimur lived. He was a great chieftain and ruled over much of the country. The village got its name from his pagan altar, Hov."

"I am glad the word for altar in Norwegian is not Trongisvasfjordur's Hov!" Cathleen burst out laughing.

"What?"

"The name of the old store that you are trying to pronounce means Thor's fjord or God's Inlet."

"Oh, then I am glad Thor didn't decide to build his altar on an inlet or we would have a place called Hovtrongisvasfjordursburg." Spencer nearly fell out of the back seat laughing.

"Dad?"

"Yes, Carson?"

"Are we always going to have this much fun on holiday?" Before I could answer, Cathleen asked him, "Carson are you sure you want to give up Spencer?"

"Yes, Mum, I have turned a new page in my life's book." I looked at Cathleen and smiled.

The next day we went west on the island to see the bird cliffs and then to the most southern tip where we found the city of Vagur. Like Tveroyri, it drew many trades people in the last fifty years. There were private houses with large gardens and commercial buildings, along with stately churches like the Norwegian inspired wooden church in Tveroyri.

A large city park was full of flower children celebrating mid-summers day festival. I asked Cathleen, "The first day of summer is June 22nd, isn't it?"

"Yes, I think they are a bit early."

We spent the rest of the day exploring the uninhabited island of Litla Dimun. We got on a day boat and had a fantastic experience on the island, walking among the wild goats, sheep and flocks of birds that would land on your head and outstretched hands and arms to be fed.

"The war seems to be on another planet, Louis. It is only a couple of hundred miles north of Scotland's Shetland Islands."

"I know, I will be sad to leave this wonderful chain of small islands tomorrow and head for Iceland."

No one talked much on our drive to the hotel. I parked the auto behind the hotel and gave the keys to the woman behind the counter in the lobby. I asked her if our tickets for Iceland had arrived.

"Yes, Sir. Here are your ferry tickets to Reykjavik and on to Angmogsslik, Greenland. They are first class, your family should enjoy this trip. I have train tickets to Sydproven for you. The Canadian ferries come there to pick up passengers to Hebron. Hebron is pretty isolated, but a train runs once a day into Nain and on into Goose Bay and Quebec. There is a nice small family inn in Hebron, I have stayed there."

I thanked her and headed up the stairs to our room for the night. It was the 11th of June and our trip had just begun. In sixteen more days we would be approaching Washington, D.C. by train from Quebec if we did not miss any of our connections.

18

Landfall in America

June 24, 1915

The ferry rides were over, we stepped foot on dry land in Hebron, Canada, on June 21st. Carson was beside himself. The main street of Hebron was dirt packed hard with a raised wooden sidewalk with hitching posts in front of the stores. Men rode horseback and the women drove buck boards. There was not an automobile in sight.

"Can I learn to ride when we get to Washington, Dad?"

"Son, if you can find a horse for sale in Washington, I will buy it for you."

"Louis, don't be telling him that!"

"We have missed the only train today. Let's ask some cowpoke if-in he knows the way to the boardin' house."

"Why is Dad talking like that, Mum?"

"Your father is trying to be funny. I see the sign for the inn right over there. Help me with this suitcase, Louis, we have bought too many things along the way."

The next day I bought train tickets to Quebec and we dragged our suitcases on the loading platform so that they could be placed in the luggage boxcar. Cathleen had bought a small bag and packed our overnight things in it. The train would go straight through and we had a sleeper compartment. We found the compartment and put our overnight bag inside and I tried to lock the compartment door.

"Look, the door slides into the wall. This compartment is larger than the cabin from Kirkwall." Carson was enjoying himself.

"We need to find the dining car, I am hungry." Cathleen and Carson looked at me and just shook their heads.

"What?"

"How can you be hungry, you just ate breakfast."

"Well, little lady, here in the wild west we catch our own food and cook it over a campfire, usually – but today, I'm-a-hankerin' fer some real train grub."

"Mum, are we going to have to put up with this, the whole time we are in Canada?"

"I am afraid so, your father has lost his mind."

Our kidding around ended when we found the dining car and a porter was calling, "Telegram for Commander Caldwell, telegram for Commander Caldwell."

"Louis, that is for you!" I raised my hand and motioned for the telegram. I gave the porter some change and he looked at it funny.

"Sorry, I do not have any Canadian money." I tore open the telegram.

LOUIS CALDWELL
CANADIAN RAILWAY SERVICE
HEBRON, CANADA

LOUIS, CATHLEEN AND SPENCER

HOPES THIS FINDS YOU TODAY. ITALY HAS DECLARED WAR AGAINST AUSTRIA AND HAVE JOINED THE ALLIES IN THEIR FIGHT AGAINST GERMANY. SINCE YOU LEFT LONDON, GERMANY HAS APOLOGIZED FOR THE GULFLIGHT SINKING. WE REPLIED TO THE GERMAN NOTE OF MAY 28TH (A COPY IS ON YOUR DESK HERE IN THE WHITE HOUSE). ON JUNE 12TH THE GERMAN FOREIGN OFFICE DECLARED THE LUSITANIA A "WARSHIP" (THOUGHT YOU AND CATHLEEN WOULD FIND THAT INTERESTING SINCE YOU WERE RETURNING TO LIVERPOOL ABOARD SHIP). ON JUNE 17TH WE GOT A NASTY MESSAGE FROM LONDON'S WAR OFFICE STATING AMERICAN SHIPPERS HAVE NO CAUSE FOR COMPLAINT. TODAY WE REJECTED GERMAN PROPOSAL TO SUBMIT CASE OF THE WILLIAM P. FYRE TO A PRIZE COURT. KNOW THIS SPOILS YOUR VACATION – BUT THIS IS WHAT YOU WILL BE WORKING ON IN

A FEW DAYS. GOD PROTECT YOU THREE AND BRING YOU HOME TO YOUR
FAMILY HERE IN THE UNITED STATES.

I handed the telegram to Cathleen to read to Spencer.

"You have an office in the White House, Dad? Can I come see it?
Where is the White House?"

"Yes, I do. I will show it to you and your Mum in a few days. The
White House is in the middle of the capitol located at 1600 Pennsylvania
Avenue."

"Louis, can you send a telegram from this train?"

"Of course, do you want to send one to your parents? Or do you want
me to answer this one from Grandpa Caldwell?"

"Yes, you should acknowledge receipt of your father's telegram, ask
him to meet our train in Washington."

"I do not have a train number or time yet."

"How many trains a day leave Quebec for the United States?"

"Hundreds."

"Oh, wait to give him details, tell him we are safe." I left to find the
porter who had delivered the telegram.

We arrived in Quebec tired and dirty, two days later. The Canadian
railway service was patched together and passenger trains pulled
to the side to allow war materials to pass to the sea coast so they could be
loaded on supply ships headed to England.

"Louis, seeing this makes me feel better for the people in Great Britain.
Canada is large and mostly agriculture, it should feed the whole of England
if the ships can arrive safely."

"That will be the first thing that I and my brother will be working on,
I am sure."

"James is in command of the submarine fleet for the Atlantic, what
can he do to protect Canadian shipping?"

"James has told me about a new invention that Thomas Edison is
working on that can detect submarines underwater. If they can get that
to work and install it in every submarine in the fleet, they can detect the
U-boats and send a wireless to the convoy of transports. The President of
the United States has about decided that American ships can return fire for
self defense. If the U-boat fires on a convoy escorted by one of my brother
submarines, they will be allowed to return fire and sink the U-boat."

"How can a submarine sink a submarine?"

"I have no idea, you will have to talk to my brother when we see him this Thanksgiving. All I know, is that the German U-boats are going to drag the United States into this war, sooner or later."

"If there is war, will you have to serve in the Navy?"

"I would consider it an honor, but I am not trained in the military, I am a lawyer. Maybe I could sue Germany for loss of life and property, while James and my father put to sea to sink the scum buckets."

19

Life in America

July - December, 1915

Words of prophecy are rarely spoken and are most often lost in the shuffle of daily life. Louis' words of prophecy would not get official status until September 12th, when the President of the United States appointed a Naval Advisory Board to aid the Navy Department in a new technical development to be placed upon a submarine for testing in the Atlantic Ocean. Thomas Edison was chairman of the board and two members each of eleven scientific organizations were also appointed. Their charge from the president was simple, "Gentlemen, we must be able to detect the presence of a German U-boat before a torpedo is released."

Louis and his family had arrived in Washington on June 26, 1915 and Emily and I met the three of them at the Union Station. They were dirty and tired and we drove them to Bellawoods in my new American Motors Limousine. Spencer, who now wanted to be called Carson, was disappointed that we did not bring a stagecoach to 'fetch' them from the station. He sounded like a cowboy and not like the little English lad we had known for seven years.

"His father started that cowpoke stuff as soon as we landed in Canada, Admiral. Can you get him to stop it?"

"Louis, stop that cowpoke stuff, right now." The entire family burst into laughter.

"Okay, Dad. You and Mom will have to take Carson where he can ride a horse before he will stop that cowpoke stuff."

"We are all scheduled to meet in Virginia City, Nevada, for Thanksgiving this year. Carson, you will have plenty of horses to ride there."

"Appreciate that pardner, truly I do."

"Spencer, that is your grandfather you are speaking to!"

"Yes, Mum. I am sorry grandfather, my mouth ran away with itself." That brought another round of laughter, because that was what his father, Louis, always said to get himself out of trouble.

L ouis and I rode into the White House in the morning and I introduced him to his boss, Secretary Robert Lansing, who took him for his orientation meetings with the rest of the staff. Louis hardly had time to get adjusted to his office before the whole capitol was in an uproar, July 2nd, over the arrest of Erich Muenter, alias Frank Holt. He was an employee of the German Embassy and was arrested for placing explosives inside the House of Representatives, for the shooting and wounding of House Members. He reported to American News Service that is was to prevent the shipment of war munitions to England. He was found dead in his holding cell on July 6th.

By August, Louis and Cathleen had moved from Bellawoods and into a newer, larger apartment in downtown Washington, D.C. Louis had been working on the proposal for Congress to appropriate funds for the return of American citizens stranded in Europe. On August 5th the bill was passed. All was quiet until August 20th when the Austro-Hungarian Ambassador to the United States was sent home for sponsoring sabotage. The proof was obtained in letters exchanged between the German and Austrian Ambassadors, "It is my impression that we can disorganize and hold up for months, if not entirely prevent, the manufacture of munitions in Bethlehem and the Middle West. In the opinion of the German military attache, this is of great importance and amply outweighs the comparatively small expenditure of money involved."

There was other proof positive of sabotage activities to have the entire Austro-Hungarian delegation recalled for cause. By the end of September, there were too many diplomatic notes exchanged between Vienna and Berlin to keep count, Louis wrote most of them. His language was strong and the messages were sent in German. Because of his work, Germany agreed to pay the indemnity for the sinking of the *William Frye*. The sinking of American merchant marines did not stop, however. In October, Louis wrote a note of complaint about the loss of the merchant marine, *Arabic*, and demanded an indemnity of 1 million dollars. This was four times the normal amount and Germany responded that she did not attack the *Arabic* and had no knowledge of who might have done this terrible act. With the approval of his boss, Secretary Lansing and President Wilson, his response was harsh and to the point. In German, he informed the foreign office in Berlin and Vienna that all future attacks on American vessels would not be tolerated. It would now be the policy of the United States government to send submarine escorts for all American shipping between the east coast of the US and European ports of call. The captains of the submarines were instructed to hunt down and sink without warning any U-boat that fired upon an American vessel on the high seas. By October 15th, a joint promise to pay Great Britain and France, a loan of $400,000,000 was negotiated by J. Pierpont Morgan and company. The loan was to be used to escort merchant marines by US naval submarines under the command of Commodore James Caldwell. Large convoys of ships bound for England and France would now have US protection.

Germany and Austria had immediate responses by sending small army units into the United States. On October 14, 1915, federal secret service officers and members of the New York Police Bomb Squad arrest two Germans near Weehawken, New Jersey. One claimed to be Robert Fay, of the German army here on leave to visit family, the other, Walter Scholz, his brother-in-law, confesses that they were in the employ of the German Secret Service and were developing means to destroy vessels carrying war supplies to Europe before they left port. Subsequently, fourteen others are arrested in other eastern seaports.

November came and Berlin shifted to attacking American shipping in the Mediterranean. In the first week of November, 27 ships are attacked, several are sunk and 272 lives are lost. During the second and third weeks, four different American manufacturing plants are sabotaged by bombs and fires set by German and Austrian agents. On November 17, 1915, the American Liner, *Ancona,* is attacked in the Mediterranean tying to reach Italy.

It sinks within sight of the coast after the life boats have been filled to overflowing. On November 29th, a US Navy wireless operator in Honolulu picks up messages transmitted from Nauen, Prussia, to Tuckerton, New Jersey, a distance of 9,000 miles. Louis had Captain Karl Boyed and Captain Franz von Papen arrested in Tuckerton and brought to Washington, D. C. for a public trial. His boss refused to press charges. Louis talked to the President and requested that the two be sent back to Germany, but not before they were sent to The Farm in Lancaster, Virginia, for some 'advanced questioning'.

December 3, 1915, for Louis and the State Department, was a very trying day. They were trying to keep us a neutral nation, while Great Britain and France were trying to get us to declare war. On December 3rd, the British foreign office sent an apology to Louis in the State Department for the seizure of the American escort vessels *USS Hocking* and *USS Geneses*. They believed them to be enemy owned, could we please provide proof of ownership. Louis sent a testy reply:

LORD ALFRED DINSMORE:

WHILE I AM LOCATING AND SENDING YOU PROOF OF THE MILITARY OWNERSHIP OF THE USS HOCKING AND USS GENESES, THE PRESIDENT OF THE UNITED STATES HAS ORDERED ALL SHIPPING CONVOYS ACROSS THE ATLANTIC TO CEASE OPERATION FROM ANY AMERICAN PORT. ALL SHIPS OF GREAT BRITAIN WILL ALSO BE DELAYED FROM LEAVING PORT UNTIL THIS MATTER OF OWNERSHIP CAN BE DETERMINED FOR THE USS HOCKING AND USS GENESES. THE PRESIDENT HAS ASKED ME TO REMIND YOU THAT THE LAST TIME BRITAIN SEIZED AMERICAN WARSHIPS WAS 1812.

I CAN TELL YOU THAT THE TWO SHIPS IN QUESTION WERE CONSTRUCTED IN THE PHILADELPHIA NAVAL YARDS AND HAVE BEEN IN CONTINUOUS CONVOY DUTY UP UNTIL THEY WERE SEIZED BY YOUR GOVERNMENT. THERE IS AN OLD SAYING IN AMERICA – DO NOT BITE THE HAND THAT FEEDS YOU!

I DO NOT KNOW WHICH IS WORSE, A NATION WHO SINKS OUR SHIPS OR ONE WHO SEIZES THEM.

LOUIS JASON CALDWELL, CAPTAIN USN
COUNSEL US STATE DEPARTMENT

That same day, Karl Boyed and Franz von Papen were arrested by NIA agents trying to reenter the United States and were taken to St. Elizabeth Hospital for 'observation'. This observation would last until November 11, 1918.

December 4, 1915, Henry Ford announced that he was forming the Peace Party to seek a conference of peace advocates to influence belligerent governments to terminate the war, he leaves New York for Europe without informing the State Department.

December 6, 1915, the State Department demands of Austria that her government denounce the sinking of the passenger ship *Ancona* as an illegal and indefensible act. Louis writes that the captain who perpetrated the deed should be surrendered to the United States for punishment and that an indemnity be paid of $1,000,000 for the American citizens who were killed or injured in the attack. On the 15[th,] Austria replies to Louis and asks to state the law broken by the submarine commander in the *Ancona* sinking, since the *Ancona* was bound for a port in a country which is at war with Austria. They further state that all US shipping bound for Italy will be sunk without warning.

On the 18th, Louis receives a reply from his inquiry to Germany. They deny claims of the US that she has "Inspired acts of spies in the United States" and encloses their reply to the American News Service articles, "To Germans abroad, to German-American citizens in the US, to the American people, and any alike peoples; whoever is guilty of conduct tending to associate the German cause with lawlessness of thought, suggestion or deed against life, property and order in the United States, is, in fact, an enemy of the very cause and a source of embarrassment to the German Government."

Louis fired off another telegram:

Baron Von Hindenkild:

The Department of State appreciates the last communication where you disavow any knowledge of spies sent from Germany. The following German-Americans working within the German Conciliates in the United States have been detained for questioning.

Robert Fay
Walter Scholz
Karl Boyed
Franz von Papen
Eric von Clausen
Erich Muller
Bernhard von Helder
Constantine Duma

SINCE THEY ARE NOT GERMAN CITIZENS, THEY WILL EITHER BE RELEASED AFTER QUESTIONING OR CHARGED WITH THE CRIME OF SPYING FOR A FOREIGN GOVERNMENT. THE PUNISHMENT FOR THIS IS DEATH BY FIRING SQUAD.

December 19th, Louis replies to Austria's note of December 15; he notices admission that the *Ancona* was torpedoed while passengers were aboard; says the culpability of the submarine commander is fully established; refuses to discuss other details of the attack as immaterial, holds the dual government in Vienna and Budapest responsible for the act of its submarine commander and reiterates his demands for denunciation and reparation for the attack. On December 23rd, England notifies Louis that she has suspended the issuance of permits for the shipment of hospital supplies of any description from the United States to Germany, Austria, Bulgaria and Turkey. Louis sends another one of his famous telegrams.

LORD ALFRED DINSMORE:

I AM CONSTANTLY AMAZED AT GREAT BRITAIN'S ATTEMPTS TO REWRITE INTERNATIONAL LAW. YOUR GOVERNMENT SIGNED AN AGREEMENT AFTER THE WAR STARTED TO ALLOW FREE ENTRANCE INTO ALL COUNTRIES OF HOSPITAL SUPPLIES. IF YOU PERSIST IN THIS NONSENSE, WE WILL ALSO NOT SHIP HOSPITAL SUPPLIES TO GREAT BRITAIN. BUT IT IS A MOTE POINT SINCE YOU HAVE NOT RELEASED THE USS HOCKING AND USS GENESES TO CONVOY SERVICE. UNTIL THAT IS DONE – **NOTHING WILL BE SHIPPED TO GREAT BRITAIN FROM THIS COUNTRY.**

I HAVE LOCATED AND SENT YOU PROOF OF THE OWNERSHIP OF THE USS HOCKING AND USS GENESES, INCLUDING THE LIST OF OFFICERS AND ENLISTED MEN SERVING UPON THESE VESSELS. IF THESE MEN ARE NOT RELEASED IN THE NEXT TWENTY-FOUR HOURS I AM FILING KIDNAPING CHARGES TO THOSE ALREADY FORWARDED TO THE INTERNATIONAL COURT IN THE HAGUE. THE PRESIDENT HAS CONTINUED THE ORDER FOR ALL SHIPPING CONVOYS ACROSS THE ATLANTIC TO CEASE OPERATION FROM AMERICAN PORTS UNTIL THE SHIPS ARE RELEASED. I HAVE RELEASED ALL SHIPS OF ANY OTHER NATION, EXCEPT BRITAIN, FROM ANY FURTHER DELAY FROM LEAVING US PORTS. THE ACTIONS OF YOUR GOVERNMENT ARE THOSE OF A HOSTILE NATION, NOT A FRIENDLY ONE. MY GOVERNMENT WILL

CONTINUE TO SEND HOSPITAL SUPPLIES TO ANY NATION THAT REQUESTS THEM. I DO NOT THINK ENGLAND WILL WANT THE WHOLE WORLD TO KNOW THAT THEY ALSO WILL SEIZE HUMANITARIAN AID TO ANY NATION WHEN IT IS MEANT TO RELIEVE SUFFERING AND DEATH.

AGAIN, I DO NOT KNOW WHICH IS WORSE, A NATION WHO SINKS OUR SHIPS OR ONE WHO SEIZES THEM. NEITHER HAS MY RESPECT.

LOUIS JASON CALDWELL, CAPTAIN USN
COUNSEL US STATE DEPARTMENT

The *USS Hocking* and *USS Geneses* were released twenty-four hours after Louis sent the second telegram to London.

On December 29th, a telegram arrived from Vienna declaring that much of the loss of life on the *Ancona* was due to a panic on the vessel, they offer to make full grants to American demands. The next day another Austrian submarine sinks the passenger ship, *Persia*, in the Mediterranean, causing loss of American lives including Robert McNeely, US Consul at Aden, Arabia. Louis has a meeting with President Wilson and asks him to break diplomatic relations with Austria.

20

Awaiting Convoy Duty

North Atlantic, 1916

M y son, James, has his office in the Army Navy Building while he waits for convoy duty to start again in the Atlantic. He is the commander of the Atlantic Submarine Fleet. James is the third member of our family to become an admiral in the United States Navy, there are probably other families with this distinct honor, but I can not recall any others off hand. James has not lived a charmed life like the rest of us. Trouble, heartache and major hurdles have been the norm for him. I love and respect him more than any of my other children. I suppose a father should not say that or even think that. Emily and I have four children. The oldest is Elizabeth and she was the joy of our life when we had no others to raise. She called herself 'busy butt' because this was how she first pronounced her name. She was a model child, the typical oldest sister of two brothers and one sister. She attended the small college where my sister taught in upper New York State, married and raised a family with her devoted husband, one definition of a charmed life. James was born next and tried very hard to imitate his father in all things, then came the twins. Louis and his sister Louise completed our family.

James is the most sensitive of our children, he feels things deeply, not at all like his mother and me. We care about things in our life, but not to the degree that James does. Here are a couple of examples:

He met his first wife in Bermuda when he was still a midshipman in Annapolis, this is how I remember it. He called me at my office in the White House to ask me for permission to marry her. He did not seem himself, he probably had never been so happy, frightened, anxious, and almost ill to his stomach in his whole, short life. He started the conversation with me this way.

"Father, did you have anything to do with the new transfer program to the War College for final year midshipmen?"

"James, hello to you, too. Yes, it was my idea."

"I just signed up today. I was also approved and accepted today. That is highly unusual, isn't it?"

"Very, I had nothing to do with that."

"I am not twenty-one and I need your permission to move into married student housing on base."

"I see. Have you thought this through, James?"

"No, I am still working my way through it. If you do not grant me permission to marry, it would be silly to ask Marisa to marry me a year earlier than we planned."

"I will need to talk with your mother, James. When I make decisions unilaterally, she comes unglued."

"I understand, Dad. I have watched you and mother from the time I can remember. I will make Marisa a good husband, I promise."

"In that case, you need to telephone your mother at home and tell her I have given you my permission subject to her approval, Son. President McKinley has asked me to attend the World Peace Conference at The Hague in Holland, my next letter to you will be from there."

"Thank you, Dad." He hung up without saying goodbye and placed a call to his mother. He talked to her and then to Marisa in Bermuda. They would be married June 2, 1899, in Newport, Rhode Island. She bought the invitations and mailed them from Bermuda.

Seems idyllic, doesn't it? It wasn't, his wife did not like living in the United States and they returned to Bermuda with their young daughter. James had to travel back and forth to continue his navy career and his wife was murdered while he was away from home. James was absolutely devastated when I told him the news. I met him at the mail terminal in Washington as he stepped off the gangway from the Bermuda mail steamer. I was alone, no other members of the family were present. He tried to shake my hand and I refused, I gave him a huge hug. At that time in my life, I was not very affectionate with any of my children and him least of all. He was surprised when I said, "James, turn around, we are going back to Bermuda."

"What has happened?"

"Marisa is dead, she died while you were in route."

"Dead, I don't understand."

"She was murdered, Son. They found her body early yesterday."

"Where is Star?"

"She is with her grandmother, Wendy. She will need you to get through the loss of her mother, Son. You and I will make the final arrangements for Marisa and when the memorial service can be held after the release of her body, the whole family will come from the States to attend. We have lots of work to do, James. Are you able to do this?"

"Of course, it is the last thing that I can do for Marisa."

"That is the spirit, Son. She is a Caldwell and a member of our family. We bury our own and move into the next chapter of life, just like your grandmother taught us. Star needs to come home, she is a US citizen and a treasured member of this family."

Three days later we stepped off the mail steamer in St. George's. We were met by WH, Wendy, Star, and the Butlers. It hit him when he saw Star trying to be brave and he let it all go. Everyone stood around, uncomfortable, waiting for him to pull himself together, except Star, she clung to him and said, "Don't leave me ever again, Daddy."

"I won't, Star. I promise. From today on, you will always be by my side." All of the adults nodded their agreement. He took Star's hand and we walked to Caldwell Place to eat a meal and plan the memorial service. John Butler was very quiet, not like himself at all. James talked with him away from everyone else and he told him what he had planned.

"James, we have a Butler family plot here in Bermuda. It is time to bring my son Zachary home to his family. I have written to the London War office with the help of your father and the remains will be shipped to Bermuda in time for the internment with Marisa, side by side, father and daughter. Wendy is remarried and will be buried with WH in Scotland, and I like that idea. Do you still have Zachary's diary?"

"Yes, I have it at the cottage, why?"

"I want to place it in Marisa's hands to give to her father when they meet in the great beyond."

"That would be wonderful, General Butler, let's plan on that."

The family was together until after the inquest into the death of Marisa and the arrest of the man responsible. Zachary came home and the service was complete. James was ready for the next chapter in his life. Star and he left Bermuda with the Caldwell members who could attend the service. Louis was in Europe chasing "bad guys". "Busy" was busy giving birth to a baby and Grandma Caldwell stayed with her to hold her hand. Other than that, the entire crew was on hand, even his Uncle Teddy and Aunt Ruth took a few days off. I paid for first class tickets on a Cunard Liner from St. George's to Washington and the family reunion continued on board, but Star and he stayed by themselves and just talked about what four year olds were interested in. It was a sad time and a time of discovery for him. The last time I had felt like this was five years ago at my father's funeral at Arlington. My mother did not let the family dwell on the loss, but instead, encouraged all of us to find new opportunities for life. Family is the key to survival in this world, not a superhuman effort to overcome all obstacles before us. James needed to pack away his former life and start a new one with his daughter wrapped in the warmth of the Caldwell Clan. Star and James must have decided this because they hugged each other and left their cabin to find the other members of the family.

The other examples I remember all start with a telephone call. Here is another one where I called him.

"Commander Caldwell?"

"Yes."

"This is the White House calling. One moment until I connect you with your father."

"Who is it, Daddy?"

"Grandpa Caldwell. Hush, I want to listen to him. Run into the kitchen and pickup the extension, you can listen." She tore off for the kitchen.

"Hello, James."

"Yes, Dad, what can I do for you?"

"Your brother is in the hospital. He is being treated for burns suffered in a car accident."

"That is too bad. Where was he driving?"

"He wasn't, the car was parked in the Navy Yard here."

"Oh, I see. Hold on a minute, Dad. Star hang up the telephone and come sit on my lap."

"Star is on the extension?"

"Yes, I thought she should not hear this. What happened?"

"Tim and your brother returned to Washington from South Hampton and reported for their debriefing at *The Farm*."

"How did Louis' car explode?"

"Tim and your brother needed to get back to the safe house and get some clean clothes. Louise was teaching in Alexandria and they had the house to themselves, until the telephone rang and Commander Morton wanted see them."

"Morton is a pain in the ass, Dad. What did he want?"

"He wasn't even there, he had a stack of case files for your brother to begin working. It never ends for him. He must have scooped them up into his arms and they headed back to their Ford. Tim must have opened the back door for him and he crawled into the seat still holding a hundred or so files, that is what saved his life. They could not have been inside the RLSO more than ten or fifteen minutes. They were not very diligent about their surroundings and they had jumped into the Ford without thinking. Tim pushed the starter with his foot. The motor did not turn over, the entire front of the Ford exploded in a giant orange ball of flames. The first thing I saw when I was called to the scene was hundreds of pages blown all over the parking lot."

"Star and I will be careful, Dad. Thanks for calling, we are on our way up there as soon as I can arrange leave."

"Don't rush, James. Your brother is stable but not awake yet. I will call you again in a few hours and let you know how he is doing. By then your mother and I will have talked to the doctors and we will have some news."

"Good bye, Dad."

"Uncle Louis is hurt, Daddy."

"Yes, he is. I need to call my office and tell them we are going to Washington on the next train.

The next few weeks of James' life, were spent with the two people he loved most in the world, his daughter and his brother. Louis and he had grown very close working together. Star and he spent the first week in the navy hospital in Maryland, because that is where Louis was. At first they did not let Star into Louis' room, but then they relented when the President of the United States took her by the hand and walked into his room. No doctor or nurse was brave enough to say, no, to the "commander and chief."

James sat in a chair in the corner of his room and slept most of the time. He did not even wake when other family members came to visit Louis. They just smiled at him and checked on Louis to see if his eyes were open. When his eyes were open, James would swear that he could see him and hear him, but Louis never moved a single muscle, not even his eye lids and then he would fall asleep again and James would go talk to Star and whoever brought her to the hospital.

Finally his sister, Louise, said to him, "James, one of us can spell you. You do not need to stay in this room day and night."

"I have already lost a member of my family by not being there when she needed me. I am not leaving Louis and that is final. Louise was standing at the foot of Louis' bed crying, when they heard a very faint sound come from Louis' lips.

"Did you hear that, James?" Louise was crying and screaming at the same time.

"I heard it, Sis! Louis, say it again. Say it again, please." Their racket brought a nurse into his room.

"You should not ask your brother to speak, Commander."

"He spoke to us."

"The noise you heard was the noise all comatose patients make."

Emily and I walked into the room just then with a doctor. The kids were talking.

"Has there been any change, doctor?"

"No, your son is still in a coma. He is responding to stimulation so he should be regaining his consciousness within a few days."

"Thank you, doctor." We left the room. Only James remained at the foot of Louis' bed rubbing his feet.

Emily reentered the room with the doctor. "How long will my son be in this coma, doctor?"

"He is semi-conscious now, Mrs. Caldwell. He can hear you, he can not respond to you, but he can hear you. Say something to him and watch his non-verbal responses, they appear before full consciousness."

"Louis, darling can you hear Mommy? Did you see that, Doctor? He moved his eyes back and forth and squeezed my hand!"

"Yes, I did Mrs. Caldwell. He will start his long way back today and the rest of his life."

That night after everyone else had left, James sat and held his brother's hand. Louis would wake, mumble something that James did not understand, squeeze his hand and then fall back asleep. James was sleeping in the corner of the room again when he heard a voice ask, "Doctor, how is my brother today?"

James started to tell her that Louis was talking when Louis said, as clear as a bell, "Hey, Louise. How come you are not in school? Wait a minute, who got rid of the wet shiny stalagmites? Why is it so bright in here?

"He is awake. He woke up last night and tried to fondle a nurse."

" Why are you telling our sister that, James. I did no such thing. I am an officer and gentleman in the United States Navy."

"Because it is true, I was here and saw the whole thing."

"Oh, my God, James. They replaced my brain, I hate the Navy and everything it stands for, I am a spy." That brought laughter from the three of us looking down at him in his bed, laughter of relief.

"Louis, I am so happy to see your eyes open!"

"Me too, why is it so damn bright in here?"

"What did you say? Louis, oh, Louis, talk to me! What happened? Why is he asleep again, doctor?"

"He has spoken his first words in over a month. His left temporal lobe is working, Miss Caldwell. Go tell your parents while he takes a little nap. Come back for evening visiting hours and I think he will say a few more words. You too, James, your twenty-four sessions are over. Go on, spend some time with your daughter, get out of this hospital."

He did and Star and he enjoyed the time together. That evening he took her to talk to her Uncle Louis.

A week later, Louis was up and walking the halls of the hospital with his brother. They walked the halls and then tried a few stairs. That really hurt his legs. Every day they could go farther and soon the doctor released him to come home, provided he signed up for outpatient rehabilitation once a day. The hospital gave him crutches to leave and he handed them back to them on the front sidewalk and asked for a cane from Grandpa Schneider. The cane and he went everywhere together. His new driver drove him and his brother to the RLSO office and helped him up the flight of steps. They walked towards his desk in the corner and someone was sitting there.

"Hello, what can I do for you, Commander?"

"I am Commander Caldwell and that used to be my desk before my automobile was blown out from under me."

"Sir, it is still your desk, should you be back at work so soon? You have been promoted to Chief prosecutor of the NLSO office next door. You are in the wrong building."

"I can still give orders here, right."

"Go ahead, Sir."

"Telephone Admiral Lowe at the NCI training center and he will fill you in. But before you do that, would you walk with me, my brother and my driver over to my new office? What is your name? I can't keep calling you my driver."

"It is Tim, Sir. Timothy Caswell."

"I will call you, Timothy. Tim is not formal enough for a Marine Scout and an expert sniper."

"How did you know that, Sir? My file has not caught up with me yet, it is still at Pendleton."

"Timothy, I have this sixth and even a seventh sense about people, you look like a sniper!"

"I do? Thank you, Sir."

"You are welcome. Lieutenant Henderson, show us the way." They began walking to a down stairwell.

"I notice that you carry a cane, Commander. How many weeks until you can get rid of it?"

"Timothy, my boy, I never plan to be without it. It will be our little secret, gentlemen, what Commander Morton does not know will not hurt him. Besides, my doctor has instructed me to carry this until my rehabilitation is complete."

"Really, Commander Caldwell?"

"Lieutenant Henderson, do not believe everything you hear and only half of what you read."

"Didn't President Lincoln say that, Sir?"

"No, I did just now, pay attention." His face dropped. "LT, that was a joke. President Lincoln said you can fool some of the people some of the time and all of the people some of the time; but you can't fool all the people all the time – unless you work for NCI."

"He did? I don't remember that last part."

"Then, maybe that last part is not true, or NCI was created after he left office and he would have added it, if it existed. The point is, in our jobs we fool all the people all the time or we are dead. I am walking proof of that statement."

"Understood, Sir."

"Good, how far is my office? I do not want you three to have to carry me."

"Not far, Sir."

They walked for what seemed like hours to Louis, but it was only a few minutes and he had to sit down behind his desk. His new office was nice, not too big, not too small, it had its own telephone and he picked it up and a voice said, "Yes, Commander Caldwell, can I place a call for you?"

"Who is this? Where are you?"

"I am the switchboard operator, Commander. I answer whenever you pick up your hand set. My switchboard is in the basement."

"Can I make a call without going through the switchboard?"

"Of course, use the rotary dial."

"Is that this thing below the hand set?"

"Yes, Sir."

"What is the number for *The Farm*?"

"Which farm is that, Sir?" He knew then, that this girl did not have a clue what he did for a living.

"The one in Alexandria that has all the turkeys at Thanksgiving, I forget its name."

"Well, without a name, I can not look it up for you, Sir."

"If I think of it, I will call you back. What is your name?"

"It is, Miss Hattie, Sir."

"Thank you, Miss Hattie, I am sure that we will be hearing a lot from each other, now that I have moved into my new office."

"I am sure that we will"....click.

"She hung up on me! James, get down to the basement and have a talk with this, Miss Hattie. Find out if she has a brain in her head." James started for the down stairs and he heard. "Sit, gentlemen, LT, open my brief case and get the number for Admiral Lowe's office."

"It is, PENN473, Sir."

"How did you know that number, LT?"

"I talk to that office at least once a day, Sir."

"What about? I already know, you could tell me but then you would have to kill me." The three of them burst out laughing.

James reached the basement, and began looking for a switchboard. He found it around the next corner.

"Are you Miss Hattie?"

"Yes, are you Commander Caldwell?"

"Yes, I am one of them. You were just talking to my brother, Louis. My name is James."

"And you both work in this building, doesn't that get confusing?"

"No, I work in Norfolk, Virginia, not here. I am visiting my brother and I think he sent me down here to talk to you because he has some telephone calls to make and he did not want me to listen in on them."

"Are they classified?" James shook his head, no.

"Here, put on this headset and you can listen if you want to." She stood up and let him sit in her chair. She was nearly as tall as he was, but had a graceful movement about her like she was a dancer. Her hair was pulled up into a bun and her face was washed so clean, James bet it hurt her. Her lips had no color, not a hint of lip stick. She obviously went out of her way to look plain. She could not hide her shape, however. She wore a loose fitting plain colored dress that hung almost to her ankles. But when she moved, you could see the size of her breasts and hips, this was a mature woman, probably older than him. "Are you going to sit down, Commander?"

He realized that he had not put the headset on and he was staring at her. "No, I think my brother probably wants his privacy. Have you had this job long, Miss Hattie?"

"A couple of years, I started right after my husband was killed."

"I am a widower myself, I have a four year old daughter. Do you have any children?"

"Yes, a son. That is his picture over there." She pointed to a framed picture on her desk.

"May I?" She shook her head, yes and he picked it up and looked at it. He was of mixed blood and looked like he could have been Star's brother. He put it down and reached for his wallet.

"This is not a very good picture of Star, my daughter." He handed it to her and she smiled a wide smile, "Which of you had the Negro ancestors, Commander, you or your wife?"

"My wife, she was about one tenth and looked like she had a sun tan year around. Why do you ask?"

"Because my father was about one fourth and my mother was white as snow. I favored her, but you can see in the picture that my son has more of my father's genes."

"Are your parents still alive, Miss Hattie?"

"Yes, they babysit with Randolph."

"I would like to meet them."

"You would?"

"Yes, I would. You must have a first name."

"It is Martha, Martha Andrews."

"Why the, Miss Hattie?"

"Because it sounds like an old maid school teacher and the sailors never come looking down here, you are the first in two years, Commander."

"And do you dress like an old maid school teacher for the same reason?"

"You don't like the way I dress?" She had a smile on her face.

"Yes, I think, the early feed sack look, will come back some day." She burst into laughter. She had a beautiful face when she laughed.

"Why are you in Washington visiting your brother?"

"You did not hear about his accident?"

"I am the last to know anything around here, only the names and voices over my switchboard." He sat and talked with her between flashes of the switchboard and her routing of calls here and there. He told her about Louis' brush with death, Star and his train ride to Washington, the time spent in the hospital with Louis and his strong recovery.

"So now you and Star are ready to return home. Just as we have managed to meet each other."

"I have ten more days of leave. Would you consider taking some days off and spending them with Star and me. I would be interested in what Star thinks of Randolph."

"I do not have any vacation time left, James. I get off at 5 this afternoon, can you meet me here and take me home to my family?"

"I can and I will, see you at five this afternoon."

That was how James met his second wife and started his life over. They have a son, Jason Arthur Caldwell, and they live close to us in Washington. James' immediate supervisor is Admiral of the Navy, George Dewey, Chief of Naval Operations. The seventy-five submarines of the United States are spread among the oceans of the earth. Admiral Dewey decided to move the majority to the Atlantic and Mediterranean to help protect American Merchant Mariners. As soon as the president lifted the embargo against shipments to England, James would be at sea in command of the secret operation to identify German U-boats by a new device installed in each of our submarines. Shipments were in route to France and Italy and the president wanted them protected across the Atlantic and throughout the Mediterranean. This would probably mean a confrontation with an Austrian U-boat.

James had talked to me several times about the German and Austrian U-boats currently in service.

"You can tell President Wilson that my information comes from Admiral Dewey and not Secretary Daniels. I am informed that the Germans have two classes of submarines, the U class and the UC class. I have a picture of U-53 taken off Newport, Rhode Island." He handed it to me.

"How was this picture taken?"

"It was taken with the periscope camera of F -34."

"One of ours?"

"Yes, it was coming out of Newport to test our new listening devices and heard what turned out to be a tender making a delivery to U-53. Can you see the tender in the back ground on the right hand side?"

"Yes, what is the size of this submarine?"

"Probably 2500 tons, in a craft of that size, reasonable habitability and good sea-keeping qualities are possible. It crossed the Atlantic by itself. We are hauling our submarines to the Mediterranean, but they are between 800 and a 1000 tons. We have nothing in our inventory to compete with U- 53. It has a length of 280 feet, beam of 26 feet, depth of 20 feet, surface horsepower of 7000, surface speed of 22 knots, submerged speed of 14 knots and a cruising distance of 6500 miles."

"That is why they need tenders."

"Yes, U-53 can carry supplies for six to eight weeks. With 8 torpedo tubes, during war time she needs new fish sooner than six to eight weeks"

"I count 8 deck guns, is that correct?"

"Yes, some are anti-aircraft, notice the covered bridge and conning tower, the two collapsible boats are hard to see. U-53 has 4 officers, 3 machinists, 1 medical officer, 50 petty officers and crew members."

"How do you know that? I know, you could tell me, but then you would have to kill me. The Farm, right?"

"Yes, do you want to see a UC class?"

"What is the difference?"

"UC's are designed for laying mines instead of firing torpedoes."

"Are you kidding? How do they do that?"

"They have tubes for 'squirting the mines out in a string.' They carry 150 contact mines and the UC's have been raising hell with Great Britain, but the Royal Navy won't admit it."

"This looks a lot smaller."

"That is because this is a snap shot taken from a pier in Germany. A UC is a lot larger, it is 5000 tons, 413 feet long, speed on the surface of 26 knots, submerged 16 knots with a radius of action of 20,000 miles."

"Good, God. The Germans could mine our harbors on both coasts with this."

"Yes, they could. Admiral Dewey wants a battle plan for sinking UC's before they reach our harbors."

"Can you give it to him, James?"

"Depends if we can locate them. Every ship gives off a sound signal when its screws are turning in the water. We have patterns for most of US shipping so we don't attack our own. We are being ordered into the Mediterranean to record the sounds made by German and Austrian U-boats. The special weapons committee headed by Thomas Edison has given us the recording equipment and a device that can be placed inside our torpedoes that will 'home-in' on any sound pattern that we have. Once the sound patterns are known we will be able to destroy U-boats underwater from a safe distance, they should not be able to detect us if we are careful."

"What is this system called, James?"

"Neff."

"I thought the Neff system was the removal of storage batteries and the venting of diesel fumes into the sea without fouling the air inside the submarine."

"It is. And let's hope that is all the Germans think it is." He had a big smile on his face.

"You look pleased with yourself, does it work?"

"Like a charm, I have never seen anything work as well during sea trials. We will continue using it this month in the Mediterranean. We will not use a torpedo with a warhead. Upon contact, the torpedo turns to scrap metal pieces and tears the submarines screws to pieces. We used it last month against the Austrian submarine that sank the *Persia*."

"Does Louis know this?"

"No, why?"

"He has gone to President Wilson and asked him to break diplomatic relations with Austria. The president said he would need proof that an Austrian U-boat sank the *Persia*. If the *Persia* is in for repair or missing that would be proof if we had a statement from your captain to include."

"Admiral Dewey would not allow one of his captains to admit that we broke our neutrality over the testing of the Neff System."

"Have the Austrians lost any other U-boats?"

"Six that we know of, total tonnage is estimated at 10,824. That would include some small coastal U-boats and not anything in the U-53 class."

"Have we lost any?"

"One, F-4, in the Pacific off the coast of Hawaii. You don't hear much about the war in the Pacific, but it is there. Japan has lost 3, Portugal 1, Belgium 2, Germany 12, and Great Britain 69."

"All in the Pacific, all U-boats?"

"All in the Pacific, not all U-boats."

"Do you have the total estimated losses so far in the war, James?" He handed me a list of vessels destroyed since July 28, 1914.

Country	*Ships*	*Tonnage*
Great Britain	684	1,419,580
Norway	90	131,488
Germany	69	177,530
France	67	162,417
Sweden	45	49,999
Holland	43	131,333
Russia	35	42,349
Denmark	33	35,605
Italy	24	49,197
Belgium	12	22.931
Turkey	12	11,831
Greece	10	17,477
Austria	6	10,824
United States	6	14,583
Spain	4	8,606
Japan	3	19,267
Rumania	1	758
Portugal	1	620

While I was reading the list, James gave me Admiral's Dewey evaluation of the naval conflict since 1914. The naval operations and incidents of the war were not, aside from the battle of Jutland, particularly noteworthy. The British fleet continued to give the world a shining example of the value of sea power by shutting off Germany from all seaborne supplies except the small quantities which occasionally came across from Norway and Sweden and even this traffic was almost stopped. The prevention of import of cotton, copper, rubber, zinc, tin, petroleum and foodstuffs greatly hampered Germany, Austria and Turkey in the production of munitions of war and it is probable that it seriously interfered with their military operations.

The German U-boat war against commerce has been modified recently, while the German government took up a new and indefensible attitude towards neutral shipping. A very considerable portion of the German people are beginning to have doubts of the advisability of ruthless U-boat war against non-combatant shipping. Notice that England has lost 684 ships, but when you look at the average tonnage of each ship, it is equal to a merchant marine vessel, not a battleship. It has also been very costly of life and vessels in the U-boat service. 150 U-boats have been lost since the German government began the new policy of U-boat engagement. Admiral Dewey believes that between 36 and 40 of the U-boats have been refloated and brought in for repairs. The most serious loss to U-boats in 1915 was the British armored cruiser *Natal*, which was destroyed December 30th. Earlier in the year, *HMS Bulwark* and *HMS Princess Irene* were also lost. The Italians have lost the battleships *Benedetto* and *Leonardo da Vinci*. The Russians have lost the battleship *Imperatritsa Maria*.

"Dad, do you remember that Admiral Dewey worked very closely with General MacArthur in the defeat of the Philippines?"

"Yes, I remember it clearly, why do you ask?"

"Admiral Dewey doubts that the navies are cooperating with their armies in the field. Especially the German Navy, except for the U-boat service, the entire navy is setting on the German coast, not even venturing out of the Baltic. The German Army has shown its superiority. In 1914, Belgium and a considerable portion of France had been overrun by the German Army. Despite reckless sacrifices of men, the German Army has failed to reach Calais   or the channel coast. In the summer of 1915, the Russian Army has been trundled back from Galicia and from Poland in a badly battered condition. In the closing months of 1915, Bulgaria has joined Germany and Austria to conquer Servia, thus giving them control of the railways from Germany through Austria all the way to Constantinople and into Turkey. Thanks to the dismal failure of the French and English to hold the Dardanelles, supplies are free to move from Asia directly into Germany.

General Joffre is planning an ambitious Anglo-French forward movement for 1916. Admiral Dewey can not understand the stubborn refusal of the defeated western allies to sue for peace, while Winston Churchill has an interesting opposite point of view."

"What did he say, James?"

He said, "It is not necessary for us to win the war to push the German line back over all the territory they have absorbed, nor even to pierce it. While the German lines extend far beyond their frontiers, while their flag flies over conquered capitols and subjected provinces, while the appearances of military success greet their arms, Germany may be defeated more fatally in the second or third year of the war than if the Allied armies had entered Berlin in the first year."

"Sir Winston, seems overconfident to me, James."

"Louis says Mr. Churchill bases his conclusion on five points: 1) Military Manhood. The Teutonic coalition, Germany, Austria and Turkey, are wasting their supply of young fighting men; 2) Economic resources. It is believed that the British blockade of German ports will have a greater affect than the opening of the railroads into the middle east; 3) Naval supremacy. Even though Britain has lost over 684 vessels, she is replacing them at a greater rate than her enemies; 4) Diplomacy. Before the war is over, additional nations like Greece and the United States will enter the war; and 5) Internal disorders. Every dictator is in danger of being overthrown because of the war. Enver Pasha in Turkey, the Kaiser in Germany, the Emperor in Austria and even the Czar in Russia may be overthrown by the peoples of those nations."

"Louis has changed his mind about wanting to join MI 5. He and Lord Alfred Dinsmore are at each other's throats over the British seizure of American shipping."

"Britain is in the fight for the long run, Germany hoped for a quick victory. Austria had no idea what they started. Russia did not answer the call against the Slavic threat and we sit and hope for the best. I will write you from the Mediterranean, Dad, I have to get home and pack my bag. My submarines are loaded on transport ships and are heading for a show down with Austria."

"God's speed, James, be careful and come home safely to us."

21

Convoy to the Mediterranean
Atlantic Ocean, 1916

W e had no idea that James would be gone from Washington for an entire year. His convoy left the Washington Naval Yard on January 18th. Louis' request for President Wilson to break diplomatic relations with Austria was being processed when the president asked his ambassador in Vienna to deliver a note of protest. Ambassador Penfield was told that Austria had no interest in helping the United States discover who sank the *Persia* and Penfield was called home for consultations with the State Department. On January 18th, Germany informed us that her U-boat commanders in the Mediterranean have strict orders to observe the principles of international law in their operations against enemy merchantmen; vessels will be sunk only when carrying absolute contraband of war, and in a manner that passengers and crew will be able to reach a port safely. German Ambassador Count von Bernstorff in Washington sent a message to his government that contained the American terms for settling the *Lusitania* Matter. They included a disavowal of the act, an expression of a willingness to make reparation for the American lives lost and an admission of the illegality of the act.

January 23, 1916, President Wilson traveled to New York City and began a series of public addresses relating chiefly to his plans for national defense. These speeches were delivered in part because Congress had delayed action on plans to raise money for defense purposes and because the midyear elections of 1914 had provided strong opposition to his plans to slowly tip the balance of power in Europe. In his first address, covered by American News Service, he declared , "The question of national defense has been clouded by passion and prejudice. Partisan politics should be excluded so that in dealing with national defense, all parties should be drawn together. While the passion of the people is for peace, I seek to maintain peace, against very great and sometimes very unfair odds. The American people would fight for the vindication of their life and character, for liberty and their free institutions. America must maintain her sovereignty and that means we must become the champion of free government throughout the western hemisphere. I propose, here in New York, and in future locations, my plans for this championship. I have in mind a system of industrial and vocational education, under federal guidance, to which will be added training in the use of arms, camp sanitation and military discipline, to make young men and women serviceable for national defense. Such a system can not be made in a short time and without the aid of Congress. I call upon the Congress to read and accept my plan for training without delay. While I admire and respect the national guard, it has the disadvantage of being under the control of the States and I can only command it in the case of actual invasion. There should be a citizens' reserve of at least 500,000 trained men and women to be available in case national emergency."

Two days later, January 25th, the president spoke in Pittsburgh, where he again advocated the reserve of 500,000. While he was delivering his speech, I received an answer from Berlin indicating that German U-boats were not responsible for either the *Lusitania* or *Persia* sinking. The following day a message from Vienna claimed that Austrian U-boats were not responsible for either the *Lusitania* or *Persia* sinking. Germany and Austria issued a joint message to Washington that indicated that all merchant men will be treated as war ships after February 29th. The president was now in Cleveland where he said that his administration had not found it easy to avoid entanglements. Here, he urged the development of coast defenses, enlargement of the navy and again the supplementing of the standing army by a trained reserve. He said with great emphasis, "Let me tell you very solemnly that we cannot postpone this war being thrust upon us. I do not know what a single day may bring forth. I feel very much like President James Buchanan in March of 1861."

January 26th, I drafted a protest to be sent to London concerning the British Act forbidding British subjects (like myself) to trade with persons or firms in neutral countries that are of enemy nationality or connection. We used my case as an example. The British response was for me to immediately return to Bermuda or give up my British citizenship. I ignored the response because the president was now in Chicago where he would provide my response by restating the Monroe Doctrine, "We are asking ourselves, 'shall we be prepared to defend our shores and our homes?' Is that all we stand for? To keep the doors securely shut against our enemies? What about the great principles that we have stood for – for liberty of government and national independence in the whole Western Hemisphere? What about President Monroe? Was he wrong?"

During the president's travel to St. Louis, a federal grand jury in San Francisco indicted thirty Turkish seamen and the Turkish Consul on a charge of conspiring to wreck ammunition factories and to furnish supplies to German warships. The president added this bit of American News Service information to his address in St. Louis. There he said, "One reckless foreign consul or even one U-boat commander, choosing to put his private interpretation upon what his government wishes him to do, might set the world on fire. The United States may have to respond, in force, to save American lives of seamen serving in the Atlantic and Mediterranean. Today, I have been informed that a US Naval task force is presently patrolling the sea lanes inside the Mediterranean. My orders of engagement are clear. Defend yourselves and all American Merchantmen. Do not engage any foreign national ships to avenge lives already taken or to protect property of American shipping companies. Respond only after the foreign vessel has fired upon our ships and respond with total effort in order to permanently remove the threat of that foreign warship from ever committing such an act of murder in the future."

Twenty-four hours after the president's address, Germany and Austria announced that they will treat armed merchant vessels of enemy countries as warships, but will not engage neutral shipping in the Atlantic or Mediterranean. All ships in Great Britain waters will be sunk without warning until Great Britain agrees to lift the naval blockage of German ports in the Baltic. On February 15th, the State Department insists that Germany withdraw her order for the sinking of American vessels approaching Great Britain.

The three arguments advanced by the president in a series of ten speeches in ten cities (New York, Pittsburgh, Cleveland, Chicago, Milwaukee, Des Moines, St. Louis, Kansas City, Topeka and Tulsa) were, first, the maintenance of the honor of the United States, second, the maintenance of the Monroe Doctrine and third, our readiness in case the nation was forced into war in either the Mediterranean or Atlantic Oceans. The president returned to Washington, making additional short speeches from the platform of his train. His reception on the return began as small gatherings at train depots and swelled to huge crowds in the major cities along the return route.

On February 21st, he was back in the oval office sending messages and replies. He asked London for an explanation of seizure of American mails containing $10,000,000 in securities, also for a reply to our note of February 15th. March 1, 1916, Italian Minister in Washington informs us that Italy will continue the arming of merchantmen, despite the Austro-German warning of February 10th. They thank us for sending Commodore Caldwell's task force to the Port of Civitavecchia.

March 3, 1916, The Senate studies a resolution of Senator Gore declaring that, "The sinking by a U-boat without notice or warning of an armed merchant vessel of her public enemy, resulting in the death of a citizen of the United States, would constitute a just and sufficient cause to break diplomatic relations with the German Empire. (President Wilson now has two requests for diplomatic sanctions on his desk, one from the Senate and one from his own State Department). March 21, 1916, President Wilson sends his position paper to Congress proclaiming the neutrality of the United States and suggests a world wide regulation of submarine attacks on merchantmen. March 22, 1916, transatlantic liner *Minneapolis* is attacked by a U-boat in the Mediterranean. The U-boat involved sends out an SOS after it develops a ruptured hull from a damaged drive propellor. March 24, 1916, Entente Allies decline to accept American suggestion for the regulation of submarine attacks. The British vessel *Sussex* is sunk by U-boat. We are informed by France that they will not disarm their merchantmen even if Germany promises not to sink them. March 27, 1916, Turkey rejects American proposal for moratorium on U-boats attacks and claims it is responsible for sinking of *Persia*. March 28, 1916, London responds to our note of protest for the seizure of $10,000,000. London claims the money was from Germany and was seized under her policy to strike at German assets. The amount is forfeited and suggests that the US stop trading with Germany.

In April, after the War Council of Paris, I was asked to prepare another position paper for the president's signature to be forwarded to Congress. I began to think about the diplomacy of the war. In a war of endurance, as the War of the Nations has clearly reveled itself, diplomacy may prove more decisive than gunnery. That the Entente Allies (England, France, Italy and Russia), would possess the important advantage of a more skillful diplomacy was at first taken for granted by President Wilson. He observed the clumsy maneuvers of the German and Austrian foreign offices during the historic 13 days of July 23rd to August 4th. Since August of last year, the Central Powers (Germany, Austria and Turkey), have tried to retrieve their diplomatic reputations by successfully enlisting Bulgaria as an active alley. They are in the process of calculating, to a nicety, the limit of President Wilson's forbearance on the U-boat question and are fostering a very influential pro-German propaganda in Sweden, Spain, Greece, US and other neutral countries. The diplomats of the Entente, on the other hand, have fatally bungled the Balkan situation; one of their intended allies, Bulgaria, has become an avowed enemy and the other two, Greece and Rumania, still remain neutral. Italy's aid against Turkey has been purchased dearly and only after protracted bargaining. Most of all, the ineptitude of Entente diplomacy has been exhibited in the failure of the Allies to subordinate their own immediate political aims to the general advantage of the coalition. Italy has striven simply for her own territorial advantage in Trentino, Trieste and Albania. France has fought with more valor than calculation to regain Alsace-Loraine. Russia's gigantic military efforts have been futile because they have not been coordinated with those of the Allies and because they have been undertaken without previous provision of adequate munitions. Servia and Montenegro have been left disastrously to shift for themselves.

The weak Anglo-French expedition to Saloniki is an example of a diplomatic, as well as a military, failure. Sir Edward Grey has suffered England's prestige in the middle east to be ruined by the failure of other ill-supported offensives at the Dardanelles and in Mesopotamia. The Pact of London (September 5, 1914), binding the Allies not to negotiate peace separately, has been a notable achievement, but it was becoming painfully obvious that a further agreement was needed.

Only by a long series of discouraging defeats were the Allies taught the necessity of cooperation. After Russia's field army had been routed by Hindenburg, after the Anglo-French offensive of September, 1915, had proved to be merely another stab at the German line, after Servia had been conquered, after Gallipoli had been evacuated, after Townshend had been surrounded at Kut-el-Amara, after the French lines around Verdun had been battered back by German attacks did the Allies decide to hold a joint council of war. France, England, Italy, Belgium, Servia, Russia, Japan, Montenegro and Portugal were represented.

Their agreement should secure the maximum effort from each of the Allies and arrange a joint plan of action to decide in advance the terms upon which the war is be concluded. Before the end of the Paris meeting, however, diplomatic issues began to heat up here in the United States and President Wilson's attention was taken away from the paper that I was preparing. He and I discussed a series of incidents.

P ort of Civitavecchia, ninety miles from Rome, February 1, 1916, Commodore Caldwell, the son of Presidential Advisor Caldwell, read his most recent communications from the army navy building and one from the White House.

The White House
Washington DC

January 27, 1916

Commodore James Caldwell
United States Naval Task Force
Port of Civitavecchia, Italy

Re: Rules of engagement

My orders of engagement are clear. Defend yourselves and all American Merchantmen. Do not engage any foreign national ships to avenge lives already taken or to protect property of American shipping companies. Respond only after the foreign vessel has fired upon our ships and respond with total effort in order to permanently remove the threat of that foreign warship from ever committing such an act of murder in the future.

Your father shared your last conversation with me. As of this date, all torpedoes are to have maximum warheads, fired for total effect. If you are able to respond, in kind, at the time of an attack upon our vessels, I expect an immediate and lethal response. I do not expect an attack upon any U-boat or surface vessel a day after an attack.

Save this and show it to any American or Italian military personnel who do not cooperate in fulfilling any of your requests for assistance of supplies.

1. Woodrow Wilson

Thomas Woodrow Wilson
President of the United States

After reading the White House communication he buzzed for his radio mate to take a message and send it to the White House.

FEBRUARY 1, 1916

RULES OF ENGAGEMENT RECEIVED AND UNDERSTOOD.

JAMES JASON CALDWELL, COMMODORE USN

He then sent the following wireless message to all submarine captains in the Mediterranean.

FEBRUARY 1, 1916

AFFECTIVE THIS DATE, YOU ARE TO REPLACE DUMMY WARHEADS ON ALL TORPEDOES. UPON ORDER OF THE PRESIDENT OF THE UNITED STATES, YOU ARE TO TRACK ALL FOREIGN U-BOATS WITHIN STRIKING RANGE OF YOUR ASSIGNED MERCHANT CONVOYS. IF A US VESSEL IS ATTACKED, YOU ARE CLEARED TO ATTACK AND SINK THE U-BOAT OR SURFACE VESSEL INVOLVED IN THE ATTACK. YOU ARE NOT AUTHORIZED TO ATTACK ANY VESSEL UNLESS THAT VESSEL HAS ALREADY ATTACKED A MERCHANT MARINE.

JAMES CALDWELL, COMMODORE USN

He then began the long wait inside the harbor at Civitavecchia aboard the *USS CurtisWright*. His patrol submarines were transported to Italy aboard ships of the line, he left Washington Naval Yard with 12 and needed another 24 to set up his patrol network. The transport ships returned for another shipment and the first 12 began to record the sounds of U-boats on the west coast of Italy. By the middle of March, eighteen foreign

U-boats had been recorded and patterns of the sounds had been given to all 36 submarines assigned to the Mediterranean. On March 22nd, F -34, an American submarine on patrol picked up the sound of a transatlantic liner headed for the Port of Civitavecchia, they also heard the sounds of U - 22 in close pursuit.

Captain David Ellingsworth of F - 34 sent a wireless message to the Liner Minneapolis, "U-boat in pursuit, take evasive action."

The Minneapolis replied, "Turning 90 degrees starboard."

Radioman Jake Turner, parroted the message back to his captain, "Minneapolis turning 90 degrees starboard at flank speed, that should send a wave towards the U-boat."

"Let's hope he is in time, Mr. Turner. Open all outer doors on tubes 1 through 6, set homing device for sound pattern U-22 on tubes 3 and 4. Wait to fire 3 and 4 upon my command."

"Sir, I hear outer doors of U-22 opening, he is going to fire at the Minneapolis."

"Understood. Wait to fire upon my command. Do not jump the gun, we are going to kill everyone on U-22, let's be justified in our actions."

"But, Sir. He is going to sink the Minneapolis."

"He is going to try to sink the Minneapolis, we are the force that will put him on the bottom if he tries."

"Sir, torpedoes in the water. U - 22 has two fish headed straight for the Minneapolis."

"Understood. Distance to impact?"

"1500 yards more or less, it is hard to tell, U - 22 is turning away from target and making a run for it."

"Close the distance between us. Prepare to fire tubes 3 and 4."

"Sir, fish one has missed the Minneapolis, fish two is not running smoothly it has exploded beside the Minneapolis before impact."

"Torpedo room, do you copy?"

"Yes, Captain."

"Are we close enough to U - 22?"

"Range is difficult to determine, U - 22 is headed for the bottom."

"Fire tubes 3 and 4."

"Both fired, Sir."

"Radio, what do you hear?"

"Two fish running hot and going after the U-boat, Sir."

"How many seconds to impact?"

"They should be there now, Sir." F - 34 rocked from side to side as their torpedoes struck the U-boat. "Sir, I am getting an SOS from the U-boat in simple morse code. Do you want to respond?"

"No, Mr. Turner, no one can help them now, they signed their own death warrants. U-boats travel in pairs, be listening for other one."

"Sir, outer doors opening of second U-Boat!"

"Calm, Mr. Turner, which U-boat is it? Match the sound patterns."

"It's U- 32, Sir. Oh my God, Sir, two torpedoes in the water headed directly for us."

"Where is U - 32, Mr. Turner?"

"Directly astern, Sir."

"Torpedo room, fire stern tubes without setting homing devices, do it now."

"Four fish in the water, Sir, approaching each other."

"Distance from each other?"

"Less than a 100 yards, Sir."

"Torpedo room, detonate stern fish now." F - 34 rocked from side to side again as four torpedoes exploded between the two submarines. The torpedo room had sent a signal to the F-34 fish and they exploded taking the U - 32 torpedoes with them.

"Torpedo room, set homing device for sound pattern U- 32 on tubes 1 and 2. Engine room, stop all engines. Torpedo room, fire tubes 1 and 2."

"Torpedoes in the water, Captain. They are turning trying to find a sound pattern. They have passed us and are heading for the U - 32."

"Distance to impact?"

"Unknown, Sir. U - 32 is trying to close on us for another shot." F - 34 rocked from side to side and the lights went out. Emergency lighting came on casting a reddish glow on the hundreds of tiny water sprays trying to fill the hull of F -34.

"All hands – man emergency shutoff valves now!"

"Calm, Captain, the men know what to do. You have drilled us repeatedly on this." Mr. Turner was smiling and he began his checklist of items that needed to be restarted. "Engine room report damage."

"Engine room is dry, no damage, Sir."

"Torpedo room, report damage."

"Torpedo room is dry, no damage. Outer doors closed, six fish loaded and ready for action. Standing by." F - 34 went through the emergency shut down and restart in a matter of minutes. Captain David Ellingsworth sent a message to the Minneapolis.

"Damage report."

"Damage to hull, starboard side, taking on water. Bilge pumps holding their own, we are underway to Port of Civitavecchia. Thank you, whoever you are."

"Radio, send a burst to the *CurtisWright*, 'scratch U - 22 and 32 from the recorded list of sounds available for tracking, this date.'"

Commodore James Caldwell read the flash message from F - 34 and wondered if he had done the right thing. United States Naval Policy had always been that ships fight in pairs, never alone. His father and grandfather had always hammered that into his head. He had sent 36 submarines into convoy duty as single ships. He had been lucky, F - 34 had taken on two U - boats and had survived, only because the Austrians were not expecting a lethal response from the convoy. Next time, the U - boats would be in packs, not in pairs. He radioed all submarines:

MARCH 24, 1916

SINGLE CONVOY DUTY ENDS THIS DATE. BEGIN PAIR ROTATIONS FOR REDUCED SHADOWING OF CONVOYS FROM GIBRALTER TO CIVITAVECCHIA.
JAMES CALDWELL, COMMODORE USN

22

Cabinet Changes

Washington, D. C.

The second split in the cabinet of President Wilson came when the, Secretary of War, Lindley M. Garrison, presented his resignation to the President. This action came as a result of the differences of opinion in regard to the proposed bills for the increase of the army. In 1915, President Wilson had requested Mr. Garrison to work with me to prepare a plan for reducing the military deficiencies of the country. We concentrated our efforts upon this problem and we finally evolved a scheme which, in the autumn of 1915, was accepted by President Wilson and made a part of the official administration policy. In his annual message to Congress delivered on December 7, 1915, the President warmly commended our plan and recommended its enactment by Congress. Our plan included, first, a considerable enlargement of the regular army and, second, the formation of a reserve body of about 400,000 men and 100,000 women.

The committee on military affairs of the House of Representatives had in the meantime prepared its own bill, the distinctive feature of which was an increase in the number of the national guard and the payment of these bodies out of the national treasury. President Wilson having delivered his message to Congress, found among the members of the committee in the House, little support for the plans that I and Secretary Garrison had formulated. Mr. Kitchin, the floor leader of the Democrats, was openly opposed to preparedness in any comprehensive form and Mr. Hay, chairman of the military committee, was entirely out of sympathy with our plan. The President did his best to present our plan when he visited ten cities in the latter half of January. On his return he conferred freely with members of Congress and allowed it to become known that he was no longer committed to any particular plan and was entirely open to conviction. On February 9th, five days after his speech tour, Secretary Garrison wrote him a letter. The President asked to see me and I met with him.

"James, come in, come in. What do you hear from Rome?"

"We are going to get a formal complaint from Vienna over the damages done to U - 22 and U - 32, Mr. President."

"Commodore Caldwell did exactly what I ordered him to do, they are very lucky the two submarines were not totally destroyed. Do you have time to read a letter from your partner in crime?" He handed me Lindley's hand written letter.

Dear Mr. President:

Two matters within the jurisdiction of this department are now of immediate and pressing importance, and I am constrained to declare my position definitely and unmistakably thereon. I refer, of course, to your proposal to create a department of defense and eliminate the department of war from your cabinet, to help settle the matter of national defense.

You know my convictions with respect to each of these. I consider the principle embodied in the Clarke amendment an abandonment of the duty of this nation and a breach of trust with the American people; so believing, I can not accept it or acquiesce in its acceptance.

I consider the reliance upon the state militias for national defense an unjustifiable imperiling of the nation's safety. It would not only be a sham in itself, but its enactment into law would prevent, if not destroy, the opportunity to procure measurers of real, genuine national defense. I will not accept it or acquiesce in its acceptance. I am obliged to make my position known immediately upon each of these questions – in a speech on Thursday afternoon upon the national defense question and in a communication to the House committee having charge of the question. If, with respect to either matter, we are not in agreement upon these fundamental principles, then I could not, with propriety, remain your seeming representative in respect thereto. Our convictions would be manifestly not only divergent, but utterly irreconcilable.

You will appreciate the necessity of timely knowledge upon my part of the determination reached by you with respect to each of these matters, so that I may act advisedly in the premises.

Sincerely yours,

Lindley M. Garrison.

"Mr. President, I am sorry to read this. Lindley and I worked very hard on a plan for you to present to Congress."

"James, I feel duty bound to keep my mind open to conviction on the national guard argument. I should deem it a very serious mistake to shut the door against this attempt on the part of the committee to form a department of defense."

"It is a blurring of the separation of powers, Mr. President. The legislative branch of government can not create departments within the administrative branch. That is Lindley's whole argument, he wants you to tell Congress that you want to rename the department of war, the department of defense."

"Don't you think it would be a mistake not to accept the committee with perfect good faith to meet the essentials of your plan set forth in my message, but in a way of their own choosing?"

"There is way to find out, Sir."

"How?"

"Issue an executive order, forming the department of defense and nationalizing the state militias under the Secretary of Defense."

"This is a time when it seems to me patience on the part of all of us is essential."

"Patience will not solve the encroachment of the legislature upon the administrative branch of government. I agree with Secretary Garrison and as his 'partner in crime', as you put it, I must render my resignation as well."

"I will not accept either resignation, James, meet with Lindley and find a compromise."

"I respect Lindley's decision, Mr. President, I will not try to talk him out of it."

"Then, I accept with regret, both you and Mr. Garrison's resignation. Can we agree that the former director of NIA and my former Presidential Advisor for Foreign Affairs can also give his friend, Woodrow, advice on foreign affairs?"

"No, Mr. President, you never needed an advisor on foreign affairs, you have one, he is called the Secretary of State. Please don't let Congress try to change his title to Secretary of Foreign Affairs." I was smiling to take some of the sting out of my last statement.

I left the oval office and realized that I would need to write a formal letter of resignation. I headed for the State Department and the office of chief consul. I needed to talk to Louis and bring him up-to-date on what just happened. I found him writing to London, again.

"How many of those complaints have you written, Louis?"

"Obviously too many, I am running out of ways to call them insulting names without hurting their feelings." He laughed.

"The President and I just had an interesting meeting." I filled him in on the details.

"Sounds like you were put in a no-win situation, Dad. What are going to do?"

"Write my letter of resignation and submit it, why?"

"Have you talked to Rodney recently?"

"Admiral Lowe, no, why?"

"He wants to return to The Farm and naval counter-intelligence, says he hates trying to run a world-wide spy network like NIA."

"Interesting development, I was eased out of that position by the President, he didn't even ask me if I enjoyed the NIA. He informed me that I had a new job, with a brand new, gigantic title and I fell for it. I let the title go to my head. I can't go backward, I need to talk to your Uncle Teddy and see if he is going to run for president. Wilson is never going to get involved in Europe, the war would already be over if Teddy Roosevelt was president."

"Uncle Teddy came home sick from his last trip to Brazil in 1914. Has he fully recovered? Does he want to be president again?"

"I will let you know. Have you heard about the other changes in the administration?"

"Well, let me see. I know that David Francis is going to replace George Marye in Russia. Henry Fletcher was approved by the Senate to go to Mexico City if the civil war ever ends there. Joe Shea is going to Chile. Abram Elkus is going to Turkey to replace Henry Morgenthau who it is rumored will be chosen by Wilson to be his next vice-president. Former Senator Garrett from Maryland is going to the Netherlands to replace Van Dyke. There are rumored to be 41 replacement of American consuls in Europe this year. Viscount Chinda was recalled to Japan and Aimaro

Sato will replace him. Another rumor, Austria will replace Duma with Adam Tarnowski von Tarrow. He was here from 1899 to 1901, remember him?"

"Yes, I do. You have the change of line up in hand, Louis. Your boss is a straight shooter, Louis. You can not find a better man in Washington than Robert Lansing."

23

Protests from Vienna

Washington, D. C. April, 1916

The loss of U - 22 and 32 was a bitter pill for the war cabinet in Vienna to swallow. They could not complain to Ambassador Penfield, he was recalled and no replacement had been sent to Vienna. The Austrian Ambassador in Washington had been sent home. The German Ambassador in Washington, D. C. was instructed to deliver the following message to the State Department.

Secretary Robert Lansing

My Dear Mr. Lansing:

Ambassador Johann Heinrich, the Count von Bernstorff, is delivering this message to you. My government must protest the damage to two Austrian war ships patrolling in international waters off the coast of Italy. Both of these vessels sent SOS morse code messages and were rescued and towed to safety after they were suddenly attacked by three surface vessels of the United States Navy. Seamen lives were lost and the damage to the vessels will need to be compensated as soon as possible.

The matter has been sent to the international court in the Hague for final settlement. A state of war will exist if any other attacks occur upon Austrian vessels in the Mediterranean.

Konstantin Theodor Dumba

Robert Lansing read the message and laid it aside. He took off his glasses and gazed at the German Ambassador.

"Thank you for bringing this to my attention, Mr. Ambassador. Are you familiar with what Mr. Duma is talking about. I have no idea. The United States is a neutral nation and does not have surface warships patrolling in the Mediterranean. We have two warships anchored in the port of Civitavecchia at the request of the Italian government. Mr. Wilson has not authorized any surface ships to travel outside of the harbor until the training mission for the Italian navy is completed."

"I have no knowledge of the loss of any Austrian ships, Mr. Lansing. I am here as a courtesy to Vienna, the diplomatic breakdown between your two countries has caused a difficulty in communication."

"The reason for the breakdown is the sinking of ships with American loss of life by Austrian warships, Mr. Ambassador. The loss of the *Persia*, *Sussex, Manchester, Berwindvale* and *Eagle Point*, have all been sent to the Hauge and Austria has not bothered to answer to any of these. You may advise Mr. Duma that I already think a state of war exists between our two countries – why else would Austria attack unarmed merchant vessels of a neutral country. Do I understand that neither of these Austrian Navy un-named vessels was lost, but only damaged?"

"I believe we are talking about two U-boats, Mr. Lansing."

"Two U-boats were attacked by an unarmed merchant vessel – let me find my report of the attack on our vessel, I had it here a minute ago – yes, here it is the *Minneapolis*. Mr. Duma claims that the *Minneapolis* attacked two U-boats!"

"No, he claims that three warships attacked the two U-boats."

"Let me assure you, Mr. Ambassador, that if three USS Warships attacked two U-boats, they would not have survived to be rescued, they would be on the bottom of the Mediterranean."

"I think so, also, Mr. Secretary. Mr. Duma is trying to save face by claiming that three ships attacked his U-boats."

"What do you think happened, Mr. Ambassador?"

"I think the Austrian Navy is in over their heads in the Mediterranean, Mr. Secretary. My government has taken Mr. Wilson's addresses, that all American convoys will be protected, to heart. Orders have been issued that U-boat commanders do so at their own risk."

"Do you think your government could send a friendly message to Vienna which says that from this date forward, all American shipping will be inside protected convoys and U-boats attacking these protected convoys will be fired upon if they approach closer than 5000 yards. That way, there can be no confusion about what will happen."

"I will send that to Vienna and Berlin, if that is agreeable to you, Mr. Secretary."

"Nice to see you again, Johann, will you have your grandchildren on the White House lawn this Easter for the egg hunt?"

"Would not miss it, Robert. My best to your wife, children and grandchildren."

A merican ambassadors in the warring countries continued to perform the duties entrusted to them as representatives of belligerent governments. The burden fell especially hard upon Ambassador James W. Gerard in Berlin and Ambassador W. G. Sharp in Paris. Ambassador Walter Page in London was engaged in the many diplomatic storms created by my son, Louis. Louis would ruffle Sir Alfred Dinsmore feathers and Walter would smooth them back in place. Louis was used to writing messages to Lord Dinsmore regarding a number of illegal issues such as the detainment of American citizens in Shanghai. I was back at my re-election office for Theodore Roosevelt and he let me read some of them.

LORD ALFRED DINSMORE:

I AM CONSTANTLY AMAZED AT GREAT BRITAIN'S ATTEMPTS TO REWRITE, MISINTERPRET OR IGNORE INTERNATIONAL LAW. YOUR GOVERNMENT HAS NOW REMOVED THIRTY-EIGHT AMERICAN CITIZENS WHO WERE SERVING AS SEAMEN ON THE MERCHANT MARINE SHIP, AMERICANA, WHEN IT LAY AT ANCHOR IN SHANGHAI HARBOR. THESE AMERICAN SEAMEN WERE BORN IN THE UNITED STATES FROM PARENTS WHO HAVE IMMIGRATED FROM TURKEY, AUSTRIA AND GERMANY. FOR YOUR INFORMATION, EVERY WHITE PERSON NOW LIVING IN THE UNITED STATES PARENTS OR GRANDPARENTS CAME FROM OTHER COUNTRIES. MY GREAT GRANDPARENTS CAME FROM GERMANY, THEREFORE, I RUN THE RISK OF BEING ARRESTED IF I EVER TRAVEL TO THE BRITISH EMPIRE, SO WILL THE PRESIDENT OF THE UNITED STATES.

IF YOU PERSIST IN THIS NONSENSE, WE WILL BE FORCED TO ARREST 38 SEAMEN OFF THE NEXT BRITISH SHIP THAT ENTERS AN AMERICAN HARBOR. I AM CONSUMED BY ANSWERING STUPID STUNTS PULLED BY

GREAT BRITAIN SINCE THIS WAR BEGAN. AS A BRITISH SUBJECT, I CAME TO THIS COUNTRY TO TRY AND ENCOURAGE THE UNITED STATES TO ENTER THE WAR IN SUPPORT OF GREAT BRITAIN. AFTER LESS THAN A YEAR SERVING IN THE STATE DEPARTMENT AND HANDLING OVER 120 COMPLAINS ARRANGING FROM THEFT OF MONEY, MURDER, KIDNAPING, PIRATING OF USS WARSHIPS, ILLEGAL DETENTION AND ARRESTS TO GOD ONLY KNOWS WHAT TOMORROW BRINGS, I NOW CONSIDER GREAT BRITAIN TO BE THE TRUE ENEMY OF THE UNITED STATES.

I HAVE LOCATED AND SENT YOU COUNTLESS PROOF OF THE OWNERSHIP OF VESSELS, THE CITIZENSHIP OF MEN AND WOMEN, INCLUDING LISTS OF OFFICERS AND ENLISTED MEN SERVING UPON THESE VESSELS. NOTHING SEEMS TO PHASE YOUR GOVERNMENT. IF THESE 38 SEAMEN ARE NOT RELEASED IN THE NEXT TWENTY-FOUR HOURS, I AM FILING 38 MORE KIDNAPING CHARGES TO THOSE ALREADY FORWARDED TO THE INTERNATIONAL COURT IN THE HAGUE. THE ACTIONS OF YOUR GOVERNMENT ARE THOSE OF A HOSTILE NATION, NOT A FRIENDLY ONE. MY GOVERNMENT WILL CONTINUE TO ENCOURAGE THE INTERNATIONAL RED CROSS TO SEND HOSPITAL SUPPLIES TO ANY NATION THAT REQUESTS THEM. I DO NOT THINK ENGLAND HAS FORGOTTEN THAT SHE IS A MEMBER OF THE GENEVA CONVENTION, YOU HAVE NO CHOICE IN THIS MATTER.

AGAIN AND AGAIN, I DO NOT KNOW WHICH IS WORSE, A NATION WHO SINKS OUR SHIPS OR ONE WHO SEIZES SEAMEN OFF OF THEM.

LOUIS JASON CALDWELL, CAPTAIN USN
COUNSEL US STATE DEPARTMENT
`

Robert Lansing received a reply from Berlin, April 12th, regarding the sinking of the *Sussex, Manchester, Silverlining* and *Englishman* in coastal waters around Great Britain. It said that in each case where German U-boats were responsible, the promises to the United States were kept and the instructions to the U-boat commanders were obeyed. Louis gave me a copy and I thought may be we would enter a cooling down period. I was wrong. The *Friedrich der Grosse*, interned at Hoboken, New Jersey, was discovered to be a workshop for firebombs. Four arrests were made, Captain Charles von Kleist confessed that more than 200 firebombs had been made for purposes of sabotage inside the United States. Money for the materials to construct the bombs had been furnished by Lieutenant Francis von Rintelen of the German Embassy.

24

Presidential Campaign
Washington, D. C. 1916

I opened Teddy's pre-convention campaign office after leaving the White House because I agreed to be his chief of staff for the White House in March of 1917. This year I was 59 years old and Teddy was 58. We had reached the zenith of our professional energies and we both wanted the mess in Europe cleaned up and put to bed. So far this year, there were three prominent Republicans mentioned as possible candidates for the Presidency; Theodore Roosevelt, Elihu Root and Supreme Court Justice Charles Hughes. Colonel "rough rider" Roosevelt was the only hope of reuniting the Republican and Progressive parties, without which reunion there could be no possible hope of defeating the sitting president. Mr. Root represented the choice of those conservative members of the party who wished to maintain the existence of the party along the same lines as had distinguished it prior to 1912. Mr. Hughes was regarded as the compromise candidate if neither Roosevelt or Root could gather enough convention votes to be nominated. Hughes was better known as the ex-governor of New York State. There were, of course, other men's names mentioned in the various newspapers, these included Senator Cummings of Iowa and Senator Borah of Idaho. We would need to campaign against them in the upcoming primaries.

The chief opposition to the nomination of Teddy centered around those identified with the Republican party in 1912, the conservative element members of the party. He was also distrusted by those who feared his possible action. In the case of his election, we would enter the war in Europe. His sympathies with the Allies were well known and he had frequently expressed his resentment toward Germany. He had not hesitated to criticize President Wilson for his failure to present a more aggressive policy toward the Central Powers of Europe and toward the civil war in Mexico.

Mr. Root, formerly the Senator from New York, was recognized as one of the most able statesmen of the Republican party. His experience as Secretary of War and State made him a tough campaigner. We would run against him, to a large extent, as the leader of the conservative element who led the opposition in the Senate against the progressive wing of the Republican party. In the mind of many, he was too strongly identified with the so-called "money interests" of the country. From the standpoint of his knowledge of international law and his experience in the handling of foreign relations, it was considered by many that he would be an ideal candidate. We would have to point out, early in the campaign, that it would be foolhardy to nominate Mr. Root.

Mr. Hughes occupied a peculiar position. He had taken no active part in politics since his appointment to the Supreme Court and efforts to draw anything from him regarding political questions would be difficult. Those who advocated his nomination, therefore, promised nothing, except what could be assumed from his performance as governor of New York and from a general knowledge of his characteristics and opinions. The so-called Old Guard of the Republican party did not view his nomination with enthusiasm. Teddy Roosevelt was the only other man whose nomination they feared more.

This in general, were the conditions facing me as I opened the campaign headquarters for Teddy. I found Elihu Root's address to the State of New York Republican delegate's convention held February 15th. He was the keynote speaker and it contained most of the arguments that would later be used in the national campaign. The address was in effect a powerful arraignment of the administration of Wilson in the conduct of both domestic and foreign affairs. In relation to the responsibility of the president in the conduct of foreign affairs, Mr. Root said, "When a president and secretary of State have been lawfully established in office, a power of initiative in foreign affairs rests with them. The nation is in their hands. Their's is the authority and the duty to adopt and act upon policies subject to such laws as Congress may enact with constitutional limits. Parliamentary opposition can take no affirmative step, nor accomplish any affirmative action. The expression of public opinion can do nothing, except as it produces an influence upon the minds of those officers who have the lawful power to conduct our foreign relations."

In regard to conditions in Mexico and the rights of the United States in that country he said, "The United States had rights and duties in Mexico. More than 40,000 of its citizens lived and worked there. Millions of dollars had been invested in that rich and productive country and millions of income from these enterprises were annually returned to the United States, not merely for the benefit of our whole country, but for its production and enterprise. Civil war has come to Mexico. Americans have been murdered, American property has been wantonly destroyed. That was the situation when Mr. Wilson became president in March, 1913. His duty then was plain. It was first to use his powers as President of the United States to secure protection for the lives and property in Mexico and to require that the rules of law and stipulations of treaties should be observed by Mexico towards the United States and its citizens. His duty was, second, as the head of a foreign power, to respect the independence of Mexico, to refrain from all interference with her internal affairs, from all attempts at dominance as he was justified by the law of nations, for the protection of American rights."

Mr. Root declared that the President had failed to fulfill any of these duties; that he interfered in Mexico, to aid one faction in civil strife against another; that he undertook to pull down Huerta and set up Carranza in his place and that when Huerta had refused a demand which was in substance that he should retire permanently from the Government of Mexico, the power of the United States was applied to turn him out. Arms and munitions of war were freely furnished to forces opposed to him and finally the President sent the army and navy to invade Mexico and capture its great sea port of Vera Cruz and hold it and throttle American commerce until Huerta fell. With the occupation of Vera Cruz the moral power of the United States over Mexico ended. We were, then and we are now, hated for what we did in Mexico and we were despised for our feeble and irresolute failure to protect the lives and rights of our citizens living in Mexico. That is why we have failed in Mexico."

Mr. Root's attitude toward the diplomatic relations with Europe thus far in the War of the Nations, was even more severe. He said, "A study of the administration's policy toward Europe since July, 1914, reveals three fundamental errors: first, the lack of foresight to make any provision for backing up American diplomacy by actual or assured military and naval force. Second, the forfeiture of the world's respect for our assertion of rights by pursuing the policy of making threats and failing to make them good. Third, the loss to the moral force of the civilized world through failure to truly interpret to the world, the spirit of the American democracy in its attitude toward the terrible events which accompanied the early stages of the war."

He contrasted the action of Switzerland and Holland into at once mobilizing their forces of trained soldiers and thus preventing their territory as independent and inviolate with the action of the United States. He said, "Ordinary practical sense in the conduct of affairs demanded that such steps should be taken that behind the peaceable assertion of our country's rights, its independence, its manifest purpose, warning the whole world that it would cost too much to press aggression too far." Mr. Root declared that while many persons saw the necessity of such action, the Democratic government did not see it. The President described those who advocated prompt measures (William Jennings Bryan, Lindley Garrison and Admiral JJ Caldwell) as being nervous and excited.

He then reviewed the course of diplomatic negotiations with Germany following the sinking of merchant ships with Americans on board. After characterizing the action of the administration as "threatening in words but irresolute in action", he said, "Measured and restrained expression backed to the full by serious purpose, have strength and respect. Extreme and belligerent expression, unsupported by resolution, is weak and without effect. No man should draw a pistol who does not dare to shoot. The government that shakes its fist first and points its finger afterward, falls into contempt. Our diplomacy has lost its authority and influence, because we have been brave in words and irresolute in action. Men may say that the words of our diplomatic notes were justified; men may say that our inaction was justified, but no man can say that both our words and our inaction were wise and creditable."

Mr. Root declared that the invasion of Belgium should have been met with strong protest on the part of the American government. He said, "The American people were in entitled not only to feel, but to speak, concerning the wrong done to Belgium. It was not like interference in the internal affairs of Mexico, or any other nation, for this was an international wrong. The law protecting Belgium, is the same law protecting us. It was violated and it was wrong to every other civilized nation except us. For generations we have been urging the adoption of international law, we have bound ourselves to it, we have regulated our conduct to it and we are entitled to have other nations observe it. Yet our government acquiesced in the treatment of Belgium and the destruction of the law of nations. Without one word of objection or dissent to the repudiation of law or the breach of treaty or the violation of justice and humanity in the treatment of Belgium, our government enjoined upon the people of the United States an undiscriminating and all-embracing neutrality and the President admonished the people that they must be neutral in all respects, in act, word, thought and sentiment. We were not to be neutral merely as to the quarrels in Europe; but neutral as to the treatment of Belgium, neutral between right and wrong, neutral between justice and injustice, neutral between humanity and cruelty, neutral between liberty and oppression. A single expression by our government, a single sentence denying assent and recording disapproval of what Germany did in Belgium would have given to the people of America that leadership to which they are entitled, in their earnest grope for the light. It would have ranged behind American leadership the conscience and morality of the neutral world. It would have brought to American diplomacy the respect of loyalty to good cause."

In conclusion, he said, "We have not been following the path of peace. We have been blindly stumbling along the road that, continued, will lead to inevitable war. Our diplomacy has dealt with symptoms and ignored causes. The great decisive question upon which our peace depends, is the question whether the role of action applied to Belgium is to be tolerated. If it is tolerated, by the civilized world, this nation will have to fight for its life. There will be no escape. That is the critical point of defense for the peace of America."

Prior to this speech, Mr. Root's name did not appear on the Minnesota primary ballot for presidential preference cast January 12, 1916, and he was an unknown national quantity.

The national attitude toward Teddy on January 12th was similar, he was an unknown national quantity for president. Most voters did not even think a president could run for more than two terms. While I was still working in the White House during the first three months of 1916, he indicated to me, that under certain conditions he would accept the nomination of the Republican party, but not the Progressive party. As the weeks went by, his position in regard to the nomination was made clearer to me. On January 30th he delivered a speech in Brooklyn. It was devoted to the attitude of the United States toward the European war. Concerning the attitude of the administration, he said, "We are asked to kiss the bloody hands of the murders of women and children and to serve as the tool of these men against those nations which have behaved more valiantly and righteously than we have." He declared that, in his opinion, the US was actually bound by the Hague convention to protect Belgian neutrality. He also made a strong plea for preparedness in universal military training. On February 17ᵗʰ he and my sister, Ruth, sailed for the West Indies. They made several appearances during their visit, in some of which they again attacked the administration. At the same time they gave a statement of their position in regard to the near impossible nomination of Elihu Root from New York or Henry Stoddard of Massachusetts. They returned to Long Island in the latter part of March, and on March 29, 1916, contacted me by telephone in the White House. They had read a statement by President Wilson that wealthy American owners of property in Mexico had attempted, by sinister methods, to bring about the intervention of the United States in that republic.

"James this is simply not true. I have reviewed the events on the border in the preceding three years and discovered that the loss of American lives in Mexico was due to the shipment of arms to "first one set of bandits and then another." I am going to make a public statement where I will charge incompetence and mismanagement on the part of the administration and I characterize the pursuit of Poncho Villa as "the second war in Mexico" the Vera Cruz incident being cited as the first. Did you have anything to do with what happened in Mexico? I will not attack my own brother-in-law."

"Teddy, I have been consumed by the world war that has been raging on three continents. Mr. Wilson has kept me completely out of the Mexican affair. You should know that I have submitted my letter of resignation to Mr. Wilson – so has Lindley Garrison."

"Oh, James, I know how much you enjoyed being the director of NIA." My sister was on the extension at Oyster Bay, Long Island.

"Ruth, I have not been involved with NIA for nearly a year, I was pulled out of there and turned for war as his presidential advisor on foreign affairs."

"James, I want you to open a Washington office for re-election of President Roosevelt, can you bring yourself to work for a Progressive?"

"If you want the job, Teddy, forget the Progressive party and secure the Republican nomination, can you bring yourself to do that?"

"I can with you and Ruth at my side, James."

On March 31ˢᵗ, Teddy and I met at the home of Mr. Robert Bacon, former Senator Root, Senator Lodge of Massachusetts and General Leonard Wood. This was the first meeting of Teddy and Elihu Root since 1912, when they parted as a result of the split in the Republican party. Elihu was the presiding official at the national convention in 1912 and his conduct in that capacity was bitterly resented by Teddy during the progress of the campaign. This reunion was to be for the reconcile of Teddy with the leaders of the regular party, although those present at the meeting later denied that there had been any effort to bring this about.

On April 5ᵗʰ, Teddy made it clear to a group of visiting reporters at his home in Oyster Bay on what conditions he would accept the nomination for the presidency. One of the reporters was from American News Service, of course.

American News Wire Service: Dateline Oyster Bay, Long Island, April 5, 1916. *Former President Theodore Roosevelt answered the question about his entering the race again this way, "Let me give you a piece of advice. If you have any doubt on the subject, do not nominate me. Get it perfectly clear in your head that if you nominate me, it mustn't be because you think it is in my interest, but because you think it is in your interest and the interest of the Republican party and because you think it is to the interest of the United States to do so. Don't be for me unless you are prepared to say that every citizen of this country has got to be pro-American, first, last and always.*

Every American citizen must be for America first and for no other country even second and he hasn't any right to be in the United States at all if he has any divided loyalty between this country and any other. I don't give a rap for the man's creed or birthplace or national origin, so long as he is straight United States. I am for him if he is and against him if he is not.

I am not for war; on the contrary, I abhor an unjust or a wanton war and I would use every honorable expedient to avoid even a just war. But I feel with all my heart that you don't in the long run, avoid a war by making other people believe that you are afraid to fight for what is right. Uncle Sam must never wrong the weak; he must never insult any one or wantonly give cause of offense to either the weak or the strong. And don't you nominate me unless you are prepared to take the position that Uncle Sam is to be strong enough to defend his rights and to defend every one of the people wherever those people are, and he can't be strong enough unless he prepares in advance. The squarest possible way to enable him to keep the peace and to keep it on terms that will enable Americans to hold their heads high and not hang them in shame, is for him to be prepared. I mean prepared in his own soul as well as his army and navy so that when he says anything, the rest of the world will know that he means it and that he can make it good.

Don't you try to nominate me unless you think that is the policy that ought to be followed and followed for your sake as much as for mine and for the sake of the rest of us here in the United States. Don't forget that isn't a course that provokes war, it is the only course that, in the long run, prevents war and secures national self-respect and guarantees the honor of this country and the rights of it citizens wherever they may be.

On April 7th, 75 prominent Republicans of New York State, including many delegates elected to the national convention, endorsed Teddy and we were off and running for president. By April 29th, Teddy and I were in Chicago speaking to the Illinois Bar Association. By May we were campaigning in Michigan where he delivered a notable address in Detroit on preparedness for our military. He said, "I believe in a thoroughly efficient navy, the second in size in the world. I believe in a small, but thoroughly efficiently regular army, an army of 250,000 men, with a proper reserve. This would give us a mobile army that must stand the strength of the people themselves, and this strength must be prepared in advance or it will be utterly useless in time of trial.

Following this address, we made a tour in the Midwest and were heard with great enthusiasm in Kansas City and St. Louis. We finished with a speech at Newark, New Jersey, on June 1st. Thus far in the pre-convention campaign, we felt that Teddy was the most conspicuous figure and best known. We were on a train to Chicago to attend the 1916 Republican Convention.

25

Republican Convention
June 7, 1916

At a meeting of the Republican national committee, it was decided that the national convention should meet in Chicago on June 7, 1916. At that same meeting, it was decided to reduce the Southern representation in the national convention to about 30 per cent, less than it had been. This was done by the application of an apportionment system uniformly throughout the entire country. In accordance with this system the apportionment of delegates from the Southern States was 174 in 1916, compared with 252 in 1912. Teddy considered this a major victory for him, since these 252 delegates had refused to vote for him in 1912, and he left the convention to form the Progressive party, which guaranteed the election for Mr. Wilson. No matter what happened this time, Teddy, assured me, he would not bolt the party.

"I do not want your resignation from this administration and your retirement from the military to be in vain, James. We are going to win this thing, first the nomination and then the White House. Are you with me?"

"To the bitter end, Teddy, to the bitter end."

The total number of delegates entitled to a vote in the convention was 984. There was a notable absence of contests for seats in the convention and in this, conditions differed widely from those in 1912, when the bitter fights for seating of rival delegates nearly disrupted the start of the convention. This 16th national convention assembled at 11 o'clock on June

8th. Over 12,000 were in the Coliseum, but there was a remarkable absence of enthusiasm in the opening hours and Teddy was worried. The chairman was Senator Warren Harding of Ohio and he called the delegates to order. The platform committee spent most of the first day reading various statements and intended messages within each plank. Then each name for consideration was placed into nomination; Borah, Brumbaugh, Burton, Cummings, Du Pont, Fairbanks, Ford, Hughes, Knox, La Follette, Lodge, McCall, Roosevelt, Root, Sherman, Taft, Weeks and Willis. Most of these were favorite son's candidates and would not attract any major votes.

The first ballot was called for on June 9th. This resulted in Hughes (253), Weeks (105), Root (103), Cummings (85), Burton (76), Fairbanks (74), Sherman (66), Roosevelt (65), Knox (36), Ford (32), Brumbaugh (20), La Follette (25), Taft (14), Du Pont (12), Willis (4), Borah (2), McCall (2), not voting 2. I was shocked, how had Teddy only gotten 65 votes out of 984? He just laughed and said, "Relax, you are used to the Democratic Convention, this is when the horse trading starts. All those starting with Taft on down will start visiting the front runners and try to buy a position in the new administration with a plum job. Be ready to talk to a lot of folks before this is over, James. I can not be seen talking with any of them, you will have to sort it out."

And sort it out we did. I bought sixteen votes from Du Pont and Willis with promises of positions within the new Roosevelt administration, after all they were talking to the new chief of staff for the White House. The second ballot was taken with Hughes (325) + 72, Root (98) - 5, Fairbanks (88), +14, Cummings (85), +0, Roosevelt (81) +16, and Weeks (79) -26. Between the second and third ballots no one came to see me to buy or sell any votes and we braced for the worst as the third ballot was counted. Hughes (949), Roosevelt (19), Lodge (7), Du Pont (5), Weeks and La Follette (3). I was numb, I had failed my brother-in-law. He just laughed and said, "This is Republican politics, James. Hughes does not have a chance against Wilson the election is over."

I sat and listened to Justice Hughes' acceptance speech that began with, "I have not desired the nomination. I have wished to remain on the bench......."

I was sitting next to Teddy in the Coliseum with 12,000 other people as Justice Hughes finished his remarks. I looked over at Teddy and he was holding his cheek.

"I think I have an infected tooth, it is killing me, let's get out of here and find a dentist." We left our seats and picked up the small group of men that always traveled with Teddy. "We are going back to the hotel, gentlemen, Amos, you go ahead and see if the hotel has a doctor on call."

"I thought you said it was your tooth."

"I did but look at my ankles." He hiked up his pants legs and he indeed have badly swollen ankles.

"Amos, wait, get us a cab. Mr. Roosevelt needs to get to the closest hospital." Within a few minutes the cab pulled up in front of Roosevelt Hospital in Chicago,

"This must be a good hospital, driver, it is named after me!"

"Sorry to disappoint you, Mr. President, this hospital was here before you were president, it is named after your father."

"Close enough, let's get in there and see what is wrong with this old body."

Teddy would never go to a doctor unless he was in a bad way. He would not admit that he could become ill and the idea of regular examinations and medical care never attracted him. He was perplexed and indignant with himself when this attack came at the convention. I knew it was serious when he fainted before he could be admitted. The staff rushed him to an examination room and I left him to call my sister, Ruth, and let her know where we were and what was happening.

"Hello, Ruth? Yes, the convention is about over, Teddy wasn't feeling well so I have him in the hospital."

"The hospital? How did you manage that, James, he hates doctors."

"I know, it is probably nothing, I will call you back after they complete their examination."

"Which hospital is it?"

"Roosevelt, the one named for his father. He didn't argue so I know he needs to see a doctor, I will call back within the hour, Sis."

I left the telephone booth and headed back to the waiting room. Amos, Teddy's closest friend since childhood, did not look pleased.

"Have you talked to the doctor?"

"Yes, it is a blood clot, caused by inflammatory rheumatism."

"Rheumatism, how long has he had that?"

"About ten to fifteen years, nobody is supposed to know about it, but I guess the cat is out of the bag now."

"I know he still carries the bullet which was fired by Schrank when he was campaigning in Milwaukee many years ago."

"The Colonel has survived many accidents and dangers to his life,

Admiral. Not only when we were in Cuba, but falling from horses did not help. Did you know he is deaf in one ear and nearly blind in one eye?"

"No, when did that happen?"

"When we were in the White House. He was boxing in the White House gym and his sparing partner nearly gouged his left eye out."

"What about his hearing?"

"The hearing of one ear was destroyed by an abscess in his ear last February. He has suffered from broken ribs and a strained ligament on a rib caused him a severe attack of pleurisy. After that attack he was ordered by his doctors to give up violent exercise, but this advice he will not follow."

"Anything else?"

"Not since his trip to South America."

"What happened in South America?"

"He tore his leg badly when he was thrown from the boat we were in on the River of Doubt. The wound became badly infected and he ran a high fever, I thought he would die then. His health has not been sound since we returned from that trip in late 1914."

"And here it is, the middle of 1916 and he still will not slow down, he should never have run a campaign for another term, Amos. If I had known, I would never have agreed to be his campaign manager."

"Admiral, you don't know him like I do. This is how he will end his life, on his feet, doing as violent an activity as he can. Do you know he wants to go to the trenches in France and teach the Frogs how to kill Germans?"

"Sounds like the 'Bull Moose' we all know and love, Amos. Sit on him if you have to, he is not going to France and that is final."

In a few days, Teddy was released from the hospital and was on a train bound for Long Island. I rode as far as Washington with him and Emily met me at the station. Carson was with her and wanted to know all about the convention.

"Why aren't you in school, Carson.?"

"It's the middle of summer vacation, Grandpa. Do you feel alright?"

"Yes, I forgot you go to public school, here in the United States. If you were home, you would be in the middle of some school project about now, wouldn't you?"

"Yes, Sir. Did you go to public school, Grandpa?"

"No, Carson, your great grandfather, my father, never believed in public school." I shot a look at Emily who was smiling. We had this conversation before our twins were born.

"If we have twins, Em, we will call them quits! Four children would be a handful when two are twins. We would need more household help and by that time we would need to hire a tutor for Busy."

"I did not have a tutor, James, and I went to college. Elizabeth does not need a special tutor unless her teachers indicate that she needs one to keep up with the rest of her class. I, absolutely, do not think that home schooling is a good idea, James. I want our children to interact with people outside the immediate household."

"I agree, Em. The contact with others is important, I missed that part of my education. Would you agree to sending them to private school? The best private school, in the immediate area where I am stationed, would allow them to take advantage of our ability to give them the finest education available."

"Only if it is a day school, James. We are not going to send our children to a boarding school like the English."

"Agreed. I will write to my mother."

We had barely arrived home when Carson wanted to know what I was going to do now that his great Uncle Teddy was not going to run for President.

"Well, the first thing I am going to do is call a CI board meeting and you can go with me to the meeting. Would you like that?"

"Sure, Grandpa, if my Mum thinks it would be alright."

"What about your Dad?"

"What about him, he does everything that Mum tells him to now that I have a baby sister. Did you know, my parents are looking for a house?"

"Yes, your father talked to me about that. Would you like that?"

"I am not sure. I would not like that, if it meant we would not be able to return home after the war is over."

"I understand your feelings. You are still two people. Spencer lives in London and Carson lives in Washington."

"I never thought of it that way, Grandpa. You are exactly right. I must feel like Winston Spencer Churchill, did you know he is the same as me. He has parents like mine."

"You could not pick a better model than Winston Churchill, Carson, he will be a great statesman before this war is over."

In a few days, Carson, Emily and I were back on the train traveling to New York City to attend the CI board meeting. The train service between Washington and New York was excellent, any member of the board of directors could get to either Washington or New York in minimum travel time. The purpose of the meeting was to discuss our last efforts to provide war support within the CI group of companies throughout the world. Before we left Bellawoods, Carson walked with me in the woods so I could show him the healed scars on the trees and the holes that had now been filled from the massacre of German agents that occurred after his father's attempted murder.

"A total of 34 men died trying to kill your father, Carson, and the diplomatic declaration of war by your great Uncle Teddy brought the German Empire to its senses with an apology from the German Kaiser."

"Wow, was my Dad involved in a shoot out, like in the wild west?"

"No, the dogs of war are silent in America, Carson. The Caldwell family can relax until the next crisis comes along." He was smiling.

"What are you smiling about, Carson?"

"I was remembering our family trip to Virginia City. I expected it to be like that little town in Canada, with dirt streets and cowboys on horses. Instead, I found a bunch of business men in suits and ties driving automobiles on paved and brick streets, just like London!"

"It wasn't always like that, Carson. It truly was the wild west not to long ago."

"When you were a little boy?"

"No, when I was a man. The first time I retired from the Navy your grandmother and I visited each of the family businesses. We had just returned from Bermuda and we on our way to Virginia City to see the watchdog of Nevada."

"What kind of dog was it? Why did you have a watchdog?"

"Not a dog, a person."

"Oh, like Winston Churchill, they call him a bulldog."

"Yes, they do. But this watchdog was a woman."

"Who was that?"

"Corine Peoples Wilson, you met her."

"The Indian woman who takes care of that old man?"

"She is not an American Indian, she was raised by them. And that old man was a CI pioneer." An hour later I had told the story of how Dewayne David Wilson had met Corine in a place called Paradise, Utah Territory.

"How did your father every get started in Nevada? Was this before he met grandma's father?"

"No, during. Your great grandfather was sent to Nevada as commander of the National Rapid Response detachment out of Washington, D. C. Your Grandmother and I were just born."

"What did your father tell you about the founding CI in Nevada, Grandpa?"

"It was Utah Territory then and it involved the discovery of gold. When tiny deposits of gold were discovered in western Utah Territory in 1857, it was not met with the same "Gold Rush Fever" of ten years earlier at Sutter's Mill, California. It was known within the White House, however, and in 1858, my father had sent his company representatives to explore this business prospect. They were guided by two of his former RR marines, corporals D.D. Wilson and Matthew James, now private citizens and retired employees of Caldwell Shipping and Trading."

"They are both alive?"

"Yes, Carson, they were just teenagers when they left for Nevada. When the Caldwell representatives, a mining engineer, surveyor and construction foreman, (now all deceased), reached Carson Canyon they found gold miners at work along the gravel banks of the canyon river with rockers, Long Toms and sluices. Most of the men complained about a heavy blue-black material which kept clogging their rockers. The Caldwell engineer thought this might be silver and when he had it assayed, it was determined to be almost pure sulphuret of silver. Traveling on up the river, they came to the town of Johnstone. Here they paused long enough to purchase a few lots upon which to build later. My father had insisted that they not pan for gold. Or they should not stake claims for silver, instead they should build a saw mill and obtain timber for the mill. He reasoned that mining required timbers cut from trees and water. They were to purchase any water rights that they could find. Then and only then, should the five of them begin to buy up played out gold strikes, turning these into silver mining operations."

"What did the five of them do, Grandpa?"

"By the Spring of 1859, those who discovered the Comstock Lode had extracted all the gold and discounted the "blue-stuff". Patrick McLaughlin, Emanual Penrod and Peter O'Riley sold their interests in the Ophir Mine to us. One year later the Ophir Mine produced one and one half million dollars in silver dividends for us. D. D. Wilson, manager of the saw mill, sold over a half a million dollars in cut timbers for the prevention of cave ins to other mine owners. Matthew James, director of Caldwell Water Company was selling sump pumps to keep the mines free of flooding from vast quantities of underground streams of hot water. The hot water was collected and sent to Johnstone through pipes and sold there to businesses and townspeople. The proceeds from these enterprises were placed in the Bank of California until a bank could be built in Johnstone and later Carson City."

"What did Caldwell Shipping do in Nevada?"

"There were no railroads into Utah Territory, Caldwell Shipping noticed this and began a shipping operation. Freight and passengers were transported by mule teams of from 10 to 16. Ore was hauled from the mines to the mills for refining by Caldwell Shipping. They brought to the mines all the timbers, mining machinery and supplies. No wagon made an unloaded run anywhere. Goods and merchandise needed by small mining towns was hauled over the Sierras from California on the return trips from deposits of pure silver and gold from the refining mills. Caldwell investments would have flourished by shipping contracts only, but it was the Caldwell Water Company that became the real 'Gold Mine.'"

"I have never heard of the Caldwell Water Company."

"It was deeded over to Mathew James and his family for twenty years of service to CI. But before that, in 1859, the flow of water from natural springs was adequate to supply the needs of the miners and small towns of Johnstone, Virginia City and Gold Hill. As population increased, wells were dug for domestic needs, and the water within several mine tunnels was added to the available supplies. As the refining, smelting mills and hoisting operations multiplied, the demand for water for use in steam boilers became so great that it was impossible to supply it without creating a water shortage. To fill this need the Caldwell Water Company began hauling water to whomever needed it. Water tank wagons became common sights as they traveled from the Sierra Nevada mountains to the Virginia ranges that lay in the Washoe Valley. The Caldwell engineer, Herman Schussler, began working on a plan to replace the wagon trains by a cast iron pipe line. The 7 mile distance between water source and water demand could be met with a 12 inch diameter pipe which would produce 92,000 gallons of water per hour. Caldwell water systems construction company now became the leading manufacturer of water systems for towns in Western Utah Territory."

"What happened to the saw mill and lumber business?"

"The saw mill was deeded over to DD and Corine for twenty years of service, also. In the spring of 1860, D. D. Wilson sent his first report back to the home office in Pennsylvania. He had the accountants provide an annual statement of saw mill production, sales and expenses. His salary was $10.00 per day, he itemized his expense account, and indicated that his profit sharing of 2% of timber production for that year was $10,000.00. Employees were paid at $1.00 per day plus expenses and ½% profit sharing or $2500.00. The cost of timber purchased that year was $40,000.00. Equipment and supply costs were $28,000.00. Transportation costs were $11,250.00. This left roughly $240,000.00 on deposit in the Bank of California for payment of outstanding debts. The mill had been constructed at a cost of $80,000. The interest on the loans for operating expenses, equipment and transportation showed a balance of zero. Not apparent to a casual reader was that the interest was paid to a Caldwell bank, transportation costs were paid to a Caldwell firm and timber purchases were to a Caldwell firm."

"Those were huge salaries, even by today's standards, Grandpa."

"Yes, Matthew James sent a similar annual report for the water company. It had a balance of $650,000 on deposit in the bank of California to pay outstanding debts, interest, transportation, machinery purchases, pipe and supply purchases. His annual salary was also $10.00 per day, plus 2% of net operating profits or $13,000.00 His expense account was not itemized, but it was modest, it included one trip to Indiana. When the copies from the lumber company, water company and Caldwell Mining and Shipping were forwarded to my mother and father in the White House that year, they were pleased. The western assets were now worth well above 14 million dollars and that year's income to them was a little over one million dollars."

"I had no idea your parents were making that kind of money when they were in the White House, Grandpa."

"Neither did I, until I began reviewing annual reports from the various companies to the home office. When my mother reviewed the statements, she saw that D.D. and Matthew had done an outstanding amount of work for them in the past two years. I think this is when they decided to reward both of them if the business' continued to grow at the same rate."

"How long did the silver last?"

"It took between fifteen and twenty years until the veins of the Comstock were completely gone."

"And what about the oil in Titusville, Grandpa?"

"That should last longer, it will not disappear in your life time.

"But, when the oil is gone?"

"Then Cranson College will have to look elsewhere for endowments."

"Did you regret leaving the Navy to take the chairmanship of CI from your father, Grandpa?"

"Carson, your father and Uncle James are keeping the Navy safe, using my plan. But the future for war with Europe, does not look good. We will have to see what happens if war comes. I certainly will be recalled to help your father."

"What happens to CI then?"

"It is in your grandmother's care, Carson."

"Can she do that, Grandpa?"

"Yes, she already has, after my first retirement. My mother ran CI when my father was gone during the Civil War."

"She did?"

"She sure did. She is the one that kept track of everything inside the company, as long as she was alive."

"What does a war with Europe do to the profits for a company like yours, Grandpa?"

"Our company, Carson, you have an equal share, I gave it to you on the day your were born."

"You did? Will I run CI someday, Grandpa?"

"You already do. That is why we are going to New York, so you can see how the company is run. You can vote on company decisions when you reach age 18. But I am not telling you the story about our visit to Virginia City when it was still the wild west."

"Go ahead, Grandpa, I am listening."

We reached Virginia City and stepped off the train to find DD and Corine Wilson waiting for us. They had a horse and buggy and it felt strange getting into it for the short ride out to the ranch house that Corine had designed and DD had built for my father. We visited all the way out to the house and I could tell something was bothering them both.

"What is on your mind, DD? You and Corine look like you have lost your best friend."

"We are concerned that you will sell all the Nevada assets like you did in Alaska and California."

"That was my father's decision before I became chairman, DD. He has a sixth sense about these things and I did not question his judgement. I am interested in finding a director for the Nevada Division of CI. That is what this trip is about. CI no longer has any interest in what Mathew James is doing with the water company, it is his to do with as he sees fit. Just like the saw mill is yours. How is that business doing?" I asked.

"That is one of our concerns, JJ. The mill does not produce anything for the mines any more. It supplies the lumber yards owned by CI and indirectly Caldwell Bankers Real Estate and Development Corp. If you sell that, we would be in trouble."

"What if you and Corine bought the lumber yards? Caldwell Bankers is not for sale, but I am sure the lumber yards would be better in your hands." Corine had not said a word. She stared straight ahead.

Finally, your Grandmother said, "Corine, what do you think?"

She turned to her and said, "I am more concerned about the hotels than the real estate development."

"What do you mean?"

"The managers at both the Johnstone Lodge and the new Tahoe Resort are using a creative system of book keeping."

"If I were to meet with them together, do you think I could get to the bottom of the questionable business practices?" I asked.

"I only have my opinions of what is going on, JJ. You really need to talk to Eugene Peters, he is your head of security at the two hotels. I think he may have some ideas for you. The few days spent here should be a focus on the hotel management not on the real estate development, I have all the data for you on that."

"Thank you, Corine. I will look at that data on our way home on the train. For now we are all on this hotel business, this directly affects my sisters' income. If they are stealing from them, they have no idea who Theodore Roosevelt is and how he handles situations like this."

They dropped us off at the ranch house and I did not sleep very well that night. The next morning I had decided what to do. I saddled a horse and rode into Johnstone like a cowboy from half a century ago. I tied up in front of Marshall Peters' office and walked in.

"Good morning, Eugene. Do you have an extra side arm that you could loan me?"

"Good morning to you, JJ. Why do you need a sidearm?"

"Personal protection. I am going to visit the banks in Carson City and here in Johnstone." He began to laugh.

"The banks make you check firearms at the door, JJ."

"How about the town Marshall?"

"No, I keep mine."

"Good, make me your deputy."

"What?"

"Eugene, do you like being the head of security for CI?"

"Of course."

"What do you know about the Bank of Johnstone helping in the stealing of income from the Johnstone Lodge?"

"That is not certain, JJ."

"But you have some evidence."

"Yes, of course."

"I would like to tell you about what CI did in Bermuda last month."

A short time later, the town Marshall and his new deputy walked into the Bank of Johnstone both carrying loaded sidearms. The Marshall did all the talking, his deputy just nodded his head yes for affect.

"Is Mr. Headings in his office, Glen?"

"Yes, he is, I will see if he is busy."

"No, we will be with him most of the day, Glen, hold all of his messages and cancel all of his meetings for the rest of the day."

Glen turned white and said, "Of course, Marshall." We walked behind the teller's counter and found Henry Headings sitting at his desk.

"Morning, Henry, I have some bad news for you. My deputy and I are here to ask you some questions about the Johnstone Lodge's accounts at the bank. It seems that the home office in Pennsylvania has found some rather large errors in accounting practices. We came here before we arrested anyone at the Lodge."

"Well, that is sure something. What can the bank do to help you Marshall?"

"I will need to have an accountant from CI audit the bank's books."

"I am not sure that is possible, Marshall. This is a State of Nevada bank and I would need someone from CI present if that were to happen."

"Would the chairman of CI be good enough for you? I would like you to meet James Caldwell. He has a warrant for your detention and questioning in the whereabouts of his missing funds." I placed a folded bench warrant from circuit court Judge Keller's office on his desk.

Henry Headings hands began to shake as he said, "They threatened to kill my family if I did not go along with their scheme, Mr. Caldwell. I am a victim here."

"I do not think so, Mr. Headings. You could have reported this is to me. Instead you took money to keep quiet, you could have refused the money. Please stand and place your hands behind your back so that I can place handcuffs on you."

"Mr. Caldwell, please help me. I do not want the bank employees to see me taken off to jail. I have everything that you need to arrest the manager at Johnstone Lodge for the theft of corporate funds. Let me be a witness for the prosecution. Please."

"You are fired as president of the bank, Mr. Headings. And you will go to jail unless you show the Marshall here everything he needs for a warrant from Judge Keller. The Marshall will decide if what you provide for him would be enough for CI not to prosecute you as a co-defendant. Your cooperation is important to us. Do you understand?"

"Yes, thank you, Sir."

Eugene Peters was correct, we spent the majority of the day in the bank president's office. Before the closing of the business day, Eugene had taken a number of documents to the judge's office and had a warrant for the arrest of the Johnstone Lodge manager and the hotel accountant. I declined to be present at the arrest as I was in route to Carson City to talk to the president of the Nevada State Bank.

After my experience in Johnstone, I did not go alone. Judge Keller was helpful in drawing up a search warrant for the Nevada State Bank. The Judge had asked the US Marshall's Office to meet us in Carson City. Carson City, the capital of the State of Nevada, was a city of over 50,000 people, while Johnstone had shrunk from 8000 to around 2000 when the silver mines closed. The Johnstone Lodge was the largest employer in the town and if it closed, then the town would disappear. It was sixteen miles from Johnstone to Carson City. The posse that rode towards Carson City contained DD Wilson, James Mathew, and assorted volunteers that I would meet later. We stopped in Silver City after 8 miles and watered the horses. I had not ridden a horse in years. I was used to driving my motorcars. We met the US Marshall at the front door of the bank and we entered.

"We are here for a meeting with the bank president. I am James Caldwell, owner of the bank. Can we meet with Carl Reynolds?" The woman behind the teller's cage was very nervous.

"Mr. Reynolds is not here, Mr. Caldwell. He cleaned out his office papers and left late yesterday." I smiled and said, "Marshall, put a padlock on Reynold's office. He could not have taken everything we need with him." I turned to the teller and said, "What other officers are in the bank?"

"Mr. Tallard, the Vice President is in." She pointed to his office. I walked over to it, the door was open and he was sitting behind his desk.

"Are you James Caldwell? I have been expecting you, Sir. I have copies of everything that Carl took with him." I smiled and said, "Mr. Tallard what is your first name?"

"Joseph, Sir."

"Mister Joseph Tallard, you are the new acting president of the Nevada State Bank. What can you tell me about the irregular deposits?"

26

Democratic Convention

St. Louis, Missouri

The Democratic convention differed from the Republican convention in that there was at no time a doubt as to who would be the nominee for the presidency. Mr. Wilson was the only candidate suggested and no other was mentioned as a possibility. Before the convention convened in St. Louis on June 14th, the Republicans had adjourned with their nomination made. Democratic leaders who had gathered in St. Louis made no effort to conceal their disappointment that Teddy had not become the candidate for the progressive wing of the Republican party again.

In the absence of any contest over the nomination process, the chief issue involved the platform. Mr. Baker, the new Secretary of War, arrived in St. Louis on June 13th with a draft of the platform which had been submitted to President Wilson and which he had already approved. Certain portions of the document, Mr. Wilson had written himself. Among these were those which discussed peace and recommended the formation of a world's peace league. It was the intention of certain of the Democratic leaders to insert in the platform a plank condemning Mr. Hughes for resigning from the Supreme Court to become a candidate for the presidency. At the request of President Wilson this was omitted.

The most suggestive feature of the convention was of the elimination of William Jennings Bryan as a conspicuous figure. In the several previous conventions he had been the outstanding figure, but his arrival was scarcely noticed and he took little or no active part in the proceedings. There were no candidates for the vice-presidency and Mr. Marshall had his second nomination. The leaders of the convention wanted some excitement to be generated so they suggested that the nominations wait to take place on June 17th. By the 15th, however, it was obvious that the delegates wanted to return home and the nominations were moved to June 15th. Both Wilson and Marshall were re-nominated by acclamation and no vote was taken.

I followed the short convention through my access to the American News Service that was a wholly owned company of Caldwell International. Whenever I could not attend a convention, I got a letter from my father who was in attendance, when he could not attend, my grandfather would write to him with details. In fact, with both Louis and James involved with the war effort, this was the first Democratic convention that a member of the family had not attended since the nomination of John C. Calhoun for vice-president. My father had accepted Teddy into the family and had funded his first run for the White House and I was convinced that he would return for a third term. Instead, I read everything that Charley Reuters forwarded to me from American News Headquarters.

American News Wire Service: Dateline St. Louis, June 14, 1916. The Democratic convention opened today with the reading of the platform upon which President Wilson will run his campaign for re-election. It looks very much like the platform we saw last week in Chicago. It contains the following planks:

Protection of American Rights
Mexico
Latin America
Right of Expatriation
Tariffs
Rural Credits
Railroads
Conservation
Territorial Officials
Suffrage

Foreign Relations
Monroe Doctrine
Philippines
Protection of the Country
Business
Merchant Marine
Economy & Budget
Civil Service Reform
Labor Laws

American News Wire Service: Dateline St. Louis, June 15, 1916. The second day of the Democratic convention convened at 11:50 am and following the report of the committee on credentials, Senator Ollie James was chosen permanent chairman and Bruce Kraemer, secretary. Senator

James then delivered his address to the convention. He made an attempt at arraignment of the Democratic platform and tried to defend the actions of President Wilson. This was followed by a demonstration which lasted 25 minutes. Following the demonstrations two speeches were made, one placed President Wilson in nomination and the other placed Vice-president Marshall in nomination. A recess until 8 pm was announced and at the approach to the night session American News found an immense crowd of people besieging the doors of the Chicago Coliseum. As soon as the doors were opened, the galleries were jammed to the danger point. Every available foot of space was occupied. There was much more cheering and excitement than had distinguished any other session. The cheering was for William Jennings Bryan who had entered the hall with the Nebraska delegation. There was chanting for a speech and a resolution was brought forward by the Kansas delegation that Mr. Bryan be given the privilege of the floor. A vote was taken on the resolution and Mr. Bryan ascended the platform.

"Mister Speaker, members of the convention; it is not often that a three time nominee for President of the United States is given a fourth opportunity to address the convention. I do so with the first hand knowledge of what this administration has done in the last four years. Granted, I have a better knowledge of what happened the first two years when I was a member of the that administration, but in just that short time, I was amazed by the leadership of President Wilson. He set his cabinet immediately to work on the problems ignored for so many years by the Republicans. We enacted a Federal Reserve act, the new income tax law and then began the unpopular panegyric effort to maintain this country's neutrality in the war of the nations that is raging on three continents. I did not fully understand Woodrow's intent and I stepped aside for new leadership from Secretary Lansing. I did not have the energy to fight the nations of Europe and the country south of our borders at the same time. Lansing and Wilson have, and if the Democratic majority had been maintained in the midyear elections, they would have solved the Mexican dilemma. You can thank the Republican majority in Congress that the solution to the Mexican problem never materialized. The American people want solutions to problems – not arguments by their elected officials on how to solve them. If the American people will send President Wilson back to the White House and Democrats to the House and Senate, this country will become the shining example of peace and prosperity for the whole world to follow. President Wilson will immediately begin a world wide effort to stop the war and instill honor among the nations presently involved in this great disaster."

The convention floor erupted in a demonstration that lasted 35 minutes. At 10:16 pm Senator James moved for the nomination of President Wilson by acclamation. At 10:50 he moved for the nomination of Vice-President Marshall by acclamation.

American News Wire Service: Dateline New York City, June 17, 1916. Supreme Court Justice Hughes sent a letter of resignation to President Wilson earlier this week and is in New York today to consult with the leaders of the Republican party in laying out the broad outline of the campaign. He has asked William Willcox, the former postmaster of New York City, to be chairman of the Republican National Committee and to manage the campaign. Cornelius Bliss was chosen treasurer. Late yesterday Mr. Hughes met with Colonel Roosevelt at his home on Long Island and they dined together. He was an overnight guest and Mr. Roosevelt expressed satisfaction at the end of this meeting and put an end finally to any doubts as to whether he would support the Hughes bid for the White House. From the front porch at Oyster Bay, Hughes said, "President Roosevelt and I desire that the Republican party as a great liberal party shall be the agency of national achievement, the organ of the effective expression of dominant Americanism. What do I mean by that? I mean America must be conscious of power, awake to obligation and erect in self respect, prepared for every emergency. We must be devoted to the ideals of peace, instinct with the spirit of human brotherhood, safeguarding both individual opportunity and the public interest. We must maintain a well-ordered constitutional system adapted to local self-government without the sacrifice of essential national authority – I mean, America first and America efficient."

American News Wire Service: Dateline Washington, D.C., June 21, 1916. The United States Department of State has called on Austria-Hungary for an apology for the attack on the American steamer *Petrolite* in the Mediterranean, Secretary Lansing was quoted as saying the act was a deliberate insult to the American flag. A source within the War Department was quoted as saying the Austrian U-boat that attacked the *Petrolite* was driven off before major damage was done to the American vessel.

A merican News Wire Service: Dateline Norfolk, Virginia, July 9, 1916. The German submarine *Deutschland* arrived here today with $10,000,000 in gold bullion as payment in full for what was stolen by the British government earlier this year. The Captain of the *Deutschland* carried a personal letter from the Kaiser to President Wilson, contents are not known at this time.

A merican News Wire Service: Dateline London July 13, 1916. Owners of the American vessel *Wilhelmina*, seized by the Royal Navy on February 15, 1915, are awarded $390,000 under arbitration. The Official British Gazette, published under the "Trading with the Enemy Act," a list of 82 American firms and individuals with whom residents of the United Kingdom are forbidden to trade. Included in the list was Caldwell International, the chairman of the board for CI just laughed when he saw his company listed. He said, "I doubt the people of Bermuda will discontinue the use of their telephones, that the people of Britain realize how many products and services are provided through CI, in fact most of the munitions shipped to England from America come by Caldwell Shipping and Trading Company.

King George received a letter from President Wilson today suggesting united relief for Poland. The letter was identical to those sent to the Emperors of Germany, Austria-Hungary and Russia. The President of France has already replied to President Wilson with his country's regrets. The US has also sent a telegram of complaint from their State Department to Lord Dinsmore protesting the seizure of mail bound for the US. The telegram was delivered even though it was sent by AT and T, a CI company.

A merican News Wire Service: Dateline Berlin, August 14, 1916. Germany today notified the US that she will not accept the proposition of the Entente Allies for the relief of Poland; Germany charges that the distress caused there is because of Russia. U-boat *Deutschland* secretly set sail for home today. The port of departure was Baltimore and British warships are searching the normal sea lanes beyond the three mile limits. England has announced today that she is not opposed to the Red Cross delivery of medical supplies to Berlin and Vienna. The Imperial Government today appealed the decision in the sinking of the *Appam*.

Officials in Berlin announced that they would join the US in appeals to Turkey on the behalf of Armenians endangered by the Turkish operations in Persia. And finally the Imperial Government noted that the US Senate has approved a bill which authorizes the President to prohibit the importation of articles from such countries as will not admit American products into their ports. England has repeatedly banned certain American companies and goods from entry to the UK. They risk the closure of all American ports to goods from Great Britain.

American News Service: Dateline Washington, D.C., September 8, 1916. The United States Congress inserted the following provision in the General Revenue Act as retaliatory measures against belligerents interfering with American commerce: "Sec. 104. That whenever, during the existence of a war in which the United States is not engaged, the President shall be satisfied that there is a reasonable ground to believe that under the laws, regulations, or practices of any belligerent country or Government, American ships or American citizens or firms composed in part of American citizens or American companies or corporations are not accorded any of the facilities of commerce, including the unhampered traffic in mails which the vessels or citizens, firms, companies or corporations of the belligerent country enjoy in the United States or its possessions, equal privileges or facilities of trade with vessel or citizens, firms, companies or corporations of any nationality other than that of such belligerent, the President is hereby authorized and empowered, in his discretion to deny to the citizens, firms, companies or corporations of such belligerent countries the use of the US mails, or the facilities of any express company engaged in interstate commerce, or of any telegraph, wireless, or cable company and in such case he shall make a proclamation stating the denial of the use of the mails and forms of communications. He will indicate the country to whose citizens such privileges are denied.

Upon the making of such proclamation the use of said mails or other communications so prohibited shall become unlawful and the President may change, modify, revoke, or renew such proclamation as in his opinion the public good may require."

American News Service: Dateline Army Navy Building, October 8, 1916. The War Department reports today that additional Zeppelin bombing has occurred on the east coast of England. The Rumanians have invaded Bulgaria but are repulsed by German and Bulgarian units. In Macedonia, Servians take Hovio, the French take Petorak and Verbeni, while the British capture Janikov. The French lost the cruiser *Rigel* in the Mediterranean.

In Belgium, General von Bissing, German Military Governor, orders all able-bodied Belgians, receiving public support, into forced labor details, while German U-boats continue to sink British shipping off the coast. Further south near Somme, British and French troops advance on a ten mile front, between the Alber-Bapaume road and Bouchavesnes. The British take Le Sars in advance between Gueudecourt and Les Boeufs. The Germans have captured Kronstadt and Szeke-lyudvarhely in Transylvania. Rumania retreats to Carpathian frontier.

By November, President Wilson was re-elected by the narrowest margin of electoral votes that had determined an election since the Hayes-Tilden campaign of 1876. So close was the result in the popular vote in several of the states, that over a week elapsed before it was conceded that he had been re-elected. On the evening of November 7th, reports came in from all over the country showing that Justice Hughes had carried what were considered by both parties as doubtful States, including New York, Illinois, Indiana, and others. On election night it was generally conceded that Justice Hughes had been elected and only the chairman of the Democratic National Committee, Vance McCormick, insisted that later returns would show the re-election of President Wilson. Returns the next day proved him to be correct. The final result hinged on the votes from California and Minnesota, both considered Republican. In California women voted for the first time and they voted heavily for the president. The president was behind in Minnesota until the re-count showed he won by less than a 100 votes.

27

Presidential Initiative
November -December, 1916

Within days of the final count and confirmation of his re-election, Woodrow Wilson sent for his Secretary of State, Robert Lansing and one of the State Department consul's, Louis Caldwell. After that meeting Louis called us at Bellawoods. He was so excited to get to meet the president in the oval office and actually get a task directly from him. Louis was instructed to contact the United States Charge de Affaires in Berlin by cablegram. The Charge de Affaires was to read the cable directly to the German Chancellor.

THE GOVERNMENT OF THE UNITED STATES HAS LEARNED WITH THE GREATEST CONCERN AND REGRET OF THE POLICY OF THE GERMAN GOVERNMENT TO DEPORT FROM BELGIUM A PORTION OF THE CIVILIAN POPULATION FOR THE PURPOSE OF FORCING THEM TO LABOR INSIDE GERMANY, AND IS CONSTRAINED TO PROTEST IN A FRIENDLY SPIRIT, BUT MOST SOLEMNLY, AGAINST THIS ACTION, WHICH IS IN CONTRAVENTION OF ALL PRECEDENT AND OF THOSE HUMANE PRINCIPLES OF INTERNATIONAL PRACTICE WHICH HAVE LONG BEEN ACCEPTED AND FOLLOWED BY CIVILIZED NATIONS IN THEIR TREATMENT OF NON-COMBATANTS.

FURTHERMORE, THE GOVERNMENT OF THE UNITED STATES IS CONVINCED THAT THE EFFECT OF THIS POLICY, IF PURSUED, WILL IN ALL PROBABILITY BE FATAL TO THE BELGIAN RELIEF WORK, SO HUMANELY PLANNED AND SO SUCCESSFULLY CARRIED OUT, A RESULT WHICH WOULD

BE GENERALLY DEPLORED AND WHICH, IT IS ASSUMED, WOULD SERIOUSLY EMBARRASS THE GERMAN GOVERNMENT.

While Louis was sending his cable in the German Language, Robert Lansing sent a secret cablegram to the heads of all governments presently engaged in the world conflict. The first response was from Berlin.

THE MOST TERRIFIC WAR EVER EXPERIENCED IN HISTORY HAS BEEN RAGING FOR THE LAST TWO AND ONE HALF YEARS OVER A LARGE PART OF THE WORLD — A CATASTROPHE WHICH THOUSANDS OF YEARS OF CIVILIZATION WAS UNABLE TO PREVENT AND WHICH INJURES THE MOST PRECIOUS ACHIEVEMENTS OF HUMANITY.

OUR AIMS ARE NOT TO SHATTER NOR ANNIHILATE OUR ADVERSARIES. IN SPITE OF OUR CONSCIOUSNESS OF OUR MILITARY AND OUR ECONOMIC STRENGTH AND OUR READINESS TO CONTINUE THE WAR (WHICH HAS BEEN FORCED UPON US) UNTIL THE BITTER END, AND IF NECESSARY; AT THE SAME TIME PROMPTED BY THE DESIRE TO AVOID FURTHER BLOODSHED AND MAKE AN END TO THE ATROCITIES OF WAR, THE FOUR ALLIED POWERS PROPOSE TO ENTER FORTHWITH INTO PEACE NEGOTIATIONS.

IT IS THE DESIRE OF THE ALLIED POWERS (GERMANY, AUSTRIA-HUNGARY, BULGARIA AND TURKEY) THAT FORMER PRESIDENT THEODORE ROOSEVELT AND HIS BROTHER-IN-LAW, ADMIRAL JAMES CALDWELL COME TO THE HAUGE AND MEET WITH ALL COUNTRIES CURRENTLY LISTED IN THE SECRETARY OF STATES MESSAGE. THE PROPOSITION WHICH THESE TWO, RESPECTED FRIENDS OF THE KAISER, BRING FORWARD FOR SUCH NEGOTIATIONS AND WHICH HAVE FOR THEIR OBJECT A GUARANTY OF THE EXISTENCE OF THE HONOR AND LIBERTY OF EVOLUTION FOR THEIR NATIONS ARE, ACCORDING TO THEIR FIRM BELIEF, AN APPROPRIATE BASIS FOR THE ESTABLISHMENT OF A LASTING PEACE.

When this was read in the Oval Office, President Wilson was not happy.

"Teddy Roosevelt is not a peace maker, he wants to bury every German soldier presently on French soil. And Admiral Caldwell was marked for murder by the Imperial Government of Germany not too many years ago. We can not put these two in charge of anything, one thinks he belongs in my chair in the Oval Office – the other believes he is a seer and can foretell the future."

"That is rather harsh, Mr. President, I have worked closely with James Caldwell and he completes his assignments with careful consideration of all those involved. He has absolutely no ego and he aspires to no public office. When he left the White House as your advisor, a door closed upon our ability to predict what the nations at war might do."

"Yes, Mr. Lansing, that might have been too harsh for James – but not for his brother-in-law. If I turn Teddy Roosevelt loose in the Hauge, we will be at war with Germany in twenty-four hours and he will make it look like Germany started it." Robert Lansing had a big smile on his face. "What did I say that was amusing, Robert?"

"I have a way to control Teddy Roosevelt."

"You do? I would like to hear it."

"Invite him to become one of your ambassadors and subject him to your control through the State Department. Louis Caldwell is amazing, not anything like his father, he can sit on Teddy, any time you would like him to."

"I should have a talk with Louis, the mad dog trainer, and tell him when to jerk the leash, so to speak."

"Exactly, Mr. President."

"Get Louis Caldwell back in here today, I want to talk to him."

"Mr. President?"

"Yes, Robert, what is it?"

"We have not heard anything from the others. There is no need to contact Roosevelt or the Caldwells until their replies are in your hands."

"Good point, Robert, wait until we get a direction from London."

Several days later another cable arrived from Berlin. It contained the basis on which Germany was willing to terminate the war, of which the following is a synopsis: The surrender of Belgium and French occupied territory; the establishment of Poland and Lithuania as independent States; the return of all German colonies taken in the Pacific and in Africa; the retention of Servia by Austria-Hungary; the restoration to Bulgaria of all territory lost in the Balkans; the restoration to Austria of territory taken by Italy; the retention of Constantinople and the European territory to Turkey.

The cable was actually sent to the State Department, Spain and Switzerland who were encouraged to forward the following message to Great Britain, France, Russia and Italy.

THE FOUR ALLIED POWERS HAVE BEEN OBLIGATED TO TAKE UP ARMS TO DEFEND JUSTICE AND THE LIBERTY OF NATIONAL EVOLUTION.

THE GLORIOUS DEEDS OF OUR ARMIES HAVE IN NO WAY ALTERED THEIR PURPOSE. WE ALWAYS MAINTAINED THE FIRM BELIEF THAT OWN RIGHTS AND JUSTIFIED CLAIMS IN NO WAY CONTROL THE RIGHTS OF THESE NATIONS. THE SPIRITUAL AND MATERIAL PROGRESS WHICH WERE THE PRIDE OF EUROPE AT THE BEGINNING OF THE TWENTIETH CENTURY ARE THREATENED WITH RUIN. GERMANY AND HER ALLIES GAVE PROOF OF THEIR UNCONQUERABLE STRENGTH IN THIS STRUGGLE. THEY GAINED GIGANTIC ADVANTAGES OVER ADVERSARIES SUPERIOR IN NUMBER AND WAR MATERIAL. OUR LINES STAND UNSHAKEN AGAINST EVER-REPEATED ATTEMPTS MADE BY ARMIES. THE LATEST ATTACK IN THE BALKANS HAS BEEN RAPIDLY AND VICTORIOUSLY OVERCOME. THE MOST RECENT EVENTS HAVE DEMONSTRATED THAT FURTHER CONTINUANCE OF THE WAR WILL NOT RESULT IN BREAKING THE RESISTANCE OF OUR FORCES AND THE WHOLE SITUATION WITH REGARD TO OUR TROOPS JUSTIFIES OUR EXPECTATION OF FURTHER SUCCESSES.

IF, IN SPITE OF THIS OFFER OF PEACE AND RECONCILIATION, THE STRUGGLE SHOULD GO ON, WE ARE RESOLVED TO CONTINUE TO A VICTORIOUS END, BUT WE DISCLAIM RESPONSIBILITY FOR THIS BEFORE HUMANITY AND HISTORY. THE IMPERIAL GOVERNMENT, THROUGH THE GOOD OFFICES OF YOUR STATE DEPARTMENT, AGREE TO THE PEACE CONFERENCE IN THE HAUGE.

President Wilson decided to send both German notes to all the capitals of the warring nations and ask for individual responses saying, "An early occasion must be sought to call out from all the nations now at war such an avowal of their respective views as to the terms upon which the war might be concluded and the arrangements which would be deemed satisfactory as a guaranty against its renewal or the kindling of any similar conflict in the future, as it would make it possible frankly to compare them.

As President of the United States, I want it understood that the suggestion is made in the most friendly spirit and as coming not only from a friend but also as coming from the representative of a neutral nation whose interests have been most seriously affected by the war and whose concern for its conclusion arises out of a manifest necessity to determine how best to safeguard those interests if the war is to continue."

After Secretary Lansing sent the cablegrams, he spoke to his consul saying, "The reasons for sending the notes were as follows: It is not our material interest we had in mind when the notes were sent, but more and more our own rights are becoming involved by the belligerents on both sides, so that the situation is becoming increasingly critical. I mean by that, that we are drawing nearer the verge of war ourselves and, therefore, we are entitled to know exactly what each belligerent seeks in order that we may regulate our conduct in the future."

The next diplomatic communication was from Switzerland.

THE PRESIDENT OF THE UNITED STATES OF AMERICA, WITH WHOM THE SWISS FEDERAL COUNCIL, GUIDED BY ITS WARM DESIRE THAT THE HOSTILITIES MAY SOON COME TO AN END, HAS FOR A CONSIDERABLE TIME BEEN IN TOUCH, HAS THE KINDNESS TO APPRISE THE FEDERAL COUNCIL OF THE PEACE NOTE SENT TO THE GOVERNMENTS OF THE CENTRAL AND ENTENTE POWERS. IN THIS NOTE PRESIDENT WILSON DISCUSSES THE GREAT DESIRABILITY OF INTERNATIONAL AGREEMENTS FOR THE PURPOSE OF AVOIDING MORE EFFECTIVELY AND PERMANENTLY THE SUFFERING OF TODAY. IN THIS CONNECTION HE LAYS PARTICULAR STRESS ON THE NECESSITY FOR BRINGING ABOUT THE END OF THE PRESENT WAR. WITHOUT MAKING PEACE PROPOSALS HIMSELF OR OFFERING MEDIATION, HE CONFINES HIMSELF TO SOUNDING AS TO WHETHER MANKIND MAY HOPE TO HAVE APPROACHED THE HEAVEN OF PEACE.

THE SWISS FEDERAL COUNCIL IS THEREFORE GLAD TO SEIZE THE OPPORTUNITY TO SUPPORT THE EFFORTS OF THE PRESIDENT OF THE UNITED STATES. IT WOULD CONSIDER ITSELF HAPPY IF IT COULD HOST THE CONFERENCE IN THE CITY OF GENEVA, WHERE THE SWISS PEOPLE COULD ACT IN ANY, NO MATTER HOW MODEST, WAY FOR THE PEACE OF THE PEOPLES NOW ENGAGED IN THE STRUGGLE AND FOR REACHING A LASTING PEACE.

The next communication to arrive in Washington was from the allied powers.

THE IMPERIAL GOVERNMENTS OF GERMANY, AUSTRIA-HUNGARY, BULGARIA AND TURKEY HAVE ACCEPTED AND CONSIDERED IN THE FRIENDLY SPIRIT WHICH IS APPARENT IN THE COMMUNICATION OF THE PRESIDENT, THE NOBLE INITIATIVE OF THE PRESIDENT LOOKING TO THE CREATION OF BASES FOR THE FOUNDATION OF A LASTING PEACE. THE PRESIDENT DISCUSSES THE AIM WHICH LIES NEXT TO HIS HEART AND LEAVES THE CHOICE OF THE WAY OPEN. A DIRECT EXCHANGE OF VIEWS APPEARS TO THE IMPERIAL GOVERNMENTS AS THE MOST SUITABLE WAY OF ARRIVING AT THE DESIRED RESULT. THE GOVERNMENTS HAVE THE

HONOR, THEREFORE, IN THE SENSE OF ITS DECLARATION OF THE 12TH, WHICH OFFERED THE HAND FOR PEACE NEGOTIATIONS, TO PROPOSE THE SPEEDY ASSEMBLY, ON NEUTRAL GROUND, OF DELEGATES OF THE WARRING STATES.

On the last day of 1916, the answer arrived from the Entente Governments of Great Britain, France, Belgium, Italy, Japan, Montenegro, Portugal. Rumania, Russia and Servia.

THE ENTENTE GOVERNMENTS, UNITED FOR THE DEFENSE OF THE LIBERTY OF THEIR PEOPLES AND FAITHFUL TO ENGAGEMENTS TAKEN NOT TO LAY DOWN THEIR ARMS SEPARATELY, HAVE RESOLVED TO REPLY COLLECTIVELY TO THE PRETENDED PROPOSITIONS OF PEACE WHICH WERE ADDRESSED TO THEM ON BEHALF OF THE ENEMY GOVERNMENTS THROUGH THE INTERMEDIARY OF PRESIDENT WILSON.

BEFORE MAKING ANY REPLY THE ENTENTE POWERS DESIRE TO PROTEST AGAINST THE TWO ESSENTIAL ASSERTIONS OF THE NOTES OF THE ENEMY POWERS THAT PRETEND TO THROW UPON US THE RESPONSIBILITY FOR THE WAR AND PROCLAIM THE VICTORY OF THE CENTRAL POWERS. WE CAN NOT ADMIT AN AFFIRMATION DOUBLY INEXACT AND WHICH SUFFICES TO RENDER STERILE ALL TENTATIVE NEGOTIATIONS. WE HAVE SUSTAINED 30 MONTHS A WAR WE DID EVERYTHING TO AVOID. THE ENEMY HAS SHOWN BY THEIR ACTS THEIR ATTACHMENT TO PEACE. THAT ATTACHMENT IS AS STRONG TODAY AS IT WAS IN 1914. BUT IT IS NOT UPON THE WORD OF GERMANY AFTER THE VIOLATION OF ITS ENGAGEMENTS THAT THE PEACE BROKEN BY HER MAY BE BASED.

A MERE SUGGESTION WITHOUT A STATEMENT OF TERMS THAT NEGOTIATIONS SHOULD BE OPENED IS NOT AN OFFER OF PEACE. THE PUTTING FORWARD BY THE IMPERIAL GOVERNMENT OF A SHAM PROPOSAL LACKING ALL SUBSTANCE AND PRECISION WOULD APPEAR TO BE LESS AN OFFER OF PEACE THAN A WAR MANEUVER. IT IS FOUNDED ON CALCULATED MISINTERPRETATION OF THE CHARACTER OF THE STRUGGLE IN THE PAST, THE PRESENT AND THE FUTURE. AS FOR THE PAST, THE GERMAN NOTE TAKES NO ACCOUNT OF THE FACTS, DATES AND FIGURES WHICH ESTABLISH THAT THE WAR WAS DESIRED, PROVOKED AND DECLARED BY GERMANY AND AUSTRIA.

AT THE LAST HAGUE CONFERENCE, IT WAS THE GERMAN DELEGATE WHO REFUSED ALL PROPOSALS FOR DISARMAMENT. IN JULY, 1914, IT WAS AUSTRIA WHO, AFTER HAVING ADDRESSED TO SERVIA AN UNPRECEDENTED

ULTIMATUM, DECLARED WAR UPON HER IN SPITE OF THE SATISFACTION WHICH HAD AT ONCE BEEN ACCORDED.

THE UNHOLY, EVIL EMPIRES THEN REJECTED ALL ATTEMPTS MADE BY THE ENTENTE TO BRING ABOUT A PACIFIC SOLUTION OF A PURELY LOCAL CONFLICT. GREAT BRITAIN SUGGESTED A CONFERENCE, FRANCE PROPOSED AN INTERNATIONAL COMMISSION, RUSSIA SENT A SETTLEMENT PAPER ON THE EVE OF THE CONFLICT. BUT TO ALL THESE EFFORTS, GERMANY GAVE NEITHER ANSWER NOR EFFECT.

BELGIUM WAS INVADED BY AN EVIL EMPIRE WHICH HAD GUARANTEED HER NEUTRALITY AND WHICH HAD THE ASSURANCE TO PROCLAIM THAT TREATIES WERE "SCRAPS OF PAPER" AND THAT "NECESSITY KNOWS NO LAW". AT THE PRESENT MOMENT THESE SHAM EFFORTS ON THE PART OF GERMANY REST ON THE WAR MAP OF EUROPE ALONE, WHICH REPRESENTS NOTHING MORE THAN A SUPERFICIAL AND PASSING PHASE OF THE SITUATION AND NOT THEIR REAL STRENGTH. A PEACE CONCLUDED UPON THESE TERMS WOULD BE ONLY TO THE ADVANTAGE OF THE AGGRESSORS, WHO AFTER IMAGINING THAT THEY COULD REACH THEIR GOAL IN TWO MONTHS, DISCOVERED AFTER TWO YEARS THAT THEY COULD NEVER ATTAIN IT.

AS FOR THE FUTURE, THE DISASTERS CAUSED BY THE GERMAN DECLARATION OF WAR AND THE INNUMERABLE OUTRAGES COMMITTED BY GERMANY AND HER ALLIES AGAINST NEUTRAL NATIONS DEMAND PENALTIES, REPARATIONS AND GUARANTEES. THE GERMAN NOTE AVOIDS MENTION OF THESE.

IN REALITY, THESE OVERTURES FROM THE UNITED STATES ARE NOTHING MORE THAN A CALCULATED ATTEMPT TO INFLUENCE THE FUTURE COURSE OF THE WAR WITHOUT ENTERING IT THEMSELVES. THE OBJECT OF THESE OVERTURES, SEEMS TO BE, TO CREATE DISSENSION IN PUBLIC OPINION WITHIN THE NEUTRAL NATIONS. BUT THAT PUBLIC OPINION HAS, IN SPITE OF ALL THE SACRIFICES ENDURED BY THE ENTENTE, ALREADY GIVEN ITS ANSWER WITH ADMIRABLE FIRMNESS AND HAS DENOUNCED THE EMPTY PRETENSE OF THE AMERICAN ATTEMPTS.

THESE ATTEMPTS HAVE THE FURTHER OBJECT OF STIFFENING PUBLIC OPINION IN GERMANY AND IN THE COUNTRIES ALLIED TO HER – ONE AND ALL, SEVERELY TRIED BY THEIR LOSSES, WORN OUT BY ECONOMIC PRESSURE AND CRUSHED BY THE SUPREME EFFORT WHICH HAS BEEN IMPOSED UPON THEM.

FINALLY, THESE OVERTURES ATTEMPT TO JUSTIFY IN ADVANCE IN THE EYES OF THE WORLD A NEW SERIES OF CRIMES – POISON GAS, SUBMARINE

WARFARE ON NON-COMBATANTS, DEPORTATION AND FORCED LABOR WHICH
ARE VIOLATIONS OF NEUTRALITY.

FULLY CONSCIOUS OF THE GRAVITY OF THIS MOMENT, BUT EQUALLY
CONSCIOUS OF ITS REQUIREMENTS, THE ALLIED ENTENTE GOVERNMENTS
REFUSE TO CONSIDER A PROPOSAL WHICH IS EMPTY AND INSINCERE. ONCE
AGAIN, WE DECLARE THAT NO PEACE IS POSSIBLE SO LONG AS WE HAVE
NOT SECURED REPARATION FOR VIOLATED RIGHTS AND LIBERTIES, THE
RECOGNITION OF THE PRINCIPLE OF NATIONALITIES AND THE RIGHT OF
EXISTENCE OF SMALL STATES; SO LONG AS GERMANY AND AUSTRIA REMAIN
ARMED AND WITH STANDING ARMIES, THERE WILL BE NO PEACE. PEACE
WILL COME WHEN GERMANY AND AUSTRIA ARE DISARMED OR THEY ARE
BURIED UPON THE BATTLEFIELD.

Robert Lansing and Louis Caldwell had brought the German reply to
the Oval Office and President Wilson had just finished reading it.

"I take this to mean a 'no'."

"Mr. President, I think you can take that as a 'Damn, No.'" Louis had
spoken without being asked anything and he continued, "The English have
something stuck in their craw. This is typical of every response I get from
Lord Alfred Dinsmore. The British Government has gone out of their way
to provoke us, they have seized our mails, refused safe passage of diplomats
to our country and arrested American citizens without cause."

"Where does that leave us, Mr. Lansing?" The president seemed
exhausted.

"Captain Caldwell and his father are both British subjects, perhaps
we should have them contact London by telephone and find out what
exactly the Entente Powers would have us do, short of declaring war on
both the Central powers and the Entente. Maybe it is time to inform the
British that we are about to sink their vessels, as well as German vessels,
for unwarranted attacks on our commerce."

"My God, Robert, you may have something there. Let's not threaten
something we can not enforce or have no desire to carry out. Let's make
our moves and then inform the Entente Powers of what we have done."
The exhaustion was gone and Woodrow Wilson grabbed a sheet of paper
and began writing. He picked up his telephone and buzzed his secretary,
"Get me Secretary Baker on the phone, please. Ring me back when he is
on." He continued to write. "I have ordered the entire Atlantic fleet to stop
all vessels approaching our convoys anywhere in the Atlantic Ocean. Your
brother will immediately bring his entire submarine fleet to hunt down and

destroy any submarines within the 15 mile limit of our shores. These vessels will be sunk without warning, no matter the nationality of ownership." He stopped writing and handed the sheet of paper to Louis.

"Mr. President, I can not repeat this to Lord Dinsmore. This is extreme, even for me." Woodrow Wilson laughed and then nodded his head. "Never ask an assistant to do what you would not do yourself." He picked up his telephone and said into it, "I wish to speak to King George of England. Ring me back when you have a connection." Louis and Robert Lansing had no idea what the president was about to do. The telephone rang.

"Yes, Hilda. Who do you have on the line? Good, tell him to mobilize for defense of the east coast. He will find that in the folder marked Operation Anvil. Have him send a wireless to Commodore Caldwell in Rome, just the following: Commence Operation Hammer. That's right, tell him I am on the line to London. Switch me to that line please." He placed his hand over the mouthpiece and winked at Louis, "Here goes nothing, Louis."

"King George, good afternoon your highness, this is President Wilson calling from Washington...... It is good to hear your voice too, your highness, the reason I called ......

28

Presidential Actions

January, 1917

The president hung up the phone and looked at his two cabinet members seated before him. He was smiling and Louis Caldwell was grinning from ear to ear.

"Mr. President, I am going down to the communications center and tell them to be waiting for the cable from Sir Cedric Spring-Rice."

"Louis, tell them not to be looking for anything before the middle of January. I know the British and they will not respond until they see our naval operation underway. I expect my orders will be carried out tomorrow or the next day and this will be reported to the War Department in London. I wish I had two of you Louis, I need you here and in London."

"I have a twin, Mr. President, but my replacement in London is not a hot head like me, he will serve you well."

"Louis, sometimes we need a hot head or two around to light a fire under us. Both of you take a few days off and enjoy the holiday with your families, I will see you next week."

"Aye, aye, Sir." Louis saluted the president and left the Oval Office.

"Now, Robert, how do I get his father back in the White House?"

"I think you should consider a position in the Army Navy Building, Sir. Admiral Dewey is near death and I know you did not want to replace him, but here is your opportunity. There is only one direction this will go now that it is started, we will be at a state of war within weeks."

"I agree, Robert, we have been neutral long enough, if the countries in Europe can not settle this, we can. I am going to beg James Caldwell to return to duty one last time as Admiral of the Navy."

On January 11th a letter arrived from Sir Cedric in London.

My Dear President Wilson,

The Government of Great Britain is in receipt of your recent cablegram and the transcription of your conversation with King George. Our government has studied both with the realization that has the gravity of the hour and by the sincere friendship which attaches them to the American people.

In a general way, we wish to declare that we pay tribute to the elevation of the sentiment with which your telephone call has inspired. We associate ourselves with all the hope with your project for the creation of a league of nations to insure peace and justice throughout the world. We recognize all the advantages for the cause of humanity and civilization which the institution of international agreements will bring. It would be destined to avoid violent conflicts between nations. It would prevent agreements which must imply the sanctions necessary to insure their execution. It should thus prevent an apparent security from only facilitating new aggressions.

A discussion of future arrangements destined to insure an enduring peace, presupposes a satisfactory settlement of the actual conflict. Great Britain has as profound a desire as the United States to terminate, as soon as possible, a war for which Germany is responsible and which inflicts such cruel sufferings upon humanity. We believe that it is impossible at the present time to attain peace – a peace which would permit the establishment of the future on a solid basis.

Great Britain is fully aware of the losses and suffering which the war causes to neutrals as well as to belligerents. It is with satisfaction, therefore, that King George takes note of the declaration that the American communication of December 19th is in no way associated in its origin with that of the Germany note dated December 18th. His highness did not doubt, moreover, the resolution of that Government to avoid even the appearance of a support, even moral, of the authors responsible for the war.

Great Britain must protest in the most friendly, but in the most specific manner, against the assimilation established in the American telephone call between the two groups of the belligerents. President Wilson, in mentioning it, certainly had no intention of associating himself with the German Government. If there is a historical fact established at the present time, it is the willful aggression of Germany, Austria, Bulgaria and Turkey to insure their hegemony over Europe and their economic domination over the world. Is it necessary to recall the horrors which accompanied the invasion of Belgium and of Servia, the atrocious regime imposed upon the invaded countries, the massacre of hundreds of thousands of innocent Armenians, the barbarities perpetrated against the populations of Syria, the raids of Zeppelins on open towns and cities, the destruction by submarines of passenger steamers and of merchantmen under neutral flags, the cruel treatment inflicted upon prisoners of war, the juridical murder of thousands of Belgians for daring to resist an invasion? The execution of such a series of crimes perpetrated with no regard for human life, fully explains to President Wilson the protest of Great Britain.

President Wilson has asked our King to affirm the objectives which we seek by continuing the war. Our object is the total and unconditional defeat of Germany and her allies, followed by the reorganization of Europe guaranteed by a stable regime in Russia. The overthrow of the Czar, and his family, by his own people, give hope to the German Emperor that he may invade and occupy Russia. This will not happen because it is our aim to remove the Emperors of all the Central Powers and replace them with democracies like those in the west. Unless the systems of government are changed in Berlin, Vienna and the other capitols of eastern Europe, the war will continue on some basis. The war must end and end in favor of free peoples throughout the world.

Awaiting your response, I remain your humble servant.

Sir Cedric Price-Rice
House of Lords
London, England

On January 16, 1917, Admiral George Dewey died at his home and was given a military funeral and internment in Arlington National Cemetery on January 19th. After a private funeral service at his home and a simple but impressive service in the rotunda of the capitol, attended by the most distinguished personages in Washington and conducted by the Rev. J. B. Frazier, who was his chaplain of the *Olympia* at Manilla Bay, the body was taken under military and naval escort to Arlington. As an extraordinary mark of honor, Secretary Daniels directed that all officers of the navy and marine corps should wear mourning with their uniforms for thirty days.

I had visited with President Wilson by telephone and he told me George was failing on January 2, 1917. He would not name his replacement while he was alive, but he wanted me to know that he had chosen me to replace him until the war in Europe ended and beyond that if I wanted to report directly to the Secretary of the Navy and not the White House. I accepted the president's request to return to full time duty until my 65th birthday. That would give me 6 years of service and no more. The president was relieved and he said as much, "James, I was very foolish to accept your resignation and retirement from the Navy. Are you familiar with operational plans, Hammer and Anvil?"

"Yes, Mr. President, my son, James, assisted in the completion of the plans for Operation Hammer. Is that going to be implemented?"

"Your son is coming home, Admiral. He is the hammer and you will be the anvil. It will be your responsibility to see that the United States Navy clears the 15 mile limit all along the east coast."

"Aye, aye, Sir. It will be done."

On January 20, 1917, I was in the uniform of the Admiral of the Navy and I was standing in the kitchen of our home at Bellawoods, Emily was smiling.

"What are you smiling about, Em?"

"I have watched you change your collar insignia, sleeve marks and shoulder boards since you were an Ensign. I sewed on the anchor with twisted rope in July, 1877, then I sewed on the single bar beside the anchor when you were promoted to Lieutenant, Junior Grade in June, 1880. I sewed on a second bar when you were a Lieutenant and sent off to Chile. I removed the bars and added an oak leaf beside the anchor when you made Lieutenant Commander after Chile and Commander when you taught at the Academy. When you were promoted to Captain, I removed the oak leaves and added an eagle so you could work for the Secretary of the Navy. I removed the eagle and added a star when you were known as Commodore Caldwell. I miss not seeing that rank in the navy anymore. Anyway, I added a second star for rear admiral, a third star for vice admiral and when you retired you had three stars beside the anchor and a forth star embroidered on top of the anchor. Now, finally, at age 60 you have the second embroidered star and the second embroidered anchor."

"I am 59.75 years old, not sixty."

"You were adopted, James, you could be 61."

"That's not very nice, Emily."

"James, I am already 60, it doesn't hurt. Life begins at 60."

"Depending upon what I find in my office today, I probably will agree with you, Em. I wonder what Secretary Daniels and Franklin Roosevelt have in mind for me?"

"What does your cousin, Franklin, do in the Department of the Navy?"

"He is not related to us, Em, he is related to our brother-in-law."

"When you find out, call me at home and tell me what Franklin does."

"There is my navy driver, Em. See you tonight with the usual bundle of manila folders." We left the suburb known as Forest Heights and headed for the Army Navy Building next to the White House. I left my driver and told him to pick me before 6 pm for the ride home. I had a brief case and a smile on my face as I entered the building.

"Good Morning, Admiral." Franklin Roosevelt was a tall, slender man who looked like a kid just out of school. He held out his hand and said, "The Secretary asked me to meet you and escort you to your office. Admiral Dewey has left you some files and a personal letter on your desk. I have all the operational plans and updates in my office when you want to see them." We walked at a brisk pace. I had much shorter legs than he and I had to almost double quick to keep up with him. "Here we are, buzz me when you need anything, Admiral, Secretary Daniels will be in to see you when he returns from the White House."

I entered a rather dark and dimly lit outer office with a couple of clerks and an Ensign sitting behind a very large desk piled high with manila folders. "Flag officer on deck!"

"As you were gentlemen, I am your new boss, Admiral Caldwell. I understand Admiral Dewey left a letter for me."

"The Admiral left a letter to the next Admiral of the Navy, Sir. It is in the middle of your desk ready for you to read, Admiral. Would you like a cup of coffee?"

"I would, Ensign, what is your last name?"

"Miller, Sir. Eugene Miller, class of 1914."

"And your name, Chief?" I was looking at one of the two clerks working at a tiny table in the corner.

"Gunnerson, Admiral." I asked him what a Chief Boatswain was doing as a clerk.

"Admiral Dewey was always going to promote me, Sir. But other things always got done first it seems, I never minded. The Admiral and I have been together since Singapore."

"You were with him at the Battle of Manilla, then. You are that Chief Gunnerson! Your boss talked about you all the time, Chief. It is an honor to meet you." I extended my hand. He smiled and saluted instead.

"Sir, Admiral Dewey spoke of you often. You wrote the operational plan for Manilla and he thought you were absolutely crazy for planning a night time attack. After the battle, he said you were the genius that was going to make him famous."

"Well, that is nice to know, Chief. Who is this young fellow that is helping you?"

"This is Andy White, Quartermaster 3rd Class, a wizard with supplies and transport, Admiral."

"Hello, Andy, nice to meet you. When you have time, I would like to hear how you plan to ship troops to Europe." He blushed and nodded his head, yes. "Show Secretary Daniels in when he comes back from his meeting."

"Aye, aye. Sir."

I walked into George Dewey's office, it was not mine yet. It still smelled like cigar smoke and old leather bound books. I walked to the wall of bookcases and found my text book for surveying among his collection. I took off my coat and hung it on a hall tree in the corner and came around the desk to sit in his chair. It didn't fit me, we were different sizes. I crawled under the desk and adjusted the chair until it felt comfortable. I sat down and scooted up to the knee well and saw the letter placed in the middle of his desk.

Department of the Navy
Office of the Admiral

December 24, 1916

If you are reading this, James, I died a happy man knowing that this office will now be filled by the most capable man alive in the Navy today. If you are not Admiral James Caldwell, you should know that I recommended to Secretary Daniels, who recommended to the President the most capable man I thought could handle this job. You might want to give him a call at Bellawoods and visit with him for advice from time to time. James Caldwell plucked me out of the unknown ranks of Commodores to implement his plan of attack for the Battle of Manilla. Over the years, I have consulted with him before I planned any operations of my own.

The United States Navy is filled with graduates from the Academy. James is one of us, Class of '77. He did not get his insight from the Academy, however, his father was also an Admiral of the Navy and Vice President of the United States, he was a graduate of the United States Military Academy, Class of '37. James has formal training at Annapolis and family training from a man who understood military operations on both land and sea.

War is being thrust upon us, and once again the Navy will be responsible for getting the Army to the battlefield a continent away, while protecting our home ports from U-boat attacks. I can rest easy that the next Admiral of the Navy will either be James Caldwell or someone who has the common sense to consult with him.

James, if you are reading this, lead the Navy and the Nation into this great struggle with the knowledge that I consider you the most capable Admiral alive today. Do not wonder what "George" would have done. George would have asked you for help.

Remembering you fondly, your friend,

George Dewey

George Dewey

I had tears in my eyes as I rose from my chair at my desk and walked to the office door. "Ensign Miller, did you type this letter?"

"Yes, Admiral. Do you like it?"

"Is there a copy for the files?"

"Yes, Admiral."

"Then get this framed and hang it in the outer office so that everyone can see it as they enter my office."

"Aye, aye. Sir, it will be done."

"Oh, and Ensign Miller, we will need a special handling crew to come in and box most of Admiral Dewey's things of a historic nature to be sent to the Naval Institute in Anapolis. I will let you and Andy go through ever thing and decide what goes and what stays. Type up the promotion papers for Master Chief Gunnerson today, we do not want George Dewey's ghost wondering if I appreciated his right arm."

"Master Chief, I will need a word with you."

"Aye, aye. Admiral, let me grab my pad and I will be in, in a second." The new Master Chief had a smile on his face.

We were inside my office with our heads together, trying to get a handle on why his former boss had kept the outer office so dark and sober, when Secretary Joe Daniels stuck his head through the door. "Can I interrupt you, James?"

"Of course, Sir. Come, have a chair. Master Chief, get those first few things done today, call the electrician and get him started hanging the light fixtures."

"Aye, aye, Sir. Morning, Mr. Secretary."

"Good morning, Earl. The boss got you working already?"

"Yes, Sir, Mr. Secretary, you are going to see some changes around here!" Master Chief Earl Gunnerson left us alone and closed the office door. Secretary Josephus Daniels and I had been cabinet members under the first Wilson administration and he was clearly uncomfortable.

"Admiral Caldwell, you are replacing a famous American naval officer, you were not at his funeral, care to explain why not?"

"I did not want to go back to Arlington, Sir. I have not been back there since I buried my father. I was at the house and talked with his wife and I was with her at the family service that you did not attend. Am I in some sort of trouble with you, Sir?"

"No, not at all. We were cabinet members together and frankly I am surprised that you accepted the President's offer. I was in his office when he called you, James. You should know that we both expected to be turned down."

"I never wanted to leave the White House, Joe, the President was wrong. Lindley Garrison was right, it was as simple as that."

"Will you leave this position, if we ask you to do something that is wrong?"

"Of course, I am my father's son."

"So was George. Did you know his father was a physician? Dr. Julius Dewey was his name. George had his 79th birthday on December 26, two days after he left this office, never to return. A week before that, George and I had an interesting conversation, I would like to tell you about it, if you have time."

"I would like to hear what he told you, Joe."

"George was proud of his Huguenot heritage. In the 17th Century, one ancestor fought in King Philip's War and in the 18th, another was a minute man at the battle of Lexington. George was sent as a boy to Norwich Military Academy and expected to go from there to West Point. But when he was ready, there was no vacancy available and he accepted an appointment to the newly established Naval Academy at Annapolis. He graduated 5th in his class in 1858 and was assigned to the steam frigate *Wabash*, flagship of the Mediterranean squadron. He made Lieutenant and was transferred to the *Mississippi* in Farragut's fleet. That is where he met your father. By this time he was the executive officer of the *Mississippi* and assigned to Farragut's fleet which had orders from your father to begin the battle of New Orleans. The *Mississippi* was lost shortly after the battle and he was assigned to command a gunboat on the Mississippi River. In 1863, he was transferred to the *Agawam*, which was helping to maintain the blockade along the Carolina coast. After the civil war he met and married Susie Goodwin, daughter of the governor of New Hampshire. That was in 1867, I think, she died in childbirth a few years later and his naval career was going nowhere, he considered leaving the Navy and returning to private life. He hated the naval assignments ashore. Did you know he was Secretary of the Light House Board?"

"He was also chief of the Bureau of Equipment and Lighting, chief of the Board of Inspection and chief of Navy Reviews."

"I did not know that, James, I knew he chafed under the system of slow promotion, he became a commander in 1872 and captain in 1884, when he was placed in command of the *Dolphin*, then a dispatch boat and one of four vessels comprising the original white squadron. By 1896, he got his first star, you were already a one star working here as the Assistant to the Secretary of the Navy. George was a late bloomer, he was twenty years older than you and was still a captain when you were here. When his appointment as commander of the Asiatic fleet was made by Teddy Roosevelt, then an assistant secretary himself, his fortune changed. He credited you and your brother-in-law with his assignments that propelled him into the national spot light. Did you know that?"

"I do now, I just read his letter that he left for me. Have you read it?"

"No, may I?" I walked to the office door and asked Ensign Miller for Admiral Dewey's letter.

"This is typical of the George, I knew. After the war, he returned to New York, September 26, 1899. He found a welcome unparalleled in

American history. The events included a naval review in the North River, receptions and a great parade. Congress voted funds for the purchase of a house here in Washington. Less than two months later, he married Mrs. Mildred McLean Hazen of Washington and deeded her the house. This raised a storm of indignation that only died down when George asked, 'Do you want me to give it back?' On March 2, 1899 he was appointed Admiral of the Navy. This rank had only been held by three other people, Farragut, Porter and Caldwell. He was supposed to retire in 1903 on his 65th birthday, but your brother-in-law told him he could keep the office until he decided it was time to retire. No president since has had the guts to fire a national hero. Now we have the second Admiral Caldwell sitting in this office."

"Thank you for telling me your conversation, Joe. I will not tarnish the office or do anything unworthy for the next six years."

"What happens in the next six years?"

"I turn 65."

"James, I think you should read what President Wilson has placed in your jacket. I have it with me, with orders to place it in your Navy file." He handed me a letter.

The White House
The Oval Office

December 24, 1916

It is my honor to forward to the United States Senate for confirmation the name of four star Admiral James Jason Caldwell as the personal choice of Admiral George Dewey to become the next Admiral of the Navy. Attached please find the letter from Admiral Dewey which describes the career of Admiral Caldwell. I fully and whole heartily support Admiral Dewey's choice. My choice would have been the same, even if this letter did not arrive from Admiral Dewey. Admiral Caldwell was the first director of the National Intelligence Agency and a member of my first cabinet. He would probably still be a member of my second cabinet, if I had not asked him to do something he felt was not in the best interests of this country.

I trust Admiral Caldwell's judgement and know he will become an excellent Admiral of the Navy. It is my recommendation that the Admiral serve in this capacity for as long as he feels he can perform in the best interests of the US Navy and the United States of America. There have only been four other Admirals of the Navy in its long and honorable history. We keep from President to President those key individuals who are destined to serve their countries without regard for their personal ambitions. James Caldwell will be the second member of this family to be so honored and who will honor the office he is about to enter.

I recommend without reservation, the name of James Jason Caldwell for your consideration and confirmation.

Thomas Woodrow Wilson

President of the United States

I handed the letter back to Secretary Daniels and blew my nose. He was smiling and said, "I have already heard from the Senate, James. Your confirmation was the shortest ever considered. Congratulations, James."

"Thank you, Joe. How many months do I have until we will be at war."

"Technically, we have just entered a state of war with any country who approaches one of our convoys in Operation Hammer. The President will address the Senate the day after tomorrow, that is when he will probably ask for a declaration. You will need to go with Franklin and me and sit together so he can see us and refer to us as the ones in charge of Operation Hammer."

"Is he addressing only the Senate."

"Yes, why? Oh, it would need to be a joint session if this is his request, anyway, I will pick you up and walk over to the Senate chamber with you, I hope it does not snow."

29

Presidential Address

January 22, 1917

G entlemen of the Senate:

On the 18th of December last, I addressed identical notes to the governments of the nations now at war. I requested them to state, more definitely than they have stated, the terms upon which they would deem it possible to make peace. I spoke on behalf of humanity and of the rights of all neutral nations like our own, many of whose most vital interests the war puts in constant jeopardy. The Central Powers united in a reply which stated merely that they were ready to meet their antagonists in conference to discuss terms of a peace. The Entente Powers have replied much more definitely, and have stated in general terms indeed, but with sufficient definition to imply details, the arrangements, guarantees, and acts of reparation which they deem to be the indispensable conditions of a satisfactory settlement.

We are that much nearer a definite discussion of the peace which shall end the present war. We are that much nearer the discussion of the international concert which must, therefore, hold the world at peace. In every discussion of the peace that must end this war, it is taken for granted that the peace must be followed by some definite concert of power which will make it virtually impossible that any such catastrophe should ever overwhelm us again. Every lover of mankind, every sane and thoughtful man, must take that for granted.

I have sought this opportunity to address you because I thought that I owed it to you, as the council associated with me, in the final determination of our international obligations. I wish to disclose to you, without reserve, the thought and purpose that have been taking form in my mind in regard to the duty of our government in those days to come when it will be necessary to lay afresh and upon a new plan the foundations of peace among the nations. It is inconceivable that the people of the United States should play no part in that great enterprise. To take part in such a service will be the opportunity for which they have sought to prepare themselves by the very principles and purposes of their polity and the approved practices of their government, ever since the days when they set up a new nation in the high and honorable hope that it might, in all that it was and did, show mankind the way to liberty. They cannot, in honor, withhold the service to which they are now about to be challenged. They do not wish to withhold it. But they owe it to themselves and to the other nations of the world, to state the conditions under which they will feel free to render it.

That service is nothing less than this – to add their authority and their power to the authority and force of other nations to guarantee peace and justice throughout the world. Such a settlement cannot now be long postponed. It is right that before it comes, this Government should frankly formulate the conditions upon which it would feel justified in asking our people to approve its formal and solemn adherence to a league for peace. I am here to attempt to state those conditions. The present war must first be ended, but we owe it to candor and to a just regard for the opinion of mankind to say that, so far as our participation in guarantees of future peace is concerned, it makes a great deal of difference in what way and upon what terms it is ended. The treaties and agreements which bring it to an end must embody terms which will create a peace that is worth guaranteeing and preserving, a peace that will win the approval of mankind, not merely a peace that will serve the several interests and immediate aims of the nations engaged. We shall have no voice in determining what those terms shall be, but we shall, I feel sure, have a voice in determining whether they shall be made lasting or not, by the guarantees of a universal covenant, and our judgement upon what is fundamental and essential as a condition precedent to permanency should be spoken now, not afterward, when it may be too late.

No covenant of cooperation that does not include the peoples of the new world can suffice to keep the future safe against war, and yet there is only one sort of peace that the peoples of America could join in guaranteeing.

The elements of that peace must be elements that engage the confidence and satisfy the principles of the American Governments, elements consistent with their political faith and the practical conviction which the peoples of America have once and for all embraced and undertaken to defend. And defend we will, a force must be created as a guarantor of the permanency of the settlement between the nations of Europe. Starting today, we will defend all shipping within the 15 mile limit of our shores. It is our hope that this type of defense will extend across the Atlantic and into the seas which open into this great ocean. It will be absolutely necessary that an international peace keeping force be created as a guarantor to the freedom of the seas. If the peace presently to be made is to endure, it must be a peace made secure by this organized major force of mankind. The terms must also depend upon whether it is a peace for which such a guarantee can be secured. The question upon which the whole future peace and policy of the world depends is this:

Is the present war a struggle for a just and secure peace or only for a new balance of power? Only a tranquil Europe can be a stable Europe. There must be not only a balance of power, but a community of power, not organized rivalries, but an organized common peace with a single armed force of a United States of Europe. All states must be equal in every respect, not some more powerful than another. It is not pleasant to say this, but until this happens, the war in Europe will continue. Only a peace between equals can last. The equality of states upon which peace must be founded, if it is to last, must be an equality of states rights, the guarantees exchanged must neither recognize, nor imply, a difference between big states and small, between those that have powerful armed forces and those that have none. Might does not make right, no state has the right to take anything from another state within Europe. No one asks, or expects, anything more than an equality of rights. Mankind is looking now for freedom of life, not for equipoises of power.

And there is a deeper thing involved than even equality of rights among the organized states of Europe. No peace can last, or ought to last, which does not recognize and accept the principle that Governments derive all their powers from the consent of the governed, and that no right anywhere exists to hand people from sovereignty to sovereignty as if they were property. If I may venture upon a single example, the people of Belgium are not property to be shipped to the state of Germany. Poland is a separate state within Europe, not the backyard of Germany or Russia. I wish frankly to face realities, any peace which does not recognize and accept this will inevitably be broken by war. So far as possible, moreover, every state now struggling toward this realization should be assured a direct outlet to the great highways of the seas and into the oceans of the world. With a right of arrangement, no nation need be shut away from free access to the open paths of the world's commerce, we will not settle for less. The paths of the sea belong to everyone and in fact be free to all. The freedom of the seas is the sine qua non of peace, equality and world cooperation. There can be no trust or intimacy between the peoples of the world without them.

It is a problem closely connected with the limitation of naval armaments and the cooperation of the navies of the world in keeping the seas at one free and safe. The limiting of naval armaments opens the wider question of the limitation or elimination of land based armies upon the continent of Europe. The concept of a single European army must be faced with the utmost candor and decided in a spirit of real accommodation, if peace is to come with healing in its wings and come to stay.

I have spoken upon these great matters without reserve, and with the utmost explicitness because it has seemed to me to be necessary if the world's yearning desire for peace was anywhere to find free voice and utterance. Perhaps I am the only person in high authority among the people of the world who is at liberty to speak and hold nothing back. I am speaking as an individual, and yet I am speaking as the head of a great government. I am holding out the expectation that the people of the United States will join the other civilized nations of the world in guaranteeing the permanence of peace upon such terms as I have named, I am proposing that nations henceforth avoid entangling alliances which draw them into competition, catch them in a net of intrigue and selfish rivalry, and disturb their own affairs with influences beyond their control. I am proposing government by the consent of the governed. I am proposing freedom of the seas. I am proposing the limiting of world navies and the elimination of large standing armies. These are already the policies of the United States. We can stand for no others. They are the principles of mankind and must prevail.

The members of the Senate were attentive, but not enthusiastic for the address. The president was not interrupted with even courtesy applause. I knew that the president was sincere in what he was reading from his notes, but the members of the Senate were almost restless after the first few minutes. It was not what they were expecting and were not certain that the address should have been sent to the printer and made available to every nation that had an embassy in the United States. I was sitting with Franklin Roosevelt, John Pershing and Joe Daniels. Franklin and John were visiting about their upcoming trip to France. People who were not members of the senate were filing out and Joe and I visited while we walked back to the Army Navy Building.

"Franklin and Black Jack are going to be heading for Europe with a small peace keeping force."

"Has the transport vessel been determined?"

"Yes, it is only 4000."

"4000?"

"That is a convoy, not a transport vessel!"

"Well, yes, I would like you to review the orders that were issued by the president."

"Why did the president decide that John Pershing would be the first American army officer to command troops in Europe.?"

"John is a graduate of West Point, class of 86, that makes him ten years younger than you, James."

"Yes, but what is his experience?"

"He fought in the last Indian Wars, Apaches I think, along the Arizona - Mexico border. He was an officer in Cuba for a year. He made Brigadier in 1906, your brother-in-law had to jump him over 862 other officers who were his senior in rank. He has fought overseas before, he won the battle of Bagdad from the Sultan of Jolo in 1913."

"I do remember that, when he returned to the United States, President Wilson gave him command of the 8th Army stationed in El Paso. The president used Pershing to make punitive raids into Mexico. This is what started the separation between Lindley Garrison and the president, Wilson was completely satisfied and his Secretary of War thought they were unjustified."

"He, Lindley, thought that? We never heard that in the cabinet meetings, did we, James."

"No, Lindley was also opposed to the forced retirement of Major General Funston, who was Pershing's immediate superior and the promotion of Pershing into his place so the raids could be made without question."

"So this is Black Jack's first command that is not desert related, I wonder how he will get along now that the President of France has accepted President Wilson's offer to send peace keepers to Europe?"

"England would not let him land anywhere in Great Britain as he wanted, so he could train his troops in his 'special mission'."

"Knowing Black Jack, he will probably have his troops make up a giant sign to hold up as they get off your troop carriers which reads, *Lafayette, we are here.*"

30

Europe Responds

February, 1917

A merican News Service: Dateline Washington, D.C., January 31, 1917. The German Ambassador in Washington delivered the response of Germany to the address of President Wilson before the United States Senate. A source inside the State Department has given a copy to the American News Service.

Mr. Secretary of State:

Your office was good enough to transmit to the Imperial Government, a copy of the message which the President of the United States addressed to the Senate on January 22, 1917. My government has given it the earnest consideration which the statement's desire, inspired as they were, by a deep sentiment of responsibility.

It is highly gratifying to the Imperial Government to ascertain that the main tendencies of this important statement correspond largely to the desires and principles professed by Germany. These principles especially include self-government and equality of rights for all nations. Germany would be sincerely glad if in recognition of this principle countries like Ireland and India, which do not enjoy the benefits of political independence, should now obtain their freedom.

The German people also repudiate all alliances which serve to force the countries into a competition for might and to involve them in a net of selfish intrigues. On the other hand, Germany will gladly cooperate in all efforts to prevent future wars.

The freedom of the seas, being a preliminary condition of the free existence of nations and the peaceful intercourse between them, as well as the open-door for the commerce of all nations, has always formed part of the leading principles of Germany's political program. All the more, the Imperial Government regrets that the attitude of her enemies, who are so entirely opposed to peace, makes it impossible for the world at present to bring about the realization of these lofty ideals.

Germany and her allies are ready to enter now into a discussion of peace, and has set down as basis the guarantee of existence, honor, and free development of their peoples. Their aims, as has been expressly stated in the note of December 12, 1916, were not directed toward the destruction or annihilation of their enemies and were, according to their conviction, perfectly compatible with what other nations have done to us in this war. As to Belgium, for which such warm and cordial sympathy is felt in the United States, the Chancellor would like to remind you that Belgium declared war on our nation and is not a neutral nation but a member of the Entente group of allies. Nothing has happened in Belgium that has not happened in occupied France. In order for peace talks to begin, Belgium should not be used again by Germany's enemies for the purpose of instigating continuous hostile intrigue. Such precautionary measures are all the more necessary, as Germany's enemies have repeatedly stated, not only in speeches delivered by their leading men, but also in the statutes of the Paris Conference, that it is their intention not to treat Germany as an equal, even after peace has been restored, but to continue their hostile attitude, and especially to wage a systematic economic war against her.

The attempt of the four allied powers to bring about peace has failed, owing to the lust of conquest of their enemies, who desired to dictate the conditions of peace. Under the pretense of following the principle of nationality, our enemies have disclosed their real aims in this way, viz.: To dismember and dishonor Germany, Austria-Hungary, Turkey and Bulgaria. To the wish of reconciliation they oppose the will of destruction. They desire a fight to the bitter end.

A new situation has thus been created which forces Germany to new decisions. Since two years and a half, England has used her naval power for a criminal attempt to force Germany into submission by starvation. In brutal contempt of international law, the group of Powers led by England does not only curtail the legitimate trade of their opponents, but they also, by ruthless pressure, compel neutral countries either to altogether forego every trade not agreeable to them or to limit it according to their arbitrary decrees.

The United States knows the steps which have been taken to cause England to return to the rules of international law and to respect the freedom of the seas. England, however, insists on continuing its war of starvation, which does not at all affect the military power of Germany, but compels women and children, the sick and the aged, to suffer for their country, pains and privations which endanger the vitality of any nation. This government can not justify before its own conscience, before the German people and before history, the neglect of any means destined to bring about the end of the war. The following memoranda regarding the details of the contemplated military actions are this, "From February 1, 1917, sea traffic will be stopped with every available weapon and without further notice within 20 nautical miles of Great Britain, France, Italy and in the Mediterranean. This will correspond to the United States intentions given to the Senate by President Wilson. Neutral freight ships are included in this new barring of materials of any type from reaching England and her allies.

American passenger ships may pass through the blockade unharmed if they send notification to Berlin one week before departing the United States and enter only the port of Falmouth. All other ports are banned, approach to Falmouth must be via the Scilly Islands and a point 50 degrees north, 20 degrees west. German mines will not be placed along this route, all other approaches to all English ports will be mined. All American passenger ships must be marked in the following way, on the hull and superstructure three vertical stripes one meter wide, each to be painted alternately white and red and the stern must have a painted American flag image. One passenger ship a week may sail in each direction with arrival at Falmouth on Sunday and departure from Falmouth on Wednesday. The United States Government may not ship materials of any kind aboard passenger ships.

Two copies of maps on which the blockade zones are outlined are attached for your reference, I remain, etc.

Johann Heinrich Bernstorff

American News Service: Dateline Washington, D.C., February 2, 1917. President Wilson addressed a joint session of congress today. An advanced copy of the address was sent to American News as, "Gentlemen of the Congress – The German Government has announced to this government and to all other governments that on and after February 1 it would adopt a policy with regard to the use of submarines and mines against all shipping seeking to pass through certain designated areas of the high seas, to which it is clearly my duty to call your attention.

On the thirty-first of January, the German Ambassador handed to the Secretary of State, along with a formal note, a memorandum, which contained the following statement, 'The Imperial Government, therefore, does not doubt that the United States will understand the situation thus forced upon us by the Entente Allies' brutal methods of war and by their determination to destroy the Central Powers, and that the United States will further realize that the now openly disclosed intention of the Entente Allies gives back to Germany the freedom of action which she reserved in her note addressed to you on May 4, 1916. Under these circumstances, Germany will meet the illegal measures by forcibly preventing after February 1, 1917, a zone around all of Great Britain, France, Italy and in the Eastern Mediterranean, all navigation, that of neutrals included. All ships found in that zone will be sunk.'

I think that you can agree with me that, in view of this declaration, which suddenly and without prior intimation of any kind, deliberately withdraws the solemn assurance given in the German communication of May 4, 1916. This government has no alternative consistent with the dignity and honor of the United States but to take the course which was given to them on April 18, 1916. I have, therefore, directed the Secretary of State to announce to His Excellency the German Ambassador, that all diplomatic relations between the United States and the German Empire are severed and that the American Ambassador and his staff in Berlin will immediately be withdrawn, and, in accordance with this decision, to hand His Excellency his passports and send him and his staff through the German blockade to a port of his choosing.

Notwithstanding this unexpected renunciation of its assurances to neutral nations given at one of the most critical moments of tension in the world, I refuse to believe that it is the intention of the German authorities to do in fact what they have warned us they will feel at liberty to do. I can not bring myself to believe that they will, indeed, pay no regard to the ancient friendship between their people and our own, or to the solemn obligations which have been made between them, to destroy American ships and take the lives of American citizens in the wilful prosecution of the ruthless naval program they have announced their intentions to adopt. Only actual overt acts on their part can make me believe it even now.

If this confidence on my part in the sobriety and prudent foresight of their purpose should unhappily prove unfounded, if American ships and American lives should in fact be sacrificed by their naval commanders in headless contravention of the just and reasonable understanding of international law and the obvious dictates of humanity, I shall take the liberty of coming again before the Congress to ask that authority be given me to use any means that may be necessary for the protection of our seamen and our people in the prosecution of their peaceful and legitimate errands on the high seas. I can do nothing less. I take it for granted that all neutral governments will take the same course.

We do not desire any hostile conflict with the Imperial German Government. We are the sincere friends of the German people and earnestly desire to remain at peace with the government which speaks for them. We shall not believe that they are hostile to us unless and until we are obliged to believe it. We propose nothing more than the reasonable defense of the undoubted rights of our people. We wish to serve no selfish ends. We seek merely to stand true alike in thought and in action to the immemorial principles of our people which I have sought to express in my address to the Senate only two weeks ago. We seek merely to vindicate our right to liberty and justice and an unmolested life. These are the basis of peace, not war. God grant that we may not be challenged to defend them by acts of wilful injustice on the part of Germany."

E mily folded the newspaper and laid it beside her cup of coffee. "James, you sat in the joint session yesterday. What was the reaction to this second speech by President Wilson?"

"It was quite different than the first one. He was interrupted with courtesy applause a few times at the beginning. The members of the House and Senate were attentive, but were lukewarm for the address. The president was not interrupted with courtesy applause when he informed them that he had broken diplomatic relations, they were expecting a declaration of war. I know that the president is sincere in what he believes to be his peaceful nature, but the members of the House and Senate were restless near the end of the speech. It was not what they were expecting and they were not certain that the address should have been sent to the printer and again made available to every nation that has an embassy in the United States. After the first speech, I was sitting with Franklin Roosevelt,

John Pershing and Joe Daniels. Franklin and John have arrived safely in France. Your son sent word to me that the convoy reached safely and all are on shore."

"Will there be war for us and our family, James?"

"There is war, it is just not formerly declared by the United States."

"But our son could not come back from one of his escort missions, is that what you are saying?"

"Our sons and many more, Em. I worry that Louis will do something rash and return to England with his family."

"Talk to him, James, tell him one son at risk in the navy is enough."

"I can not tell him that, Em. I think he enjoys what he is doing for President Wilson in the State Department. I will talk to him if we declare war on Austria and Germany to erase the break in diplomatic relations. It will all depend on what Germany does in the Atlantic and Austria does in the Mediterranean, if they attack, or God forbid, sink an American vessel, it will be immediate war. We have no intention of honoring the blockade of Great Britain or Italy."

War of the Nations

Part V

Black Jack Pershing's Peace Keeping Force Reaches France.
American New Service Wire Photo

31

America Responds

March-April, 1917

E mily and I held our breath while the newspapers carried the "headlines" of our lives. I went to work everyday including the weekends to make sure that the United States Navy was doing everything they could to control the events that were spiraling out of our control.

UNITED STATES RECOGNIZES NEW RUSSIAN GOVERNMENT – March 22

Until March, 1917, Russia was an empire. On the 11th, two ukases issued by the czar suspended the sitting of the Russian Duma and of the Council of the Empire. The Duma unanimously refused to dissolve and the Council appealed to the czar to reconsider. The czar, who was at the Austrian front, immediately started for the capital. He never reached Petrograd. At Pskov he was taken from the train and forced to announce his abdication and that of his heir-apparent in favor of the Grand Duke Michael, who declined the honor. Meanwhile a new government was formed with Prince George Lyoff as Premier, Miliukoff became minister for foreign affairs and Kerensky as minister of Justice. The new government imprisoned the czar and czarina in Tsarakoe-Selo.

GERMAN CHANCELLOR HOLLWEG ADDRESSES REICHSTAG – March 29

"After bluntly refusing our peace offer, the Entente Powers stated in their note addressed to the Americans that they are determined to continue the war in order to deprive us of our provinces in the west and east, to destroy Austria and annihilate Turkey. In waging war with such aims they are violating all rules of international law. We have not so far made unrestricted use of all the weapons which we possess. Since the Entente have made it impossible to come to an understanding based upon the American equality of rights for all nations as contained within the Wilson doctrine, we are no longer unable to forego the full use of our weapons.

I have notified the United States that the use of poison gas for our armies and the unrestricted use of U-boats for our navy, will give back to Germany the freedom of action which she reserved in her note addressed to the United States on May 4, 1916. Under these circumstances Germany will meet the illegal measures of her enemies by forcibly preventing, after February 1, 1917, in a zone around Britain, France, Italy and Greece, all navigation, that of neutrals included. All ships met within this zone will be sunk."

US Summons Citizens in Search of German spies – March 30

"I do hereby proclaim and direct that the conduct of all German aliens be observed by US citizens. All German aliens are enjoined to preserve the peace toward the government and are to refrain from crime against the public safely and from violating the laws of the United States. All aliens are to refrain from actual hostility or giving information, aid or comfort to Germany. As ordered by the President of the United States, all aliens violating this order will be deported."

U-boat Sinks American Freighter Aztec – April 2

The reality of the German threat soon became evident. On April 2 the commercial freighter *Aztec* was sunk without warning. A communication was received from Germany through the Swiss minister suggesting negotiations to arrange a modification of the U-boat policy, but Secretary Lansing replied that no negotiations would be undertaken until Germany withdrew her blockade order.

U-boat Sinks American Freighter Missourian – April 5

Germany again sends a message through the Swiss, Secretary Lansing sends a simple reply - a state of war now exists between our two counties.

President Wilson Signs Congress' War Resolution – April 6

President Wilson signed the following resolution submitted to him by the congress. "Whereas the Imperial German Government has committed repeated acts of war against the Government and the people of the United States of America; therefore be it resolved by the Senate and House of Representatives of the United States of America in Congress assembled, that the state of war between the United States and the Imperial German Government which has thus been thrust upon the United States is hereby formally declared, and that the President be and he is hereby authorized and directed to employ the entire naval and military forces of the United States and the resources of the government, and to bring the conflict pledged by the Congress of the United States."

Admiral Caldwell orders mobilization - naval forces – April 6

The naval force on April 6, 1917 consisted of 64,680 men. Admiral Caldwell has given the orders to increase this number to 149,169 which will come from the active reserves. The US Marine corps will be increased from 13,266 to 30,000. The hospital corps will be increased from 2000 to 7000. The National Naval Volunteers will be called upon to supply 16,000. These increases are necessary to fully man the surface fleets which consist of over 800 vessels.

On April 6, a destroyer and patrol fleet was rapidly prepared and sent to sea under the command of Vice-admiral W. S. Sims. They arrived in Britain on May 4 and joined the Allied anti-submarine forces.

Army Bill for 1,000,000 men is approved – April 7

The chief war measure of the government introduced in Congress was a bill to increase temporarily the military establishment of the United States. Its main feature was the provision for a selective draft called the "Selective Draft Act". This act authorized the president: First, immediately to increase the regular army to the full strength provided by the "National Defense Act" of June 3. 1916, only one increment of which had so far taken effect. Second, to draft into the service of the United States the entire National Guard of the several states. Third, to raise by draft a force of five hundred thousand enlisted men with the necessary officers and another similar size force at his discretion. The draft is applicable to all male citizens between the ages of twenty-one and thirty years of age.

US seizes 91 German vessels in US ports – April 8

The attorney general has cleared the way for Admiral Caldwell to give the orders for the seizure of all German vessels now in American ports of call anywhere in the world.

GERMAN CRUISER *CORMORAN* DESTROYED IN PACIFIC – **April 9**

During the attempted seizure of the German auxiliary cruiser *Cormoran* interned at Guam, the crew set explosives and blew it up so the ship could not be used for Operation Hammer.

HERBERT HOOVER NOW FOOD CONSERVATION CHAIRMAN – **April 10**

Mr. Herbert C. Hoover, Chairman of the Commission for Relief in Belgium, is appointed chairman of a committee on food conservation within the United States.

NAVY BEGINS OPERATION HAMMER ALONG ENTIRE EAST COAST – **April 11**

By far the most important event of the spring is the entrance of the navy into the war and the addition of its forces to those of the Entente Powers. In April, US battleships are not needed in Europe as the British battleships alone are vastly superior to the German's, which do not venture beyond the protection of their own harbors. All battleships will take up positions to begin the blockade of US ports from enemy entrance. The American destroyers and patrol ships will be of enormous value, particularly the destroyers, which are the most effective enemy of the U-boats either in chasing and destroying them, or passively in protecting merchant ships against attack. All destroyers and patrol vessels are leaving their ports of call to begin the protection of the east coast of the United States.

AMERICAN COUNCIL OF NATIONAL DEFENSE IS FORMED – **April 12**

Captain Harry S. Truman, of the Missouri National Guard, shares with American News Service his first meeting with Admiral Caldwell.

"It was during the 1900 Democratic Presidential Convention. Before the admiral left the convention, he posted a notice in the page's cloakroom. It announced that Caldwell International would grant small amounts of funding for any Democrat that would like to run for state or federal office. The age range for those attending should not exceed twenty-five years. His idea was to meet the youngest, most active members of the party. He reasoned that if a young man or woman took the time to attend the national convention and work as a page, they were the future of the party. I was one of twenty-two pages and some other young delegates that came to the room indicated in the announcement. He introduced himself and asked each of us to stand and introduce themselves and tell him why they thought they would like to run for a state or federal office. I was the first one on my feet. I was a short, young man from Missouri, most of the pages were from Missouri, Iowa, Kansas and nearby. What I said must have impressed him."

"Admiral, I knew your father and if you are anything like him, I would like to throw my hat in the ring."

"What is your name, son?"

"Harold S. Truman, Sir. I am from right here in northwestern Missouri. There are so many Republicans in this part of the state you have to be careful not to step on one in your rush to make it to the back house to take a shit."

He began laughing. "Mr. Truman, the first thing I would do is change the Harold to Harry. No one knows who Theodore Roosevelt is, Teddy, on the other hand was just nominated for Vice President!"

"What is second thing, Admiral?"

"I would never admit that you still used an outhouse!"

"Too colorful, Admiral?"

"The third thing that I would do, if I were you, is not be impressed by other people's titles. My name is James Caldwell and I have so much money it would scare you to death. Most admirals and generals do not have a pot to pee in. Teddy Roosevelt was a colonel and he too is beyond worrying where his next meal is coming from. It takes lots of money to run for public office, that is why I am meeting with you today. What office are you going to run for, Harry?"

"The first office will be state representative and the last will be President of the United States, James."

"Well, then, Mr. Truman. You will need to have military service on your record. No man has ever served as the President of the United States without it. When you get to the White House, Harry, give me a call in Pennsylvania. Either myself or one of my sons would like to be a member of your cabinet! In the meantime, come up here and see the treasurer sitting at the end of this table and sign the conditions for the funding to run for the Missouri House of Representatives."

Admiral Caldwell welcomes allied naval officers – April 13

Secretary of the Navy, J. Daniels, met with his counterparts from England, France, Belgium, Russia, Greece and Italy in the Army Navy Building to discuss America's role in the expanded war. The Entente naval heads decided that the United States Navy should take charge of patrol work in the entire Western Hemisphere, using British and French ports in the West Indies for bases.

President proclaims defense zones along east coast – April 14

A Presidential executive order was made public today announcing the establishment of defense areas at the entrance to the chief harbors of the Atlantic and Pacific coasts, the Gulf of Mexico and in insular colonies and US territories. One of the reasons for the restrictions in these areas was the presence of German commerce raiders in the western Atlantic.

US Passes $7,000,000,000 war-loan bill – April 17

Congress continued the debate of war measures and the House on April 14, passed without a dissenting vote, a bill providing for a war loan of $7,000,000,000, the largest single loan in the history of the United States. The Senate will now debate the house bill. Three billion are to be invested in war bonds for the Allies. Secretary McAdoo, of the US Treasury, has already announced the offering of first "Liberty Loan" which is to consist of two billion for 30 years at 3.5 per cent. The Senate has already approved the sale of war saving stamps for the purpose of raising funds for the US military. The stamps may be purchased in denominations, 25 cents (thrift stamp) or 5 dollars. The large stamps can be fixed on a war bond and will earn one cent per month.

Entrance into war welcomed in British Parliament – April 18

Simultaneously with the departure of Arthur James, the British Foreign Secretary to the United States, the entry into the war was celebrated in London. For the first time in history, a foreign flag was raised over the Houses of Parliament. Both houses passed the following resolution: "This House desires to express to the government and the people of America, their profound appreciation of the action of their government in joining the Allied Powers and thus defending the high cause of freedom and rights of humanity against the gravest menace by which they ever have been faced."

British and French Secretaries visits Washington – April 20

About the middle of April, the expected envoys from France and Britain reached Washington, D. C. The British mission arrived first and was headed by Arthur James Balfour, the foreign secretary, and included a number of noted military and naval officers and financiers to discuss details of the war loans to both countries.

Two days later, the war commissioners from the French Republic reached Norfolk, Virginia, and were taken to Washington on the President's yacht, the Mayflower. The movements of the commission have been kept a secret in order to prevent any interference. As soon as their secret was known, their journey to Washington became a triumphant procession. It was on a parallel to the visit of Lafayette. The French delegation is headed by former premier Rene Viviani and other members are Marshall Joffre and the Marquis de Chambrun.

ELIHU ROOT APPOINTED TO RUSSIA – April 25

The Russian revolution, which occurred in February, created the most sympathetic feeling and interest in the US. President Wilson has resolved to send to Russia a war mission, to consult with the authorities of that country and to assist in the establishment of a stable government. Elihu Root, former secretary of state, was appointed chairman of the commission, which included representatives of the army and navy, financial and transportation experts.

WAR COMMISSIONERS FROM PARIS AND LONDON TOUR US – April 30

Following the conference in Washington, the war commissioners began an extensive tour in the eastern and mid-west states. The commission was received with enthusiasm, especially in Chicago. It became known in Chicago, that Marshall Joffre and other members of the French commission had laid stress upon the necessity of at once sending an army to France in support of General Pershing's "Peace Keeping Force." In a statement given to American News Service, he expressed his belief that American recruits could best be trained behind the battle lines in France.

FRANKLIN ROOSEVELT HOME FROM FRANCE WITH ILLNESS – May 1

The undersecretary of the Navy was sent home from Paris today with what is reported to be a sever case of influenza. He is, of course, only one of many cases of the 1917 strain of influenza that is now world wide. The undersecretary was unable to walk and reported that his legs had become numb when he visited French troops along the battle lines in eastern France. He has been granted a leave of absence from his position in Washington and he will begin his treatment and recover, at his home in Skaneateles, New York.

32

Submarine Warfare

Germany, 1917

When in February, the German campaign against American merchant shipping was first launched, it was immensely popular, both with the nation and the navy. It was looked upon by the starving people as the final relief of the blockade of the German coast. Service in the submarine branch was encouraged by increased pay, promotion, honors, decorations and prize money for ships sunk. Volunteers were plenty and the service was popular. The sinkings increased from an average of five a week in February to twenty-two a week in May, and then steadily dropped to two a week. The reduction was brought about by several causes. First, Operation Hammer's submarine nets, submarine chasers and destroyers were said to have disposed of 50 per cent of all U-boats that had been sent into the Atlantic and Mediterranean. Second, Operation Anvil added a considerable number of U-boats destroyed by mines, chased aground by patrol vessels and internment in US ports.

While the magnitude of the losses could be concealed from the German people, the personnel of the German Navy could not be deceived. Even the most ignorant of the enlisted men were tolerably sure of the facts. They had seen U-boat after U-boat sail away and never return. It required no mathematics to deduce the danger of the service. It began to be noised about that U-boat duty was not dangerous – it was fatal, because any man who survived a year of it, was endowed with marvelous luck. Volunteering stopped entirely and the new crews were taken from the surface fleet which rested at anchor due to British blockade of German ports. As these were green hands, it became necessary to establish larger schools for the instruction of officers and men to replace those who were disappearing so fast. Long before this, the naval authorities realized that the U-boats, built before 1916 were too small and too weakly armed. A new and larger U-boat building program was begun mid year 1916. These new U-boats were all sent to the western Atlantic and Mediterranean, where the field of operations was wider if less intensive and the anti-submarine defenses were not yet as effective as the British and French navies.

During the five months between October 1, 1916, and the end of the next February the number of U-boats was heavily increased. More than half of the U-boats built were over 800 tons. The smaller U-boats that were built were assigned in the North Sea and throughout the Baltic. During this period, the Entente Allies and the neutrals became convinced that the danger of the U-boat menace was decreasing and the German people were losing faith in the U-boat as a decisive factor in the war. By January, 1917, the number of new U-boats had reached a figure satisfactory to the German War Council, led by Tirpitz and Reventlow and they demanded a renewal of U-boat operations on a great scale with all humane restrictions as to non-combatants removed. They carried the day against the wishes of a large part of the government, including, it is believed, the Chancellor.

In February, just as the United States was congratulating itself on the favorable conclusion of the Lusitania Affair, in which Germany acceded to the demands of the US, the new threat was secretly launched. This was followed by the declaration of Germany on February 1, 1917. This new offensive developed slowly. Tirpitz and his followers were wholly dissatisfied and urged unrestricted warfare against all vessels trading with the Entente countries. When approval was slow in coming, Tirpitz resigned and Vice-admiral von Capelle now ordered all ships of any nation torpedoed without warning. President Wilson informed Vice-admiral von Capelle that unless he would declare and effect an abandonment of his existing method of submarine warfare, the United States would sever diplomatic relations.

On April 2, the commercial freighter *Aztec* was sunk without warning. A communication was received from Germany through the Swiss minister suggesting negotiations to arrange a modification of the U-boat policy. They would agree to the US demands and stated that "vessels both within and without the area of the sinking of the *Aztec* would not be sunk without warning and without saving human lives unless the ship attempted to escape or offered resistance." But if the US should fail to secure "freedom of the seas" from Britain, "the German government would then reserve to itself complete liberty of decision." The promises against Entente and neutral merchantmen – especially the latter – was short lived as another U-boat was in the process of sinking the American Freighter *Missourian*. Germany again sent a message through the Swiss, Secretary Lansing sent a simple reply - a state of war now exists between our two counties.

A large force of destroyers and patrol vessels was sent to Europe, where they arrived on May 4. The effect of this order by the Department of the Navy had a very considerable affect on the Allied efforts to clear the U-boats out of the declared kill zone around Britain. Vice-admiral Sims and rear-admiral Caldwell were given the joint task of clearing the zone. Admiral Sims was in total command of the operation and drew up the plan of attack for all surface vessels. Admiral Caldwell was the Operation Hammer Commander in the Atlantic and together they sat aboard Sims' flagship and sent the following sets of orders:

To all surface vessel captains:

Tomorrow at sunrise we will commence operation Dragon Fly. We are in search of the German Commerce Raiders known as *Moewe* and *Secadler*. These two groups are composed of several surface ships and several U-boats known as a wolf pack. These two groups have sunk almost 600 merchant marine vessels, let's see how they do against us. Background on the captain of the Moewe Raiders is this: His name is Count Schledien, his success in passing through the British blockade is almost legendary, he passes his U-boats through first and they surface and are chased by the British, while this is happening his surface group makes an end run. That group of raiders is now in port close to Burges, Belgium, to refuel and take on munitions. We will intercept them as they leave port on or before May 20th. The Captain of the Secadler Raiders is Lieutenant Von Luckner. His favorite trick is to set a harmless fire on the deck of his lead vessel (the captured American *Pass of Balama*) she is fitted to look like a cargo hauler with tarps pulled over stacks of lumber to conceal her wireless rigging and gun mounts. Once the tarps are removed she no longer looks like a freighter in trouble on the high seas. By this time the ships coming to her aid are torpedoed

BY THE WOLF PACK. USE YOUR WIRELESS COMMUNICATIONS WHENEVER YOU HAVE A QUESTION FOR ME OR ADMIRAL CALDWELL.

GOOD HUNTING,

ADMIRAL W. S. SIMS

TO ALL VESSELS IN OPERATION HAMMER SUBMARINE FORCE:

TO THOSE WHO HAVE LEFT THE ATLANTIC WITH ME AND JOINED ADMIRAL SIMS, WELCOME TO OPERATION DRAGON FLY. TOMORROW WE WILL ASSIST VICE-ADMIRAL SIMS BY LOCATING THE U-BOATS WHO ACCOMPANY THE COMMERCE RAIDERS KNOWN AS MOEWE AND SECADLER. THE WOLF PACKS THAT ACCOMPANY THESE GROUPS HAVE A NUMBER OF FAMOUS U-BOATS AMONG THEM, IN PARTICULAR U-42 AND U - 20, WE HAVE THE NEFF SOUND PATTERNS FOR THESE TWO BOATS AND SEVERAL OTHERS. IT WILL BE OUR JOB TO KEEP THE U-BOATS OFF THE SURFACE DESTROYERS OF ADMIRAL SIMS. KEEP IN TOUCH WITH THE FLAGSHIP AND RECORD EACH KILL AS IT HAPPENS – GOOD HUNTING!

REAR ADMIRAL CALDWELL

The sunrise of May 17, 18 and 19 brought no sign of the commerce raiders or any U-boat soundings. On the morning of the 20th, a flash wireless message was sent to Admiral Caldwell from the *USS Seawolf* and Captain Daniel Wells.

ADMIRAL CALDWELL:

NEFF RECORDINGS FOR U-20 AND THREE OTHERS (U-24, U19 AND U42) HAVE BEEN FOUND LEAVING THE PORT OF BURGESS – CAPTAIN WELLS

"Ensign, send this to Admiral Sims on his flagship. Radio, send the following flash to the *Seawolf*: Follow U - 20. Send the following to the *Starfish, Rapier* and *Saratoga*: Find neff sounding for *Seawolf* and follow him to rendevous point blackjack."
"Aye, aye. Sir."
"Sir, radio has another message from the *Seawolf*."
"Read it to me, radio."

"Unknown sounds of surface vessels leaving Burges, count at least ten."

"Get that off to Admiral Sims as soon as you can, the battle has begun."

"Aye, aye. Sir."

"Engine room, full speed ahead, head for the port of Burges."

"Engine room here, Admiral, engines at full speed."

"Thank you, guys. I want all the speed this old bucket can give us. Torpedo room, load all tubes, but keep outer doors closed."

"Navigation, let me know when I can see the entrance to the port."

"You should be able to see it now, Admiral."

"Captain, this is your submarine, I am just along for the ride. Take a look and give us a reading on the number of ships leaving the port."

"Thank you, Admiral. It is hard not to take command when the fight is about to start, isn't it."

"Yes it is. Radio, be ready to send the count and types of vessels leaving to Admiral Sims."

"Aye, aye. Admiral."

"I count nine surface ships, the lead looks like an older S type destroyer, that might be the Count's ship, Admiral."

"Our job is to relay information to Admiral Sims, not sink the bugger, Captain, relax. Radio, get that off to Admiral Sims as the captain gives you the ship's number."

"Another message from the *Seawolf,* Admiral."

"Read it to me, radio."

"U - 20 has surfaced near Admiral Sims' surface ships and has started to run on the surface. The other three U-boats have outer doors open and ready to fire."

"Send that to Admiral Sims."

"But, Sir, if Admiral Sims chases U - 20 he will run right into the wolf pack."

"Relax, radio, that is part of the plan."

"Aye, aye. Admiral. A flash coming in from the *Seawolf!*"

"Calmly read it, radio."

"*Seawolf* has surfaced and is chasing U - 20. Less than 500 yards separate them, Sir."

"Daniel Wells is an old hand, radio. Listen and learn."

"Admiral, the surface group of raiders is making an end run."

"Are they tightly grouped?"

"Yes, just as you said they might. Good you know what to do Captain."

"Torpedo room, open all outer doors. Fire all torpedoes for a spread of 800 feet on my mark."

"Torpedo room, Captain. Outer doors open. Ready to fire for spread of 800 feet."

"Let's break them up and send them right into Admiral Sims waiting destroyers. Fire all torpedoes."

Captain Henry Claypool watched as his spread of torpedoes raced toward the group of S type destroyers. Before any could reach their targets the surface ships tried to take evasive action. Two collied with each other and exploded before any of Claypool's shots could take effect. One stopped dead in the water and was shelled by one of Admiral Sims' approaching destroyers. Only one of the enemy surface ships was struck by a torpedo, but the damage was done as Admiral Sims's ships pounded the survivors into surrendering their ships to the Americans.

The battle between the wolfpack and the Hammer squadron had just begun. The *Saratoga* killed U-42 before U - 20 realized it was a trap. U - 20 crash dived and the *Seawolf* followed him as fast as she could. U - 20 was larger and tried to settle on the bottom. The *Seawolf* crashed onto the U - 20 conning tower and both boats began to take on water. In the confusion, U - 19 and the *Rapier* collided bow first. U - 19 was a smaller, older U- boat and this saved the lives on the *Rapier* but they were both out of the fight. Only U - 24 was still able to fire torpedoes, but she was blind and fired in a spread formation in a desperate attempt to hit an enemy submarine, she came close. One found the slowly rising U - 20 and killed everyone on board. In wild panic, U - 24 turned to run toward the Port of Burges and was killed by the captain of the *USS Starfish*. The following flash message was sent to Admiral Caldwell: ***Scratch neff readings for U - 19, 20, 24 and 42.*** The submarine of Daniel Wells was brought under control and surfaced to find all of his squadron in tack except the *Rapier*, her entire forward bow section was missing, only the locked flood doors from the forward section had saved their lives.

"Radio, send a message to Admiral Sims for the *Rapier* to be loaded on board a transport and returned to England."

"Aye, aye. Captain. Any other messages?"

"Yes, to the *Rapier, Saratoga* and *Starfish* – well done. Thank you for saving my ass."

Captain Claypool returned Admiral Caldwell to Admiral Sims' flagship and after action reports were sent to London and forwarded to the Army Navy building in Washington. W. S. and James were in the ward room having a cup of coffee and discussing where they might find the *Secadler* when a radioman brought them a message which accounted for the demise of the *Secadler* group. After sinking thirteen vessels in the Atlantic she passed around Cape Horn, sank three American schooners and then was wrecked on Mopeha Society Islands. The *Secadler* Captain Von Luckner, three officers and two seamen put to sea in an armed motor boat and were soon captured. The remainder of the officers and men seized the small French schooner *Lutcee* which put in at Mopeha, armed her and proceeded to return to Germany, they have not been found.

"Well James, it appears that Operation Dragon Fly is at an end. I wonder what your father will have us do next?"

"I would think that we would be assigned either the *Asturias* or the *Gena* sinking problems to try and resolve."

"Refresh my memory, what was the *Asturias* sinking?"

"On March 20, a German U-boat sunk the British Red Cross hospital ship. She carried navigating and other lights, the Red Cross signals and had the Red Cross flag brilliantly illuminated by a search light. The sinking was, therefore, deliberate. The Germans alleged that they were sinking hospital ships because the British were using them to carry munitions and troops across the channel."

"Why would the Germans commit such a faithless breach of law and humanity when they expect it of others?"

"The same reason they release poison gas upon the battlefields of France, knowing that the change in wind direction could kill their own troops."

"How was the *Gena* sunk?"

"On May 1, the *Gena* was sunk by a German seaplane that carried a torpedo. We think this was the first use of a seaplane as a torpedo carrier in the war, though the idea was suggested by Admiral Fiske, USN, several years ago."

"I remember Fiske and his plans for a 'torpedo-plane' for carrying, directing and dropping what he called automatic torpedoes. Leave it to the Germans to make it work and use it successfully."

With the elimination of the German surface commerce raiders like Moewe and Secadler, the German Navy was reduced to only U-boat wolfpack attacks. This greatly reduced the radius of action of the wolkpack and caused them to return at shorter intervals to their bases. It also threw strain on the German supplies, for a torpedo requires several months to build and adjust. Zigzag steering, the depth charge and the smoke-box, that can quickly obscure a steamer from the U-boat's view, each played its part. The combined results of the various adverse factors gradually diminished the number of large (over 1600 tons) British vessels sunk each month until in November, 1917, the average was only 13 per week. Moreover, the average tonnage of the ships sunk was lessening. Admiral Sims was ordered out of the North Sea and into the Irish Sea and Admiral Caldwell was ordered back to the east coast of the United States to continue Operation Hammer in that part of the Atlantic.

Beyond question, the German naval authorities at the end of 1917, were preparing to meet the new conditions. Their remaining U-boats were all larger and faster, and were said to have some hull armor and to carry much larger guns than the older, now destroyed, vessels. With the shift to torpedo planes, an increase in torpedo supply was naturally to be expected and it was quite likely that the new torpedoes would have a greater range. Two defects the new U-boats may posses, are being larger they might be more easily detected by the new neff system of the USN, and they might not be built at the same rate of speed and in the same numbers as were the American smaller types.

If the German sinkings do not rise above the level of the first half of 1917, the total tonnage of shipping lost will be 3,320,000 tons. While it is probable that the new German U-boat fleet will be stronger than ever, it would have to be in order to meet the enlarged and constantly growing force of American destroyers and large patrol vessels being supplied to Admiral Sims and Admiral Caldwell.

33

American Expeditionary Force

France, 1917

After the declaration of war by the United States on Germany, April 6, 1917, public opinion in the United States and abroad wondered what part the new member of the Allies would play in the world-wide war. The opinion at home and in the Allied countries seemed to be, that not very much help on the battle fronts would be quickly forthcoming from the great republic on the Western Hemisphere. They looked for financial and economic aid rather than for manpower and gun power. Before the declaration of war, the American army consisted of less than a 100,000 men and experience on the continent had proved that it took from six to nine months to turn out an efficient soldier. In order to make the United States army an efficient fighting force, preparations on a gigantic scale were immediately entered upon. The State National Guard was called into federal service, the regular army and marine corps recruited to full war strength, and the Selective Conscription Act was passed. In Germany, these preparations and the very entrance of the United States into the ground war was laughed at. The American army, in comparison with the well-trained and seasoned German millions, was an object of ridicule. Well known German military experts put the effect of the United States' entrance into the war on a par with that of Rumania's. The feeling was widespread in Germany that even if the United States did raise and equip a big army, she would be unable to transport it to Europe and keep it supplied with materials and provisions, because of the big inroads made on the shipping of the world by U-boat activity. The fact that General Pershing and a peace keeping force of 4,000 arrived safely in April did not mean that an army of a million could survive the crossing of the Atlantic.

The first contingent of an army from the United States to ever fight on European soil disembarked at a French port on June 26 and 27. Major General William L. Sibert, who commanded this force, and his men, received a tremendous ovation. The town and port authorities had declared a holiday, and the khaki clad men marched to their barracks through lanes of men, women and children, waving tiny American flags and shouting, "Vivent les Etats Unis." The transports had several narrow escapes on their way over to France. They were twice unsuccessfully attacked by U-boats, which were driven off by the convoying destroyers of Operation Anvil. Black Jack Pershing had been in France since April, preparing for the coming of the "Sammies" as the French people nicknamed the American soldiers.

Training camps had been located in various parts of France and were ready for occupancy when the troops arrived. Infantry, artillery, cavalry, aviation and medical bases were established. Besides these newly arriving branches, special regiments had been formed in the United States and sent to France as early as 1916. These regiments included engineers, railroad men, lumbermen, laborers and airplane mechanics. The volunteer American ambulance drivers and the Lafayette Escadrille flying squadron in the service of France, were given to General Pershing in April. The number of troops sent "over there" was never divulged by the War Department, Secretary Baker announced that the number being sent over exceeded the Navy's ability to transport them.

The Missouri National Guardsmen were in the first contingent sent to France. The infantrymen were under the command of Captain Fred Wilson who was a baker in Kansas City two months ago. The artillery was under the command of Captain Harry Truman, a local politician from Independence. The cavalry was sent without horses and was under the command of Captain Chase Miller, a shoe salesman from St. Louis. The aviation members were sent without airplanes and joined the Lafayette Escadrille as replacement pilots and the medical members joined the medical corps already established by Black Jack. The Missourians joined the other national guard units in an intensive system of training, consisting of trench digging, bayonet fighting, bomb throwing and the use of gas masks. The instructors were officers and men of the British and French armies, who had seen considerable service at the front. The American transport service took over all railroads leading to the American training bases and a section of a French national forest was turned over to the lumbermen to supply the needs of the expeditionary force.

The news that units of USEF (United States Expeditionary Forces) were in action "somewhere in France" was given out in a dispatch on July 27, 1917. This stated that American artillerymen, under the command of Captain Truman, had fired their first shots into the German lines and that American infantry, under the command of Captain Fred Wilson were in first line trenches. This report of active participation in the war did not mean that American forces had taken over a section of the front, but that they were completing their training under actual war conditions. American patrols, a few nights later, crept out into "No Man's Land" on reconnoitering patrols. At stated intervals the troops in the trenches were changed so that as many of them as possible could be initiated into the real conditions of war. On November 3rd the Berlin official report announced the capture of American troops, when an advance trench in which they were located was cut off from the main trench by a heavy barrage fire. Three Americans were killed, eleven missing and about the same number injured. Although no official after action reports were filed with the War Department, the location of this action was in the Vosges Mountains, where the Rhine-Marne Canal crosses the boundary line of France and Lorraine. During the next few weeks, intermittent artillery duels and patrol engagements occurred but no conflict of any size developed.

After the defeat of the German thrust at Calais, called the battle of Ypress, in early June, the position of the German and Allied lines was very peculiar. They resembled a huge S made backwards. Ypress was in the upper arc and Messines Ridge was in the lower arc of the S. The Allied line was really a great salient bulging into the German line. Messines Ridge in German hands was a serious menace to the entire Allied army at Ypress as there was the ever present danger of an attack in force which could crush the southern side of the Allied defenses and, as a result, reopen the way to Calais. All the high ground artillery positions were in the hands of the Germans and the manner in which the Allies had held on to the Ypress position was almost miraculous.

The objectives of the Allied attack on these positions in late June were to straighten out the lines south of Ypress and to get control of Messines

Ridge which was about 250 feet high, the highest within a radius of 10 miles of this section of the front. General Herbert Plumer was in command. Very careful preparations were made to accomplish the objectives. For over 15 months British and America volunteers had been digging tunnels under the ridge. They placed 19 mines, containing nearly 500 tons of ammonite, under the principle German fortifications, the forward positions consisted of elaborate systems of wired trenches covering an area a mile wide. These were protected by artillery in the rear made up of newly arrived American National Guard units. Early in the morning hours, the mines were set off by electrical contact and a man-made earthquake, awesome and gruesome, occurred. The tops of the hills were blown off and the earth rocked like a ship rolling at sea. The roar of the explosion could be heard within a radius of 150 miles. At the same time the American artillery reached the height of intensity. The greater portion of the German first line trenches and dugouts were obliterated. Then the infantry, composed of English, Irish, Australian and New Zealand units, swept forward on a front extending from Observation Ridge, south of Ypress, to Ploegsteert wood, north of Armentieres. The Americans were held in reserve in case another attack would be needed. Within minutes the entire first line positions were captured on a ten mile front. These included the villages of Messines and Wytschaete. Within a few hours the entire ridge had been cleared and later in the day the back side of the ridge was cleared. The fighting here was stiffer than any yet encountered, but after fierce fighting the village of Oosttaverne and the entire defenses on a five mile front and three miles deep were captured. During this process the American infantry held in reserve, helped move the American and British artillery to the top of the ridge with the result that the Germans were compelled to abandon their lines between the Lys River and the village of St. Yves. Seven thousand prisoners fell into Allied hands and the estimated German casualties were 30,000. The British lost about 10,000 and the Americans none.

The next American involvement was the Battle of Flanders which lasted from July until December of 1917. The successful operations against Messines Ridge in June and the deadlock in the Battle of Arras caused the Allied General Staff to start another offensive in the Ypress section. As in the Messines Ridge Battle, the United States National Guardsmen were held in reserve. General Pershing complained but to no avail. The victory at Messines Ridge enabled the British and French to take their first offensive action of the war, instead of continually being on the defensive.

The British and French did not want the American News Service to report that the offensive was because of the American entrance into the war. Consequently, on July 31, the British and French began an offensive which lasted intermittently to December 31st. The immediate objective of the battle was to get control of the high ground in front of Ypres, called the Passchendaele Ridge. The ultimate objectives were to compel the Germans to retire from the Belgium coast and thus give up their U-boat bases at Ostend and Zeebrugge, and also to envelop the industrial center of Lille and the railway center at Roulers. The entire country in this section is flat with the exception of Passchendaele Ridge. Heavy rains were frequent which made the terrain a veritable sea of mud. Allied troops foundered along up to their knees in it, and artillery was moved only with the greatest difficulty and with the aid of the Americans again.

Twenty days later, on August 20th, the Verdun line became active again, after nine months of comparative quiet. The French were not with any British units to support them and they welcomed the American units sent to them from General Pershing. The combined units started one of their quick thrusts, which would later be their trademark, with a three day American artillery bombardment. When the bombardment lifted, they advanced on both sides of the Meuse River and penetrated a mile across an eleven mile front. Using Teddy Roosevelt tactics, they captured Avocourt Wood, Le Mont Homme, Corbeaux and Cumieres Woods, Cote de Talou, Chapneuville, Mormont Farm and 4,000 prisoners. In the next four days, smashing blows were delivered which resulted in the capture of Regneville, Samogneux, Cote de l'Oie and more than 15,000 prisoners. By September the French and American support units had recovered more than 100 of the 150 miles of territory, which the Germans, under the Crown Prince, had seized in their great, but unsuccessful, offensive. The French army now held all the dominating positions in the Verdun sector.

On October 20, 1917, the United States War Department issued a statement concerning the number of men bearing arms in the great war. The estimates were as follows: Germany 7,000,000; Austria 3,000,000; Turkey 300,000; Bulgaria 300,000; France 6,000,000; Britain 5,000,000; Italy 3,000,000; Japan 1,400,000; United States 1,000,000; China 550,000; Rumania 320,000; Servia 300,000; Belgium 300,000, Greece 300,000; Portugal 200,000; Montenegro 40,000; Siam 36,000; Brazil 32,000 and Cuba 11,000. The most noticeable missing figure was the number of armed men for Russia. When the war started, Russia sent 9,000,000 men into the conflict and during the first two and one-half years, the Russian armies had played a tremendous part in lessening the pressure on the western front. They had proved as a fighting force, that they were superior to the Austrians, although they were defeated invariably by the German armies that they faced. After the Bolsheviki revolution, all fighting ceased. There was a strong undercurrent of pacifism and desire for peace throughout Russia. The Marxist party was opposed to war and negotiated a separate peace. They demobilized their army and ordered all munition factories to stop the manufacture of war material. The collapse of Russia's armies put a burden on the armies of her Allies, especially Italy.

Austria and Germany turned their attention to Italy with the same plan in mind as what happened in Russia. The *Great Italian Retreat* began in October and ended in December. The main Italian army was located in narrow front on the Bainsizza Plateau. The entire line of active fighting was scarcely more than 12 or 15 miles long. With the Bolshevik peace completed, the Austrians and Germans were free to transfer two armies and a great quantity of heavy artillery to throw against the Italians. Faced with superior numbers and superior guns, the Italians began a slow retreat. The Austrian forces opposing them lost no opportunity to harass this retreat as much as possible. On the 27th of October, Vienna announced that they had captured 60,000 men and 500 heavy guns. According to Rome, in a report sent to Paris, most of these prisoners were non-combatants used in repairing mountain roads and were caught behind the battle fronts. The cause of their capture was the seizure of Monte Matajur and the beautiful lake front city at its base. The rapid advance of the Germans and Austrians made the retreat from the Bainsizza and Carso plateaus across hastily constructed bridges over the Isonzo River look like a rout. This first retreat jeopardized the fourth Italian army, which was guarding the frontier in the Arnie Alps. They were compelled to join the first army in a much larger scale retreat. Further German reports announced the capture of 250,000 prisoners and 2300 guns. The retreating Italians prayed for winter snows and on the 23rd of December their prayers were answered and snow closed the mountain passes into lower Italy. The rout of the Italian armies was at a halt.

Before the end of 1917, there was an Allied conference held in Rapallo, Italy, the purpose was to try and save Italy. The shaken Allied members in attendance were Lloyd George (British Premier), the French Premier (Painleve), the Italian Premier (Orlando), Chief of the British Imperial Staff (Robertson) and assorted generals from France, Italy and Britain. No Americans were invited to attend.

War of the Nations

Part VI

Final assembly point for the Caldwell Avenger, near Combles, France American News Service Wire Photo, January 4, 1917

34

Aerial Warfare – Western Front

France, 1917

The year 1917, marked the ever-increasing importance of the modern airplane as a military asset. New and improved types were being produced in great numbers in the United States by the Caldwell Aviation Corporation of America. Jason Edwin Caldwell had founded the parent company, Caldwell Shipping and Trading in 1857. It had endured for the last sixty-one years because he started it as a wholly owned family group of small companies. He encouraged his entire family, starting with his wife, the sister of President James Buchanan, to take an active part and voting member of the board. At his death in 1900, the chairmanship passed to his wife and then his son, James Jason Caldwell, Admiral of the Navy.

The aviation was founded shortly after his second son, Louis Jason Caldwell, visited an assembly plant in Stuttgart, Germany, late in 1905. The American assembly plants were based upon his report and began production in 1906.

Caldwell International Report

Valkyrie Assembly Plant
Stuttgart, Wurtemberg
November 20, 1905

This report may never reach the home office, I will mail it. When I do, the German state security will open and read it. I have begun to protect myself by speaking less and letting Hans do most of the communication. State security is certainly following us on this train. We need to keep them in tow, we can not afford to lose them. It will cause a panic and that is when people can get hurt. I got our letter of introduction from the Kaiser and read it again, it will outline the sections of the plant that we are allowed to visit. It says we are going to get a guided tour of the frame building section, wing assembly area, elevators and rudder sections. There is no mention of the roll control, keel and propulsion, and landing gear assembly points. We will not ask to see them. The photographs that I took of the Valkyries from the zeppelin windows should be enough for my report. I wonder how the new 'idiot proof' hidden camera will work? I can not get a very good photograph with a regular camera.

We needed to keep to the schedule laid out for us by the Kaiser. If we suddenly cut our trip short, that would send a signal to Berlin that we are in some sort of trouble. I decided to lull them to sleep and hope that they will not wake up and bite us in the butt!"

It was a short distance from Kaiserslautern to Stuttgart and the train was entering the station. We waited for our luggage to be brought from the baggage car, we were in first class. We did not notice anyone watching us. We picked up our bags and walked slowly through the train station. We hailed a cab and asked for the hotel that the Kaiser and the Princess had recommended to us. Our driver said he could take us, but it was only one block over and two up. We thanked him and we began walking. We continued slowly up the street towards the hotel. We entered the lobby of the hotel and showed the front desk our letter from the Kaiser. Our room was waiting for us. Once inside, Hans motioned to me that a recording device was probable. I nodded my head, yes, and opened my suitcase so that it could be examined later after we left our room, this we expected, anything we did not want to have seen by a German agent was placed in my brief case. We checked our watches and picked up the hotel telephone in our room and asked if our automobile had arrived from the Valkyrie assembly plant. It had and I thanked them.

A black Daimler was waiting at the curb. Our driver introduced himself and we were there in a few minutes. The plant manager was waiting to greet us as the Daimler stopped outside the factory. He welcomed us to the Stuttgart Valkyrie Assembly Point, SVAP is stamped on every part made and assembled in this plant. He handed us a black leather covered notebook with gold letters SVAP on the cover. I opened it and it contained an outline of the visit. Photographs of all the assembly points, starting with the frame point were clearly identified all written in German.

The Frame Point

A very fine quality of Honduras mahogany is used almost exclusively in the framework. The main members of the frame are two long skids, upon which the rest of the frame is built. These skids are wide apart and take the place of a central chassis. The joints of the frame are made up of aluminum and are very easily bent. All aluminum joints are wire wrapped to increase their ability to withstand the forces of take offs and landings.

As we walked around the framing point, I realized that this plant did not believe in Henry Ford's assembly line. Each assembly point was set up like a giant checker board throughout the plant. Workers moved from point to point rather than have the item moving. Henry's moving assembly line started with a model A frame and ended with a finished automobile. In this German plant, all the frames were started at the same time and workers brought items to be mounted to the frame, in a few days all of the checker board locations had completed aeroplanes. These were rolled out and filled with fuel and the engines started and the process started all over again. A different concept, to be sure.

The Wings

The wings and rest of the body of the Valkyrie are made in three sections, the one between the frames and back of the propeller has a similar chord and less incidence than the other sections because of its position in the slip stream of the propeller. The two outer sections of the plane are turned up slightly, giving a dihedral angle effect. The surfaces are made of one layer of Egyptian cotton fabric stretched tightly over the numerous wooden and aluminum ribs. The plane is braced by cables to the struts and frame of the central section. The spread is 32 feet, the chord is 6.5 feet and the surface area is 190 square feet.

We had walked from the Frame assembly point and watched the workers assemble the wings and the remainder of the fuselage. I read the description in my notebook and examined the photographs provided for us. There was no need for Hans to practice with his brand new, super secret spy camera.

THE ELEVATORS

Out at the front, under the horizontal front fixed keel plane, is the single surface elevation rudder. This is operated by wires leading to a lever which is moved to and fro, as on the H. Farman model biplane. The elevator is 8 feet wide, 2.5 feet deep and 20 square feet in area.

Hans and I stood and watched the workers come to this assembly point with their tools and parts to be placed at the front of the aeroplane. I wondered why the Germans were using this system of assembly, it was exhausting for the workers. We walked on to the next assembly point.

THE DIRECTION RUDDERS

Two identical surfaces at the rear serve as direction rudders. They are controlled by a foot pedal or by the side to side motion of a lever.

I began to see the logic of this method of manufacture. It took about an hour at each assembly point. There were eight assembly points, in eight hours the workers had assembled eight Valkyrie fighters that were ready to fly. The plant was producing 40 aeroplanes a week, that was more than the entire inventory of aeroplanes in the United States Military in the fall of 1905. This was just one model being assembled throughout the German Empire. Hans and I had seen three different models on our flight from Berlin to Kaiserslautern.

THE ROLL CONTROLLER

Ailerons fixed to the trailing edge of the main surface at either end control the transverse balance. They can be operated by pedals or by side to side motion of the lever, as desired. These ailerons are 5 feet wide and 2 feet deep.

Hans looked at me and smiled. He was thinking the same thing that I was thinking, this is not spying, the whole plant is open for anyone who wants to tour the plant and purchase an aeroplane. This is not a military secret, it is a commercial enterprise to improve the economy of the German Empire.

The Keel

The Valkyrie has a large horizontal keel placed well out in front and called the "leading plane", it is 14 feet wide and 3 feet deep. It exerts a considerable lift and is set at a greater incident angle than the main surface, thus employing the principle of the dihedral angle for longitudinal balance. The incident angle of this plane can be altered at will. There is no rear tail.

At this assembly point I understood the genius of the German design. The rear seat of a two seated Valkyrie would machine gun off a rear tail when in a dog fight. I wondered how the pilot fired his forward machine guns without destroying the propeller.

The Propulsion

A 30 horse power Benz engine, placed at the center in front of the main plane, drives a 7.5 foot propeller at 900 rpm. The position of the propeller is a curious one, working as it does in a slot in the framework. The rotation of the propeller is timed so that the firing pin of the machine guns does not engage when the propeller is vertical to the ground.

All I had to do was read my notebook, this was the secret of how the forward pointing machine guns worked.

The Landing Gear

The landing gear is purchased from the United States Wright factory and attached directly to the skids. This combination of serviceable skids and the Wright gear make this the safest aeroplane in the world. On each skid at the front, below the seats, is fitted a pair of wheels attached by springs and at the rear are two smaller wheels.

I noticed that the seats were very conveniently placed out in front of the motor. In case of an accident, this position appeared to me to be extremely dangerous for the pilot. The center of gravity appears to me to be very far forward and would necessitate a considerable lift on the part of the leading plane.

I closed my notebook and handed it back to the plant manager. He told me I could keep the notebook with the Kaiser's complements. I thanked him, asked him jokingly if he had any aeroplanes for sale. He did not seem surprised. He began writing out a factory order for a two seat Valkyrie. I again asked him, jokingly, if he accepted bank drafts. He nodded his head, yes. I opened my brief case and wrote him a check from the Caldwell International Account, Copenhagen. I told him I would like the certificate of ownership to be made out in the name of Caldwell Trading and Shipping, Copenhagen. I also told him I would like the plane delivered to our airfield in Copenhagen next month. I asked if he saw a problem with that. He shook his head, no and told me that I could have it next week, if I liked. He also gave me a heads up that the Danish would not allow an armed aeroplane to land in Copenhagen. The aeroplane would be flown to our airfield and the guns would be sent separately in crates marked *spare parts.*

We left the Valkyrie Assembly Plant with the notebooks under our arms and a bill of sale for a Valkyrie to be flown to Copenhagen next week. Hans was shaking his head and said, "Louis, CI just wanted photographs and specifications, not the whole aeroplane."

"I think my father will be overjoyed when we ship him the plane in large wooden crates to be reassembled and test flown in the United States. It is time that our military sees what they are up against from the Europeans."

James Caldwell decided to build aeroplanes and airplanes based upon his son's report. He met with his family controlled board of directors and explained it this way, "Your brother, Louis, and I have just finished writing the 1906, report of *Naval Progress/Aviation* for your Uncle Teddy. It is probably an accurate accounting of progress within the United States, but it is not the progress made world wide. France, Germany and Japan are far ahead of the efforts made in the United States. The trap we fall into, is believing that anything worthwhile must have been invented in the United States. In the case of the automobile and aviation, this is certainly true. The record of accomplishment in aviation did not begin with the flight of the Wright brothers, December 19, 1903. That is the date of the first flight in the United States. It took us nearly two years, September 26, 1905, before a flight of an hour's duration was made by these American inventors. Compare our progress with that made by the German Empire. A flight of four Valkyries left an airfield and met the zeppelin Louis was riding in and escorted him for over an hour. This flight was replaced by a different flight of different manufacture and then escorted him for another hour. A third flight of still another model of aeroplane escorted him the final hours of the flight. These were called long range aeroplanes. You may want to review the report sent to you of his tour of the Valkyrie assembly plant in Germany.

Henry Farman in England has made longer, cross-country flights, while Louis Bleriot, of France, has flown from France to England across open ocean. Japan destroyed the Russian fleet with bombs dropped from their aeroplanes. Some countries have developed separate air forces, which operate independently from their armies and navies. The number of pilots within the United States is estimated at less than a hundred. The number of pilots being trained in Germany, for example, is 220 per month to keep pace with the number of airframes being produced.

The effort within the United States is research. The effort throughout Europe is development, from your brother's observations. I shudder to read from US reports, statements like, *From such beginnings and early flights, the use of the aeroplane, as well as the mechanical efficiency and construction of the machine itself, will be researched until the beginning of 1906. Further research and theoretical knowledge of aviation must be completed to a point where the problems of the air and its navigation are well recognized.* This is what I read about bi-winged aeroplanes!

Meanwhile, in Germany, the mono-wing airplane is being researched and tested. An airplane is not like an aeroplane with two wings. The airplane has a single supporting surface, whose possibilities far surpass anything presently built in America, England or France. If an aeroplane and an airplane meet in combat, it will be suicide for the pilot of the aeroplane. It is the purpose of the airplane to fly anywhere from 10 to 20 times faster than the bi-wing. A bi-wing frame is made of wood in the United States and wood and aluminum in Europe. Both versions fall apart upon emergency landings and the pilot dies upon impact with the earth. There is no wood construction in an airplane. An airplane has hollow, high tensile steel tubes for its framework. By the end of 1906, I see a gradual development in all fields of aviation throughout Europe, not just Germany.

This, as will be shown in this CI report, was in general, the tendency throughout the world, except the United States. There was not an undue imitation of successful machines by the many world manufacturers, but more or less development along original lines. This was evidenced by the fact that during the year it was estimated that some 100 different types of aeroplanes were in use. Naturally, there was also an increased number of aviators. In all branches of aviation there was considerable development, and the machines produced were of greater efficiency than in previous years. A large number of exhibitions were held in all the leading countries of the world and various competitions took place. The United States did not win a single competition. The reason for this is obvious. Vast amount of investments were made by manufacturers of machines in Europe, which already had begun to number long-established engineering firms, yet it was considered that the commercial possibilities would rest rather in the military use than in more general fields. Numerous sales were made to foreign governments, including our own purchase of a German Valkyrie. It is presently undergoing military tests in England, under US supervision. I would recommend the purchase of any and all foreign made aircraft for comparison testing.

Owing to competitions and military applications, the main aim in the design and construction of machines during the year was to increase speed, and this naturally required engines of greater horsepower, so that motors from 140 to 200 horsepower were being fitted to the more recent aeroplanes. With the increase in speed, the dangers of flight were diminished, especially under unfavorable conditions of weather and changes of wind directions. The most apparent shortcoming in the aeroplane of 1905, was the inability of the aviator to control his speed as desired, and especially to start his motor again in case of stoppage or sudden failure.

An interesting feature is the construction of aeroplanes and airplanes with bodies more closely resembling that of a bird, which became most marked in the Austrian Etrich airplane. These completely covered bodies with enclosed cockpits, were first developed in the case of the German airplane design mentioned earlier. The enclosed fuselage was found much more useful to support the propeller and side planes than a construction of spars and at the same time it diminished wind resistance. Furthermore, such covering naturally involved the enclosing of the motor, and at the

Paris Aviation Salon, held in December, it was noted that most of the more advanced types of machines were built with enclosed motors.

Another tendency of the year was the replacement of all cloth covered wings and fuselages with thin sheets of aluminum. At the Paris Salon, 42 airplanes were exhibited, six were built entirely of hollow steel, the rest were a mixture of steel, aluminum and wood frames. In the general design of the planes, various conditions had to be taken into consideration. The ability to warp the wings being controlled by the Wright patents, some other means was required by other manufacturers. Yet the flexibility of the planes themselves was no longer desired if smaller controlling planes or ailerons could be used. These have been found very satisfactory, and they figure in most of the aeroplanes of the day. Some device for reducing the size of the surface plane, or reefing them, was also suggested, as by telescoping, but nothing practical along these lines was forthcoming.

Taken all in all, the great tendency of aeroplane design was the reduction of wind resistance and supporting surfaces, and using the power of the motor to compensate for it. With the increased power and means of control at their disposal, aviators during the year were able to fly under conditions of wind which previously would have been considered impossible. Flights in winds up to thirty miles an hour were not uncommon, and in the long-distance trips the amount of time lost by bad weather was being greatly diminished."

The sub-assembly of airplanes for the war in Europe began inside Caldwell Aviation in late 1914, not April 6, 1917, when war was declared by the United States. The first shipment of airplane sections (frame, wings, elevators, rudder/roll controller, keel, propulsion and landing gear) were sent to France in early 1915 when the American flyers showed up to join the Lafayette Escadrille flying squadron. Caldwell engineers and mechanics were on the ground in France to supervise the final assembly of the American version of the German Valkyrie called the *"Avenger."* Of course the French immediately renamed them the " Les Liberator's"

Le Liberator was called the eyes of the French army and lived up to this name more and more as the great battles of January to December, 1917, were fought. During the battle of Somme and the great German withdrawal, General Haig depended on his air service to find out just what the Germans were doing and where the strategic points of the "Hindenburg Line" were located. A large aeroplane, manufactured by Caldwell, and intended to carry the US mail was also sold and delivered to the Rome assembly point, the Italians renamed it the *Caproni*. Fleets of 150 or more *Caproni* would fly low to the ground and drop bombs on the advancing Germans chasing the retreating Italian army. They bombed German lines of communication and munition dumps or they would rake the enemy below with heavy machine-gun fire.

The ability of the Caldwell machines to be mass produced and supplied in great quantities changed the progression of the war and naturally stimulated the discovery and use of methods to counteract their activities. One of the most effective was the use of camouflage. This was the covering of trenches, artillery and other things of military value with netting containing limbs from trees, painted objects and other ground clutter, so that it would be hard to distinguish them from the landscape.

Very few Caldwell machines were involved in "dog fights" over the western front. They were considered to be too valuable to risk in individual, pilot to pilot, engagements in the air over the battlefront. Hundreds of them, spectacular and daring, occurred every week of 1917, and the deeds of any one airman did not stand much above those of others. To give an idea of the activity, the official reports for a few months might provide an example; April, 717 machines were lost on the Western Front alone. In May, 713, In July, 467 and in September 704 were lost in single combat.

About 25 aerial raids were made over England during 1917, which destroyed a considerable amount of property and killed a number of civilians. The military damage was practically nil. Probably the most successful raid from the German point of view was that on June 13. It was carried out in broad daylight and resulted in 437 casualties and the death of 97 persons, including 26 school children. The most disastrous from the German point of view was the one made on the night of October 19th. At least 11 Zeppelins participated and on their way home five were lost in French territory. One was captured undamaged at Bourbonne-les-Bains. Twenty-seven were killed and 53 wounded as a result of this raid. Since the beginning of the war to January 1918, a compilation of British reports show that as a result of air raids 616 persons have been killed and 1630 wounded in England.

35

Death of a Son

France, 1917

Not a single extended family could escape the news that one of their loved ones "over there" was sick, injured, or was dying. In 1917, when the "dough boys" received their selective service notices, boarded trains for the training camps all over America, some of them died of influenza, training accidents or died in France. When Teddy Roosevelt's youngest son, Quentin, decided to use his private flying skills and volunteer for the Lafayette Escadrille, his father and I were naturally concerned. Our son, James, was already at risk in a submarine and now another member of the family wanted to be a pilot. The life expectance of an American volunteer in the Lafayette Escadrille was less than six months. The odds were against him that he would ever return home. Teddy was a personal acquaintance of hundreds of the American air pilots, especially those on Long Island, many of whom had been home with his son to Oyster Bay. Every week that Quentin, Kermit, Archie or Teddy Jr. were home since the war began, they had been visited by men from all branches of the service. After Quentin left for France and his tour of duty, the War Camp Community Service made a practice of coming out to Oyster Bay to visit with Colonel Roosevelt every Saturday afternoon. Some of Quentin's buddies would bring their letters from Quentin and share them with Ruth and Teddy. My sister and Teddy would be on the front porch waiting to give them a real Roosevelt welcome.

When these flyers left for France, Ruth and Teddy were in regular correspondence with them. Teddy took the deepest pleasure in the letters which he received from many of these flyers. When the telegram from the War Department arrived at Oyster Bay, Teddy refused to open it. He handed it to his wife and said, "Ruthie we have lost him."

Only the members of Teddy's extended family and his most intimate friends knew how deeply he suffered because of the death of his youngest son in France on July 14th. This news, I believe, coupled with his attack at the Republican Convention caused Teddy Roosevelt to loose his zest for life and he began a slow slide toward his own death in January of the next year.

Teddy had refused to open the telegram because two days before, an American News Service Correspondent had given him his inkling that this had occurred when she asked him about the report of a Roosevelt family member killed in France. As soon as the reporter asked him, he took her by the arm into another room so his wife should not learn the topic that was under discussion.

"Theodore, our oldest son, and Archie are both in hospitals, wounded. Kermit is on his way from Mesopotamia to France. It must be either Quentin or Kermit killed in an accident."

When the news was confirmed the next day, Teddy, who had always declared that families should accept cheerfully the sacrifice of their sons in the war, went to his office at 347 Madison Avenue as usual, attended to his work and later issued a statement in which he said that he and my sister, Ruth took pride in their son's service to his country. In truth, he was shattered emotionally but he wanted to continue with his life's work. The following week he kept his engagement to address the Republican State Convention at Saratoga Springs, New York, where the enthusiasm for him resulted in an attempt to nominate him to run for Governor of New York. His response was typical Teddy Roosevelt, "Been there, done that. Too bad my cousin Franklin is not a Republican, he would make an excellent Governor of New York!"

Franklin Roosevelt had other ideas as to what office he would like to hold. Before working in the Woodrow Wilson campaign for president in 1912, he was a state senator from New York. In the State of New York election of 1910, Franklin ran for the state senate from the district around Hyde Park in Duchess County, which had not elected a Democrat since 1884. He had the Roosevelt name, with its associated wealth, prestige and influence in the Hudson Valley, and the Democratic landslide that year carried him to the state capital Albany. Franklin took his seat on January 1, 1911. He became the leader of a group of "Insurgents" who opposed the Tammy machine which dominated the state Democratic Party. The US Senate election which began with the Democratic caucus on January 16, 1911, was deadlocked by the struggle of the two factions for 74 days. On March 31, James O'Gorman was elected and Franklin had achieved his goal: to upset the Tammy machine by blocking their choice, William Sheehan. Franklin soon became a popular figure among the New York Democrats. He was re-elected for a second term in the state election of 1912, but resigned to accept his appointment as Assistant Secretary of the Navy.

In 1914, Franklin ran for the US Senate from the State of New York, but was defeated by Tammy Hall-backed James Gerard. He returned to his post as assistant to Josephus Daniels and remained in that position until the end of the second Wilson term. He was not out of politics, however, he was active in the presidential primary campaign and worked for Governor James M. Cox of Ohio. Cox had promised him a spot on the upcoming ticket and the race for president and vice-president in 1920.

36

Presidential Address

Congress, January 8, 1918

President Wilson addressed Congress outlining the war aims of America on January 8, 1918. The message met with universal approval and was instantly hailed as the Magna Charta of future peace. In conjunction with Premier Lloyd-George's similar utterance, it laid the war aims of the Allies for the first time clearly before the world.

"Gentlemen of the Congress:"

"Once more, as repeatedly before, the spokesmen of the Central Empires have indicated their desire to discuss the objectives of the war and the possible basis of a general peace. Parleys have been in progress at Brest-Litovsk between Russian representatives and representatives of Germany and Austria, to which the attention of all the belligerents have been invited for the purpose of ascertaining whether it may be possible to extend these parlays into a general conference with regard to terms of peace and settlement. The Russian representatives presented not only a perfectly definite statement of the principles upon which they would be willing to conclude peace, but also an equally definite program for the concrete application of those principles. The representatives of the Central Powers, on their part, presented an outline of settlement which, if much less definite, seemed susceptible of liberal interpretation until their specific program of practical terms is adopted. That program proposed no concessions at all, either to the sovereignty of Russia or to the preferences of the population with whose fortune is dealt, but meant, in a word, that the Empires of Germany and Austria were to keep every foot of territory their armed forces have occupied – every province, every city, every point of vantage – as a permanent addition to their empires and their political power. It is a reasonable conjecture that the general principles of settlement, which they at first suggested, originated with the more liberal statesmen of Germany and Austria, the men who have begun to feel the force of their own people's thought and purpose, while the concrete terms of actual settlement came from the military leaders, who have no thought but to keep what they have obtained. The negotiations have been broken off. The Russian representatives were sincere and in earnest. They cannot entertain such proposals of conquest and domination."

"The whole incident is full of significance. It is also full of perplexity. With whom are the Russian representatives dealing? For whom are the representatives of the Central Empires speaking? Are they speaking for the majorities of their representative Parliaments, or for the minority parties, that military and imperialistic minority which has so far dominated their whole policy and controlled the affairs of Turkey and of the Balkan States, which have felt obliged to become their associates in this war? The Russian representatives have insisted, very justly, very wisely, and in the true spirit of modern democracy, that the conferences they have been holding with the Teutonic and Turkish statesmen should be held with open, not closed, doors and all the world has been audience, as was desired. To whom have we been listening? To those who speak the spirit and intention of the resolutions of the German Reichstag of the 9th of July last, the spirit and intention of the liberal leaders and parties of Germany, or to those who resist and defy that spirit and intention and insist upon conquest and subjugation? Or are we listening, in fact, to both, unreconciled and in open and hopeless contradiction? These are very serious and pregnant questions. Upon the answer to them depends the peace of the world."

"But whatever the results of the parlays at Brest-Litovsk, whatever the confusions of council and of purpose in the utterances of the spokesmen of the Central Empires, they have again attempted to acquaint the world with their object in the war and have again challenged their adversaries to say what their objects are and what sort of settlement they would deem just and satisfactory. There is no good reason why that challenge should not be responded to, and responded to with the utmost candor. We did not wait for it. Not once, but again and again we have laid our whole thought and purpose before the world, not in general terms only, but each time with sufficient definition to make it clear what sort of definite terms of settlement must necessarily spring out of them. Within the last week Mr. Lloyd-George has spoken with admirable candor and in admirable spirit, for the people and Government of Great Britain. There is no confusion of counsel among us, the adversaries, of the Central Empires, no uncertainty of principle, no vagueness of detail. The only failure to make definite statement of the objects of the war, lies with Germany and her allies."

"The program of the world's peace, therefore, is in our hands and that program, the only possible program, as we see it, is this:

1. Open covenants of peace, openly arrived at, after which there shall be no private international understandings of any kind but diplomacy shall proceed always frankly and in public view.
2. Absolute freedom of the seas.
3. Removal of all economic barriers and the establishment of trade between all nations consenting to the peace agreement.
4. Adequate guarantees that national armaments will be reduced to self-defense status.
5. A free, open-minded adjustment of all colonial claims to include the right of self-determination of the peoples involved.
6. The evacuation of all Russian territory.
7. The evacuation of all Belgium territory.
8. The evacuation of all French territory.
9. The evacuation of all Italian territory.
10. Austria-Hungary shall cease to be an empire and its people are free to develop autonomous development.
11. Rumania, Servia and Montenegro are to be evacuated.
12. The Ottoman Empire shall cease to exist, the Dardanelles shall be permanently open as a free passage to all the ships of the world.
13. The state of Poland shall be erected which includes all the Polish speaking peoples.
14. The League of Nations shall be formed under specific covenants for the purpose of affording mutual guarantees of political independence and territorial integrity to all states alike."

"In regard to these essential rectifications of wrong and assertions of right, we feel ourselves to be intimate partners of all the governments and peoples associated together against the imperialist empire builders. We cannot be separated in interest or divided in purpose. We stand together until the end.

For such arrangements and covenants we are willing to fight and continue to fight, until they are achieved; but only because we wish the right of prevail and desire a just and stable peace, such as can be secured only by removing the chief provocations to war, which this program does remove. We have no jealousy of German greatness and there is nothing in this program that impairs it. We grudge her no achievement or distinction of learning or of specific enterprise, such as have made her record very bright and very enviable. We do not wish to injure her or to block in any way her legitimate influence or power. We do not wish to fight her either with arms or with hostile arrangements of trade, if she is willing to associate herself with us and the other peace-loving nations of the world in covenants of justice and law and fair dealing. We wish her only to accept a place of equality among the peoples of the world. Neither do we presume to suggest to her any alteration of modification, but it is necessary to say, that we must know for whom she is speaking. Is she speaking for a free peoples, or is she speaking for the Reichstag and the military whose creed is imperial domination. We will not deal with the latter.

We have spoken now, surely in terms concrete enough not to be misunderstood. An evident principle runs through the 14 points I have outlined. It is the principle of justice to all peoples and nationalities and their God given rights to life and liberty of choice. The people of the United States will not act upon any other principle. To this end, I pledge our very lives, honor and everything that we possess. The moral climax of this the culminating and final war for human liberty has come, we are ready to put our own existence to the test."

37

American News Service Clips

January, 1918

January 2 – Secretary Lansing makes public a resume of the work accomplished by the American War Mission abroad. A coordination of war plans, a pooling of resources and a speedy dispatch of large American fighting forces (300,000 a month) are the salient features. London reports that German raids on the British lines between Lens and St. Quentin are repulsed with heavy loss of the enemy. American artillery has been active in France in Belgium, but there has been no infantry action.

The English loss in ships week ending today is 18. The average number of vessels of more than 1,600 tons sunk weekly during the last year is 16.6.

Italians disperse flotilla loaded with Austrian troops attempting to cross the Piave River at Intestadura.

Officials from Petrograd state that Germany demands Russia cede Poland, Courland, Esthonia and Lithuania to the German Empire. A Russian refusal is said to have caused a rupture of the peace negotiations at Brest-Litovsk. A Petrograd dispatch states that thousands of officers of the regular army are flocking to the standard of General Kaledines, the Cossack commander, who is said to have organized a corps of 20,000 men.

January 3 – General Korniloff, former Commander-in-Chief of the Russian Armies, who was unofficially reported dead, arrives in the district of the Don Cossacks to join with Kaledines. Foreign Minister Trotzky declares the Russian workers will not consent to the German peace terms and enslavement in German work camps. The new Russian sentiment is for the resumption of hostilities with Germany.

January 4 – A growing disposition to recognize the Lenin Government, if it can demonstrate a fair degree of support from the Russian people, is reported in London. Concerning the rejection of the German peace terms, Chancellor Von Hertling, before the Reichstag Committee, says, "Germany can afford to wait further developments, relying on her strong position, her loyal intentions and her just rights."

January 5 – American aviators dropped bombs over the German lines in reprisal for the killing of two American News Service reporters. Leon Trotzky returned to Brest-Litovsk to resume peace negotiations with Germany. Turkey offers Russia free passage of the Dardanelles in return for Russian evacuation of Turkish territory and the demobilization of the Black Sea fleet. Turkey is to retain her army because of the continuation of the war with the Allies. Premier Lloyd-George, in a speech before delegates of trades-unions, again sets forth Britain's war aims. The "reconsideration" of the Alsace-Lorraine seizure, the restoration of Belgium and reparation for injuries inflicted is required. The restoration of Servia, Montenegro and the occupied parts of France, Italy and Romania are the principal demands. Russia, he declares, can now only be saved by her own people, but an independent Poland is urgently necessary for the stability of Europe.

January 6 – Rome announces a vigorous fire all along the Italian front with great aerial activity. Because the request of the Russian Government that the peace conference be transferred to Stockholm, all negotiations have been temporarily suspended by Berlin.

January 7 – The United States Supreme Court delivers decision upholding the constitutionality of the Army Draft Law. Increasing activity on the Asiago Plateau, where Italians bombard enemy transports and moving columns is reported. British patrols cross the Piave at various points. The Bolshevik Government is prepared to resume the offensive against Germany. All points on the Russian front are being strengthened and disaffected troops are being sent into the interior. The British War Office issued the following statement of captures and losses in 1917: captures are 114,544, losses are 28,379.

January 8 – President Wilson announced in a speech before Congress his famous 14 points which alone could be the basis of peace with Germany. The British and French Governments expressed their entire agreement with the groundwork for peace as established by President Wilson.

January 9 – The French penetrate German positions on a front of a mile and to a depth of half a mile in front of Flirey and westward to St. Mihiel, 130 villages reported razed by Germans as they retreated.

January 10 – The Republic of Finland was recognized by Denmark, Norway and Switzerland.

January 11 – Trotzky resumes talks with Germans at Brest-Litovsk. Baron Von Kuhlmann announces that, owing to non-acceptance by all enemy powers, the Central Powers had withdrawn their offer to conclude a general peace, without forcible annexations or indemnities. At the suggestion of Trotzky, the armistice was extended for another month, beginning January 12.

January 12 – Two German attacks, accompanied by liquid fire, were driven back by the French before Chaume Wood.

January 13 – Russian Black Sea fleet at Sebastopol defect to Turkey.

January 14 – Joseph Caillaux, former Premier of France, and two of his associates are arrested on a charge of treason.

January 15 – Italians deliver surprise attacks in the Monte Asolone region and east of Capo Sile.

January 16 – Secretary Lansing makes public, the secret code correspondence between Count von Bernstorf and Caillaux and agents of Germany.

January 17 – A dispatch from Berlin reports that an official statement on the peace negotiations at Brest-Litovsk says that the withdrawal of troops from the occupied Russian territories is impossible while the war lasts.

January 18 – The War Trade Board makes public, drastic regulations for the supplying of fuel, coal and stores to vessels in American ports.

January 19 – An attack by the enemy, on a wide front on the lower Piave, is stopped with the exception of a few groups which are wiped out on reaching the Italian wire entanglements.

January 20 – German raids at St. Quentin and Courtecon are repulsed. The French are active again in the Verdun sector.

January 21 – The British Admiralty announces that action with Turkey at the entrance of the Dardanelles results in the sinking of the Turkish cruisers *Midulla* and *Selin*.

January 22 – Berlin claims continued success in reconnoitering expeditions on the French front and states that the artillery fighting in Flanders below Lens is particularly heavy.

January 23 – The French freight transport *La Drome* and the trawler *Kervihan* were sunk by mines off Marseilles.

January 24 – The German and Austrian governments replied to President Wilson's presentation of the 14 points. Germany objected strongly to any proposition that would entail loss of territory of the Empire. The reply of Austria was more favorable, but neither country accepted the terms outlined. The Supreme War Council at a meeting held at Versailles decided that by force of arms only could any equitable peace be reached. The sinking of the British troopship *Tuscania* caused a loss of 200 American soldiers.

January 25 – German Foreign Minister, Von Kuhlmann, speaks in the main committee of the Reichstag, justifying the policy pursued by the German representatives at Brest-Litovsk and denounces the Bolsheviki as ruling by force.

January 26 – French troops repulse raids west of St. Gobain between the Oise and the Ailette Rivers.

January 27 – The Cunard liner *Andania* is torpedoed off the Ulster Coast.

January 28 – The Irish steamer *Cork* is sunk Germany.

January 29 – French penetrate deep into Upper Alsace.

January 30 – Paris is bombed by German airplanes.

January 31 – Increasing unrest in Germany, one million workers on strike and munitions factories are closed. Immediate peace with Russia are worker's demands.

38

President Responds to Germany
February 11, 1918

President Wilson asked to address Congress a second time to outline the war aims of America on February 11, 1918. The president wished to reply to speeches of Von Hertling and Count Czerin.

"Gentlemen of the Congress:"

"It will be our wish and purpose that the processes of peace, when they are begun, shall be absolutely open and that they shall involve and permit, henceforth, no secret understandings of any kind. The day of conquest and aggrandizement is gone. So is the day of secret covenants entered into in the interest of particular governments. It is this happy fact, now clear to the view of every public man whose thoughts do not still linger in an age that is dead and gone. We make it possible for every nation, whose purposes are consistent with justice, to avow now the objectives it has in view.

After all, the test of whether it is possible for either government to go any further in this comparison of views, is simple and obvious. The principles to be applied are these:

First – That each part of the final settlement must be based upon the essential justice of that particular case, and upon such adjustments as are most likely to bring peace.

Second – That peoples and provinces are not to be bartered about from nation to nation as though they were cattle to be traded at market.

Third – Every territorial settlement involved in this war must be made in the interest and for the benefit of the populations concerned and not as a part of any mere adjustment or compromise of claims among rival States and finally....

Fourth – That all well-defined national aspirations shall be accorded the utmost satisfaction that can be accorded them without introducing new or perpetuating old elements of discord and antagonism that would be likely in time to break the peace of Europe and of the World. These four principles do not replace the 14 points previously presented to Germany – they are an application of those 14 points.

A general peace erected upon such foundations cannot be discussed, until such a peace can be secured. We have no choice but to go on with this war. So far as we can judge, these principles that we regard as fundamental are already everywhere accepted as imperative except among the spokesmen of the military and annexationist party in Germany. If they have anywhere else been rejected, the objectors have not been sufficiently numerous or influential to make their voices heard. The tragic circumstances is that this one party in Germany is apparently willing and able to send millions of men to their deaths to prevent what all the world now sees to be just. Who will we offer peace to after the last man in Germany is dead?"

The members of congress bolted to their feet and interrupted the President's speech for 20 minutes. This is what they expected two years ago from the White House. Members of the military establishment of the United States were invited to hear President Wilson's address to Congress and I was sitting beside Franklin Roosevelt. He turned to me and said, "Finally, he is willing to give the Huns a clear choice, peace or death, take your pick."

"Franklin, what did you report to the president about your observations in France?"

"He never requested a report and I did not offer to write one. I was home in the finger lake district of western New York and he did not even come to see me. He has never seen these." He place his hands on the metal braces inside both pants legs. "I cannot work an entire day without the use of these. My legs are still too weak, they need the support. My doctors said that the Guillain-Barre syndrome I brought back from France could reappear at any time and if it does, I should use a wheelchair – but that is out of the question. I am always going to be an elected politician, and no voter has ever voted for someone in a wheelchair."

"You move around the Army Navy Building with ease, Franklin. Do you remember the first day I reported for duty?"

"Yes, I do, why?"

"You took off with those long legs and long stride and I could barely keep up with you!"

"You would have no trouble doing so now, James. I believe people reap what they sow. I went to Groton, an Episcopal boarding school in Massachusetts, as an only child, my parents wanted me out of the house and I became close with my headmaster, Endicott Peabody, who preached to me everyday about my oversexed pursuit of the opposite sex. I never listened to him and when I entered Harvard, I lived in the 'gold coast' area where wealthy and privileged students lived in luxurious quarters. As a member of Alpha Delta Phi fraternity, the binge of sex continued. There was never a shortage of young women wanting to marry a millionaire. While I was at Harvard, my cousin, Teddy, moved into the White House. You moved with him as I remember."

"Yes, it was after the death of McKinley and the place was in an uproar, I remember you coming to see Teddy in 1902. That is when you met Eleanor, wasn't it?"

"No, I knew her as a child when we went to our great grandparent's reunions, but that is the first time I ever noticed her as a woman. We are both descended from Claes Martensz van Rosenvelt who arrived in New Amsterdam from the Netherlands in 1640. The Rosenvelt's had two grandsons, Johannes and Jacobus. These two started the Long Island and Hudson River branches of the Roosevelt family. Eleanor and Teddy were descended from the Johannes branch and I am from the Jacobus branch. When did your ancestors arrive in America, James?"

"1701, from Ireland, they entered the Colony of South Carolina and made their fortunes from large land holdings, merchant marine shipping and various other enterprises in the western territories."

"Caldwell Industries is well known today, James. Both our families have done wonderful things for this country. I always look to the future but right now, mine is rather bleak."

"Bleak, you just recovered from polio. It will take sometime to put your life back together."

"So, you heard about my separation from Eleanor?"

"No, what happened?"

"It is a continuation of my life of sin, I guess. I managed to graduate from Harvard in 1904. I entered Columbia Law School that same year, but dropped out in 1905, because I passed the New York State Bar exam. By that time Eleanor and I were married, we were married in March, 1905, I do not remember the day. It was not important to me at the time. I was getting married to produce another branch of the Roosevelt tree. We moved into my mother's house in Springwood and started having children; Anna, 1906; James, 1907; FDR jr., 1909 still born; Elliot, 1910; FDR again in 1914 and finally John Aspinwall in 1916 just before President Wilson wanted me to go to France with Black Jack Pershing."

"That sounds like you were happy, Franklin."

"I was not, my mother was terrible to try and live with, always trying to take charge of everything, Eleanor hated her. Eleanor was always pregnant and in a foul mood. Things came undone for me when I traveled with Black Jack and met a French woman, Marguerite LeHand. I hired her and sent her to Springwood as my personal secretary. Eleanor saw right through that sham, she saw that Marguerite was in love. She wrote to me in France and offered to give me my freedom to marry the woman I loved. Before I could write and lie about my affair, my legs went out from under me, literally. I was shipped home on one of your transports and my mother, Sara, had a little talk with me. She said if I divorced Eleanor, I would bring scandal upon the family, and that she would not give me another dollar."

"So what happened, why are you separated?"

"Separated may be too strong a word for what it is, James. It is a marriage of convenience, she bought an estate in Hyde Park, called Valkill, where she devotes herself to various social and political causes."

"How is this going to affect your political future, Franklin?"

"It already has affected it, my opponents will use it against me when ever I run for public office. I have a bright future in the Democratic Party, James. There is talk of placing me on the ticket as Vice-president in the next election. I need to complete the next assignment that Woodrow Wilson has asked me to do. If I am successful with the demobilization of the Navy after the war, maybe my political career will not be a shambles."

"I have spent the last few years trying to build the Navy into something respectable for national defense. It is interesting that President Wilson is already considering taking it apart." I didn't say anything else as the demonstration for the president's speech died down and he completed his address. I returned to my office in the Army Navy building and realized why it looked so "dog eared." Admiral Dewey was trying to keep the place afloat after the demobilization of the last great naval war for America. I decided that I did not want to become a 'care taker' and I started making plans for what I would do after the War of Nations was history.

The remainder of February contained the following news clips:

February 12 – Germany announces that the Bolsheviki has declared the state of war with the Teutonic powers is at an end and has demobilized the Russian army. Lloyd-George replies to Chancellor von Hertling and Count Czerin in a speech before Parliament.

February 13 – Washington reports $50,000,000 loaned to Italy, making the total of $550,000,000 to Italy and $4,734,400.000 to allied nations. American News Service has estimated that the number of German troops massed on the Western front is 2,100,000.

February 15 – Eight British patrol boats hunting U-boats in the straits of Dover are sunk by a flotilla of enemy destroyers.

February 16 – Dover is bombarded by German aircraft. In Belgium and France, British repulse German raids south of the Scarpe while French forces penetrate the German lines near Vauquoise. German aircraft cross the Kent coast of the Thames estuary at night to bomb London.

February 17 – Night raids on London continued, while French raids increase along the fronts in France and Belgium.

February 18 – A third consecutive air raid on London, this time during the day time and they were driven off by the Royal Air Force. This marked the 100th air raid over London. Germany invades Russia on the expiration of the armistice agreement between Russia and Germany.

February 19 – The Bolshevist Government issues a statement, signed by Lenin and Trotzky, announcing that Russia has been forced to surrender. The German terms included the retention of Poland, Lithuania, Estonia, Livonia and Moon Island.

February 20 – British advance to three miles east of Jerusalem. The French capture a large part of Lorraine.

February 21 – British capture Jerusalem. Germany invades Finland, while British troops take over for the exhausted French army south of St. Quentin.

February 22 – Turkey retreats across the Jordan. The German army tries to occupy Russia, resistance is ordered by Bolshevist Government, and Petrograd declared in state of siege. Germany makes new peace offer, calling for the cession of more Russian territory.

February 23 – Germany demands unconditional surrender of Russian army and navy.

February 24 – Russia accepts Germany peace terms, while the German cruiser *Wolf* returns to Kiel after sinking eleven Russian vessels.

February 27 – Germany begins bombing campaign of French territory behind the lines around Nancy. Germany army fails to capture Butte de Mesnil.

February 28 – Germany begins bombing campaign of Belgium territory behind the lines north of Dixmude.

39

Future Planning

March, 1918

As Germany was launching her long delayed super-offensive, I was planning the family's future. I walked over to the White House and entered the Department of State office and asked to see Captain Caldwell. The office receptionist smiled and said, "Your son is writing his 'butt kicking' memos to England again, Admiral. I doubt you will disturb him, he is on a roll. Go right in."

"Dad, what are you doing here, is the navy taking the day off?"

"I am, the navy can take care of itself for a few hours while I talk to my sons."

"Where is James? Did he report back to Washington?"

"Yes, and that is where I intend to keep him until this peace agreement is signed, sealed and delivered."

"What happened, why are you so down?"

"I just heard that the president is already making plans to demobilize the navy."

"Does he have a crystal ball? Has he gotten word that the war is over? He better tell the Germans to give back Camgrai, St. Quentin, La Fere and Vimy and the captured British first army."

"The British first army has been captured? I did not know that. Russia has been eliminated as a factor, this released an entire German army to transfer to the western front. It was only a matter of time before the disorganization among the Allies would become a tool for the Germans.

Pershing's troops are still not used as a front line army. Pershing has over 1,000,000 now and I am sending him 300,000 a month. He should be given a section of the front, or better yet, turn him loose to clear the trenches like your Uncle Teddy did in Cuba."

"The Allied High Command has their collective heads-up-their- asses, Dad. They will not accept any suggestions from here in Washington or from Pershing in France. I am wasting my time trying to write to them."

"Louis, put your pen down and pay attention."

"It is down, what is up?"

"I have a question for you. When a peace agreement is signed, would you and Cathleen like to return to London?"

"Yes, we plan to."

"Good, are you staying in the US Navy, or would you like a position with one of our companies in London? We are going to need a good lawyer to make sure all the debts due Caldwell Aviation are paid by England and France. We will no doubt have to sue both countries in their court systems in order to settle what is owed us."

"I will not be very popular in England if I do that, Dad."

"You, personally, will not represent us in court, you will hire the lawyers in England and France to represent us. I will take all the heat."

"I will think about it. I would really like to go back with NIA as station chief in London."

"First choice, I would agree. But what if NIA is disbanded by Wilson before it should be, in order to save some money?"

"You think we will enter a period of isolation from Europe?"

"I do."

"What is James going to do?"

"He can stay in the US Navy if he wants to, or he can join us in building the future of the family here and in England."

"He will want to see the end of the war, first, just like you and me, right?"

"All three of us will do everything we can to see an end of this, but when that is done, we need to regroup, just like the companies that we own."

I returned to my office in the Army Navy Building and Secretary Daniels was waiting to see me.

"James, we have a problem."

"Is it the German offensive?"

"Yes, they split the French and English armies and have taken Peroune, Chauny and Ham. They are marching on Albert and if they push to the sea and capture our landing sites, General Pershing will be without your 300,000 troops a month."

"If that happens, I have plans to land them in Belgium."

"Are you referring to Operation Lion's Gate?"

"Yes, but before that happens let's play some of our trump cards. Suppose you convince the president to send an emergency cablegram to the Premier of France and the King of England stating that the German offensive threatens to capture our landing sites. In order to protect these landing sites, the president, as commander-in-chief of all American forces anywhere in the world, has ordered General Pershing to stop the German advance, then push them back into Germany. In a nice way let the British and French know that he is going to give the green light to Pershing to drive all German forces from occupied allied territories in France, Belgium and Italy."

"That is a great idea, James, would you like to go with me to see the president?"

"No, I would not. When were you going to tell me about the president's plans to demobilize the navy?"

"What? I have heard no such thing! I would be the first to know about that, what a stupid idea."

"When you see the president, tell him his assistant Secretary of the Navy thinks he is charge of the demobilization as soon as the peace agreement is signed. I will not be a party to that."

"Nor, will I. The cease fire may only last a few months and we could be up to our asses in Huns again." I looked at Joe Daniels and realized that either he or Franklin was lying, the use of the word Huns, does not come up that often in casual speech. That probably had come from a conversation in the White House and in that conversation was what to do with the massive military buildup and how soon it could be drawn down to peace time levels.

"I am the Admiral of the Navy, Joe, I take my orders from you. As soon as you have an order let me know."

J oe Daniels walked slowly across the melting snows of the last days of March, towards the White House as I watched from my office window. I wondered if the president would actually do what Joe would suggest to him. It would hinge on two critical points; had the president seen

Operation Lion's Gate that I had worked on for four months and would he hold up the third Liberty Loan in the amount of 4 billion dollars if the British and French did not agree to participate in Lion's Gate.

T he next day the Germans forced the evacuation of Albert. My landing sites would be gone if they renewed their attacks from Arras to the Somme. The next two days, I had no contact with either the White House or either of the Navy Secretaries. I called Louis in the State Department.

"Hello, Dad. Do you want to meet me somewhere for coffee?"

"Yes, I would. Where and when?"

"I am leaving my office now, see you across the street in ten minutes."

"Good, see you then." I hung up and looked out my window at the White House. I put on my winter coat and cover and walked out into the outer office. "Master Chief, do you feel like a walk with me?"

"Aye, aye. Sir, let me get my jacket. Where are we headed?"

"Across the street and into the hotel coffee shop, Louis has something he can't talk about over the office telephone. Are we ready to send out the orders for Operation Lion's Gate?"

"Yes, Sir. We can commence the naval operation part of the plan whenever you want."

"Do it now, get it off our decks before we find out something from the White House that would make it impossible to implement. I have a bad feeling about Joe Daniels avoiding me." Master Chief Gunnerson picked up his telephone and talked to someone for a few minutes, hung up and said, "Your orders are on their way to Admiral Sims. The war department has already sent orders to General Pershing, Sir. Operation Lion's Gate is already underway!"

"Good, let's find out what the State Department knows about the German offensive and the execution of Lion's Gate. It would be nice if the War Department notified the Department of the Navy."

"Maybe they have, Admiral. Do you want me to check with the sources I have inside Secnav's office?"

"Make it so, Master Chief, but I do not want to know about it. Come on over for a cup of coffee and bring your information with you."

"Aye, aye. Sir."

I left the office and headed down the stairs and out into the street, it was the first of April, but you would never know it. The wind howled about me as I put my head down and trudged through Lafayette Square across from the White House. I found Louis and Joe Daniels waiting for me.

"I brought a friend with me, Dad. He has been inside the White House most of the last three days, in fact we both slept there the last two nights."

"What has been happening?" I asked Joe Daniels.

"The president has been ganged up on, James. Secretary Baker was already in conference with Louis and Secretary Lansing deciding when to use Operation Lion's Gate. We all considered it would not work when you presented it to us."

"Even you, Louis!"

"Even me, Dad."

"But all that changed when the German High Command ordered an all out offensive and left their trenches behind and headed for the coast of France."

"I have ordered Admiral Sims to begin his portion of Lion's Gate, he will attack all the harbors in Belgium, he has several captured S-type German Destroyers, he will on top of them before they can respond. He will enter the narrow channels into each of the U-boat pens, open the sea cocks and sink them to block the U-boats from entering or leaving. He will then continue on to a point on the coast between Belgium and France. Here he will land the Marine Division we have been holding in England. This will be close enough to where we have been landing army troops. If the German's manage to make it all the way to the coast, they will find an entire division of US Marines waiting for them. If the Germans never make it to the coast, then the Marines will be free to take the seaports along the Belgium coast."

"When was this order given, James?"

"About ten minutes ago, why?"

"I was on my way to your office when you called Louis."

"Why didn't you give me the order when I talked to him?"

"We were both completely frantic to get out of the mad house, everyone else calls the White House. Louis suggested this instead and I agreed. Thank you for sending the orders to Admiral Sims, it is your right, you are the Admiral of the Navy!"

"I know Joe, but I told you I would wait for any orders you might have for me, I am sorry. It will not happen again. So, fill me in. What has happened in the last 72 hours?"

"The president has delayed the third Liberty Loan, the Allied high command has a new single commander-in-chief. He is not British, thanks to Louis here, he is General Ferdinand Foch and he has assumed command of all Allied forces, even General Pershing's. He has made General Pershing his field commander after Black Jack showed him a copy of Operation Lion's Gate. He has told Black Jack to use the US Marine division and the 1,300,000 troops under his command to spear head a counteroffensive to trap the invading German armies out in the open and drive them from all allied territories. General Foch has ordered you, Admiral Caldwell, on the next troop transport to France. You are to assume command of the allied naval efforts to support General Pershing's part of Operation Lion's Gate."

"The British will not like taking orders from you, they will call them suggestions and do what ever they please, Dad." Louis was smiling.

"No, they won't, that is where the third Liberty Loan comes into play. If the British drag their feet at all, President Wilson has informed me, that you will inform them, that if they do not cooperate, the loan will be cancelled not delayed."

"Sounds like the golden rule, Dad, 'those that have the gold, make the rules!'" Louis could always see the bright side of things – I was headed into the lion's mouth on the shores of France. The door to the café opened and Master Chief Gunnerson walked in with a smile on his face. He had undoubtedly learned the same thing I had just been told.

"Admiral, Mr. Secretary, Captain, do you mind if a seaman joins you for a cup of coffee?"

"You can have my chair, Master Chief, Mrs. Daniels has just driven up in front. I can see her waving to me, she probably wonders when I am coming home."

"Thank you, Mr. Secretary."

"You can call me, Secnav, chief, I know everyone does."

"Thank you, Mr. Secretary, I will keep that in mind." Everyone laughed as Joe Daniels drained his coffee cup and put on his coat and left.

"Master Chief, you will need to pack your seabag, you are going to France with me."

"Ensign Miller and I have been packed for two days, Admiral."

"How did you know I would be assigned to command Operation Lion's Gate?"

"Master Chief's have their own source of information, Admiral."

A s my staff prepared to move our office to Paris, the war raged on.

March 10 – Russia protests against German occupation of Finland as a breach of the peace treaty, while the British fire bomb Daimler motor works and other industrial sites in Stuttgart.

March 11 – Paris suffers first German air raid, thirty-four people killed by explosions, another seventy-nine are killed in the panic of the city. American forces enter the trenches near Toul sector, hundreds of troops are captured.

March 12 – Americans raid German trenches at Luneville, hundreds killed in flanking machine gun fire. Germany bombs Hull, England, industrial sites.

March 13 – British bomb munition plants at Freiburg, Germany. German troops enter Odessa, Russia.

March 14 – Americans occupy Luneville and advance on trenches located at Badonviller. Thousands are captured trying to escape Badonviller.

March 15 – Japan and China signified their willingness to intervene in Siberia for the protection of allied interests.

March 18 – Germany announces that all American property in Germany has been seized in reprisal for the seizure of German property in the United States.

March 19 – French penetrate German lines near Rheims, while British navy carry out first order of Operation Lion's gate at Villers-Guislain, La Vacquerie and Bois Gienier. Germany navy takes a pounding off Ostend, Belgium, two destroyers and two U-boats are sunk.

March 20 – German aircraft drop balls of liquefied mustard gas on American lines at Toul. Americans shell the trenches at Lahayville where a heavy concentration of mustard gas is stored. A heavy explosion causes the German troops to flee their own mustard gas clouds.

March 21 – Germans open a gap in the British lines along a fifty mile front from southeast of Arras as far as La Fere. Peace treaty with Russia is ignored as German troops advance toward Kherson in the Ukraine.

March 22 – Germans claim 6,000 British prisoners, British General Haig reports German advancing along entire 50 mile front.

March 23 – Germans take Moncy, Cambrai, St. Quentin and La Fere, they are advancing towards Fontaine les Croisilles and Moeuvres.

March 24 – Germans capture Peronne, Chauny and Ham and cross the River Somme. Paris is bombarded by artillery located in the Forest of St. Gobain.

March 26 – Germans take Noyon, Roye and Lihon and cross the battle line of 1916 at many points.

March 27 – British army begins counter attack and there is fierce fighting around Morlaincourt and Chipilly, north of the River Somme.

March 28 – British counteroffensive continues at Arras and Montdidier.

40

Operation Lion's Gate

France, 1918

I had given the orders to Admiral Sims on April 1, it was now May 1 and I was on the staff of General Foch. Paris had been bombarded intermittently by long range guns that carried for over a distance of 74 miles. Master Chief Gunnerson slept on a cot in my room. He had a loaded, double barreled shot gun under his cot. I wondered what he planned on doing with it if our headquarters was leveled by German Artillery, 70 miles away. It must have given him comfort because he checked it every night before falling asleep.

The great push to the sea by the German armies lasted from March 21rd to April 20th when the second battle of Somme made it obvious that the onrushing German forces had fought themselves to a standstill. On April 12th, General Haig, the commander of the British forces under General Foch, issued his historic order to the allied troops to stand firm against the German onslaught, using the phrase, "with our backs to the sea, we will fight to the last man." On April 15th, General Foch eliminated the designation of British French and American Expeditionary Forces and replaced the titles with Allied army divisions, Britain, Allied army divisions, France and Allied army divisions United States. When the Italians landed on the Mediterranean coast of southern France on April 18th, they became known as the Allied army division, Italy. General Foch now assumed command of the four armies and coordinated them from Paris while I assumed command of the American, British, French and

Italian naval forces in Europe. On April 20th, I ordered the British navy to block the Channel at Zeebrugge that was held by German troops. April 24, General Foch turned back a drive started by German forces against Amiens. The next day they were turned back from Ypres. The month of May saw heavy fighting along the Italian fronts in France and Italy. May 10th the US Marines drove the Germans out of their naval base at Ostend. May 22nd the French division capture Kemmel. By May 28th the American division recapture Cantigny and Montdidier held by the Germans. The first week in June the Americans captured Chateau-Thierry and Venilly-la-Poterie. The Americans pursue the retreating Germans into Belleau Wood. By June 11 the Americans cross the River Marne. A German counterattack is defeated by the American 1st Division. June 22nd the Italians defeat the Austrians in northern Italy. Austria begins her retreat. June 25th Italians now occupy all the conquered territory of the Austrians.

Letters from home with newspaper clippings kept me aware of what was happening in the United States. The American News Service, dateline July 4, 1918. The following address was delivered by President Wilson at the grave of George Washington at Mount Vernon.

"I am happy to draw apart with you to this quiet place of old counsel in order to speak a little of the meaning of this day of our nation's independence. This place seems very still and remote. It is as serene and untouched by the hurry of the world as it was in those great days long ago when General Washington has here and held conferences with the men who were to be associated with him in the creation of a nation. From these gentle slopes they looked out upon a much different world. It is for that reason that we cannot feel, even here, in the immediate presence of this sacred tomb, that this is a place of death. From this green hillside we also might be able to see with comprehending eyes the world that lies around us and conceive anew the purpose that must set men free."

"We take our cue from Washington and his men – do we not? We intend what they intended. We here in America believe our participation in this present war to be only the fruit of what they planted. Our case differs from theirs only in this, that it is our inestimable privilege to concert with men out of every nation who shall make not only the liberties of America secure but the liberties of every other people as well. We are happy in the thought that we are permitted to do what they would have done had they been in our place. There must now be settled once and for all, what was settled for America in the great age upon whose inspiration we draw today. This is surely a fitting place from which calmly to look out upon our task, that we may fortify our spirits for its

accomplishment. And this is the appropriate place from which to avow, alike to the friends who look on and to the friends with whom we have the happiness to be associated in action, the faith and purpose with which we act."

"This, then is our conception of the great struggle in which we are engaged. The plot is written plain upon every scene and every act of the supreme tragedy called war. On the one hand stand the peoples of the world – not only the peoples actually engaged but many others, also, who suffer under mastery but cannot act; peoples of many races and in every part of the world – the people of stricken Russia still, among the rest, though they are for the moment unorganized and helpless. Opposed to them, masters of many armies, stand an isolated group of Governments, who speak no common purpose, but only selfish ambitions of their own, by which none can profit but themselves."

"There can be but one issue. The settlement must be final. There can be no compromise. No halfway decision would be tolerable. No associated peoples of the world are fighting and which must be conceded them before there can be peace:

1) The destruction and elimination of every Central Empire,
2) The settlement of every question put before the Central Empires,
3) A common law of civilized societies and,
4) A true League of Nations."

"These four objects can be put into a single sentence. What we seek is the reign of law, based upon the consent of the governed and sustained by the organized opinion of mankind. I can sense that the air of this place we stand today carries the accents of such principles with a peculiar kindness. Here were started forces which the great nation against which they were primarily directed at first regarded as a revolt against its rightful authority, but which it has long since seen to have been a step in the liberation of its own people; and I stand here now to speak – speak proudly and with confident hope – of the spread of liberty to the great stage of the world itself!

The first week of July the Americans captured Vaux and Bois de la Roche. English division defeated Germans at Hamel and south of Ypres. The Germans counterattack at Rheims and the Americans suffer 85,000 casualties in the defeat of the Germans, but the turning point of the war had come. The great German armies of the Empire had been defeated. General, now Marshall Foch, immediately ordered a series of allied offensives that practically covered the whole war front. It was destined that his orders would roll the German armies out of France. The

American divisions engaged in this drive were the 1st, 2nd, 3rd, 4th, 26th, 32nd and 42nd. By July 29th, the Germans were forced to begin their retreat. The entire month of August consisted of one allied victory after another. By September 12th the Americans spearheaded the last push of Operation Lion's Gate with victories at St. Mihiel, Rhiems and Sedan-Meziers. On September 22nd the entire Turkish army surrenders to the British and Turkey asks for a peace agreement. September 28th Bulgaria surrenders unconditionally to the Allies.

The first week of October, Damascus surrenders. The Germans retreat from Lille, Armentiers, Lens and in Argonne regions. October 5th Austria sues for peace and sends letter to President Wilson asking for terms of surrender. October 6th, Berlin contacts Washington and asks for terms of peace. October 8th, the Hindenburg line of German defense is shattered and over run by American, British and French forces. October 12th, Germany accepts President Wilson's statement of October 8th that all invaded territory must be surrendered before any peace terms could be considered. The German government requires that a commission be appointed to adjust the invaded territories and attach them to the German Empire. October 13th, President Wilson emphatically replies to the German government that he will discuss that idea after the German armies are entirely defeated and driven from all Belgium and French territories. He orders General Pershing to "liquidate' the remaining German armies in France and for Admiral Caldwell to have his Marines remove all resistance still around Ostend, Zeebrugge and Bruges and to clear the entire Belgian occupied territories.

By the first of November, the American forces in Belgium and France have captured forty-five villages and have taken more than 20,000 prisoners. The final battle of the Meuse-Argonne was beyond comparison the greatest ever fought by American troops and there have been few, if any, greater in the world's history. October 31st, Turkey signs armistice. November 3rd, Austria signs armistice. November 6th German envoys start for Marshal Foch's headquarters to arrange terms for armistice. November 9th, Kaiser Wilhelm II abdicates and seeks asylum in Holland. November 11th, Germany signs armistice at Marshal Foch's headquarters as I watched the German authorities accepted and signed the terms of the Armistice and at 11 am, hostilities ceased. The following is a summary of the terms of the Armistice: (1) The immediate evacuation of all invaded countries. (2) The imprisonment of all German troops not so withdrawn. (3) The repatriation, within two weeks, of all citizens of Allied or associated countries imprisoned in Germany. (4) The surrender of 5,000 guns, 25,000 machine guns, 3,000 Minenwerfer, and 1,700 airplanes. (5) The occupation by Allied troops of the German Empire on the left bank of the Rhine, with frequent bridgeheads, making the further invasion of Germany comparatively easy. (6) The support of the Allied army of occupation to be at the cost of Germany. (7) All poisoned wells and mines in evacuated territory are to be revealed, and no damage shall be done by the evacuating German troops. (8) Surrender of 5,000 locomotives, 150,000 railroad cars and 5,000 motorcars. (9) Surrender of all German U-boats (including torpedo boats and all mine-laying submarines) now existing. (10) Repatriation of all war prisoners in Germany without reciprocity. (11) All German troops are to withdraw from German frontier borders. (12) German troops immediately to cease all requisitions. (13) All stolen money from Belgium and French banks must be restored. (14) Treaties of Bucharest and Brest-Litovsk are to be abandoned. (15) Unconditional surrender of German forces in East Africa. (16) Reparation for damage done in invaded countries world wide. (17) Location of all German ships is be revealed. (18) Six German battle-cruisers, ten battle-ships, eight light cruisers and fifty destroyers of the latest type are to be disarmed and interned in neutral ports. All other surface warships are to be concentrated in German ports, completely disarmed and placed under Allied supervision. (19) All naval aircraft must be concentrated, disarmed and deeded to the US Navy. (20) Allied Powers have access to Baltic Sea without interference from Germany. (21) Allied Powers will occupy German shore defenses. (22) Blockade of German ports is to be continued with the search and inventory of all relief ships headed to German ports. (23) Germany must evacuate all Black Sea ports. (24) Germany must locate all marine mine-fields. (25) All neutral merchant vessels must be released from German ports. (26) All damaged merchant vessels of Allied Powers must be restored without reciprocity. (27) No transfer shall be made of lost German merchant shipping. (28) All restrictions on neutral commerce must be withdrawn by Germany. (29) Armistice runs for thirty days, with option to extend in thirty day increments. (30) Armistice may be denounced on forty-eight hours notice.

I was exhausted. I was too old for what my president and my country had asked me to do. I was a happy man that the war, to end all wars, would now become a fact of history. It was time for my family to enjoy their lives and fortunes without the shadows of military life interrupting the ebb and flow of family dynamics within the Caldwell Clan. I sent a cablegram to Washington requesting that my wife, Emily, our sons and their families be included in the December 4th sailing with President Wilson and his large staff to attend the Peace Conference in Paris.

I got a return message from Secnav, stating that my request had been approved and that President Wilson was pleased with the outcome of Operation Lion's Gate. "The war thus comes to an end; for, having accepted the 30 points of armistice, it will be impossible for the German command to renew the war."

The next day I read the text of President Wilson's address to Congress.

It is now possible to asses the consequences of this great war of the nations. We know only that this tragic war, whose consuming flames swept from one nation to another until all the world was on fire, is at an end and that it was the privilege of our people to enter it at its most critical juncture in such a fashion as to bring about a swift and just conclusion. We know, too, that the object of the war is attained; the object upon which all free men had set their hearts; and attained with a sweeping completeness which even now we do not realize. Armed imperialism such as the men conceived who were but yesterday the masters of Germany is at an end.

The arbitrary power of the military caste of Germany which once could secretly and of its own single choice disturb the peace of the world is discredited and destroyed. And more than that – much more has been accomplished. The great nations which associated themselves to destroy it have now definitely united in the common purpose to set up such a peace as will satisfy the longing of the whole world for disinterested justice, embodied in settlements which are based upon something much better and more lasting than the selfish competitive interests of powerful states. There is no longer conjecture as to the objects the victors have in mind. They have a mind in the matter, not only, but a heart as well. Their avowed and concerted purpose is to satisfy and protect the weak as well as to accord their just right to the strong.

The humane temper and intention of the victorious Governments have already been manifested in a very practical way. Their representatives in the Supreme War Council at Versailles have by unanimous resolution assured the peoples of the former Central Empires that everything that is possible in the circumstances will be done to supply them with food and relieve the distressing want that is in so many places threatening their very lives; and steps are to be taken immediately to organize these efforts at relief in the same systematic manner that they were organized in the case of Belgium. By the use of the idle tonnage of the former Central Empires it ought presently to be possible to lift the fear of utter misery from their oppressed populations and set their minds and energies free for the great and hazardous tasks of political reconstruction which now face them on every hand. Hunger does not breed reform; it breeds madness and all the ugly distempers that make an ordered life impossible.

For with the fall of the ancient Governments, which rested like an incubus on the peoples of the former Central Empires, has come political change not merely, but revolution; and revolution which seems as yet to assume no final and ordered form, but to run from one fluid change to another, until thoughtful men are forced to ask themselves, with what governments and of what sort are we about to deal in the making of the covenants of peace? With what authority will abide and sustain securely the international arrangements into which we are about to enter? There is here matter for no small anxiety and misgiving. When peace is made, upon whose promises and engagements besides our own is it to rest?

Let us be perfectly frank with ourselves and admit that these questions cannot be satisfactorily answered now or at once. But the moral is not that there is little hope of an early answer that will suffice. It is only that we must be patient and helpful and mindful above all of the great hope and confidence that lie at the heart of what is taking place. The present and all that it holds belongs to the nations and the peoples who preserve their self-control and the orderly processes of their governments; the future to those who prove themselves the true friends of mankind.

41

Midterm Elections

November 5, 1918

The results of the midyear elections in the United States reached Paris on November 12th. The election occurred at the midpoint of President Wilson's second term. The elections resulted in a decided defeat for the Democratic Party and the present administration. The Republicans secured a substantial majority in the House and a two member majority in the Senate. This meant that the Republicans had to gain seven seats. I searched the newspaper article, sent by Em, to see who these new members were.

Lawrence Phipps (Colorado)
Heisler Ball (Delaware)
Joseph McCormick (Illinois)
Arthur Capper (Kansas)
Selden Spencer (Missouri)
Henry Keyes (New Hampshire)
Irvine Lenroot (Wisconsin)

The only Democrat to replace a Republican was David Walsh of Massachusetts. The change in control would be particularly important, since it meant that the sweeping changes planned during the last two years of the Wilson administration would not be rubber stamped by the Senate and it probably meant that the Republicans would listen to Teddy Roosevelt about the dangers of demobilizing the country's navy. I was hopeful that I would not have to resign in protest over the 'scuttling' of the navy.

I would return to Washington after a tour of Europe with my family. I was looking forward to seeing James, his wife Martha and his children, Star, Randy and Jason. Louis would bring Cathleen, Carson, and little Elska. I had written to our two daughters and their families, but I had not heard back from them. I was going to hold a family conference with the entire clan if I could get them all together in one place. I was going to suggest that the Caldwell companies that were listed on the New York Exchange be cut free to function on their own. Emily and I still owned the majority of stock in these companies and it was time to consider what we would like to do in retirement. Retirement meant not having to be responsible for Caldwell International Holding. Our children, Elizabeth, James, and the twins could buy or sell stock as they pleased. My sisters had long since been given a huge portion of Caldwell Shipping and Trading. My sister Carol was given Seneca Oil to fund Cranson College for Women, where she was the first president. My sister Ruth had married Teddy Roosevelt and had six children, four boys and two girls. She and Teddy were happily retired in Oyster Bay, Long Island. All four of their sons had served in Europe. Our two sons had served as well, now that it was over we could thank the Lord that only one perished in the War of the Nations.

I wrote to Emily and told her of my plans for the family. She wrote back and said that she would begin selling shares of the companies that I indicated and place these funds in our bank in Bermuda. From this bank we could then use the money to purchase a family compound south of London. I had asked Louis before I left for Paris, where he would like to locate the international office for the remaining Caldwell companies. We had discussed his opportunities for employment after the war before I left for Paris.

"Louis, put your pen down and pay attention. I have a question for you. When a peace agreement is signed, would you and Cathleen like to return to London?"

"Yes, we plan to."

"Good, are you staying in the US Navy, or would you like a position with our companies in London? We are going to need a good lawyer to make sure all the debts due Caldwell Aviation are paid by England and France. We will no doubt have to sue both countries in their court systems in order to settle what is owed us."

"I will not be very popular in England if I do that, Dad."

"You, personally, will not represent us in court, you will hire the lawyers in England and France to represent us. I will take all the heat."

"I will think about it. I would really like to go back with NIA as station chief in London."

"First choice, I would agree. But what if NIA is disbanded by Wilson before it should be, in order to save some money?"

"You think we will enter a period of isolation from Europe?"

"I do if the Democrats are defeated in the midyear elections. The Republicans will not allow Wilson to complete his plan for Europe."

"What is James going to do?"

"He can stay in the US Navy if he wants to, or he can join us in building the future of the family here and in England."

"He will want to see the end of the war, first, just like you and me, right?"

"All three of us will do everything we can to see an end of this, but when that is done, we need to regroup, just like the companies that we own. London is the natural choice for this location."

"In one of London's Boroughs, of course. Cathleen suggests we chose from Reigate, Redhill or Merstham."

"I have no knowledge of any of these, do you have information for me to read?"

"I do, each has its own Chamber of Commerce. I wrote to all three last month. Here is the printed material from Reigate. I hope to have the other two before you leave for Paris, Dad."

"Are you alright with living in England, Louis? You will be responsible for all foreign Caldwell company operations and debt collections."

"I promised Cathleen that we will return to England and continue to have as many children as she wants, either natural born or adopted. How do you feel about that?"

"As an adopted son of a wealthy family, I think you and Cathleen are about to make some war orphans very happy and their futures insured. I will read this material as soon as I can, once I am in Paris. I will try and contact a land broker in one of these boroughs while I am in Paris."

"I can write from the White House once you have selected a broker and before Cathleen and I return to England."

"Remember we are looking for an estate that already has three houses that are livable, one for each family."

Borough of Reigate
Chamber of Commerce LTD

SHOPS

OFFICES

INDUSTRY

SERVICES

WHEREVER YOU GO
IN THE BOROUGH

THERE ARE MEMBERS
of the

Borough of Reigate
CHAMBER OF COMMERCE

Ready to help you ......

Secretary:
R. Lutman

Registered Office:
24 Clarence Road, Redhill
Surrey RH1 6NG
Telephone: Reigate 44828

Borough of Reigate

History

Reigate is popularly, but erroneously, supposed to derive its name from Ridgegate, i.e. ridge way, an allusion to the old track, known latterly as Pilgrim's Way, traversing the top of the Downs. Other possible derivations trace the first element to the "roe-deer" or to "rie" meaning water. The first mention of Reigate by that name occurs in 1170. Long before that date, however, a Saxon village, called Cherchefelle or Churchfield, had risen near the site of the present church. The field after which the village was named included part of the cemetery. This in turn was named after the church, and, though no church is mentioned in Domesday, it is safe to assume that one had previously stood here, if no longer standing in 1086.

The early history of Reigate, the precursor of the present town, is bound up with that of its Lords, the Norman family of Warenne. William de Warenne the first fought at Hastings and was rewarded by the Conqueror with lavish grants of land in Sussex, Norfolk and other counties. In 1088 he was created Earl of Surrey and probably at the same time received a grant of Reigate and Dorking. He built, or rather dug for early Norman castles were usually devoid of masonry, the castle of Lewes, and also, it is said, Reigate Castle. His loyalty was strengthened by his marriage to Gundrada, the step daughter of the Conqueror. Their son, William de Warenne II, married Isabella of Vermandois, a Norman heiress, and took her family coat of arms. On the death of the third Earl in 1148 the male line became extinct. The enormous possessions descended to the daughter, who thus became the richest woman in England. She married William of Blois, son of King Stephen, and brought to the royal family several castles, including Reigate, a large slice of Sussex, and over 200 manors in other parts of the kingdom.

The neighboring towns of Reigate and Redhill, though two miles apart, are both located within the London Borough of Reigate, an area which comprises, within its ample limits of 10,255 acres, some of the choicest scenery to be found in the County of Surrey. Surrey lies at the base of the chalk-capped Downs, which serve as a barrier against the outward thrust of London's suburbs on the north, the towns stretch east and west along a broad valley. This part of the lovely vale of Homesdale celebrated for its supposed rout of the Danes. On the south the valley is bounded by a prominent ridge of sandstone, running parallel with the North Downs, and broken at its eastern end between Redhill Common and Redhill Hill by a wide gap, through which the Brighton Railway thrusts its main line, and Redhill is one of its busiest arteries.

The Borough is thus beautifully diversified by hill and dale, and the succession of soils ranging from chalk to sand and clay adds richness and variety to its flora. The subsoil is mainly the lower green sand, which makes an ideal formation for buildings and gardening, being firm yet easy to work, and both dry and fertile. The district is attracting a yearly increase in the number of residents since the outbreak of the war in 1914. They are appreciative of its amenities, which are not marred by any disfiguring industries. To those seeking the conveniences of a town with the health and freedom of the country, either Reigate or Redhill can be confidently recommended to meet their need. Situated within 20 odd miles of London and 30 to Brighton Beach, and served by four stations on the Southern Electric Railway – one of them (Redhill) is an important junction with the branches of Reading and Tonbridge. The district also makes a wide appeal to the business man as well as to those in quest of a pleasant home in which to spend their retirement. Merstham is a rapidly growing village on the northern confines of the Borough and is attracting mostly retired couples.

Motor buses run at short intervals between Redhill, Reigate and Merstham, and there are excellent daily services by train, bus and coach, linking up the Borough with all the surrounding districts and with London and Brighton Beach.

ABC Guide to Public Services

Almshouses, Clerk to the Governors: Miss K. Ashurt, 19 Victoria, Deering Road, Reigate (Reigate 49953)
Ambulance Service: Burgh Heath 53491
Baths: Reigate at Castlefield Road, Redhill at London Road
Car Parks: Reigate at Bancroft Road, Redhill at Cromwell Road
Cemeteries: Reigate at Chart Lane, Redhill at Philanthropic Road
Centenary House: Warwick Road at Redhill, Day Care Centre for elderly
Chamber of Commerce: 24 Clarence Road at Redhill
Council Offices: Town Clerk (Reigate 42477)
                        Borough Treasurer (Reigate 42477)
                        Borough Engineer (Reigate 42477)
                        Medical Officer (Redhill 61265)
                        Housing Manager (Reigate 42477)
                        Parks Superintendent (Redhill 64525)
                        Chief Inspector (Redhill 63574)
Day Nursery: Cromwell Road, Redhill (62661)
Department Employment: Crown Building, 75 London Road, Redhill (65020)

Department Health: Crown Building, 73 London Road, Redhill (65020)

East Surrey Water Co: London Road, Redhill (66333)

Education Office: 123 Blackborough Road, Reigate (66441)

Electricity Office: 20 High Street, Crawley (31188)

Fire: Wray Park Road, Reigate (42444)

Gas: 3 London Road, Redhill (65065)

Hospital: Redhill General (65030)

Land Broker and Surveyor: Idris Jones, 6 Bell Street, Reigate (42286)

Masonic Lodge: Albert Edward Lodge, No. 1362, Reigate (45026)

Parliament Representative: The Rt. Hon. Sir Richard Edward Howe, Q.C.

Population of Borough: 57,820

Post Offices: 33 London Road, Redhill and 20 Bell St., Reigate

Rateable Value of Borough: 3,383,993 pounds sterling

Red Cross Society: Mrs. L. Wood, Dean Oak Lane, Leigh (Norwood 22212)

Registrar of Births: 44 Reigate Hill (42259)

Rotary Club: Redhill meets every Monday, Reigate meets every Tuesday

Women's Royal Voluntary Service: Mrs. D. Brett, 7 Linkfield Street, Redhill

Youth Employment Bureau: 7 West Street, Reigate (46811)

42

Paris Peace Conference

December, 1918

A year ago, there was an Allied conference held in Rapallo, Italy, the purpose was to try and save Italy. The shaken Allied members in attendance were Lloyd George (British Premier), the French Premier (Painleve), the Italian Premier (Orlando), Chief of the British Imperial Staff (Robertson) and assorted generals from France, Italy and Britain. No Americans were invited to attend. I was sure that this conference would be different, for one thing, President Wilson was placed in charge.

I remembered the last world peace conference that I attended in 1899.

World Peace Conference

The Hague, 1899

On May 18, 1899, ninety-eight delegates met at The Hague to form the greatest conference of the century, and Admiral George Dewey and I were chosen as part of the delegation to represent the United States. World leaders were very concerned about the global scale of the recent conflict between the United States and Spain. In fact, for the last quarter of a century the nations of the world had been devoting all their ingenuity to the invention and perfection of means of destruction, with the result that a point at last was reached, which meant that the next great war must terminate in the ruin of one combatant and annihilation of the other.

The signatures on the peace agreement in Washington, between the United States and Spain, were hardly dry when this question was asked by the world powers. How will the next war between belligerent nations end? The answer came from the least expected quarter. The foreign ambassadors to the Court of St. Petersburg were handed a printed document from Count Muravieff, the Russian Minister for foreign affairs. This document has since become famous as the Czar's Rescript. It contained an invitation to all the world powers who were represented in the Russian capital, to hold a conference to discuss the possibility of putting "some limit to the increasing armaments, and to find a means of averting the calamities which threaten the whole world."

At the same time the Czar's circular pointed out that, "The ever increasing financial burdens attack public prosperity at its very roots. The physical and intellectual strength of the people, labor and capital are diverted for the greater part from their natural application and wasted unproductively. Hundreds of millions are spent to obtain frightful weapons of destruction, which, while being regarded today as the latest inventions of science, are in fact, destined tomorrow to be rendered obsolete by some new discovery. National culture, economical progress and the production of wealth are either paralyzed or turned into false channels of development. Therefore, the more the armaments of each world power increase, the less they answer to the purposes and intentions of the people. Economic disturbances are caused in great measure by this system of extraordinary armaments."

The Czar went on to say, "It should be a happy augury for the closing of the nineteenth century. It will powerfully concentrate the efforts of all countries which sincerely wish to see the triumph of the grand idea of universal peace over the elements of trouble and discord."

His comments were printed in the London Times and an editorial comment is worth noting: "The documents which Count Muravieff has presented to the representatives of the Court at St. Petersburg, are remarkable and most unexpected. On the eve of inaugurating a memorial to his grandfather, Czar Liberator, the present autocrat of Russia seizes the opportunity to appeal to the civilized world in the still more lofty capacity of the Czar Peacemaker."

All of the countries which received the Czar Rescript, agreed to the conference with the following agenda.

1. An agreement not to increase military and naval forces for a fixed period; also not to increase the corresponding war budgets; to endeavor to find means for reducing these forces and their budgets in the future.

2. To interdict the use of any kind of new weapon or explosive, or any new powder more powerful than which is at present in use for rifles and cannons.

3. To restrict the use in war of existing explosives of terrible force, and also to forbid the throwing of any kind of explosives from balloons or by any analogous means.

4. To forbid the use of submarine torpedo boats or plungers and any other similar engines of destruction, in navel warfare; to undertake not to construct vessels with rams.

5. To apply to naval warfare the stipulations of the Geneva Convention of 1864.

6. The neutralization of ships and boats for saving those shipwrecked during and after naval battles.

7. The revision of the declaration concerning the laws and customs of war elaborated in 1874 by the Conference of Brussels.

8. To accept in principle the employment of good offices in mediation and optional arbitration in cases which lend themselves to such means in order to prevent armed conflict between nations; an understanding on the subject of their mode of application and the establishment of some uniform practice in making use of them.

With the agenda in place, the ninety-eight delegates met at The Hague, where they were welcomed by the Queen of the Netherlands. I wrote my first letter to my son, James.

The Hague
May 18, 1899

Midshipman James Caldwell
United States Naval Academy
589 McNair Road
Annapolis, Maryland, USA

Dear James,

Your mother and I arrived in the Netherlands in time for the conference to open and we met Queen Wilhelmina. President McKinley has visited here before and I gave the Queen a letter from him. We are prepared for the conference to last about two months. The agenda is not an easy one to agree upon. For the English, French and German delegates, The Hague is as convenient a meeting place as could well be devised, and with the close proximity of Scheveningen, one of the most delightful of seaside watering places, will enable your mother and I to combine the pleasantness of holidays with the execution of our diplomatic and conference duties.

Many of the delegates are accompanied by their families and what with the reception by the Queen and entertainment at the British Embassy, the Kurhaus at Scheveningen and the residences of the leaders of the conference, ample provision has been made against the dullness which is proverbially known to accompany all work and no play.

The conference is so novel and so little is expected to come of the proposed deliberations, that I was not surprised by the question I got from the New York Times correspondent that is covering the events.

"Is the conference at The Hague anything else than a huge international junketing picnic party?"

I told him, " I hope not. It is my hope that an international peace agreement can be reached." Your mother sends her love, she is writing to your sisters and brothers.

Your loving father,

J. Caldwell

My second letter contained a few more details.

The Hague
May 28, 1899

Midshipman James Caldwell

United States Naval Academy
589 McNair Road
Annapolis, Maryland, USA

Dear James,

Slowly, but surely, things are beginning to take shape. It has been seen that the Czar's proposal, far being confined to disarmament, is based on three distinct ideas, which might be roughly classed as the Means to War, the Horrors of War, and the Prevention of War. Strange to say, only one of the eight points on the agenda concerns itself with the prevention of war. As soon as this fact was pointed out, we began to see our way. Our work was then divided into three sections. To the first section was given the discussion of points 1 - 4 (Armaments for armies and navies). The second section will undertake points 3 - 7 (Rules of War, Geneva and Brussels accords). The third section, of which I am the chairman, will consider the possibilities of arbitration.

The section chairmen report to the conference presidents for each section. One, M. Beernaert, the Belgian Minister of Finance; two, M. Marten, a Russian linguist and three, M. Bourgeous, Prime Minister of France. The super president of the whole conference is M. De Staal, the Russian Ambassador to the Court of St. James.

I must run, your mother wants to take a bike ride along the seashore.

Your loving father,

J. Caldwell

My fourth and final letter contained all the details of the agreements.

The Hague
July 30, 1899

Midshipman James Caldwell
United States Naval Academy
589 McNair Road
Annapolis, Maryland, USA

Dear James,

The final act was drawn up and presented to the delegates yesterday. Each section was voted on separately, here are the results:

Section one; signed by 88 countries, those who abstained were, Germany, Austria-Hungary, China, Great Britain, Italy, Japan, Luxemburg, Servia, Switzerland and Turkey. What this tells me is that these countries are in the process of building their armies and navies for a future war.

Section two; signed by 87 countries with those abstaining being the same as section one, plus Portugal. Why any country would object to the Geneva Convention is beyond my understanding.

Section three; signed by the same 87 countries that signed section two. Why anyone would object to arbitration is also beyond my understanding. I am in the process of sending my recommendations to the President of the United States. I will recommend that those nations not signing the agreement to be placed on a "watch list". I predict that these nations will be at war with each other or some other nation within the next few months.

Your loving father,

J. Caldwell

The delegates parted with mutual expressions of encouragement and goodwill, M. De Staal, as President of the conference gave the farewell address with these closing words, "For myself, who has arrived at the term of my career and decline of my life, I consider it as a supreme consolation to have been able to witness the advent of new prospects for the welfare of humanity, and to have been able to cast a glance into the brightness of the future."

I wondered if this peace conference would end any differently. General Pershing and I had received a cable from Washington on November 18th informing us that President Wilson would require our services from December 4th through the 18th. He had announced from Washington that he would personally attend and chair the Peace Conference to be held in Paris to settle the world political remaking brought about by the outcome of the World War. President Wilson held that inasmuch as his speeches had been made the basis for negotiations that it was due the American people that he should take personal charge of the deliberations leading to a permanent peace. On December 4, 1918, he sailed for France accompanied by a huge staff, he was determined not to have a repeat of the conference held in Italy a year ago. His immediate staff in Paris awaited his arrival, while his staff on board the Presidential Task Force included: Robert Lansing, Secretary of State; Henry White, ambassador to France; Bainbridge Colby, US Shipping Board Chairman; Colonel Henry House, my replacement as Presidential advisor; General Tasker Bliss, Chief of Staff US Army; Oscar Crosby, Secretary of the Treasury; Vance McCormick, Chairman of the War Trade Board; Alonzo Taylor, Chairman Food Control Board; and Thomas Perkins, Chairman of the Priority Board.

Sandwiched in between all these important members of the president's staff were the wives and family members invited to join them for a month in Paris and London. I had received a cable from my wife, Emily, saying that she purchased passage for the following members of the Caldwell family:

Herself – Mrs. Emily Schneider Caldwell

Our Son – Admiral and Mrs. James Caldwell, Star, Randy and Jason.

My youngest sister – President Carol Cranson and her family.

My sister Ruth – Widow of Theodore Roosevelt and her daughters..

Our daughter – Elizabeth Caldwell Harding and her family.

Our twin daughter – Louise Caldwell Penscott and her family.

Our twin son – Captain Louis Caldwell, Cathleen, Spencer and Elska.

I was a happy man. I would attend those meeting and sessions required of me and then the family would travel with the president's party to London where we would begin a new chapter in the Caldwell family saga.

The world peace conference of 1918 began with the arrival of President Wilson and his entourage in Paris on December 14th. The first thirty day cycle of the armistice ended on the 11th and was extended for another thirty days, plus one week, or until January 17, 1919. General Pershing and I met the President as he docked at the sea port of Havre because we were ordered to do so. A huge crowd of English, French and Belgian newspaper reporters were assembled to hear the remarks of President Wilson upon landing and before boarding the train for Paris. Black Jack and I stood at the foot of the gangway. Thomas Woodrow Wilson saw us there and did a very gracious thing. He turned and said something to someone and Mrs. Pershing and Caldwell appeared at the head of the gang way, smiling and waving to the crowd of well wishers. They marched down the gang way hand in hand and gave their husbands a huge kiss, to the delight of the crowd. Emily whispered in my ear, "The president says that you and the General should greet the reporters and answer any questions before he leaves the ship. Then you are take me to the nearest hotel and get me between the sheets."

"The president said that!"

"Not the last part, I added that myself. I have missed you so much James."

"Then let's do what the president says." Black Jack and I walked to the podium meant for the president's address and introduced ourselves. The reporters were overjoyed and started asking us question after question. I do not remember most of them, because I was still holding Em's hand and wishing that we on our way to that imaginary hotel.

One reporter asked Black Jack a routine question, "General, what do you consider the most decisive battles of the last hundred years?" He was probably thinking that Pershing would include some of his own from this war or in Mexico.

"You will get two different answers to that question, I will give you the army's point of view and my companion, Admiral Caldwell will give you the great sea battles."

"Austerlitz, December 2, 1805. The French defeated the Austrians and Russians that resulted in the peace of Presburg. The French newspaper reporters began to clap for this remark.

Leipzig, October 19, 1813. The Russians, Prussians, Swedes and Austrians defeated the French. Secured the first abdication of Napoleon. The French reporters spotted clapping and a couple of Russian reporters cheered from the crowd.

Waterloo, June 18, 1815. The British defeat Napoleon for the second time, ending the Napoleonic Wars." The French reporter probably wished he not asked the question.

"Sebastopol, September 8, 1854. Ended the Crimean War.

Gettysburg, July 3, 1863. Federal forces under Meade defeated the Confederate forces under Lee. It decisive because it ended the Confederate invasion of the north.

Sedan, September 1, 1870. Ended the Franco-Prussian War.

Paardeberg, Feburary 27, 1899. Ended the Boer War.

Marne, September 5-9, 1913. The French, English and Belgian troops stopped the German invasion of France which imperiled Paris. I regard this as a decisive defeat for the German armies as it completely shattered the plan on which they had based the war." The entire crowd bust into applause as Black Jack motioned for me to take the podium.

"Thank you, General. Here are my picks of the decisive naval battles.

Trafalgar, October 31, 1805. The British fleet under Nelson defeated the French and Spanish fleets under Villeneuve and Gravina. Nelson was killed in this battle but it ended the sea power of Napoleon.

Monitor and Merrimac, March 9, 1862. The battle of Hampton Roads was the true turning point for the northern navy during the American Civil War.

Yalu River, September 17, 1894. The Japanese fleet under Ito defeated the Chinese fleet under Ting. This battle resulted in the reorganization of the Japanese Navy.

Santiago, July 3, 1898. The American fleet under Sampson defeated the Spanish under Cervera. This resulted in the Spanish loss of Cuba.

Port Arthur, January 1, 1905. A total defeat for Russia and ended the war between the two countries.

Operation Lion's Gate. Spring of 1918, resulted in the capture of the entire Belgian coast and the landing of over a million United States forces for the final push against the German offensive. This is why we have the present armistice."

The next question caught us off guard and President Wilson stepped up behind me and said, "I would like to answer that question." I had not seen him come down the gang way and I was glad to let him try and answer the reporter's question about the money cost of the war.

"Various attempts have been made to estimate the cost in money of the war just completed, but no acceptable results have been obtained, and it is doubtful if any ever will be. There have been so many lines of necessary expenditure, so much destruction of property, both wanton and unavoidable, so much economic territory devastated, and so many demands for the relief of the destitute and starving peoples in the many war zones and of the incapacitated man-power of the belligerents, that the aggregate of even the known expenditures are almost beyond comprehension."

"The United States, Great Britain and Germany, in addition to their own war appropriations, were obliged from time to time to advance enormous sums of money to their respective allies. The United States alone, up to the end of 1917, had granted credits to its allies for purchases here that total four and one-half billion dollars, those for the single day of December 29 amounted to three hundred and fifty million dollars."

"According to estimates made by the Caldwell National Bankers of America, covering the period of August 1, 1914 to December 31, 1917, and based solely on direct appropriations for military purposes and loans to allies, the average daily expenditure was 97 million dollars. This is based upon the total military cost of 121 billion dollars." President Wilson stopped and turned to me and said, "That is correct, isn't it, Admiral Caldwell?"

"Right on the money, Mr. President." Emily Caldwell, Chairman of Caldwell Bankers of America, replied. The reporters began to laugh because women in Great Britain had the right to vote and own business' years before the United States had even considered granting the right to vote. Women had picketed the White House in November's midyear elections and President Wilson had some of them arrested. He was truly embarrassed and he motioned for Emily to take his place at the podium.

"As chairman of Caldwell Bankers of America during my husband's absence working for Marshall Foch, I have been keeping track of how he is spending my money!" This got a loud round of laughter from those assembled.

"Let me put it this way for your readers, the war has shown to cost England 74 cents a day per capita, France 50 cents, Germany 45 cents and the United States 28 cents per person per day." This brought a round of clapping from the reporters – finally something they could print for the common person to understand.

"This could be misleading to your readers because the United States was not in the war as long as the other nations. The military cost I just gave you must be apportioned among the belligerents as follows: United States, six billion dollars, Great Britain, twenty-six billion, France, twenty billion, Russia, eighteen billion, Italy, six billion and 1.5 billion each for Belgium, Servia, Rumania and Portugal. This totals over eighty-one billion dollars spent by the allies. Germany, Austria, Turkey and Bulgaria spent over forty billion dollars total. That means that over 121 billion dollars was spent on the war to end all wars, enough to send every child in the world to college."

The president had heard enough, he stepped forward and said, "Gentlemen of the press, please join us on the train waiting to take us to Paris. I will be glad to finish answering any questions that you might have. Unfortunately, Mrs. Caldwell, and the Admiral and their extended family will not be able to join us in Paris. I have managed to locate hotel rooms right here in Havre so that they may begin their reunion from the long separation caused by this war." He nodded to his advisor and I knew that no hotel rooms were waiting for us unless Colonel House could pull a rabbit out of his hat and find us some. Then a strange thing happened, one of the reporters said he would like to accompany us to the hotel so he could continue his interview with the Admiral and his wife. The group of reporters split into two groups, one boarding the train with the president and the other standing with Colonel House.

"President Wilson always books rooms where ever he docks, just in case is there is a delay in his travel plans. I have the reservations here for the Admiral and his family. They will be staying at the King Louis Hotel in downtown Havre."

"Have you ever been to the King Louis Hotel, Colonel House?" The reporter from Havre was smiling.

"Certainly not, but it must be the finest in Havre in order to have a presidential suite." He handed Emily the reservation for the presidential suite and two adjoining rooms and hurried to board the train for Paris.

"I am sorry, James, I know how much you would have enjoyed attending the Paris Peace Conference."

I swept her into my arms and kissed her passionately while standing among the extended Caldwell family. She was still holding the reservation in her hand. The reporter slid it out of her hand and said, "Let me see if I can get you the presidential suite at a slightly better hotel, Admiral."

I reached for it and said, "Are you out of your mind, this reservation is paid for by the United States Government. I will rent all the rooms on the same floor for my family."

When the Caldwell family and the members of the press arrived at the King Louis we gathered in the lobby while I showed the presidential reservation to the desk clerk. Emily had gathered the reporters around her and I could hear her answer additional questions.

"How did you arrive at the daily cost per person per day, Mrs. Caldwell?"

"Please call me Emily, or Em if you like. All my friends do, it was simple mathematics actually. I used the reported populations for each country which were US 104M, GB 47M, FR 40M, RU 175M, IT 36M, BE 8M and so on."

"Excuse me, what are the initials and numbers followed by the letter M.?"

"Shorthand I learned in Georgetown School of Business; US stands for United States, 104M is the population in millions for the last census count."

"Sorry, go on please."

"Once you have the populations you divide by the costs involved. I already gave you those at the pier, but here they are again for you slow writers; US 29.4MY, GB 35.5MY, FR 20.2MY, RU 18.1MY, IT 36.0MY, and BE 5MY."

"Oh, I get it, MY stands for millions of dollars spent that year!"

"Clever, boy you could have graduated from Georgetown School of Business."

"What year was that, Em?"

"That would be telling you my age, now wouldn't it?. Let me say that I graduated one year before my husband."

"That makes you a year older than your husband?"

"No, it makes me smarter!" Em had them eating out of the palm of her hand. She could have sold them the Brooklyn Bridge, sight unseen. Maybe I would have to rethink my plans for the family businesses and put her in charge of the whole thing. No wonder I loved this woman.

"Why are you smiling, Mon Admirale?"

43

Presidential Party Arrives in Paris

December 14, 1918

M y orders from President Wilson had been to remain on call from December 4th to December 18th. Today was the 14th and he was on a train to Paris with General Pershing and I was in a hotel with my family in Havre, France. Most of the newspaper reporters had left to take the next train to Paris. The family was finally alone and probably would be until the 18th. On the 18th, I was to be released for my thirty day leave. My leave could be extended as needed, unless Emily had really irked the president and he called me to Paris or changed my present orders. My sister Ruth and I had a private conversation and she told me what Teddy had said before his death. He knew that he was failing and that I was in France in charge of the final operational plans to push Germany out of Belgium.

"Teddy was so proud of you, James."

"He was? I thought he put up with me because he loved you so much. Did you know, I told Teddy how to win your hand and convince you he had enough money to support you?"

"Was that the family trip to Nevada?"

"Yes, the family decided to spend the month between Thanksgiving and Christmas at the lodge. Emily and I gave our household staff the month off with pay and they were all pleased. We bought train tickets directly into Virginia City. Daddy had written D.D. Wilson and told him of the various arrival times and points of origin. Two tickets from Seneca Hill were my parents. Two tickets from Albany, New York were you and Teddy."

"I remember, James, Teddy and I arrived two days before you and Em got there. He had bugged me for several days about why I didn't love him and why I did not want to get married. Who else came that year?"

"A single ticket from New York City was our sister, Carol. That meant that our mother's holiday dining room table would have to seat nine members. If you and Carol got married and started having children, then the holidays would indeed be a large event. Right then, you and Teddy were a couple and I suspected that you were deeply in love with him and probably already sleeping with him."

"Yes, I was. Teddy was busy trying to build a base of support in the Republican Party. This did not endear him to daddy, who thought all Republicans were 'shady characters' looking for some way to make a profit without working hard for it. This vacation would prove interesting just listening to them debate the various views of the two different political parties."

"Let me tell you what I remember of that vacation."

I remember that four years away from the operations of the Johnstone Lodge proved to be instructional for us. So did the fact that we checked in as guests for a month, instead of going to the ranch house and staying there with our parents. The ranch house would not hold all of us and daddy wanted his family to get a first hand impression of what our guests got for their hundred dollars a night! Em and I were shown to a suite on the ninth floor.

"Is this a penthouse suite?" Emily asked as we stepped off the lift.

"It is, Madam. The Admiral and Mrs. D. D. Wilson wanted you to get the full effect of what they designed."

The bellman opened the double doors to 904 and they swung open revealing a huge foyer with a center staircase directly ahead and rooms off to either side. "I shall place the bags in the bedrooms upstairs, you each have a separate room. Miss Elizabeth, you are in the first one to the right, Master James will be in the first one to the left. Lieutenant, you and Mrs. Caldwell are in the master. If your son gets lonely in his room, there is a connecting door into your room and a day bed for him."

We stood dumbfounded at what daddy and Corine had designed. When they furnished the lodge years ago, they selected a western motif with lots of tanned leathers, braided rugs, earth tones and Russian antiques from California.. They and mother must have bought everything for sale in Northern Mexico, because the place looked like it belonged in Monterey.

"It is absolutely beautiful, James. It must be nice to have the kind of money your parents have to spend on a project. This must be a gold mine for them."

"Hello, my parents do not own this lodge. My sisters and the four of us own this place. Remember the quarterly check from the Carson City Bank?"

"Yes, but your father owns that bank!"

"Yes, Caldwell International has several banks and we get a monthly check from them, also. My father does not think in terms of personal wealth. He thinks in terms of his extended family and what income is necessary to support that segment of the family in comfort."

"Still, it must be nice to have that kind of money. How do you think of family money?"

"Emily, we are Caldwell International. My father has given each of us stock in the company. You own Caldwell International."

"I do. I mean, we do?"

"Absolutely, get used to it, honey. The United States Navy is a hobby for the Caldwell men in this family."

"Good God, you are full of yourself, James. I married a career Navy man who will be an admiral one day - not a shameless, money grubbing, robber baron of a man. I am going to take a bath and wash some of this travel dust off my body."

I stood there with my mouth open, ready to say something, when she cut me off by saying, "Someone is ringing the door chimes, James. Can you get it?"

I walked down the stairs feeling ashamed of myself and pulled open the door. You and Teddy were standing there smiling from ear to ear. You hugged me and kissed me on the cheek. Teddy did an imitation of a bear and tried to crush me in his arms.

"James, this lodge is absolutely brilliant in design. Teddy had removed his glasses and was wiping them with a small cloth he had taken from his vest pocket. He continued, "Ruthie and I got here yesterday and I have been walking around with my sketch pad, stealing ideas for the ranch in North Dakota."

"You have a ranch in North Dakota?"

"Just bought it. When I was younger, my father sent me to work summers on a cattle ranch in North Dakota. I absolutely fell in love with the area. I dropped out of Harvard for an entire year and got a job as a deputy sheriff there. My father was not amused. Anyway, when a ranch came up for sale, I bought it."

You said, "Welcome back to Nevada, James. It is so good to see you again. Where are your children? Is Emily upstairs?"

"My sister seems happy, Teddy. When are you going to make an honest woman of her?"

"I have asked her to marry me three times, James. She keeps saying, not now. When I press her, she says when I have enough money to support her, she will."

"Ruth has a fear of running out of money, Teddy. Come into the parlor and let me fix you something to drink and I will tell you where she gets the fear. You should also try what my father tried with her."

"What was that?"

"It was at the close of the war and Ruth was not very old. She and my father were riding on a ferry in South Carolina when she asked him why he was retiring from the Navy. She was afraid that the family would not have enough money to live on."

"She did not consider the wealth of Caldwell International?"

"Little girls have no idea of what a corporation is worth. Neither do big girls sometimes. I just had a conversation with Emily about the board of directors at CI and who sits on it. She has no idea that she has a seat on the board, Teddy."

"She, meaning Ruthie or Emily?"

"They both do. It would be a good idea if you encouraged Ruth to attend a CI board meeting next month. In fact, I will try to get leave so that all the Caldwells can attend."

"Bully idea, James. What can I do to help?"

"Tell her you are busy in Albany and can not attend one of the boards that you sit on. Have her take your proxy vote and attend. That should open her eyes to corporate America."

We found a liquor cabinet in the corner of the room. I grabbed two aperitif glasses and poured two small schnaps.

"What is that wonderful peppermint smell?" Emily, you and the two children were standing behind us, I had not heard you enter the room.

"Pour us one of those will you, James?"

I reached for two more glasses, filled them and placed them on a silver serving tray. "Allow me, Madams." I passed the tray to Emily and you. We all found seats and began a conversation. The door chimed again and I went to answer it. Mother, Carol and our father came into the parlor with us. I got three more glasses while Carol scooped up James into her arms and told him how much she loved him. Busy was not going to take a back seat to her brother and asked Carol to play with her.

Father wanted to know what your job was on the new magazine called, New Yorker. " I own it, Daddy. You always said, do not work for someone else, work for yourself!"

"Do you go to work everyday, or do you have someone hired to run it?"

"I am the editor, Daddy. I took journalism at Harvard, remember? I not only own the magazine, I run it, too. I hire and fire the writers and the production staff. We are only a monthly magazine with a small circulation, but someday we will be one of the largest in the country."

I could see that Teddy was listening to every word between the two of you. "Admiral, can you and Mrs. Caldwell come to New York City and see for yourself? The folks at Albany can get along without me for a few days. I have an apartment in the city with guest rooms. You are welcome to stay there with me. Ruth's apartment is smaller and is not as close to her office building. We are thinking of buying her office building, 270 Madison Avenue, as an investment, and we would like your opinion."

"About what?"

"If it would be worth our while to convert some of the office building to executive apartments. Is there a benefit to living in the same building where you work? Or would you never get away from the work? I think best when I am on the ranch in North Dakota. I need to get away from the rat race of a city - it frees my soul. Does that sound corny?"

"No, it is how you feel, Teddy." Mother was looking at Teddy with new respect. "My daughter is addicted to work, always has been. Her father and I brought her here to ride horses and experience nature as only Nevada can provide. When would be a good time to plan this trip into New York, Teddy?"

I could see that Teddy had made a convert of mother. Now, if he could only get father to forget that he was a politician and a Republican, he might have a chance with my you."

My sister looked at me and smiled. "It must be nice to have a photographic memory, James. I do recall most of what you just told me, with one exception."

"What did I forget?"

"Nothing, it is something you did not know. The reason Teddy and I were smiling from ear to ear when you opened the door was that I was pregnant and I just agreed to marry Teddy."

"All this time, I thought it was my sage advice that moved you two together. Why didn't you tell me?"

"Are you kidding? Father would have beaten Teddy to within an inch of his life. Besides, I had a miss-carriage the next week and the wedding was planned and everything worked out as planned without having Admiral Jason Caldwell have a stroke."

"Did you ever tell Teddy about your fear of financial support?"

"Yes, you have never heard this either, James. It was when Daddy and I spent all that time together in Beaufort. You and Uncle James Buchanan were spending a lot of time together and Carol was a baby with mother. Daddy and I had an adventure. This is what I remember."

D addy and I spent a great deal of time together. You and Uncle James worked at Saint Helena's Church. Mother and Carol were busy with the restoration of the Church and the house at 353 Bay Street. So, daddy and I went to Port Royal to check on the location of the grave described by John Butler's aunt. We checked with the sexton's at the Port Royal Churches and various graveyards to find where the "defenders of Fort Beauregard" were buried. We were told that no such grave existed. Daddy asked if they remembered the firing on Beauregard during the US Navy invasion of Port Royal. Sure, they remembered it alright, "The cowards defending the fort ran at the sound of the first shot fired, no one was killed because the fort was empty!"

"Where did they go?" He asked dumb founded.

"In all directions, some went back to Beaufort, others made their way to the uninhabited islands like Fripp and Pritchard."

I had never seen our father look that upset and I asked, "What is wrong, Daddy?"

"Your Aunt, Uncle and cousins may be alive, if I can find them."

"If WE can find them." I corrected him.

"If we can find them." He said with a smile.

The next day, he and I were on the ferry to Lady's Island. We hired a "two-wheeler" and searched the little villages like "Frogmore"until we reached the ford crossing to Datha Island. We stopped and talked to people asking them if they knew of anyone who had escaped from Beaufort or Port

Royal in 1861. We explained that we were looking for Robert Caldwell's daughter and her family. They all knew of the Caldwell plantation on Pollawana, but they had not heard of anyone escaping to locate there. We crossed over to Pollawana and found Tobias Caldwell and his family still on the plantation. Daddy asked him if he knew anything about his sister, Carol.

"She was blowed up over in Port Royal, Mr. Jason. She is buried in a mass grave somewheres over there."

"Thank you, Tobias. Can I show my daughter the old deserted house where I was born? Is it still standing over in the grove of live oaks?"

"Yes, Sir. Mr. Jason. It is still there. Folks 'round here says it is haunted, it has lights at night."

My heart jumped. Maybe that is where she is, I thought. We hurried over the sandy road until the horse was winded and we stopped before the old plantation house. No one could live here, it was deserted and beyond repair. We got out of the carriage, tied the horse to the hitching post and walked up to the front steps.

"Be careful, now honey, these steps look rotten, we do not want to fall through them."

"Lift me up on the porch, Daddy." He did and hoisted himself up after me and we stayed away from the steps. The front door stood ajar and we pushed it open and birds flew in all directions. They frightened us and we jumped. We were standing in the great foyer that our grand mother was so proud of when she greeted her guests forty years before.

"Over here is the parlor, Ruth. And upstairs are bedrooms where my brother, your Uncle Robert and my sister, your Aunt Carol, used to sleep and play with our toys."

"You had toys, Daddy?"

"Of course, I was little just like you when I lived here."

"I am not little. I am small for my age!"

"Yes, I keep forgetting that you are really six going on twenty-one."

"What does that mean, Daddy?"

"You are six years old, but think like an adult."

"Oh, is that good?"

"Sometimes."

We finished our tour of the house, untied the horse and started back to Tobias' house on the other side of the island. We ate lunch with them and then continued on to the Fripp Island ferry. This ferry was a privately owned means of getting from Hunting Island to Fripp. We talked to the man in charge and asked about visitors that might have come and gone.

"This is a working plantation, Admiral. You remember Captain John Fripp's kids inherited it from him. There is only one main house, close to the beach. They have servants, but they are former slaves that have been with them for years. There are no white people, other than the owners. I do not think your sister and her family are here. I know you want to find them, Admiral. The truth is there were only a handful of casualties at Fort Beauregard, the survivors ran for their lives. They did not find any remains to bury, Admiral. Your sister died inside Fort Beauregard, let her rest in peace. The folks in Port Royal made up a nice story about the 'defenders of Fort Beauregard' for future generations. The truth is the Fort was not defended, it was destroyed by US Naval cannon fire."

"I think you are right, besides it is getting past time to get back to Beaufort."

"You and your daughter should hurry so you catch the ferries between Hunting, Saint Helena and Lady's Islands."

"Will do, thank you for what you said. It helped me clear my head."

As we rode from ferry to ferry, I asked, "What was Aunt Carol like, Daddy?"

"Well, let me remember. Her hair was about the color of yours. She liked to talk nonstop, like you. We had left the plantation and moved to Beaufort so that Robert and I could go to elementary school. She was too young and she was upset that she was left at home. Your Grandpa hired a private tutor to come to the house in Beaufort so she could begin her lessons early."

"Just like me, I have a tutor."

"Yes, you do. You learn everything as quickly as she did. When it was time to go to first grade in Beaufort, she lasted only about three days and Grandma was called to school for a visit with her teacher. It was decided that she should be moved to the second grade because she already knew how to read her letters and make her numbers."

"Just like me. When will I go to second grade, Daddy?"

"You have a private tutor that lives with us. I am sorry to tell you that you will be stuck with her until you pass your exams into second level."

"What is second level, Daddy?"

"The first level is beginning, or elementary. Second level is for really smart children, like you. You will get a new tutor and your tutor will become your little sister's tutor."

"Oh, goodie. I would hate not seeing Miss Templeton every day."

"But you can not bother her, she will be busy with Carol."

"Carol, same name as Aunt Carol."

"You figured it out, your sister is named in honor of Aunt Carol."

"Why do James and I have tutors? Why are we at home and not in school?"

"If we lived in one house, in one location, then you would be in a school. Your daddy's job takes him all over the world. And because I love you so much, I take you with me."

We had by this time found our way to the livery stable where we had rented the carriage for the day. Daddy paid the livery hand and we walked to the Beaufort Ferry.

"Daddy?"

"Yes, Ruthie."

"I love you."

"Me, too, 'Ruthie Two Shoes.'"

"Why do you call me that?"

"When you were a little girl, not like the big girl you are now, you kept losing one shoe under your bed or wherever and I had to help you find it. So I started called you, 'Ruthie Two Shoes'."

"Daddy, will it make you mad if I tell you that I used to hide one shoe so that you would help me find it?"

"I think I figured that out after the umpteenth time, Ruthie. And no, I will never get mad at you for wanting to spend time with me. There will be a time, many years from now, when you will meet a nice young man and fall in love with him, like I did with your mother."

"Then what happens?"

"Then, I hope the nice young man holds on for dear life, because life with you will be one hell of a ride."

"You swore, Daddy!"

"I know. Do not tell your mother!"

"Where are we going for Christmas, Daddy?"

"To your home in Bermuda, the flotilla is back in Port Royal and it is time that the crew members get back to Bermuda to be with their families for Christmas."

"Why do you call the ships a flotilla?"

"Because there are not enough of them to be a fleet, and they are unarmed merchant ships."

"Then why is one of them called USS Providence, it has cannons."

"Yes, it does. It was built for the US Navy about 70 years ago. I bought it and changed it into a merchant ship and used it for many years. When the war broke out, I loaned it back to the Navy."

"Do they pay you rent?"

"Yes, they do. You know, it seems I have had this same conversation with your mother!"

"Are we rich, Daddy?"

"In more ways than you can imagine, honey. This family is truly blessed."

"Will we ever run out of money?"

"Never!"

"Promise, Daddy."

"Promise, Ruthie"

My sister looked at me with tears in her eyes and said, "I made Teddy make me that same promise on the day you opened that door at the lodge so many years ago. What is this family meeting in Europe all about, James? Do you need money? I can loan you a million or two if you need it."

I hugged my sister and said, "No, I thought maybe you and the girls might need money from me." We both started laughing until Emily walked into the room and looked at both of us.

"What did I miss?"

"Family history." We repeated our stories with added tidbits that we could remember.

"The reason I came looking for you, James, is that Spencer wants to tell you about the school report that he wrote about Winston Churchill."

"The father Lord Randolph, or his famous British son?"

"Both, I think. Go and find him and I will talk to Ruth about what you have planned for Caldwell International."

"What WE have planned." Ruth began to laugh.

I found Spencer in the game room of the hotel and I asked him to show me his report on Winston Churchill.

THE CHURCHILLS

CHURCHILL, Randolph Henry Spencer, Lord, statesman, born in

Blenheim, England, Feburary 3, 1849; died January 24, 1895. He was the third son of the seventh Duke of Marlborough. He was educated at Eton, and Merton College, Oxford, and entered Parliament in 1874 as member for Woodstock. The same year he married the brilliant Miss Jennie Jerome of New York, who was a prominent member of the Primrose League, and gave him valuable assistance throughout his political career. He was a quiescent member of Parliament until 1880, when the Conservative defeat roused him to action as the leader of the Fourth Party – a small band of keen-minded Conservatives. He distinguished himself as a ready, unconventional debater, attracting particular attention by his audacious criticism of Gladstone's foreign policy. He became still more prominent as chairman of the Conservative Union (1884), and in 1885 unsuccessfully attempted to defeat Mr. Bright in Birmingham, but was returned for South Paddington, which was kept in reserve for him. He became Secretary of State for India from June , 1885, to January, 1886, but the speedy downfall of the Salisbury administration caused him to return to England. With the return of Salisbury to power, in 1896, he became Chancellor of the exchequer and leader of the House of Commons, but after successful work he resigned at the end of the year. In 1887 he made a trip through Europe, seeking to form an alliance against Germany, and in 1891 visited South Africa. During his absence he was re-elected, but died in 1895 before serving another term.

CHURCHILL, Winston Spencer (1874-). An English author and politician, son of Lord Randolph Churchill and Lady Jennie Churchill. He was educated at Harrow and Sandhurst, entered the army in 1895, served with the Spanish army in Cuba, and fought with distinction in India (1897) and the Sudan (1898). On the outbreak of the Boer War (1899) he went to the Transvaal. On November 15, he was taken prisoner by the Boers while acting as a correspondent for the Morning Post. He was imprisoned at Pretoria, but escaped later in the year. In September, 1900, he was elected Conservative member of Parliament for Oldham. He opposed Mr. Chamberlain's tariff reform proposals, and in the sessions of 1904-5 acted with the Liberals. He became parliamentary secretary for the colonies under the Campbell-Bannerman ministry in December, 1905, and in the general election of the following month was chosen as a Liberal from Manchester, Northwest. He has written; The Story of the Malakand Field Force (1898), The River War (1899), Savrola (1900), London to

Ladysmith via Pretoria (1900), Ian Hamilton's March (1900) and Lord Randolph Churchill, 2 volumes in 1906.

I handed the report back to Spencer and asked, "What have you learned from this report?"

"Well, Sir, my case is a little different. My father is the American, not my mother. My mother is a commoner from London, while my father would have been royalty if he was born in England."

"Why do you say that, Spencer?"

"Because of the wealth of the Caldwell family, Grandpa. In England most millionaires are Lords and Ladies – not commoners."

"Spencer, my father was as common as could be. He was a very good judge of character and my mother was the brains behind the business empire that they built together. She was almost as shrewd a business woman as your Grandmother Caldwell. Your Grandmother created the great wealth for this family. You need to talk to her about what she thinks about royalty, here in Europe or in the United States."

44

Presidential Party Arrives in London

December 26, 1918

According to the newspapers President Wilson arrived in Paris on the 14th of December and was made a citizen of Paris. The peace conference was held without any United States Senators present. They were not part of the official visiting Presidential party that left us in Havre. Not a single Republican from either the house or the senate accompanied the president. The president thought that his popularity in Europe would be reflected at home – it was not. The Republican Senate would be asked to ratify any agreements that the President signed in Paris – they did not. Democrats who would be seeking re-election in two years began to distance themselves from the president and his actions in Europe.

On December 23, there were hunger riots in Berlin. The new German President, Ebert of the newly formed German Republic, upheld order but not before citizens died in the streets of Berlin. President Wilson seemed not to care what was happening in Berlin and German/American citizens at home burned him in effigy. By Christmas Eve, and ten days later the peace celebration continued with the president visiting General Pershing and his American army troops. Pictures appeared in the French newspapers and were widely circulated at home showing the president's official party with the American "dough boys" eating Christmas Eve dinner in French Villas and Chateaus.

On Christmas day, the official presidential party took the train for the coast of France and boarded a ferry for the coast of England. The president was met by King George and Queen Mary at Charing Cross Station. I was standing in the crowd watching the official welcome by the King and Queen. My family had taken the train from Havre to Calais on the 18th and then the ferry crossing to Dover, England. From Dover we again took the train to the Borough of Reigate station and were met by Mr. Idris Jones who I found listed in the Reigate Chamber of Commerce materials that Louis had given me.

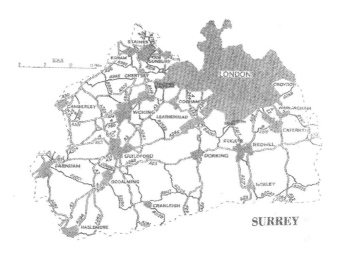

I had phoned him from the King Louis Hotel in Havre, France and asked him to meet us and show us property for sale in the borough. He took us to the Prince of Wales on Holmesdale Road where I had made reservations for ten hotel rooms. We settled in and began to visit with our land broker, Idris Jones when it began to rain. He was prepared to give us his undivided attention for as many days as we needed him.

When Spencer found out that his great grandfather was Sir Jason Caldwell, Knight of the Realm and protector of Bermuda with dual citizenship, he began to ask questions, first of his father and then of me.

"My great grandfather was a knight of the realm?"

"Yes, Spencer, we have been telling you since you were born that you are special."

"I know, but that is what all parents tell their children. How did grandpa's father get his knighthood?"

"Actually, my father was in America and I was in South Hampton on a Naval Academy cruise and I was asked to come to London so Queen Victoria could knight me in my father's place."

"You met Queen Victoria, Grandpa?"

"Yes, Spencer. This is how I remember it."

O ur last stop on the USNA cruise was South Hampton, England. As the Superintendent of the Naval Institute my father spent his summers in Nevada at the ranch house in Virginia City. He received a cablegram from Admiral Nevelle Napier in London informing him that he was meeting my ship, the USS Nispic, in South Hampton. He would meet with Admiral Hagood and request his permission to have me leave my ship long enough to travel with him to London.

When the USNA cruise arrived in South Hampton, England, we were paid a courtesy call from Lord Napier. He asked for permission to come aboard the USS Nispic and introduced himself to Captain Evans. He asked to see Ensign Caldwell so he could deliver a missive from Admiral Hagood. The Captain of the USS Nispic sent for me and asked Admiral Napier if he would like a cup of tea in the wardroom.

"An excellent idea, I had no idea that American sailors drank tea."

"Tea is easier to prepare and serve at sea, Admiral. We have something stronger if you would like."

The captain showed Lord Napier to the wardroom and asked the steward to prepare three cups of tea. I appeared in a few minutes and saluted the captain and then the Admiral. Captain Evans said, "Sit down for a minute Ensign, Admiral Napier has orders for you from Admiral Hagood."

"So you are Jason's son, I have heard a lot about you. Your father talks about you, nonstop."

"He does?"

"Yes, says you live and breathe US Navy from sun up until sun down."

"I watched my father for the last twenty-one years. I learned everything about what the Navy was between 1833 to 1873. He was my history instructor at the Academy and it helped that he owns a merchant marine fleet stationed in Bermuda. Have you ever been to Bermuda, Admiral?"

"Yes, to meet with your father during the war and , of course, to visit the Royal Naval Dockyards on the west end."

"Of course, I remember my father talking about how much he admired you when he returned the HMS Resolute to you."

"Your father is a remarkable man, James, please give him this letter when you see him. It is the official invitation to London. The Queen has recognized the fact that Jason Caldwell is a dual national and wishes to reward his 40 years of service to the US Navy and the Bermuda Crown Colony."

"Thank you, Lord Napier."

"And here are your orders for the next few days, from Admiral Hagood. You are to accompany me to London for the knighthood to be bestowed upon your father. You will kneel before the Queen and accept on his behalf and his rightful heir."

"Rightful heir?"

"That would be you, son."

"Oh."

"Yes, the next time I see your father, I can address him as Sir Jason Caldwell, Knight of the Realm, Protector of Bermuda. And upon his death, you James Jason Caldwell will become Sir James Caldwell of Bermuda."

Spencer was wide eyed, "I had no idea, Grandpa!"

"Spencer, calm down. I am only a knight in Bermuda. Not here or in America. We do not have royalty in America."

"You mean except for King Woodrow Wilson."

"Spencer, watch your mouth!" Louis was angry with him, but I could not keep from laughing.

"Spencer, you will apologize for that last remark." His mother was angry with him now.

"Sorry, Grandpa, my mouth ran away with itself."

"That is not good enough, Spencer. The President of the United States is the most important man in the world right now and your grandfather is in command of the entire United States Navy and reports directly to him as commander-in-chief." I had never heard Louis defend the military establishment, in fact he always made fun of it. Maybe he was becoming an adult.

"I am sorry Grandpa, I should not have made fun of your boss. Can I ask another question?"

"Of course, Spencer, you are in trouble with your parents, not me."

"Does this mean that my father will become Sir Louis Caldwell?"

"No, sorry, Spencer, that dubious honor goes to your Uncle James here upon my death."

"This conversation is depressing. Let's find an estate for Sir James here in England." My son James was smiling and holding Martha close to him as she realized that one day she would become Lady Caldwell.

It became overcast and the clouds opened up once more and the rain fell upon the Prince of Wales tiny hotel in Reigate. It had rained everyday since we arrived in southern England and it did not look like this was going to be any different. The rain pounded upon the leaded glass panes of our rooms as solemnly as drums in a military funeral cortege. Whenever we ventured out of the hotel we kept to the many overhangs, sheltering from the worst of the wind and rain. The evenings came earlier than usual for winter time and the air smelled of ozone and roses. Rosebushes twined around support stakes along the sides of the hotel, most varieties bloomed in southern England, even in winter. The flowers drooped, soggy and heavy in the rain. When we came inside for the night, we headed for one of the many coal fired heaters located throughout the first floor of the hotel. We warmed our backsides and dried our coats before hanging them in our rooms. Each of the ten rooms that I rented in the Prince of Wales had a fireplace and we welcomed the heat. The hotel did not have a central heat source like a boiler to supply radiator heat to every room. It was winter in England, I decided to avoid visiting Louis and Cathleen in winter time.

The family ate an evening meal together each night and then retired to our individual rooms. Emily and I stood in the dark of our room and looked out the large leaded glass window that overlooked a garden. Rain struck the window panes and streamed down the glass. When an occasional flicker of lightning brightened the night sky and passed through the window, it briefly projected the random rippling patterns of water from the glass onto the walls around us, which made the room seem as amorphous and semitransparent as a mirage. Emily spoke first.

"Why are you letting some of the Caldwell companies go public, James?"

"I want only those in the United States to be on the New York Stock Exchange and fend for themselves. Louis will handle all the international companies from here in England."

"Why Louis and not James?"

"Because Cathleen is English and she wants to remain so and Louis is devoted to her and will live anywhere she wants him to. She is European not North American. She could not survive in Canada. James is married to the Navy, just like I was before the war started. He is not a lawyer and it will take a lawyer to keep the international companies afloat when the next depression hits."

"I don't understand. Why do you think a depression is coming? Business has never been better."

"The huge economic surge was war driven, it was artificial and will collapse within a few more months. Now is the time to sell what stock we have and buy right after the fall – say somewhere between 1920 and 21."

"I trust President Wilson, James. His economic measures have proven to be just what the country needs."

"That is true, but I doubt he will run for a third term. His health is not good, I doubt he is alive in 1921."

"So, the next Democratic president will follow in Wilson's foot steps and set in place economic measures for the times. The United States is going to be the leader in the League of Nations and world policy creating business opportunities in Europe and at home."

"I hope you are right, Em. What I see is much different. The Republican controlled congress will never agree to join the League of Nations, let alone lead it. In fact, a new Republican President will not even sign the peace treaty that President Wilson is writing in Paris. I am afraid that the next president will be the US Senator from Ohio."

"Busy's father-in-law? James, no setting Senator has ever been elected president of the United States. Where will he get his support?"

"Women will vote for the first time in states throughout the union. Warren Harding is an influential newspaper publisher, or rather his wife, the former Florence Kling DeWolfe is the influential force behind him. She was a divorcee, five years Harding's senior, and the mother of a young son, Marshall Eugene DeWolfe."

"You mean our Marshall is Warren Harding's stepson?"

"Yes, she pursued Harding persistently until he reluctantly proposed. Florence's father, Amos Hall Kling was furious with his daughter's decision to marry Harding, forbidding his wife from attending the wedding and not speaking to his daughter or son-in-law even after he was elected to the Senate. In 1912, Harding gave the nominating speech for incumbent President William Taft at the Republican National Convention and he is well liked within the party. Now that Teddy is dead, there will be no one to oppose his nomination next year."

E xcept for the drifting fog and rain, the night remained perfectly still. Emily and I were fast asleep as they sky began its transition from black to gray-black. Dawn hadn't crawled out of its hole yet, but it was creeping close, and it would crest the wall of the garden in an hour. When it finally peaked over the garden wall and into our room, it painted the floor in shades of brass and copper.

"James wake up, you have to travel into London and say farewell to President Wilson, he is speaking at some guildhall or another before he takes the ferry back to France."

45

Presidential Party Returns to Paris

December 31, 1918

O n the last day of 1918, the presidential party returned to Paris, he had worn out his welcome in London. When he spoke at the Guildhall just before he crossed the channel to France he was given the United Kingdom Medal of Freedom. He wore it as he waved goodbye to me and my family saying, "Admiral Caldwell, your service to your country is very much appreciated. I know you and Louis have family here in Britain. Please extend your leave for another thirty days. I will have Joe Daniels send you the paperwork. Do you have an address here in London?"

"No, Mr. President, my family has found a land broker that we think will be showing us some properties in next few days. Have Joe send the papers to me, in care of the Hotel Prince of Wales on Holmesdale Road in Reigate."

"Prince of Wales – Halstead Road – London, got it." He turned to walk away and I did not correct him. I knew Joe's address and I would send him a telegram with the new address once the land purchase was complete. I turned to Emily and said, "You know you were right about our president when we were sitting listening to his address on Inauguration Day, March 4, 1913."

"Part way through the address, I leaned over and asked you if he always used such bombastic words when he spoke one on one to you, James."

"I did not understand the term 'bombastic', I had to go and look it up after the address was over and I was alone in my office."

"Do you think he has a chance getting anything ratified by the Senate?"

"I would venture to say that he has lost any chance of getting his ideas approved at home or back in Paris. I think he is wasting his time in Europe, he should be at home trying to mend fences."

"Do you think he will return in time?"

"No, I think your grandson Spencer was correct, 'King Woodrow has no clothes.'"

Emily began to laugh and then reminded me that our oldest daughter and her husband wanted to talk to me about something. We have four children, all married and most of them are normal, young adults in need of advice or guidance in one form or another from time to time. With our oldest it was probably what to do with her "spend thrift" husband, Marshall Eugene Harding. Marshall was the son of Warren G. Harding, the United States Senator from Ohio. His wife, our daughter, Elizabeth Louise Caldwell was born April26, 1878. Baby Elizabeth came to live with us in the two story brownstone that Emily found four blocks from her parents. She was tiny, six pounds, four ounces. Em said it was still like trying to push a watermelon through her body. She also said that, fashion be damned, she was not going to wear a corset or a bustle again!

"You can not sit comfortably in either one. They are designed to make your waist smaller and your butt bigger. Do you like the size of my waist and butt, James?"

I lied. One or the other grandmother was at our house from April 27 until May 27. The baby was named after each one. So, naturally, each grandmother tried to out do the other. I finally had to ask them both to stay at home and we would come and visit them. We had hired a household staff, including a nanny for the baby so that Em could have a break during the night feedings. I was gone from the office to inspect the harbors all over the country. These were never less than a month of travel. The other harbors assigned to us could be visited by train and I was gone a week or two depending on the distance.

Elizabeth was healthy and grew like a weed. It seemed like every time I got home, she could do some thing else.

"James, she rolled over while you were gone. She sat up while you were gone, James. She stood by herself while you were gone, James." Emily was getting tired of telling me everything I was missing.

When she started to talk and Em was pregnant again I said, "Enough of this absent husband and father business. I am asking for an assistant to run all over the country inspecting harbors and waterways."

I was holding Elizabeth on my lap, trying to get her to say her name. She could manage, "Mama", "Dada", "No" and some other simple one words commands like, "Up", "Down".

"Say, Elizabeth." I looked at Em with a concerned look on my face when Elizabeth said, "Busy butt". We both started to giggle and then laugh out loud. Elizabeth thought she had suddenly caused her parents great joy and she repeated, "Busy butt, busy butt, busy butt." Her grandmothers could not get enough of this tiny bundle of joy who called herself "Busy butt". She was their first grandchild, until Naomi announced that she and JR were expecting.

We managed to see the Schneiders most weekends that we were in Georgetown. Elizabeth loved the train ride to Grandma's house in "psylvia" as she managed only that for Pennsylvania. She could not sit on her mother's lap, as her mother had no lap. The train ride was not comfortable for Em. Busy butt climbed all over me, slept on my lap or draped over my chest like a wet shirt. I loved it.

She learned to ride a pony and do all sorts of "country" things at Seneca Hill with her Grandpa Jason, as she could not manage her last name yet. It came out "allwill". Busybutt Allwill could tear your heart out when she cried because she had skinned her knees. Her grandpa would hold her in his arms and cry with her telling her, "It is alright, Busy, you are not going to die, it is a long ways from your heart." After he had put her to bed for the night, my father would talk to me about what was going on in the White House. As the National Affairs advisor, he was privy to the latest 'scuttlebutt'.

"I take the train into town for all the regularly scheduled cabinet meetings and skip the others. President Hayes is trying his best, but the house and senate now have simple Democratic majorities after the midterm elections. The railroad strike, the summer you and Em were married, caused him a lot of head aches and now the miners are going to do the same thing. The riot in Pittsburgh required sending federal troops."

"The cabinet had quite a discussion on gold and silver coinage verus paper money, I heard from Uncle Ben."

"Yes, we did. How often do you see Ben Hagood?"

"I am in the Annex, but I see him in the Army Navy about once a week. Did you know that he is going to retire after the election - even if Hayes wins re-election. He is moving back to Savannah. He has been exchanging letters with his ex-wife. He told me that she has not had much luck with husbands. Her first, Uncle Ben, she abandoned, claiming he was never home. The second was killed in a hunting accident. The third went missing on a cruise from Savannah to Cuba. The fourth was a rich merchant who had a ship's supply warehouse on River Street. He was nearly twenty years her senior and died of old age. In her last letter, she said she always loved him and if he ever wanted to move back to Savannah she would deed the ship's store to him."

"Is he considering it?" My father had a bemused look on his face.

"I would think it could go either way, depends what he finds on his next trip to Savannah."

"He has been seeing her?" The look changed to amusement.

"He spends his leaves there. He seems ready to give her another chance."

"Well, I will be damned!"

"Jason Caldwell! Watch your language, my name sake is in this house." My mother had entered the room.

"Yes, Louise."

"What have you two men been talking about? Emily has laid down for a rest. She will be up in about an hour. How is she doing with this baby, James?"

"Her doctor in Georgetown, says she is on schedule for delivery in June. She is larger than she was with Busy, probably a boy this time or girl twins."

"Oh, James, bite your tongue, I would not wish twins on anyone."

Our second child, James Jason Caldwell II, was born on June 2, 1880, while the National Republican Convention was meeting in Chicago. He weighed six pounds and eleven ounces, small for a boy but large for someone as small as Emily. She slept for two days after the birth and awoke on June 4th to find that Rutherford B. Hayes was not re-nominated for president by his own party. A determined effort was made to re-nominate General US Grant instead. Grant's campaign manager, Roscoe Conkling, was masterful and managed to secure 306 delegates to vote for President Grant. The fraud and deception of Grant's previous administrations were brought up by James Blaine, of Maine and John Sherman, of Ohio. They convinced the convention to nominate General James Garfield and Chester Arthur.

The campaign was a heated one with both sides forgetting most of their platform planks. Hancock was quoted as saying that the tariff issue was not part of his campaign and was a "local issue". Garfield stated he favored cheap Chinese labors. These two statements drove the voters away from both parties. Each candidate carried nineteen States in November. The electoral votes were split; 214 for Garfield and 155 for Hancock.

I had until March to clean out my personal things from my office at USCGS. So I did not hurry to box and send personal items to my next assignment or to my parents for storage at Seneca Hill. My sister Ruth's intended, Teddy Roosevelt was elected to the New York Assembly that fall. He had graduated with her from Harvard in '79. His ability, courage and honesty were conceded by his political opponents. He was quoted as saying, "All Americans admire pluck, fearlessness, frankness, unassailable integrity and aggressiveness in the expression of one's convictions. You will not have to guess what I am thinking, or be surprised by what I do for the voters of New York." As the leader of the Republican minority this was like a breath of fresh air for the New York State Assembly.

After the election, Emily and I discussed where the US Navy might send us. "We should keep this brownstone here in Georgetown until I get my assignment, Em. I no longer have the shield provided by Uncle Ben, outgoing Secretary of the Navy or the White House National Affairs Advisor. For the first time in my life, I will be assigned according to my merits and service record of the last four years.

"Do you care that you were not promoted from Ensign to Lt JG in '79, James? You would have been a JG in '79 if you had gone to your sea trials."

"Not at all, Em. Kiro went to sea and is now a JG, but he has only two years of service. As soon as I am promoted to JG, I would out rank him because of my time of service. I think we made the right choice by starting our family when we did. Kiro is still telling his girl friend in California to wait until he is finished with his tour of sea duty."

"He is on the USS Ranger doing hydrographic work off Baja California, Central America and in the north Pacific, correct? What if you get assigned to the Ranger as his assignment?"

"We would be given adequate notice to move our household to anywhere along the west coast."

"What is the home port for the Ranger?"

"It might be Mare Island, San Francisco. Or it could be at the new naval base in San Diego."

"Then I will write to a staffing agency in either place and try to replace our household staff."

"Good idea, Em. You are going to have your hands full with two children."

Busy would be five years old on April 26, 1883, and Emily was not pleased that I would be gone for that important milestone in her life. I told her I would also be gone on June 2 for James's birthday and I would probably miss the birth of our third child. I could not see how I could be in charge of a marine survey in Alaska and be home for birthdays in the summer. I told Em, "If the Navy will approve survey chiefs to take command of each of the three survey ships, I could be in overall command from Mare Island or the *USS Ranger*. Rodney Lowe is the captain of the Ranger and he could take me to the nearest port that has a coastal railway into Canada. The train systems in Canada are good. I could be in San Francisco in a couple of weeks. Ask your doctor to try to pin point the delivery date and I will be here for that."

"Unless I deliver early. Once you have given birth, babies can come at any time. I will give you a date. You see if you can get a thirty day leave. Fifteen days before and fifteen days after the birth would be great for me and the children. One thing for sure, if you are gone for two more summers, we do not want to have a fourth child!"

"I understand, Em. How large a family should we consider? Your parents had two, mine three. What is the ideal number?"

"There is no ideal number, James. I enjoy our family. Write to your mother and ask her if she wants to come to San Francisco for a few weeks while your father plays 'Admiral' again in Washington. Tell her that if this is a girl, we plan on naming her Louise Ann Caldwell. That should get her and a traveling companion on the next train out of Oil City!"

"And what if it is a boy? Do you think he will mind being called Louise?" I was smiling but Em was not amused.

"James, we have not talked about this, but what if it is twins? I am huge already."

"If we have twins, Em, we will call them quits! Four children would be a handful when two are twins. We would need more household help and by that time we would need to hire a tutor for Busy."

"I did not have a tutor, James, and I went to college. Elizabeth does not need a special tutor unless her teachers indicate that she needs one to keep up with the rest of her class. I, absolutely, do not think that home schooling is a good idea, James. I want our children to interact with people outside the immediate household."

"I agree, Em. The contact with others is important, I missed that part of my education. Would you agree to sending them to private school? The best private school, in the immediate area where I am stationed, would allow them to take advantage of our ability to give them the finest education available."

"Only if it is a day school, James. We are not going to send our children to a boarding school like the English."

I was on the *USS Ranger* headed north along the coast to the ports of Alaska when the twins were born, a month early. Louise weighed just over 4 pounds and Louis was nearly five pounds. Her doctor indicated that they were both in danger of under developed lungs, time would tell. I was very grateful that my mother was with Emily and that the Schneiders came as soon as they heard the news. My father pulled some strings in Washington and I was sent home from Port Townsend on the steamer, Victoria ,on her return run to San Francisco. The *USS Ranger* continued along the inside passage. It was summer time but the nights were cool and the survey crews had to be bundled up to go on deck. They passed Canadian Indian villages and white trading posts until they came to the Port of Metlakatta. It was the first Alaskan water to be mapped and the Ranger dropped anchor. The Puritan continued on to Ketchikan and dropped anchor, the Palinurus dropped anchor in Hydaburg.

I rejoined the group in Cape Yakataga after my thirty day leave. Rodney Lowe asked me, "How are the new twins progressing, James?"

"They are so tiny, they both lost weight after they were born and it was touch and go there for awhile. Emily finally got a doll's baby bottle and fed them every hour until their body weight stabilized. In a couple of weeks they were gaining weight."

"How did big sister and brother react to them?"

"They asked if they were that small and helpless when they were born. It has been a good thing for them to see how small babies manage to stay alive. Emily is exhausted and I hired another nursery helper for her. When her mother and my mother leave, the extra set of hands will be a great help to her."

"What will you do if the twins do not progress as expected?"

"I will resign my commission and return to San Francisco. My father, of all people, suggested that I do that. I agreed with him and the relief on Emily's face was very apparent."

"I hope that you do not have to do that, James. The Navy will loose a valuable engineer."

"Thank you, Rodney. I have got to go look over all the data that you have gathered in the last several trips to this part of Alaska. We will not be able to map the Yukon River basin in the time allowed and that is a shame. Did you know that the Yukon is third in length in the United States? It is the fourth longest in North America and the seventh in the Western Hemisphere! It is 2,044 miles long, and drains an area of 200,000 square miles."

"Good God, James! That is larger than the United States east of the Mississippi."

"I know, it is even bigger than Texas." I said this because Rodney's parents lived in Houston.

"Are you sure about that, James? The Republic of Texas included the now states of Arizona and New Mexico."

"I know that, Rodney. Let me put it this way, if you divided the Territory of Alaska into two equal parts, each part would be bigger than the Republic of Texas."

The memories of those three births and the four children that composed our family were running through my mind as I agreed to meet with Busy and her husband Marshall. I asked Emily, "How did time pass so quickly? Wasn't it just yesterday that we were entering those four in college? First Busy and then the rest?"

W hen our daughter was making applications to attend colleges on the east coast that year, it still had not hit me that I was thirty-nine years old. Her mother was forty. How could that be possible? I was standing on the front porch of Emily Schneider's brownstone in Georgetown only yesterday.

What am I doing here? What if Tom Jr. and Emily are not home? I reached for the door knocker and let it fall a few times. No one is home, not even a servant. I need to get to Philadelphia. I turned to go and the door opened.

"James Caldwell, is that you?"

Emily Schneider was standing in the doorway. "Your father wanted me to check on you and see if you and Tom needed anything. I am on my way to the Philadelphia Shipyards and it was right on the way."

"You are the same poor liar, JJ. Washington is not on the way from Seneca Hill to Philadelphia. Why did you come here?"

"To see you, Emily."

"That is better, come inside, Tom is home and will want to talk to you about the Naval Academy. I want to know what your future plans are JJ."

I felt a large lump forming in my throat, so I did not respond. I grabbed my bag and walked into the Schneider home. I sat the bag down in the foyer in front of a center stairway and waited for Emily to tell me where her brother was. I turned and she had her arms around me hugging the breath out of me. My knees turned to jelly but my mouth met hers and I did not run away to the stables this time.

Elizabeth and her mother poured over college catalogs, visited three co-educational institutions and in the end picked the college that Emily had graduated from in 1876. We were already living in Washington and Emily insisted that Elizabeth spend the first year at home. There were no women dormitories on campus, she would have to live in an apartment with other roommates, and Em put her foot down.

"Elizabeth you are only seventeen years old. You have a choice here. One you wait a year before entering Georgetown or you enter this year and live at home. Remember, I went to Georgetown and I was eighteen nearly nineteen when I left home. Make up your mind."

Elizabeth chose to enter college and live at home for a year. I breathed easier, I did not know about her mother. Classes began in September that year and Elizabeth seemed happy with her course work. She went to class every day, studied in the library and at the end of the first semester she announced that she wanted to transfer to Aunt Carol's college in New York. My Sister, Carol, had graduated Magna Cum Laude from Columbia Teachers College. She had also finished her master's degree and had taken a professorship in a small college in upstate New York. Em was beside herself. "Which college, Columbia Teachers in New York or where she teaches now?"

"Where she teaches now. I want the experience of living in a dormitory with other girls my age."

Before Em could explode, I said, "That is a wonderful idea, Busy! We should have sent you there last semester. Pack your bags, your mother and I will drive you to Aunt Carol's house tomorrow."

Elizabeth was so grateful for what I said she did not even complain about the Busy moniker. Her mother, on the other hand, was not amused. When Busy was out of sight, she said, "James, we need to talk about these things before you announce a unilateral decision. I happen to agree with you, this time, but in the future she will come to you and you alone when she wants something she feels she can not get from me. Do you understand?"

"Perfectly. Elizabeth, come down here a minute and talk to your mother and me, will you?"

"What is it, Daddy?" She did not look at Em.

"I was very premature with a trip tomorrow. You need to call your Aunt and ask about the possibilities of transfer, first. Once that is done and you and your mother decide what you will need in a woman's college that far away from home - then you can start packing. I am sorry, honey. I was so happy for you that I jumped the gun. No wonder the navy has never given me anything important to do. I am way too impulsive."

"James Caldwell, you are not impulsive. It took me and my father two years to get you to propose to me!"

"Really!" Busy was enjoying this. "Tell me more."

"That is enough for now, Elizabeth. Get on the telephone and place a call to Somerset College, Oswego, New York. Before I change my mind. Your father and you ganged up on me this time. Remember, both of us care very much about what happens to you, Elizabeth."

September 1896, saw a new crop of fourth class cadets arrive at Annapolis, Maryland. One plebe was already following in the footsteps of his father and grandfather before him. He was the son of Commander Caldwell, the hero at Valpariso, Chile, and later Admiral Caldwell head of Naval Intelligence, Department of the Navy. He was also the grandson of a five star Admiral. He was excited about his appointment to the academy and we were in the process of moving him into the fourth class barracks as described by the cadet hand book pages 14-22. Em and I went with him to see his common living space. He met his room mates; William Henderson, Rudolph Hayes and Kiro Kunitomo II. Kiro was the son of my room mate from San Francisco, I wondered who had arranged that circumstance. I knew the four of them would became instant friends and spent a great deal of time together.

"Admiral Caldwell?"

"Yes, Kiro."

"My father says to ask you about what life was like here in this barracks in the olden days."

"Yes, James. Tell us what it was like that many years ago." Em was smiling.

"1873 was not the olden days, gentlemen. You will not believe this, but you will blink your eyes and you will be standing in a college dorm with one of your children. Mrs. Caldwell and I just went through this with James' sister Elizabeth."

"I know, Admiral, but when I ask my father what to expect, he just smiles and says, 'When you leave San Francisco your life will change."

"Maybe you plebes might want to sit down and I will tell you what it was like in September 1873 on this very spot, different room of course.

We were not to leave the barracks for any reason without the permission of an upperclassman. We needed permission to attend classes, walk to mess, shower and shave, and even permission to relieve ourselves in the head. All this has changed, of course, for you fellows. I remember one episode our plebe year that will illustrate what I mean...

All that went out discipline went out the window when your father, Kiro, saw President Grant cross the Academy grounds. We poured from the barracks onto the lawns without permission. The upperclassmen were too busy gaping at the security detail and President Grant to care. We began following President Grant en mass as he walked towards Wise Hall. That was where my father taught his history classes, Kiro."

"Why was the President be on the Academy Grounds?" Asked Bill Henderson.

"He is was here to see your father." Kiro replied.

"Have you heard this story, Kiro?" I asked.

"Yes, but the others have not, finish it, it is good one."

"Very well. We continued along with the mass of plebes, cadets and midshipmen until a security agent held up his hand and asked us to stop."

"The President is going to attend a Naval History class this morning in Wise Hall. He will be inside about an hour and if you would like to wait to talk to him after he is through you are welcome to do so. This many cadets can not occupy the first floor of Wise Hall. So come back if you like and the President will shake your hand and find out how you like attending the United States Naval Academy."

"By this time the midshipmen had recovered and began herding us plebes back towards our barracks. 'You heard what the officer said. Go about your business. You plebes left without permission, drop and give us twenty. Now double time back to rooms or where ever you should be at seven bells, move it, move it.'"

"I asked for permission to go to class?" I had grabbed my books and was trying to get back on the parade grounds. I began a brisk pace for the classrooms directly across from Admiral's row. I watched for upperclassmen and when no one noticed I cut across the street and into #2. Mom, President Grant is on the grounds. He went to see Dad in Wise Hall. Wow, Dad must be in some kind of trouble. What is Dad's classroom number.?"

"James, you can not just walk into your Dad's classroom. You have to have permission."

"Got it. I will be right back. I ran out the rear door of #2 and crossed along the rear to #1, my Uncle Ben's house. I knocked until a steward answered the door. I did not wait for the steward to ask a question, I said. 'The President of the United States is on the grounds, is the Superintendent aware of this?'"

"Wait here, cadet, I will see if the Superintendent is aware of the President's arrival."

"Admiral Ben Hagood, out of uniform, came rushing to the back door. 'JJ, Is this some kind of prank?'

"No, sir. I saw President Grant go into Wise Hall."

"Come inside, JJ, I do not want an upperclassman to see you at the rear of my house. Let me finish dressing and we will walk over together."

"In a few minutes, the Superintendent of the Naval Academy and I walked past the Presidential security and into Wise Hall. We pulled the door to 147 open quietly and tip toed into the back of the lecture hall. In front of the class was the President telling the seniors, 'The rest of my story can be found in the Naval Institute Building here on campus. Look for messages sent to: Edwin Stanton from Commander Western Naval Theater, subject, end of naval campaign to free Mississippi and Tennessee River Basins. In one of these messages you will find a recommendation from Admiral Caldwell for my promotion from one star to three stars - an almost unheard of thing, even in war time.'"

"President Grant walked back up the aisle towards Superintendent Hagood and me. As he passed he said, 'Superintendent Hagood, JJ, nice to see you both this morning.' He did not stop walking until he had picked up his security detail in the hallway and made his way out onto the steps of Wise Hall. Here he stopped and raised his hands above his head and said in a clear voice, 'Cadets and midshipmen line up, I want to shake the hands of the future United States Naval Officer Corps.' He moved slowly along the line, shaking hands and asking questions. He answered questions when he could, laughed with the cadets and joked about coming to Annapolis to escape the 'madhouse called the White House.' He was making his way towards a waiting carriage, opened the door himself and sat down to be driven to the train station."

"What happened then?" A wide eyed Em asked.

"Three people stood watching from the top of the steps to Wise Hall, two Admirals and myself. I was sort of in a daze until my father asked, 'JJ, what are you doing out of barracks without permission?'"

"He has the permission of the Superintendent, Admiral Caldwell. I would have missed the whole thing if JJ had not shown some initiative and come to my house."

"You went to Admiral Hagood's house?"

"Yes, sir. I went to our house first, but you were not home."

"JJ, you can not come to Admiral's row every time you want to, you have to have permission. That is how the system works. You have ten demerits to work off before tomorrow. Dismissed, Plebe."

"I answered, aye, aye, and I mixed in with the group of plebes that had talked to the President and tried to listen to what the two admirals would be saying to each other."

"What am I going to do with him, Ben. He thinks he runs the place."

"Scary thought, he is going to be running the place before we know it, Jason. These young men are not like those of us who showed up in '37. They are a new breed, determined to do better than those that came before them. Some will die young in the service to their country, a pray JJ, is not one of them. He is so much like you, Jason. If I had a son, I would want him to be just like James."

"Thank you, Ben." Was all my father could manage to say.

Ben and my father walked across the street towards #1 and #2. He carried his briefcase full of unfinished notes for that day's lecture."

"And what about these young men here, James?" Em had a tear in her eye.

"The torch will be passed to you four today. Your father is correct, Kiro, your life will never be the same again. You four are starting on your life's adventure.

Two years later, the twins, Emily and I stood on the campus of William and Mary College in Williamsburg, Virginia. We were looking at a large monument and bronze statue of Reverend James Blair. Louis was reading from his college handbook.

"It says here that William and Mary was founded in 1693. It is the second oldest college in America. The charter was granted from King William and Queen Mary to Reverend Blair who became the first president. The institution received a penny a pound tax on exports of tobacco. The college prospered until the American Revolution of 1776 when the tax disappeared. During the Civil War the campus was occupied by federal troops and it was not in session. Many of the buildings were destroyed and rendered useless by the occupation. The college reopened in 1869, but it was so crippled financially that it could not offer courses of instruction. The State of Virginia approved an annual appropriation of ten thousand dollars and the Congress approved an indemnity of $64,000 for its losses during the war."

"What about the division of instruction for men and women?" I asked.

"The college is divided into two schools. The men attend the collegiate college, leading to the degrees of BA and MA. The women attend the Matthew Whaley Normal and Practice School. This fall the college will have 244 students, 21 instructors, a library of 15,000 volumes and an income of $49,000. Its endowment is $150,000 from a single corporation made this year and its buildings and grounds are valued at another $150,000. I wonder who gave a $150,000 this year?"

Emily smiled at me and whispered, "Thank you, James, for convincing your father that William and Mary is just as deserving as a small college in northwest Pennsylvania."

The country was still unsettled from the assassination of President McKinley and my brother-in-law was now the President of the United States. The twins were home all summer and it was time for Louise to start her teaching career. She and Emily left to set up her apartment near her school. Louis and I drove down to Georgetown and I was to drop him off at the Schneider's brownstone. General Schneider was retired and I think he missed out on his own children growing up and he wanted to spend time with those grandchildren that were left. Louis seemed to humor him and spent any free time with him, I think he missed my father.

On the drive down to Washington, Louis asked a lot of questions.

"Why did you decide to apply to Annapolis, Dad?

"It was in my blood, I guess. Your grandfather spent a lot of time with his children. He was older when he adopted me in '57, I was born in '56 and was about 18 months old or so when they took me home from the orphanage."

"What day were you born?"

"I have no idea, your grandmother chose the date she first laid eyes on me, all covered with chicken pox."

"You had chicken pox when they first saw you?"

"That is what they tell me, I do not remember anything about coming home to the White House or even the years that I lived there with your great uncle – or would that be your great, great Uncle James Buchanan. He was the fifteenth president."

"He was followed by Lincoln, the 16th, Johnson, the 17th, Grant, the 18th, Hayes, the 19th, Garfield was killed but he was the 20th, Arthur took his place just like Uncle Teddy did this week and he was the 21st, Cleveland, 22nd, Harrison, 23rd, Cleveland again for the 24th, McKinley must have been our 25th president and Uncle Teddy is our 26th. Is that right?"

"That is correct, Louis. Why are you concerned about the progression of presidents?"

"I am not. It just got me to thinking about presidential protection and the large number of criminals that go unpunished."

"Is that something that you might like to do after law school, be a prosecutor like your Uncle Teddy? He went to law school, also. His military career was very short. He is seen as a reformer. He began his career in New York City trying to fight the political corruption that was rampant."

"I have not decided about what field of law I might like, but I have been talking to Grandpa Schneider."

"I know, thank you for doing that, by the way."

"Did you know that grandpa killed an unarmed man because he refused to do what grandpa told him to do?"

"Oh, Louis, I think that is probably a tall tale repeated so many times that grandpa thinks it is true."

"I don't think so, Dad. He says he still has nightmares about it. I don't think he has told anyone about it, except me."

"Why did he tell you?"

"I asked him if he had ever killed an unarmed man when he was in the marines. He said once, he had to. Grandpa Caldwell had sent him into Mexico to get a handle on the strength of the French in northern Mexico."

"I remember my dad, telling me about that, Louis."

"Anyway, he needed horses to transport all these boxes of guns that he stored in a warehouse. He asked grandpa to take him and his men down the coast a ways and up a river and wait for him to return. On his march to find horses he came across a troop of French cavalry coming down the road. He had his men hide and then ambush them."

"The men he shot were probably armed, Louis."

"No, wait, this is the interesting part. One of his men said he knew French and that they would capture the troops by making them stop along the road to help some wounded Mexicans. He passed the word that the French phrase, 'Ferma La Fenettra' meant surrender your arms."

"That means 'close the window', Louis."

"I know, the French had dismounted and were totally confused when they were captured without a shot."

"So why did General Schneider shoot an unarmed man?"

"He was a Major then, Dad. He wanted the horses and was going to let the troopers go."

"What happened?"

"Grandpa Caldwell had ordered him to take all dead, wounded and live prisoners back to the boat so he could 'make them disappear at sea'".

"What?"

"That is what grandpa said. Your father made French soldiers 'disappear' during the Civil War. Grandpa Schneider had his Mexican troops, that he was training, take the horses overland to the warehouse and he started marching the prisoners back to the ship that was 'up-the-river' so to speak. These cavalry troops were used to riding and they refused to march on foot. So grandpa pulled his gun and pointed it at the head of the French Officer and motioned for him to walk. The captain laughed and sat down on the ground. Grandpa shot him in the head and had his body loaded on a wagon. He then walked to the next trooper and that trooper said in perfect English, 'Please sir, we need to rest'. Grandpa shot him in the foot and threw him along side the officer. The rest of the French hot footed it back to the waiting ship."

"Louis, do you believe your grandfather was a killer?"

"Which one?"

"Both. No, I mean either one."

"I think it is a true story, Dad. My question to you, is this. Do you think what they did was murder?"

"I have no idea, Louis. It was war time and it could have happened, but shooting an unarmed man is never justified. And if my father threw live French soldiers over the side of his ship, then that is murder. Now, I am going to have nightmares."

"Sorry, Dad. I did not mean to upset you."

"I am upset with myself. Your Grandfather Caldwell is gone and we can not get any answers from him, but your Grandfather Schneider is alive and well, we will ask him." We continued on traveling in silence until we reached the outskirts of our nations capitol and we slowed down from road speeds. It was amazing how many automobiles were on the streets of Washington. We pulled up in front of the Schneider's brownstone in Georgetown and unloaded James' suitcases. He had a few days to find an apartment close to campus before his classes would begin that fall. The three of us sat down to have a conversation, grandfather, father and son.

"General, I never asked my father the questions that James has been asking you. He is concerned about the legal, moral and ethical questions when one man takes the life of another. Can you help us understand what you and my father faced serving in the military during peace time?"

"What about war time? There are times that a helpless prisoner of war is simply executed so that the captors do not have to feed him, and that, gentlemen, is murder, pure and simple. It happened all the time during the Civil War on both sides."

"Grandpa, war time is not my problem area for now. I am about to enter law school here and I want to focus on deaths in the military during peace time. Do they happen? Are they required for service? Are there times when the President or a superior officer orders his troops to kill people, to stop a riot, for example."

"Yes, yes and yes. Let me give you an example of each. I assume this involves your Grandpa Caldwell as well as me, correct?"

"Correct."

The amazing story followed.

Cruise to Turkey
USS Bearing Sea and USS St. Louis

It was peacetime and your grandfather met with Stephen Szirom, Hungarian defector, every day of the cruise from Potomac dockyards to the port of Smyrna, Turkey. I had never met Captain Caldwell until that cruise. He also met my marine commandos that were assigned to the USS St. Louis. I was a third generation Navy Marine. I am well over six feet, six inches tall and weighed about twice your grandfather's weight. I towered over him, but somehow I always felt smaller than him whenever we stood side by side. I did not have an ounce of fat on my body and he didn't look like he could punch himself out of a wet paper bag. My commandos were young and came from various backgrounds, there were former members of the Potomac dockyard shore patrol, medics from Georgetown, USMC riflemen who were former snipers and sharp shooters, demolition experts, and others whose specialties he had not learned yet. There were eighteen members of my detachment and your grandfather tried to get to know and understand each of them before he led us on this mission. While he did that, I exercised. I would remove a naval deck gun from its mount and carry it around while he had the others performing routine training exercises. One day he asked me about the gun and why I carried it.

"Sergeant, why are you carrying that piece of ordnance around with you?"

"This is a modified Dahlgren, model 1440 Naval deck gun, Sir."

"I can see that, Sergeant, why are you carrying it about?"

"I have one of these back at the dockyards, Sir. The detachment uses it to increase our firepower. Are you familiar with it, Sir." I handed it to him and he nearly dropped it at my feet. He had never tried to lift a deck mounted gun, of course.

"Sir, the English Navy has had a weapon of this type for many years. They used eight barrels which rotated into position for firing, it was a musket, not a heavy caliber rifle like ours. They could get off eight shots and then it needed to be reloaded with musket balls, wadding and powder. It was not very effective in a fire fight. Hand that to me and walk with me to the rail, Sir." I hoisted the gun like it was a toy and let go with a burst from the weapon. We heard forty eight shots ring out and the sea was churned with the reports.

"If there had been a long boat out there, Sir, what do you think would be left of it?"

"Not much, Sergeant, stay close to me in a fight."

"Aye, aye. Sir. What does the Office of Navy Counter Intelligence do? When I was assigned by Lieutenant Lewis, he said to talk to you, he had never heard of ONCI."

"ONCI has always been there, Sergeant. I was assigned from Mare Island Naval Yard in California on March 4th of this year after foreign agents killed a co-worker. I guess the new Secretary of the Navy must have decided that he needed a full-time officer and a detachment. Can you tell me a little about each one."

"They are your men, Sir. Lieutenant Lewis picked most of them for you, since you were not in Potomac Dock yards when the orders came down."

"Jerome Lewis is in charge of shore patrol for the dockyards, is that true? Did a policeman pick my detachment?"

"When you meet Mr. Lewis, I think you will find that he is more than a policeman, Sir." We were walking along the deck and watching the detachment during the training that I had been instructing.

"Attention on deck! Captain Caldwell is the new skipper of this outfit, come to attention and salute your captain!"

"At ease, Gentlemen. I will start over here to my right and work my way around the detachment." He walked to the first man and shook his hand. "What is your name?"

"Corporal Sam Mason, Sir, USMC." He moved to the next man.

"Private First Class, Dwayne Wilson, Sir, USMC." He managed to remember some of them, there were seventeen names and faces besides mine. They were mostly privates, but some corporals with names like Keets, Mathews, James, Peters, Mahoney, Russell, Dempsey, Cornell, Wendleson, Turnsbill, Grantham, Rivers, Alexander, Fryerson, and Miller. He had not learned, at this point in his career, to forget to memorize every face and name before a mission where some of them might not be coming home to family and friends. So we spent the first few days of the cruise learning from each other. For example, he had no idea what an EOD did for the Navy.

"You see, Cap'n Caldwell, a torpedo or a floating mine is a device waiting to make a big hole in your boat. The job of an Explosive Ordnance Disposal [EOD] is to make that device harmless to us or it can be turned on our enemy to make him pay for setting it."

"Thank you, Corporal Miller, I had no idea that an enemy mine can be used against him."

"We should see some devices on this trip, Sir. Them foreigners are not to be trusted."

"Tell the lookouts to keep a sharp eye, Mr. Miller, we do not want a big hole in the St. Louis!"

"Aye, aye. Sir."

He talked with a former member of Lieutenant Jerome Lewis' command and he gave him high praise for his novel approach to problem solving. This was followed by a visit with "Doc" Rivers, a medic from Georgetown. He asked him if he ever got on campus or to the student clinic but he indicated that he was assigned to the care of veterans at the other hospital there. He got me to question Stephen Szirom about what Martin Koszta's physical appearance was like. Koszta was the man we were sent to rescue from kidnappers. I asked Stephen where Martin Koszta would most likely go on shore leave. Who might be assigned to guard him on shore leave. I asked him if Martin liked to read or do research in a library. I asked him several questions that your grandfather might not have thought to ask.

"Captain Caldwell, we are going to be in Turkey, soon. It is the only country with its capitol city in two continents. Constantinople is located on both sides of the Bosporus Strait. The Bosporus separates Europe from Asia. If we have to leave the St. Louis, for any reason, we are going to stand out like a sore thumb. I can not think of a way to make our white faces look like someone on the street in Turkey."

"Natives of Turkey are not dark skinned like an Arab, Tom. They look like us. The problem will be the language. We have no one on board who can speak the street language. Lucky for us, there are many foreigners in Turkey. If we are careful we should be able to keep watch on those that need watching. We need to identify the source of the leak of information from the USS Bearing Sea *our companion ship on this rescue cruise. If anyone leaves the* USS Bearing Sea *and speaks the language we have identified the source. The Presidential Warrant states that these individuals are to be eliminated so that a message will be sent to foreign capitals, that if you send agents into our country, they will disappear. The bodies are not to be found by anyone in Turkey or the US, that means they are to disappear at sea. The trouble is, we are still in the process of identifying the agents on the* USS Bearing Sea, *when we do we will throw them overboard."*

"Give me the names and descriptions, Captain, and I will make sure that no one finds their bodies in Turkey"

The Navy JAG recruiters had a representative at the Georgetown Law School for interviews and Louis stopped and filled out an application. He was using an ink pen and trying to make a neat and professional looking job of the process. He was about halfway through the first page when this Navy officer in his dark blue uniform stopped him. He was reading over Louis' shoulder.

"You are Admiral Caldwell's son?"

"Yes, let me finish this, please. Can I schedule an interview with someone?"

"I think you can, Mr. Caldwell! Have you graduated yet?"

"I should be finished in June, why?"

"Do you have any time today?"

"No, I am really jammed up with this crazy contracts course."

"Are you free any time tomorrow?"

"In the morning, sure."

"I will give you this card and I will sign it on the back. This will allow you into the Army Navy Building and the ONCI office."

"I am applying for the Judge Advocate General's Office, not the Office of Naval Counter Intelligence. I am going to be a lawyer not a spy." I was smiling.

"The ONCI has lawyers working for them ,too. In fact, there is one division that is shared by both, the Criminal Investigation Division."

"What time do you want me there?"

"8:30 hours will be your appointment, Mr. Caldwell."

Louis took his card and turned it over, it was signed **Rodney Lowe**. Louis looked up at him and he was smiling.

"I sandbagged you Louis. I know your father and he said you might be applying this week. I have been here every day. I thought you might have changed your mind."

"How do you know my father?"

"I was his first commanding officer when he graduated from the academy. All I do now is look for talent."

"You are a talent scout?"

"Sort of, if you decide to join us, you can not mention that I talked to you on the Georgetown Campus. Is that alright with you?"

"What? Why?"

"It is a matter of national security. If I tell you why, I will have to kill you." He was not smiling, all the warm fuzzy emotions were gone. He looked like he had just swallowed something bitter. His jaw was pulsating like he was screwing marbles.

Louis looked him square in the eye and said, "You look just like my Grandpa Schneider, only younger."

"I am younger than retired General Schneider. He is a pussy cat. I am still an old lame tiger with a bad attitude. Piss me off and I will bite you in the ass. We understand each other, Son?"

"Aye, aye. Sir."

"Wait until after you have joined the Navy to use that phrase, Son, only a few are strong enough to understand what it means and the total commitment it implies."

"Yes, Sir. Sorry to offend you."

"Show up tomorrow ready to listen and learn, all will be forgiven if you do that."

That afternoon Louis left the law school with every intention of catching a cab over to the Army Navy Building and asking me to give him some background on this Commodore Lowe. He changed my mind and headed for his Grandpa Schneider's. When he asked about Commodore Lowe, his grandpa smiled and said, "Be careful of what you wish for, my Son. Sometimes you get it. This is what you told me you wanted the last time I threw you on your ass in my basement."

"I love you, Grandpa, I was letting you throw me around the mat down there."

"Sure you were! I had to be careful not to break your neck. You probably can not cut the program that Rodney Lowe has laid out for you. When you see him tomorrow, he will ask you to sign away your right to about every freedom we Americans hold dear. Then he will tell you that you need some introduction to the USN, via San Diego, eight weeks worth. Then they will test you for language aptitudes and send you up the coast to Monterey. A year later you will end up in OTC, probably in Virginia at the ONCI 'farm'."

"What is that?"

"Commodore Rodney Lowe's school, 'so you want to be a spy.'"

"Who is this, Commodore Lowe? I never heard of him."

"Ever hear of the *USS Maine*? Rodney Lowe was the Commodore in command of that fleet when the Maine was sunk."

"I thought Admiral Sampson had the fleet?"

"After the board of inquiry, Captain Sampson became Admiral Sampson and the rest is history."

"Why is Commodore Lowe a recruiter for JAG?"

"He is not, ONCI does not exist, he can not recruit for something that does not exist. They have to put you somewhere and guess what, you are a lawyer, so off to JAG you go like a good little boy. ONCI officers are housed all over the Navy depending upon where they went to college and what their 'cover' can be. If you 'wash out of the farm' - then you have a permanent home in JAG."

"Because, I can no longer return to the civilian life because I 'know too much'."

"I always knew you were the smartest of all my grandchildren, Louis. Keep your wits about you. Remember, when facing the bad guys, close the ground between you, never take a step backwards, it screws up the timing for converting self-defense to instant death for your attacker. Want to go down in the basement?"

"No thanks, Grandpa. I want to show up for my interview tomorrow without any marks on my body!"

At 8:00 hundred hours the next day, he was at the Army Navy Building and showed the guard at the entrance Commodore Lowe's card. He turned it over and said, "Report to Room 378, that's on the third floor." He waved Louis through and he found the steps and took them two at a time. He hit the landing at the third floor and found the room marked 378. Two large men in army green stood in front of the door. He handed them his card. The guard on the left looked at it and slammed it back into his chest. Louis took a step backwards and his grandpa's words came back to him, *"Never take a step backwards, it screws up the timing for self defense."* Louis took a quick step forward and was face to face with the two shaved gorilla types that barred the door.

"Which one of you ass holes would like to apologize for wrinkling my dress shirt?" Louis had a giant smile on his face. The words and the facial expression were in conflict. The man on the right began to relax and began to return his smile. The one on the left still had a scowl on his face. He folded his fingers on his right hand at the first joint just like his grandpa had showed him and he drove them as hard as he could, just above the Adam's apple of the guard on the left. As he was going down, he drove his right foot into the side of the right guard's knee. Louis heard a soft crunch and the guard bellowed in pain grabbing his knee and hopping around like a little girl.

The office door flew open and a naval officer, Louis did not know bellowed, "What the hell is going on out here?"

Louis said nothing. The left guard was red in face and could not speak a word, Louis' grandpa said it would be one or two days before his voice would return. The guard on the right was now sitting on the floor still bellowing something none of them could understand. Louis thought maybe it was time to say something. "Hello, I am reporting to the Navy Recruiter's office and I ran into these two."

"I can see that. What happened?"

"I handed my card from Commodore Lowe to this man here." Louis pointed to the one unable to speak. "He dropped the card and we both tried to pick it up and we bumped heads. Don't you just hate it when that happens? Then this other recruit over here tried to help us and we bumped knees, you know knee cap to knee cap, boy that smarts." The officer dropped all pretense and said, "Rodney said you were a smart ass. You

two get down to first aid and send the next two up here on the double."
He motioned me into his office.

"How did you manage to get the drop on both of those marines?"

"Those were US Marines? Maybe I better rethink my choice of military options for someone like me with a brand new law degree from Georgetown."

"You did not learn how to disable those two in law school."

"I am General Schneider's grandson."

"Your application says, Caldwell not Schneider."

"My mother was a Schneider, you want to see someone tough, recruit her!"

He burst into laughter. "Rodney said you would not agree to join us after you were given the conditions of service, but that I should meet you anyway. We have not been introduced, Mr. Caldwell, I am Captain Yandle. I run this office." He offered his hand and Louis shook it.

"Tell me the conditions of service for joining the Judge Advocate's Office, Sir."

"You will begin your service at JAG, but you may be transferred to any other unit within the Navy at your commanding officer's discretion."

"That is totally out of the question, Commodore Lowe was correct, I can not accept those conditions. I want a law career not a Navy career. Tell me the conditions for joining another branch of the Navy, like the Office of Naval Counter Intelligence."

His eyes widened and he said, "I can only tell you about JAG since that is what your application indicates."

"Can I fill out an application for ONCI?"

"There are no applications for ONCI, all members are selected from other branches of the armed forces."

"Can I modify my application to JAG to indicate that I will accept a transfer only to ONCI, after a trial period of service? I do not want to waste four years of time when I could be practicing in a law office."

"No one has ever asked me that, Mr. Caldwell. I will find out and contact you. Are you still at Georgetown Law School?"

"No, I am staying with my grandpa until I ship out for San Diego and Monterey."

"His eyes widened even further, do you a speak foreign language?"

"Yes, the Schneiders are German and my great grandmother taught me the lower version of German before she died. I have spent some time in France and seemed to get along alright there. I am not sure about my accent, though."

"Was war thre UrgoBmutter der namin?"

"Sie war aus Bayern. Sie war aus haus der Von Hingleburg."

I had not realized that we had slipped into German until Captain Yandle returned to English, "Mr. Caldwell, I am going to go ahead and recommend to JAG that you be accepted with the proviso that you share your assignment only with ONCI. If you are transferred anywhere other than ONCI, then you will muster out at the time of transfer. How does that sound to you?"

"Sounds like that will work."

"Good, read and sign this. You will leave for San Diego on Monday of next week."

Louis graduated with the rest of the July recruits and boarded the train for the Monterey Training Center. I had heard of the war department's language school at Monterey. They accepted only those who spoke a foreign language already and wished to learn one or more additional. They reasoned if human brains already contained English and another language, it could learn to accept as many as were adequately introduced. Louis had passed his entrance exam in German and was there to learn French and all the others that he could absorb in twelve months.

Louis found his billet in the "old barracks building". The US Army was in the process of building new barracks for their detachments that would be training in some new form of cavalry which did not make use of horses. Louis had no idea how they were going to have a cavalry without horses. His roommate was already checked in, his name was Hans Becker. He had passed his test in German also and he spoke English with a slight accent.

"Mine name is Ensign Hans Becker. What is yours, please?"

"My name is Louis Caldwell. Are you native born?"

"JA, mine family has been in Pennsylvania for a long time."

"Do you speak German at home, Hans?"

"JA, how can you tell?"

"Just a wild guess, my grandmother Schneider spoke German to me all the time."

"Schneider, that is a good old German name from southern Bavaria, JA?"

"It is. You were not in my basic training session in San Diego, Hans. Where did you do your basic?"

"It was five years ago in South Carolina. That has to be the armpit of the nation, Louis. Do not go there unless you have to. The insects are so large there that three of them can suck you dry! I was a radio operator and I had to string wires at night through the woods on Pritchard's Island. What a hell hole that was."

"My father was stationed at Port Royal during the last war. I know what you mean about the mosquitoes on Parris Island. Whenever I had a break from college I would ride the train as far as I could and he would come get me at a place called Yemassee."

"I know that damn place, too. Louis Caldwell. There was an Admiral Caldwell at Paris Island. He is your father, JA?"

"Afraid so, Hans. You got some really good training at Port Royal. Were you sent to Cuba?"

"JA, but the war was over before I got there. "

"Me too. I mean, the war didn't last very long. I was in college and missed it. But I am ready to 'go to war' whenever Uncle Sam needs me."

"You have an Uncle Sam in the Navy?"

"No, just an expression. You know, US stands for United States or in my case, it can also stand for Uncle Sam."

"What is your father doing now that the war is over, Louis?"

"He works for my Uncle Teddy."

"UT, what does that stand for, please?"

"My father's sister, married Theodore Roosevelt."

"So, you have friends in high places, Louis Caldwell!"

"My Uncle Teddy does not know I am alive, Hans. I have never been to the White House."

"But your father works in the White House, JA?"

"Yes, he does. I have been in college and then law school, I have not been invited to see where he works."

"Louis Caldwell, shame on you! See if you can get both of us an invitation to the White House during our Thanksgiving break, I want to meet the President, your Uncle Teddy!"

"I will see what I can do, Hans. My father likes to write and receive letters. You can help me write one to him right now."

We cleaned off a place on our study desk and got a piece of paper and a pen.

Monterey, California

September 2, 1903

Dear Father,

I arrived here from San Diego last night. My belongings still fit into one suitcase and I have gotten everything I own into a chest of drawers. My roommate is Hans Becker. He was one of the recruits that passed through Port Royal five years ago when you were in command of Paris Island. He says you should remember him, he was the one complaining of the rather large mosquitoes found in South Carolina. His family lives in Philadelphia and we plan on taking the same train back east for our Thanksgiving Vacation.

I have invited him to stop over in Washington with me for a few hours so we can tour the White House together. Neither one of us have ever been there and we decided that it might be nice to see the "People's House" up close. I hope that you will still be in your office on the 21st of November, so that Hans can get a peek at a real live Admiral at work.

We start our saturation in languages on Monday. I will write again next week and tell you how it is going.

Your Loving Son,

Louis

Hans and Louis forgot about their letter and it was nearly two weeks later that they got a reply from the White House.

The White House
Washington DC

Ensign L. J. Caldwell
United States Naval Training Center
Monterey, California

Dear Nephew,

Your father shared your last letter with me. I remember how much I looked forward to letters from your Aunt Ruth when I was serving in Cuba. I will be looking forward to your visit with us here in the White House on or about November 21, 1903. I have no idea what will be on my schedule that day, but tell your roommate that he can stick his head in my office and see the commander-in-chief hard at work!

Save this and show it to the Marine guards at the east portico. They will admit you both and set up a tour for you.

1. Roosevelt

Theodore Roosevelt
President of the United States

Hans kept reading the letter over and over again.

"I am going to see the President." He repeated this to himself over and over again, also. We managed to get several weeks of study under our belts before the time came to board the train for Washington that November. Hans was in a talkative mood and asked me about the Judge Advocate General's Office.

"Louis, what is this JAG thing?"

"It started during the Civil War, Hans. Secretary Welles of the Navy, named a 'Solicitor of the Navy Department.' By the Act of March 2, 1865, Congress authorized President Lincoln to appoint, for service during the rebellion, a 'Solicitor and Naval Judge Advocate General'. The Congress maintained the billet after the war on a year to year basis until 1870. In that year it was transferred to a newly established Justice Department."

"Has it changed much in the last 33 years?"

"Yes, it has. In 1870, there was one office, located in the Washington Navy Yard. When this became overloaded with cases, Naval Legal Service Offices, called NLSO's, were established. They divided the area of Naval Responsibility within the US and world into the following branches; North Central, Mid-Atlantic, Southeast, Central, Southwest, Northwest, Pacific Coast, Europe and Asia."

"So which one are you headed for after you finish at Monterey?"

"You didn't let me finish how the JAG offices grew. After the NLSO branches were formed, RLSO offices inside each of the NLSO offices were formed. These Regional offices further divided the legal loads within the Navy. I hope to work in one of the trial judiciary offices. These are located in Washington DC; Norfolk, Virginia; Camp Lejeune, North Carolina; San Diego and Pearl Harbor, Hawaii."

"You do not care where you are sent? These are really different locations."

"No, I do not care where I work. I still have officer's training to complete and I have no idea where that might be or how long it will take. You have to be patient if you are in the Navy. Right, Hans?"

"Right, Louis!"

"Tell me more of how you got sent to Monterey, Hans. How did a radio operator in Cuba get selected for special training?"

"It's a long story. Are you sure you want to hear it?"

"What else have we got to do during this cross country train ride?"

"I was a radio chief when we landed in Cuba at Guantanamo Bay. The Marines had established their base near there and needed help with captured messages. They had stacks of them. They had separated all the Spanish into one pile and assumed the others were sent in some kind of code. I picked up the first one off the coded pile and it read.

"**Opermerking**: *Zorg ervoor dat uw vingers droog en schoon zijn wanneer u met het keyer werkt. Zo houdt u het keyer zelf ook droog en schoon. Het keyer is gevoelig voor vingerbewegingen. Hoe lichter de druck, hoe beter de respons. Het keyer functioneert niet beter als u harder drukt.*"

"That sounds like German in some sort of code."

"JA, only it was Dutch sent in the clear."

"You read Dutch?"

"Of course, I am a graduate from Penn College!" He had a smile on his face that told me he did not learn Dutch in college.

"So, you are from Pennsylvania and you learned Dutch from a family member. Right, Hans!"

"Right, Louis!"

"Why were the Spanish sending messages in Dutch?"

"Do you remember the commanding general in Cuba?"

"The butcher of Cuba, Weylor, wasn't it?"

"General Valerano Van Weylor to be exact. The Valerano is Spanish from his mother and the Van Weylor is Dutch from his father."

"So these were messages from Van Weylor or to Van Weylor!"

"Right again, Louis!"

"What did you do with them?"

"I translated them."

"And?"

"And, I was no longer a radio chief. They promoted me to Navy Intelligence and sent me to Havana to be part of the American occupation forces in Cuba."

"So why did it take you so long to get more training at Monterey?"

"I could tell you, Louis, but then I would have to kill you." He was smiling.

"You continued to work in Naval Intelligence."

"You said that, Louis, I did not."

"Where did you get your officer training?"

"Lancaster, Virginia.

L ancaster is the name of a county in eastern Virginia and the name of an estate that was taken under the Confiscation Act of 1861. It is now federal property and no longer the Fairfield family estate. The Fairfield estate was built prior to the American Revolution and they had an excellent view of the design and layout of Washington City. As the city was constructed and spread out from its center like a giant wheel it nearly engulfed the Fairfield estate. The 1100 acres of rolling forest and farm land was like an oasis just outside the capitol city. This was the ideal place for Commodore Rodney Lowe to establish his training center he called *The Farm*.

Louis had graduated from the language school and was about to enter the ONCI phase of training which would be similar to OTC for any other normal naval recruit with a college education. This Officer's Training Center would be one of 'dirty tricks' and 'staying alive in a foreign country.' Not every agent could, or should, be assigned to a US Embassy abroad. Since the founding of the United States, immigrants from all over the world came to these shores to seek their fortunes. His OTC class of 1904, contained at least one of these grandsons of immigrants. They had German, Italian, Japanese, Chinese, Philippine, Cuban, French, Spanish, African and Russian representation. Louis got to practice his German, Spanish and French every day.

The first day of orientation was an eye opener. Louis was walking into the morning breakfast and he noticed a wall of photographs. He stopped dead in his tracks, there was Hans Becker's smiling face. He took a step closer and read the information below the photograph.

Ensign Hans Becker, communications instructor, 1899-1903.

A conversation, on a train, in November of 1903 came back into his memory. *"I could tell you, Louis, but then I would have to kill you."*

A voice behind him said, "We got a letter from Hans yesterday. He said your German was terrible and your Dutch was impossible to understand." Louis turned to face Rodney Lowe, Commodore USN and director of The Farm and me.

"Hans would know, Sir. His English is terrible and his Dutch is excellent! Hello, Dad, I did not know you would be here."

"I work for your father, Louis. How is your room?"

"On the top floor, a large bedroom with french doors that open onto a balcony that looks across a meadow and a stand of pine trees. Lancaster is a palace compared with the language barracks at Monterey, Sir. How long can I live at The Farm, Dad?"

"As long as you are a bachelor and assigned to the Washington NCI district, this is your home. I know what you mean about Monterey, a few months of language polishing and you are ready to leave there for greener pastures. We have not changed the inside of the Fairfield estate much, the bedrooms for example, are as they left them in 1861. Let's go in to breakfast and then I will take all the officer candidates on the grand tour of the place. I think you will like it, Louis."

An hour later, Commodore Lowe took his fork and clanged it against his water glass and the dining room became very quiet. He rose and said the following. "Those of you who came down for breakfast this morning are a special breed of young men. Each one of you will be sitting in a foreign country one year from now or you will be dead. Look around the tables this morning, some of you will be sent to London, others to Berlin, Rome, Tokyo, Singapore, Manila, Havana, Paris, Madrid, Marrakesh or Moscow. The list of foreign capitols is almost endless, and we need to send at least two agents to each. The graduates of the Naval Counter Intelligence Training Center are prepared to do many things. For example, the young man on my right will be given a cover placement inside the Judge Advocates Regional Legal Services Office here at the Washington Navy Yard. He will not spend much time there, that is his cover assignment. He will be in charge of catching those foreign nationals who are in this country as spies. His language skills will permit him to travel unnoticed into Germany, Holland or France in pursuit of these individuals. If he ever has to travel to see another of you in your theater of operations, God help him to remain mute!" I looked up at the Commodore and smiled. He continued, "Not everyone is cut out for this type of Navy life. I sure as hell was not when President McKinley asked me to form this unit and to track down and kill everyone involved with the sinking of the *USS Maine*." A few heads jerked towards him. "Don't look so shocked. You think that the United States never found out who sank the Maine. Not true, Admiral Caldwell turned everything he had over to me and I got the ones who attacked our vessel. I personally pulled the trigger of the pistol that I placed beside their heads. I was given a Presidential Warrant to be the one in charge of finding and finishing the guilty parties. There was no trial, the President wanted an excuse to enter Cuba and clean up the mess left by Spain. We clean up messes, Gentlemen. Your training begins today. You are all physically fit or you would not be here. You all have cover Naval assignments after you leave here, but you work for me. You will learn how to send a radio signal from inside a foreign country, contact foreign agents and retrieve sensitive information. That information can get you shot as a spy. You are not spies, however. Spies work for you gathering the data. They risk their lives within their home countries for you. These folks are called your assets. The training inside Lancaster is so specialized that once you have completed it, you have no option but to serve your country for the next thirty years. If you do not feel you can do that, I expect to see you in my office within the hour. That is all Gentlemen."

Louis spent the next five months training in "the spy school" as his Grandpa Schneider called it. He learned to send Morse code with a key pad and how to string an antenna in the attic of an abandoned house or barn. They learned how to create a 'dead drop' and how to spot someone following us. They were sent to Montreal and Quebec on classroom missions that involved how to blend in with the local population. Louis' French was not very good on those trips and everyone he talked to there assumed that he was from western Canada or the United States. Louis would be stopped on the street and asked directions, so he looked like a local, but the minute he opened his mouth, it was over. They would say, never mind, I will ask a local. Louis learned to use nonverbal communication as much as possible. A nod of the head, a shrug of the shoulders or the occasional, "Ca Va" was all that was needed. Or, this worked really well, he began to cough before uttering any French phrase.

Finally, by the beginning of the fall, he was released to his day time cover assignment as long as he continued to return at night to The Farm barracks and for weekend courses and refreshers. Louise kept her tiny apartment and Louis often stopped to see her after she completed a day in the classroom. Sometimes he took her out to dinner, other times she cooked something for them. She asked how he liked being a JAG lawyer, he did not have the heart to tell her he had no idea what a JAG lawyer did. Louis reported in on November 1, 1904. He found the office of Commander Sheldon Morton. He was Louis' immediate supervisor and was unaware that his training at Lancaster was not complete. In fact, he had no idea that Louis still lived there while he completed some, but not all, the training at The Farm. Louis' weekends were spent there taking what Commodore Rodney Lowe called his short finishing courses. Louis would take a day or two of 'on the job training' and other unmentionable exercises in how to eliminate a human being without a trace. Louis had taken one of these short courses at St. Elizabeth Hospital where he met Dr. Eli Waters, chief medical examiner.

"Lieutenant Caldwell, come in, sit down and take a load off. I have your file right here, let me open it. I have several notations that I made in it last night."

"Thank you, Sir."

"You graduated from William and Mary, pre-law, first in the class. Very impressive, Mr. Caldwell."

"Thank you, Sir."

"Law School from Georgetown, again number one!"

"Thank you, again, Sir." I smiled to relax him.

"Why did you join the Navy, Mr. Caldwell, you could have had your choice of any job on the east coast?"

"I am a Caldwell, Sir. My father is Admiral Caldwell, he works in the White House for a member of the family, my Uncle Teddy."

"You are the nephew of the President! I better make that notation in your file."

"My Grandfather was also an Admiral, the first superintendent of the Naval Institute after it was moved to Annapolis."

"Oh, my. That is missing also." He was busy with his pen adding notes here and there. "Now that you are assigned to me, I have the usual backlog of cases that I need to assign to you." He reached behind him and grabbed a stack of thirty or so manila folders with a red strip running across most of them. "You need to sort these into those you will be defending and those you will be prosecuting. None of these are earth shaking and I imagine you can plea-bargain most of them. If you have any questions come see me or your senior partner that is shown inside each case folder. Bring these back one at a time when they are cleared."

"Thank you, Sir. Where can I see each of these men?"

"If they are in a holding cell, it is indicated inside each folder. If they have been released to return to duty, pending a hearing or trial, that is indicated, also. Good luck, Lt. Caldwell."

"Thank you, Sir." I rose to leave his office and hefted the stack of files. "Do I have an office or a work desk somewhere, Commander."

"Yes, let me show you where it is in the bullpen." He rose and walked with me into a large holding area with lots of gray metal navy desks, some of them pushed back to back. You are over there in the corner by the window, Lieutenant."

"Oh, good. An office with a window!" Louis walked over to it and threw the stack of folders into the corner, under the window. Louis really did not think he would like defending navy misfits who could not keep themselves out of the brig and he reached into the pile and took out the first red stripped folder. He placed it on his desk and began to read. The navy does not have a case here, this will never be brought to a hearing or a trial and he placed it on the right corner of the his desk. The left corner was for those interesting cases that he might like to defend. The losers in both piles were placed on the bottom of each stack. In a few minutes, he had two stacks with the winners on the very top. He reached for the first red strip and began to read it in detail. The crime was assault and battery with intent to kill, striking a superior officer and drunk on duty. Chief Malcomb Denny was being held in his cell pending a hearing to determine how he might plead. Louis saw that he had no partner assigned to this case so he tucked the file under his arm, found his briefcase and asked the lawyer next to him, "How do I find the holding cells?"

The holding cells were really the basement area of the RLSO building at the Washington Navy Yards, how convenient for the JAG defense and prosecution, he thought. Louis walked down the stairs to the holding area and asked to see Chief Denny. He was brought into a small interview room, handcuffed and chained through the wrists and ankles.

"Remove the chains and cuffs will you?" Louis looked at the SP who dragged him into the room.

"You do not want to do that Lieutenant, this is a real mean son of a bitch."

"What do you think, Chief Denny? Do you want to get out of those cuffs?"

"Suit yourself. I never laid a hand on that Ensign that they claimed I decked."

"Well, just so we understand each other, Chief, if you touch me I will put you in sick bay." Louis glared at him.

"Sure you will."

As soon as this was out of his mouth, Louis slapped him across the face as hard as he could. The SP had a shocked look on his face. Louis looked over at him and said, "To bad this man slipped and fell down the stairs on his way to this interview." Louis slammed his foot into the side of the chief's knee and heard a soft pop, a dislocation for sure. Dislocations are extremely painful but not permanent.

"I am a busy man, Chief. Make up your mind. Do you want to be released from your cuffs or not?"

"Yes, Sir." He said this through gritted teeth.

"Release him, and leave us alone." The SP was not sure what he should do. Louis asked him again and he released Denny and left the room.

"Chief Denny, I am here to get your statement on how you want to plead your case. I have read your file and I think you struck the Ensign just like it states here. I also think the Ensign was probably a prick and deserved every thing that you gave him. What do you say to my dropping the assault and battery charge and you plead guilty to striking a superior officer while you were drunk. You will serve some days in the brig, you may even get credit for time served. You have been here nearly a month. The Navy may give you a dishonorable discharge, but what do you care, you will be away from that Ensign for the rest of your life."

"Where do I sign?"

Louis fished the proper forms out of his briefcase and went through them with the Chief. He waved his rights to legal counsel. He pled guilty to striking a superior officer and to be intoxicated while on duty. He signed every thing in triplicate. Louis shook his hand and said, "I doubt this goes to a hearing, Chief, if it does I will see you again at that time. Please behave yourself in here, do not strike another officer or we will have to go through this all over again. Remember, some superior officers will take your lights out without batting an eye. You are very lucky you did not strike me or you would be in the morgue." Louis looked him straight in the eye and said, "Do you have any questions, Chief?"

"No, Sir. Thank you, Sir. I expected to be found guilty of the whole list of charges and spending time in a naval prison."

"You are welcome, Chief."

Louis packed up his things and headed back up three flights of stairs to his desk in the corner of the bullpen. Louis dropped off the paper work to Commander Morton.

"What is this, Lieutenant?"

"It is a plea agreement for Chief Malcomb Denny. He pleads guilty to striking a superior office and drunk while on duty, the case is cleared waiting processing on your end."

"That is marvelous work, Lieutenant. I met with him and I got nowhere, he even tried to strike me even though he was handcuffed and chained."

"I had the SP remove the handcuffs, Sir."

"You what?"

"He had slipped and fallen when the SP was dragging him from his cell and he was in no mood to strike me. Ask the SP how docile he is now, Commander."

Louis' second and final case as a JAG lawyer was a little harder. I remember him telling me, "The four of us were sitting in an interview room. I was sitting directly beside Seaman Dempsey, Commanders Morton and Wentworth were sitting across from both of us. Dempsey was not what I expected. He was smallish, almost like a young boy. I asked him, 'How old are you, Mr. Dempsey?'"

"I am thirty-one years old."

"Have you ever been trained as a prize fighter?"

"Prize fighter?"

"Yes, have you ever boxed in a ring for payment or as an amateur?"

"No, why?"

"Because your file states that you killed your shipmate with your bare hands. How did you do that? Did you choke him to death?"

"No, Sir. I have been telling these two officers here that we were involved in a pushing match, the deck was wet and his feet went out from under him and he fell back and hit his head. I never struck him, Sir."

"Seaman Dempsey, I believe you and the navy medical examiner agrees with you. Would you like to read what I found in the examiner's office? It was not in your file, I had to go and get a copy." Commander Morton was not happy.

"When did you get that report, Lieutenant? And why have you not given a copy to the prosecution?"

"I got it today, Sir. I did not know who the prosecution was in this case." I handed a copy to him. "I suggest that we drop the charges against Seaman Dempsey and clear this case."

"I will take it under advisement, I need to study the report first before we even consider dropping the charges. I have to get back to my office, I will need to see you sometime today, Lieutenant Caldwell." He rose from his chair and left the interview room.

"What does this mean?" asked Seaman Dempsey.

"It means that the prosecution is embarrassed, Mr. Dempsey. You will be released and returned to duty shortly." Commander Wentworth said with a smile on his face. "It also means that Lieutenant Caldwell will have to undergo a chewing out by his commanding officer."

"Thank you, Lieutenant. I am very glad you believed me and checked with the medical examiner's office."

"You are very welcome, Mr. Dempsey, I have no intention of being a whipping boy for Commander Morton. I will forget to go see him this afternoon, if he wants to see me, he can come to my little corner of the world."

A few hours later, he did just that. "Caldwell, give me the remainder of the files I gave you. A new man is being assigned to me and I want to give these really simple cases to him. I have something much more difficult for you." He held his hand out and I placed the stack of files from the left corner of my desk.

"That leaves me without any cases, Sir."

"Yes, I know. I am assigning you to one of the higher profile cases that needs immediate investigation. Have you completed your courses in forensic science at Lancaster?"

"Yes, Sir."

"Good, let me introduce you to your new, permanent partner."

46

Purchase of Springwell

January, 1919

A few miles north of the village of Penshurt, Kent, in what we would call a county, a combination of tree covered foothills rises to the summit of the Kent hill country. Its suave green slopes evoke a sense of pastoral and, somewhere about the 600-foot contour, it is flanked by sheltering woods. Fertile soil overlays the local sandstone, and the trees, mainly chestnut, beech and oak, grow to a great size. Their shadows at dawn and sunset are thrown far across the lower combination of foothills. Southward the view stretches to the Wealden deposits of the Lower Cretaceous Glacier created by the last ice age.

This was the view that Louis, Cathleen, Carson and his sister Elska were enjoying. Beside them stood James, Martha, and their children. Louis turned to me and said, "Well, what do you think, Sir James? It is for sale, but I am not an English nobleman and your broker here says you will have to take possession and deed it to Cathleen and me."

Idris Jones was a land broker from the London Borough of Reigate, he came highly recommended as honest and trustworthy. We had met him in his office at 6 Bell Street. Reigate, Surrey RH7 7BG.

"Sir James, it is an honor. I have never been to Bermuda, but I hear it is beautiful. Why do you wish to purchase an estate in England?"

"Mr. Jones, our family is about to make some major changes in our corporate holdings world wide and we have decided to locate the world headquarters near London, but not in the city. The train service is excellent in Britain and we are looking for an estate that is about a 25 minute ride into town."

"I have three estates that you should look at during the next week or so, the first is called Springwell, it is the largest and it can be divided into several smaller estates if you wish."

"How large is Springwell?"

"1600 acres in two separate parcels, it could be two 800, or as many as ten 160 acre country estates."

"Where is it located?"

"In Kent, I can show it to you today."

With a cold and gusty wind blowing scraps of litter along the morning streets of Reigate, and with the portent of rain heavy in the air, the family members loaded themselves into the motorcars that Idris Jones had waiting outside his office. Once we were all inside the cars our breath steamed the inner surfaces of the glass side windows and wind screen. The rain began to fall and streamed down the exterior of the windows. The lights from Idris' office shimmered in the rippling film of water and were diffused through the opalescent condensation. That curious lambent of the rain storm, gave us the extraordinary sensation of being encapsulated and set adrift outside the flow of time and space as we drove into the English countryside.

As the entire Caldwell family, stood on the site described in his office, Idris Jones was smiling, the rain had stopped. "On one side of this little valley rises a clear spring, from which the name derives. It contains one 800 acre parcel. The wooded, smooth pastured parcel on the opposite side is the other 800 acre parcel. This estate with the houses and barns must have commended itself to the eye and spirit of the very first owners."

"What is the history of Springwell, Mr. Jones?"

"The earliest recorded owner, about 1350, was William At-Well, so called from the spring which rose on his property. From the second half of the fourteenth until the reign of James I, the property belonged to a family named Potter from which it passed by marriage to Sir John Rivers. At about the time of the Restoration he conveyed it to Thomas Smith, described by Hasted, the Kent historian, as a scrivener of London. For most of the eighteenth century it was in the ownership of the Ellison's. After passing through several hands, it was bought in 1848 by Sir John Campbell Colquhoun and remains in his family estate until it is sold."

"You said there were three country mansions built on the 800 acres."

"That is correct, Sir James. In the eighteenth century the roadway which passes the property was appropriately known as Well Streetroad and a small hamlet of the same name was situated near the top of that hill over there. On this side we see two lakes and several ponds used when the property was an operating Kent farmstead."

"How are the houses located?"

"One on each side of the valley and another farmhouse on 160 acres at the beginning of the Weald, over there, can you see it?"

"Yes, how close are our neighbors?"

"This parcel is surrounded by National Trust land. To the east is *Toy's Hill* to the west is *Crockham Hill*, both were purchased by the government when times were better. The national debt keeps the Trust from purchasing Springwell and Chartwell which is further south from here."

"Should we looking at Chart Well, as well?"

"It is to be sold at Auction and you might want to bid on the place just to keep the neighbors at a minimum."

"What do you think the opening bid will be?"

"Probably 6,500 or 7,000 thousand pounds sterling."

"And today's exchange rate?"

"You would need to multiply by 3 or so to be on the safe side."

"And how big is Chart Well?"

"800 acres with a decaying manor house and many fallen down out buildings of all types."

"I think you said the magic word, Mr. Jones, we are not looking for a decaying manor house. My sons and I are looking for something that we can move into, hire the household staff and start enjoying my retirement."

"Sir James, two of the three houses are in excellent shape for their ages, the third will take some loving care to restore. I would recommend that you restore it, Sir. Lewis Carroll leased the third house from Sir John Campbell Colquhoun, while he was writing Alice in Wonderland."

"Oh, Louis, we have to see that house!" It was nearly a scream from Cathleen. "That is my favorite children's story, I want to read it to Elska in front of the fireplace or in the study where Lewis Carroll wrote it." The adults were smiling, the decision to purchase Springwell had been made.

"Lady Caldwell, I would recommend that you interview Philip Tilden. He is the leading architect and local expert on restoration of fine old homes." Emily smiled and said, "I will defer to my daughter-in-law."

"Let's all get back in our motorcars and I can drive you past each of the two most impressive. And then we will walk through the Tilden project."

O nce we were all in our motorcars, I asked Idris to give us the history of the Manor House in England.

"Well, Sir James, a Manor is the district of a lord and his non-noble feudal dependents. The term began to be used here after the Norman conquest. A Manor consists of two parts: (1) The inland or home-estate, which the lord held in his own hands, and upon which his house was built and (2) The outland which was held by tenants for rent or for service performed for the lord of the Manor. The tenants were usually all villeins (workers who dwelt together in groups), these groups became know as villages. This part of England formed villages and Manors at about 1350 and this is the date I gave you of your property. In the fourteenth century, the lord of the Manor often was removed three degrees, sometimes even five degrees, in the feudal scale from the King. When the King bestows knighthood even today, the degree of knighthood is spelled out as the distance in property holdings away from the crown. Only a first degree knight can assume to hold as much wealth and property as the King. These knights were known as Court Barons."

"My father was knighted after the American Civil War, I have no idea what degree he held, or even what degree I am."

"You inherited your knighthood from your father, Sir James. Your father could not have been a Baron of the Court, because the Statute of Marlborough had the effect of preventing any further Barons in the kingdom, but in order to inherit a title, your father had to have been at least a second degree knight that held several properties in Bermuda."

"I interrupted you, Idris, please go on with the history lesson." Em shoved an elbow in my ribs and I remained quiet until we reached the gates to the first of two manor houses.

"The Manors were the great reservoirs of customary law, and each Manor modified the common laws of England. Manorial courts were established and the Lord of the Manor became the judge for every citizen living within his village. Some of these larger Manors gave names to districts which are preserved to this day. Do not be surprised, Sir James, if after you purchase your two Manors, you are called upon to settle disputes between neighbors that live in the village of Well Streetroad."

"The village still, exists?" Louis asked with amusement.

"Of course, Your Worship." Louis was taken aback to be addressed in such a manner and Cathleen was snickering.

"I am glad my big brother James is in the other car, he would not let me live that title down."

"Is your brother older than you?"

"Yes, he is."

"Then the title goes to him, not you, Louis. First born and all that old rot, you know."

"That is wonderful, wait till I refer to brother James as 'Your Worship'."

"Oh, you shan't do that. Only a commoner can refer to him as, Your Worship, he is the future Earl of the Manor and your father is the present Lord of the Manor." Idris Jones was pulling Louis' leg and we all started to laugh as we entered the gate to the oldest surviving manor house on the estate.

47

Future Navy Retirement
March, 1919

Winter was nearly gone and it looked like early spring. I had not returned to Washington, D.C. and my office in the Army Navy Building. President Wilson had said for me to take as much time with my family in England as I felt I needed. He had said that the immediate demobilization of the Navy would be minor and that his assistant Secretary of the Navy, Franklin Roosevelt, had his instructions on what to do and when to do it. I had not decided if I wanted to serve this president, in the last months of his "lame duck" tenure. I was more than old enough to retire, 63 and it was time to enjoy my life and my family. I had researched my family tree in 1912 right after President Wilson was elected and I had an artist make a colored diagram of the entire family. I decided a few modifications should be made.

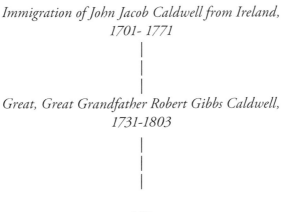

Immigration of John Jacob Caldwell from Ireland,
1701- 1771

Great, Great Grandfather Robert Gibbs Caldwell,
1731-1803

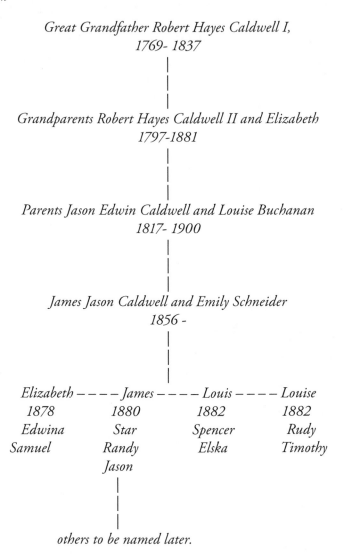

Great Grandfather Robert Hayes Caldwell I,
1769- 1837

Grandparents Robert Hayes Caldwell II and Elizabeth
1797-1881

Parents Jason Edwin Caldwell and Louise Buchanan
1817- 1900

James Jason Caldwell and Emily Schneider
1856 -

Elizabeth – – – – James – – – – Louis – – – – Louise
1878   1880   1882   1882
Edwina   Star   Spencer   Rudy
Samuel   Randy   Elska   Timothy
             Jason

others to be named later.

48

Navy Assignments
April, 1919

By April fools day I was back in my office in the Army Navy Building in Washington, D.C. Emily and I took a cruise liner from South Hampton along with our two daughters and their families. The Secnav, Joe Daniels, had sent me my orders to return to active duty. James was assigned to the US Embassy in London and his brother, Louis, was assigned as the NIA Director for Europe, based in London. James' wife, Martha, and Louis' wife, Cathleen, were put in charge of the restoration, or at least decoration, of the two manor houses at Springwell. The household staffs remained in both houses and began their service to the Caldwell family instead of the estate of Sir John Campbell Colquhoun. Emily and I turned a blind eye to what was going on in both houses after all, these were the homes of James and Louis Caldwell. Em and I would hire the architect recommended by Idris Jones when he said, "Lady Caldwell, I would recommend that you interview Philip Tilden. He is the leading architect and local expert on restoration of fine old homes."

Emily had smiled and said, "I will defer to my daughter-in-law." She had said this because of Cathleen's reaction when she heard Mr. Jones say, "Sir James, two of the three houses are in excellent shape for their ages, the third will take some loving care to restore. I would recommend that you restore it, Sir. Lewis Carroll leased the third house, a cottage really, from Sir John Campbell Colquhoun, while he was writing Alice in Wonderland."

"Oh, Louis, we have to see that house!" It was nearly a scream from

Cathleen. "That is my favorite children's story, I want to read it to Elska in front of the fireplace or in the study where Lewis Carroll wrote it."

It was at that point that the decision to purchase Springwell had been made. Cathleen and Emily became very close during the winter months and their meetings with Philip Tilden. The plans were drawn up for the smallest of the three houses at Springwell and reconstruction would begin shortly after the spring rains had ceased. Cathleen and Emily were in constant contact by telephone and letters. Cathleen realized that Grandma Caldwell would live in the smallest of the three houses whenever she would travel for extended stays in England, but her home was Bellawoods in Washington, D.C.

It was nearly a month later when I found my fathers unpublished manuscript and every scrap of paper ever sent to him. After my mother died at Seneca Hill and was buried on the grounds of Seneca Hill, now Cranson College, Emily and I moved a number of storage boxes, pieces of furniture and steamer trunks from my mother's quarters at the college to Bellawoods. Emily wanted to ship some of my mother's keepsakes to Cathleen and Martha at Springwell so they could place them in the two manor houses or set them aside for her use in the Lewis Carroll Cottage. When I opened one of the steamer trunks, I found a bundle of papers and a note from my father. The note had never been sent to me, but it was in his handwriting.

Dear James,

If you are reading this account of my memories of Hiram Ulysses Grant, better known as Ulysses S. Grant it means that your mother has not thrown away my unpublished manuscript. I want you to read it, if you like it, send it on to the publishers in St. Paul, Minnesota. The Western Book Syndicate has already published three accounts of my career. The first was entitled **Calm Before the Storm** and it dealt with my career from 1855 to 1863 and your adoption into our family. In 1855, I was working out of the Army Navy Building and reporting to President Pierce. I worked for three different Presidents during those years; Pierce, Buchanan and Lincoln. I met Ulysses during the Buchanan and Lincoln administrations.

The second book was entitled **Death Before Dishonor** and it is an account of my time with Presidents Lincoln, Johnson and Grant. The third book, **Lull After the Storm**, covers my time working for President Grant and President Hayes as director of the Naval Institute in Annapolis, Maryland. In this volume, **The General**, I have attempted to tell General Grant's story very much in my own way. I fully and heartily endorsed his positions from the first time I met him when he was a captain and in command of a volunteer group from Illinois until my retirement. I also shared in his enthusiasm for life. My task has consisted of nothing more than merely writing the notes for this book. My memories of this captain of volunteers from Illinois and the pleasant contemplation of the brilliant deeds of the General during the war between the states and his time in the White House take me back to that time and places often forgotten by others. There is something positively inspiring in the following of his career and when I declare that the enthusiasm of Captain Grant is nothing more than just and reasonable, I remember it with careful examination of the grounds on which it is based. After a patient, but exceedingly agreeable, study of the character of the man whom you and I knew as a General and a President during our years at Annapolis, I thought it fitting to put my memories to paper. (Your mother used to think I went into my study to take a nap after I fully retired).

I have twice read all that I have written, and I find no occasion to add any qualifying words, and no reason to moderate the warm enthusiasm that I felt for the man. As the elected candidate for the presidency from the Republican party, General Grants sayings and doings have been subjected to the closest scrutiny by his political opponents. As we approach the year 1900 and the turn of the century, all that he has said and all that he has done as president has been remorselessly criticized. Partisan prejudice and hatred pursued him until his death. Maybe my memories of the man will not hold up to the gaze of the American people, who I have always found stand the test of time. In his private life the General was guileless, while in his public history he has sometimes been animated by the most noble and exalted patriotism.

The research and study of the General has been exceedingly refreshing to me, as well as to my editor in St. Paul, as we analyzed together the influences which shaped the General's life. We were unable to find any of those selfish and belittling springs of action which often rob great deeds of more than half their glory. We could see in him a simplicity of character which amazed us; a strength of mind, a singleness of heart, which caused us to envy Sherman and Sheridan the possession of such a man's friendship.

I was his commanding officer during the early part of the war between the states and we were not friends. We became friends after he asked me to move the Naval Institute back to Annapolis after the war was over. I found him to be a lovable man, an attitude in which we are seldom permitted to regard for a president or a hero among our midst. I found him to be modest, gentle hearted and always approachable. There was none of the frigid reserve in his manner which awes common people in the contemplation of those exalted by mighty deeds or a lofty position.

I believe my friend, Hiram Grant, was somewhat afraid of the Republican politicians inside his own party. He was an outsider as he never had the honor to belong to their meetings during the war. During his entire time at West Point he was a Democrat. And this matter of facts, the unclothed skeleton of reliable history and biography, is a point I wish to make in this book. My editor and I used a library of reference in the agreeable task we have jointly performed including all the works bearing on the subject now available in the country as of this date, July 4, 1895. We have used them liberally and faithfully, and animated by a desire to set forth the truth about the General. My editor is entirely confident that we have produced a reliable history of all the important phases in his life. I have plentifully besprinkled the pages of my manuscript with anecdotes, some of which have never been related before, certainly not the private conversations between the two of us.

My editor and I jointly acknowledge our indebtedness to General Adam Badeau's "Military History of Ulysses S. Grant," at once the most interesting and exhaustive work on the subject which has yet been issued. We tender our personal *thanks to General Badeau for additional facts, suggestions and anecdotes.*

Jason Edwin Caldwell, former Vice President of the United States
Seneca Hill, Pennsylvania

July 11, 1895

I sat aside the note to me and read the first page of the manuscript.

One
Point Pleasant, Ohio
April 27, 1822

I was born five years before Hannah Grant gave birth to her son, Hiram, in a village on the Ohio River, twenty-five miles from the city of Cincinnati. Many people have a fanatical veneration for bloodline as such, I confess I yield no allegiance to this sentiment, for I expected to be what I made of myself, rather than what I am made by my distinguished ancestor, John Jacob Caldwell who immigrated from Ireland in the eighteenth century. But for those who attach any weight to pedigree, may be reasonably gratified in the solid character of the progenitors of Hiram Grant. He came from the Grants of Aberdeen, Scotland, whose heraldic motto was, *stand fast, stand firm, stand sure.*

Mathew Grant was a passenger in the clipper ship *Mary and John,* and settled in Dorchester, Massachusetts, in 1630. Noah Grant a descendant of that stout Puritan, emigrated to Connecticut and was a captain in the Old French War. He was killed in battle, in 1756, having attained that rank. His son, also taking the patriarchal name, was belligerent enough to have been killed in battle, for he was a soldier in the revolutionary war from Lexington, where he served as a lieutenant. This faithful soldier was Hiram's grandfather. He had a son name Jesse Root Grant, who was Hiram's father. In 1820, Jesse married Hannah Simpson and moved to Point Pleasant, Ohio.

I searched for and found the letters to and from his editor.

Caldwell International
Seneca Hill, Pennsylvania

July 4, 1895

Mr. Edward S. Ellis, editor
Woolfall Publishing Company
260 Hennepin Ave.
St. Paul, Minnesota

Dear Edward,

I took your advice and finished the last chapter with The Grand Army of the Republic encampment from the 19th to the 22nd of September, 1892. Our national capital was given over to the twenty-sixth annual encampment. The gathering was the largest that has taken place since the memorable review of the Union forces at the close of the war in 1865. Washington was elaborately decorated, and thousands of visitors from every section of the country vied with me and my aide in honoring the heroes who proudly kept step to the "music of the union" more than a quarter of a century before.

Grant, of course, was not there, he died at Mount Macgregor, near Saratoga, New York, (not far from my home, here in Pennsylvania) July 23, 1885. He was only sixty-three years old, but with cancer of the throat, your time is short. I was born 1817 and am still going strong seventy-eight years later. You never know what God has planned for you. I was sworn in as Vice-president, November 24, 1886, after my sixty-ninth birthday. President Cleveland and I had a short time together in the White House and he wanted me to run with him for re-election, I probably should have because he got beat and had to run again in four years.

I will mail the completed manuscript in a few days.

Sincerely yours,
Jason

Woolfall Publishing Company
260 Hennepin Avenue, St. Paul

July 11. 1895

Admiral Jason Caldwell
Seneca Hill, Pennsylvania

Dear Jason,

I received your letter of July 4th . What are you doing working on a holiday? I agree that the last chapter will be stronger with the 1892 encampment scene rather than the encampment right after the war ended. It was estimated that fully 67,000 men were in the parade that you describe marching past the stand in front of the Treasury building. Vice-President Morton reviewed them. The mortal illness of Mrs. Harrison prevented the president from meeting his old army comrades, as he earnestly wished to do.

The route taken was that followed by the 150,000 survivors of the Armies of the Potomac and the West, when they marched by under the proud gaze of President Johnson and his acting Secretary of State, Jason Caldwell. On that historic occasion, the vast procession was thirty miles long and lasted fourteen hours. The parade described in your last chapter, twenty-seven years later took about eight hours to march over the same ground.

I will be looking for your manuscript in the next few days.

Sincerely yours,

Edward

49

Contacting the Publisher

May, 1919

I wondered if Edward Ellis was still alive. My father lived until late in 1900 and was eighty-four years old when he died. If they were the same age, then Edward Ellis would be 102 now. Even if he were twenty years younger than my father, he would be 82 and retired. I would try and contact the editor who replaced him at Woolfall Publishing, and I had the perfect way to do it, American News Service. I telephoned Charlie Reuters at American News in my sister Ruth's headquarters in New York City.

"Hello, this is Admiral Caldwell. I am trying to reach Charlie Reuters. Can you connect me, please?" I waited.

"Hello, James, how can I help you?"

"Hello, Charlie, how is my sister treating you?"

"Like she owns the company, James. What else is new?"

"I found some old letters from my father to his editor at Woolfall Publishing in St. Paul. They were discussing a manuscript that he was writing about General Grant."

"When was this, James?"

"The letters are dated July, 1895."

"Are you sure the book has not been published? I can check titles in the Library of Congress for you, James. Every book that has a copyright has a Library of Congress control number, for example, your father's first book entitled Calm Before the Storm has a control number of 2009905274."

"How in the world would you know something like that?"

"Because American News bought the rights to publish his book chapter

396

by chapter in the newspapers that we service. Each editorial piece had to have the Library of Congress control number appearing in the credit lines. Newspaper printers and typesetters were always forgetting the number and calling me to get it, I memorized the damn thing."

"What do you think of publishing this lost manuscript in the same way?"

"You mean bit by bit in newspapers?"

"That is exactly what I mean. How much trouble is it to get a copyright and a Library of Congress control number?"

"American News can do that for you, James. A copyright is only something like seventy-five dollars. Are you sure you don't want Woolfall to publish it as a book, first. That is the normal procedure."

"Of course. But if Woolfall is no longer interested, I would like to offer it to the public. I have read it, Charlie. I liked it, and I think others will also."

"Alright, James, I will find the contact information at Woolfall Publishing, they should be impressed by hearing from us. I will let you know what I find in a few days. I will telex it to you, okay?"

"Thanks, Charlie, good talking to you again."

He hung up and I bet he was on his way to my sister's office to tell her about our conversation. An hour later my telephone rang and it was Ruth Roosevelt from the New Yorker Magazine on the line.

"James, don't you dare let Charlie cut up Daddy's last book and peddle it to the newspapers. The New Yorker will publish it as a series of chapters month by month. How many chapters do you have?"

"Ruthie, you know our father, he goes on and on, chapter after chapter. There must be a hundred chapters here."

"Good God, that is eight years worth! Can you edit it for me?"

"Charlie is trying to contact Woolfall Publishing for me to see if Dad had a contract with them. We have to clear it with them first. I would like to see it as a book first and then I will edit it into 12 issues for the New Yorker, alright?"

"James, you have not written a book since your surveying book for John Wiley. Are you up to doing a history book?"

"Ruthie, I think I may know someone at Wiley that can help us. Let me have a few days and I will get back to you, alright?"

"Can I get a copy of this lost manuscript? I would like to read it."

"Of course, Ruthie, I am sending a telex of the note that is in Dad's handwriting that I found attached to the manuscript. I will also telex the first page of the manuscript. I think you can get an idea of what Dad had in mind from just those two things. Charlie is running down Woolfall Publishing for me. I should hear from him in a few days."

"Woolfall Publishing is a British company, James. Charlie has already found that much out for you. He has no response from the Western Book Syndicate in St. Paul. He thinks it is now Western Publishing, also known as Western Printing and Lithographing Company. It seems two brothers, Edward and Albert Wadewitz, owned Western Printing and bought Western Book Syndicate in 1907."

"Where is Western Publishing located?"

"The printing plant is in Racine, Wisconsin, but they have editorial offices in Los Angeles and here in New York City. I will contact the office here and see if I can find a contract between Daddy and the book syndicate. This is getting exciting, James, it is like having him back in our midst."

"I think that was his idea all along, Ruthie. He was always better with the written word than he was in talking directly to us. Oh, another thing that I found, you might like. It is a letter that you wrote to him during the Civil War."

"Do you have it handy?"

"Yes, I have it right in my hand."

"Read it to me, James."

SENECAHILL
Januarey 4, 1865

Dear Daddy,

Mommy says my printing is very good. I try hard to do what my tutor say to me. Do you know she has only one ear ring on today. James still hits me. I told him you will tell him NO, NO. I asked Mommy why you are away from me. She says to me that some people do not like to follow the rules. The rules are for so we can all live together. She said you were telling some people NO, NO. Do you miss me? I miss you all the time. I give you a big hug when you are back to me.

Ruth Louise Caldwell

"Are you there, Ruthie?"

"Yes."

"What is the matter?"

"I am crying. I forgot I ever wrote that to him, but now I remember."

"See, that is what I am getting at."

"I don't understand?"

"Let me read you another letter."

BELMONT HOTEL
St. Louis, Missouri

November 12, 1857

Dear Louise,

I am spending a couple of days in St. Louis. My detachment is in route back to Washington City. This assignment into the West has given me an opportunity to think about my future. I have decided that I will finish my Navy Career at the end of your brother's administration in 1865. I have been away from South Carolina for far too long and I miss it. I wrote to my parents in Beaufort and told them how I feel about you. Actually, I wrote that I had finally met someone with whom I could share the rest of my life . I just needed to find out if she felt the same way.

If you will have me, as your life's partner, I will bring you to our future home in Beaufort. It is 353 Bay Street, overlooking the inter-coastal waterway. At high tide it is beautiful, at low tide it smells like shell fish - but I love it and I hope you will too. I do not need the Navy to make my life complete now that I have found you. I am the owner of the Caldwell Shipping and Trading Company of Port Royal, South Carolina. I co-own with my father and brother, a sea island plantation. You and I will be kept very busy with the business and social activities of Beaufort. It is a long time until '65 – but I wanted you to know how I feel.

Lovingly,
Jason

"Oh, James. That is a proposal of marriage to our mother! Don't lose that letter, I want to hold it in my hands the next time I am at Bellawoods. Don't risk sending it through the mails, you know how unreliable they can be."

"Do you want to hear what mother wrote back to him?"

"Yes, James we need to write a book of our own, just for the family with reproductions of everything you have. Go ahead, read it."

THE WHITE HOUSE

WASHINGTON CITY

November 18, 1857

Dearest Jason,

Your heartfelt letter arrived to day and I am answering you immediately. My answer is, I will wait for you until you ask me to marry you. I do not think that you will have to wait until 1865 to retire, however. I am telling you this in confidence, my brother will not seek the nomination from the Democratic Party in 1860. He too, says he misses spending time with his life's partner and he plans to retire from public life after the election of '60.

My brother has accepted your invitation to visit you in South Carolina. He will bring us on the USS Charter Oak via Charleston. He will drop Secretary Toucey in Charleston and continue on to Beaufort. He has also told me that you are a man of honor and I would be fortunate to have you as a husband. I can not wait to embrace you again and to make our future plans together!

With all my love,
Louise

"Oh my God, James, that is her letter of acceptance of his proposal. That settles it, I am on the next train to Washington. I want to read every scrap of paper that you found in the trunk."

"Before you hang up and get on the train, Ruthie, did Charlie talk to you about purchasing American News Service from us?"

"Yes, I think that fits into your plans for the American holdings of Caldwell International. Charlie plans to call the new company, Reuters News. Is that alright with you?"

"I think that would be an excellent name, Charlie can keep it in his family for many years to come."

50

The White House

June 1, 1919 - January 20, 1921

The remaining months of the Wilson administration were spent in two different parts, those months before his stroke on September 26, 1919 and those months after. After the armistice, President Wilson made several major trips abroad. His visited France, then England where I spoke with him for the last time. As I look back on it now, his actions, method of speech and exhaustion were all clear signs that a stroke was coming. He did not pace himself as he formed with Premier Lloyd George of England, Premier Clemenceau of France, and the Premier of Italy, Orlando, the "Big Four" on whose decisions all matters of supreme importance were final in the Inter Allied Peace Conference in Paris in 1919.

The outcome of the Peace Conference was the forming of the League of Nations. This proposed League, however, aroused intense opposition in the United States. The president not only had to face the opposition of the Republican Party but he also met with much antagonism within his own party. To combat this contravention to this cherished project for world government and world betterment as he saw it, Thomas Woodrow Wilson began to tour the country to appeal directly to the people. Here is what he faced.

January: he visits Rome, Genoa and Milan, Italy, he attends the first formal meeting of the Supreme Council of Peace Congress in Paris and he votes the adoption of Prohibition offered from the Senate. The senate over-rides his veto.

February: he visits President Friedrich Ebert of Germany, returns to

Paris to read aloud to the Peace Conference, the completed draft of the League of Nations. On the 15th he sails from Brest, France on his way back to the United States, arriving on the 23rd.

March: he makes an address in New York City on the League of Nations covenant. March 5th he again sails for Europe on his second trip to the Peace Conference at Versailles.

April: the Italian delegates quit the Versailles Peace Conference when Italy was denied the city of Fiume, and President Wilson travels to Rome to seek a compromise. The president presents revised draft of the covenant of the League of Nations to the Congress in Washington, D. C.

May: Italy agrees to rejoin peace conference and the Congress votes to submit Woman Suffrage Amendment to the states for ratification but ignores action on the revised draft of the League of Nations.

June: President Wilson returns to the peace conference without senate action and is amazed by the flight of the US Navy hydroplane NC-4 from Trepassey Bay, Newfoundland to Horta in the Azores, he realizes that trans-Atlantic flights are now possible. In late June the peace treaty is signed by German delegates, and those from France, Great Britain, Italy, Japan and the President. He leaves Paris for Brest on return to the United States for Senate approval.

July: he arrives July 10th and presents the signed treaty to the US Senate. The Senate refuses to ratify the treaty.

August: he entertains foreign visitors in the White House; Prince of Wales, King Alfonso of Spain and President of Germany, Friedrich Ebert.

September: he leaves the White House on his Peace Treaty speech-making tour through the country. He signs the bill, making General Pershing a permanent grade officer. The only others in the history of the country are Washington, Scott, Grant, Sherman and Sheridan. Still on the road tour of speeches, he signs the bill incorporating the American Legion. On September 26th he collapses while making a speech at Wichita, Kansas. The American public is not told of the seriousness of his attack and he is brought back to the White House.

October: he is bed fast and unable to move his left arm and left leg. The vice-president is not told of the president's condition, his White House chief of staff, Colonel Henry House, keeps even the cabinet members away from his bedside saying that the president is exhausted and needs his rest. While the president rested, the United States Senate killed the peace treaty by a vote of 55 to 35, they voted in favor of establishing a national budget system and Henry House signed the president's name vetoing the Prohibition Bill. The House and Senate over-ride the veto by a two-thirds majority.

November: he is able to sit up in bed after six weeks of recovery, the Senate nullify the covenant of the League of Nations and at the end of the year he is confined to a wheel chair and meeting with individual cabinet members. Secnav, Joe Daniels, comes to my office and reports the president's condition.

December: he is unable to attend normal Christmas functions in the White House or in Washington, D. C.

January: he begins a letter writing campaign to various organizations urging them to pressure the Senate and House into affirmative action on the Peace Treaty and the League of Nations.

February: his illness is reported Reuters News Service as being due to a blood clot on the brain, which affected the use of his left arm and leg. The League of Nations meets for the first time without a US delegate.

March: Senate refused to reconsider the peace treaty with Germany and the acceptance of the League of Nations.

April: the House of Representatives passes by vote of 242 to 150 the Republican peace resolution officially ending the state of war with Germany. President Wilson is not seen outside the White House.

May: he vetoes several bills passed by the Republicans and they are passed over his vetoes.

June: Republican National Convention meets in Chicago and nominate Senator Warren Harding of Ohio.

July: he does not attend the Democratic Convention to see the nomination of Governor James Cox of Ohio.

August: he signs the federal suffrage proclamation but does not campaign for Cox during the summer months.

September: he is elected an honorary delegate to the League of Nations but is unable to travel to Paris.

October: Poland and Russia are the last two nations except the United States to sign and accept the peace treaty ending the world war.

November: Harding and Coolidge are swept into office with the largest popular vote in the history of the country.

December: Argentina is the first nation to resign from the League of Nations.

Author's Note

War of the Nations is a work of fiction. The names, characters, places and incidents portrayed in this novel are the product of the author's imagination or have been used fictitiously. The characters are placed within the historical perspective of World War I. The photographs depicted in this novel are all actual photos reproduced from The Peoples Standard History of the United States. President Wilson and his cabinet are faithfully represented, but a director of the National Intelligence Agency was not part of that cabinet. Any resemblance to actual businesses, companies, governmental departments, agencies or locals is entirely coincidental. The American News Service does not exist.

President Wilson's addresses have been edited and shortened to fit the flow and sequences of the novel. President Wilson was a typical educator and could talk for hours on favorite subjects, he did not have his Secretary of State, William Jennings Bryan, write any of his remarks or coach him in the delivery of them as indicated in the novel. President Roosevelt did not ask him to become Ambassador to Germany, but it is true that Dr. Wilson did take a leave of absence from Princeton and he did enter the White House from the governor's chair of New Jersey.

My research on Sir Edward Grey, Secretary of State for foreign affairs and Winston Spencer Churchill, first Lord of the Admiralty, are faithfully presented in the novel. Their addresses and remarks are imagined, only the dates of these addresses have survived in the history books of England.

James Caldwell was not one of the passengers on the Lusitania, but an American diplomat was aboard the fated ocean liner when it was sunk. The German U-boats did sink the British passenger steamer, Falaba, on

March 28, 1915; the American Cushing was sunk by air attack, not by a U-boat as depicted in the novel; the American Gulf Light sinking on May 1, did happen, but only two crew members were lost.

To better understand the use of characters the following listing is based upon their appearance in the novel.

Fictional	Real
James J. Caldwell, NIA director	Thomas Woodrow Wilson
Louis J. Caldwell, NIA London	President's cabinet members
Hans Becker, NIA Berlin	Sir Edward Grey
Vladimir Lenardovich, NIA Petrograd	Winston Spencer Churchill
Commodore James J. Caldwell II	Herr von Jagow
Emily Schneider Caldwell	Kaiser Wilhelm II
Cathleen Whither Caldwell	King Edward VII (1901-1910)
Admiral Rodney Lowe	Theodore Roosevelt
Elizabeth "Busy" Caldwell	Franklin Roosevelt
Elska Van Mauker	Otto von Bismark
Admiral Rodney Lowe	Count Zeppelin
Louise Emily Caldwell	Czar Nicholas II
Frederick Bernhardi, NIA Vienna	Raymond Poincare
Edwardric Scziorm, NIA Budapest	Bethmann Hollweg
Captain Mick Merfield	Radko Dimitryev
Spencer Carson Caldwell	Prince Karl Lichnowsky
Captain Hans Nedimeyer	King George V
Captain Ludwig Schmitz	William Jennings Bryan
Captain David Ellingsworth	Ambassador Frederic Penfield
Lord Alfred Dinsmore	Johann Heinrich Bernstorff
Sir Cedric Price-Rice	General John Pershing
Captain Daniel Wells	Admiral W. S. Sims
Captain Henry Claypool	Marshal Ferdinand Foch
Elska Whither Caldwell	Idris Jones

Preview of Dan Ryan's new novel

CATYWAMPUS

Guide to the James Jason Caldwell II papers, 1896 - 1906
United States Naval Institute
589 McNair Road
Annapolis, Maryland

The United States Navy's Submarine Service dates from the War of 1812, if you don't count the use of David Bushnell's Boat used on September 7, 1776. A revolutionary soldier by the name of Ezra Lee used this devilish product of Yankee ingenuity to attach a mine to the bottom of Admiral Lord Howe's ship, HMS Eagle, which was at anchor in New York harbor. The War of 1812 was primarily a naval war fought by the British and American Navies. When war was declared with Great Britain on June 19, 1812, our navy consisted of only 17 ships of the line which totaled 15,000 tons. The officers and men of the United States Navy consisted of 5,000. Great Britain had 1,048 ships of the line which totaled 870,000 tons. The officers and men of the British Navy consisted of 150,000. How were the victories in our harbors, rivers and in the Atlantic Ocean achieved, then? The answer was through the use of small boats and submarine mines, called torpedoes. A naval torpedo in 1812 consisted of an explosive device designed to destroy a ship by blowing a hole in the hull below the water line. There were two types of torpedoes used against the British. A small boat was used at night to fasten the torpedo to the hull of the British ship, these were called torpedo boats. Those men who operated these boats and fastened these mines were known submariners, because they worked below the water level. The second type of torpedo was fastened to the bottom of the river or harbor and attached with a rope of varying lengths. Some of these floated on the surface and some were a few feet below the surface. These mines contained a set of pins, when one of the these pins was struck by a passing ship, the pin was driven down upon a fulminate primer and exploded the charge within the casing of the torpedo. The two types were known as self-acting (a ship comes in contact with it) or controlled (these were set by divers under a stationary ship and a timer allowed the diver to escape before the torpedo exploded).

Not all of the sea battles of the War of 1812 involved the use of submarine charges, but many did. Here are a few that did; USS President vs HMS Belvidera, USS Essex vs HMS Minerva, USS Constitution vs HMS Guerriere, USS Wasp vs HMS Frolic, USS United States vs HMS Macedonian, and the USS Constitution vs HMS Java. The total number of British ships captured or sunk during the war was reported in the London Times of March 20, 1813, as 504 captured in seven months, 527 merchant vessels sunk during the same period and 3 men-of-war sunk.

How did the Americans do it? They used one of Robert Fulton's inventions, called the Nautilus. Fulton used a plunging mechanism which was invented in France in 1795 and added his own mechanisms for vertical and horizontal rudders and he provided for the artificial supply of air. The Nautilus could descend to a given depth and re-ascend at will. The torpedo boat concept was popular in Germany (1851), England (1887), France (1889) and the United States. In 1854 the periscope was made practical and added to all US torpedo boats. The next naval conflict within the United States was the Civil War (1860-1865). A total of eight submarines were built during this period. The most famous of these was the CSS H.L. Hunley, built by J.W. McClintock. The Hunley was hand propelled and carried a crew of eight. It attacked a number of wooden Federal ships in and around Charleston Harbor. The Hunley attacked the USS Housatonic on February 2, 1864. There were 160 men on the Housatonic and five were killed in the torpedo explosion. The captain of the Housatonic ordered kegs of gunpowder with lighted fuses thrown overboard. The Hunley was sunk, history's first successful use of the depth charge. The Housatonic sank an hour later.

Four types of submarines were designed in late 1890's. The first was the Plougeur-Marin, built in Germany by H. O. Bauer. During a test dive at Kiel, Germany, one of these models was crushed by the sea's depth and increased water pressure. Bauer concluded that was because of the shoe box like design and changed to a circular cross-section design for all further production runs. The second was the HMS Nordenfeldt, built in England by a Norwegian designer. It was rectangular and could not reach proper diving depths until the cross sectional shape was made circular. The third was the Goubet, built in France. Its cigar shape proved to be the design for all future submarines. The fourth was the Holland, built in the United States by Robert Fulton and it was the submarine design used by James J. Caldwell II from 1897 until 1906.

So what does catywampus mean? It is a common term used by all men who served in the submarine fleet of the United States from 1896 until 1906. The submarines used during this period were small war vessels, with crews of less than a dozen. These vessels were fitted to use the torpedo as its primary weapon of attack. The principal requirements of a torpedo boat were high speed, efficient means of launching torpedoes, handiness and fair sea worthiness. To attain these essentials the boats were long, slender, very lightly built and low in the water. The torpedo tubes, which contain the torpedoes to be fired, could be pivoted on deck. When the torpedo boat is on the surface of the water, the tubes may be pivoted to any position. When a tube was fired diagonally across the deck, the men on the boat referred to this as a catycorner shot. This was basically a two-dimensional shot in a flat plane. When a submarine of the Goubet or Holland class were submerged under the water, the shot became three-dimensional, this was known as the catywampus shot.

Balkan Peninsula
November 1900

A small task force was sent to the Balkan Peninsula by President McKinley in August before the national election. The presidential election of 1900 was unique in that it was the first of the twentieth century and it would be the first election where I could vote. The Republicans held their nominating convention on June 19th in the Exposition Auditorium, Philadelphia. The incumbent, President William McKinley, was unanimously named the party's candidate for President. No candidate ran against him, although George Dewey considered a run. My Uncle Teddy was nominated for Vice President.

My father had gone to the Democratic Convention in Kansas City on July 14th. The convention nominated William Jennings Bryan again over many objections from a minority of delegates, including my father's objections made from the floor of the convention.

"Mister Speaker, members of the convention, and distinguished guests and visitors. A member of my family has been a member of this national convention for nearly a hundred years. Some of you delegates may remember my father, the former Vice President, when he spoke at the last convention. He is no longer with us and he warned us of that fact when he said, "I do not plan on attending the next convention, my son, James, is now a delegate and will take my place for the next convention."

I am here today, not to support any candidate that has already lost an election. I come before you to remind you that everyone in this great hall is a Democrat first and something else second. What we do for a living is not as important as improving our living standards. It has never been the policy of the Democratic Party to 'get rich quick ' upon the backs of the worker. We are the workers of America. There are no 'robber barons' inside this hall. They were all present at the Republican Convention held in Philadelphia in June.

I think Republicans see things in a very conservative, light. They see things the way they were a hundred years ago. Then world powers controlled their colonies around the globe. The Republicans say - good, we need to keep things that way. Democrats see things the way they are and say - things can be better, we need to improve things. The rest of the political parties see things that will never be. (Interrupted by some clapping)

We are here today to nominate the next President of the United States. Whenever the Democratic Party stays together and does not split into separate groups, a Democratic President is elected. I warn each and every one of you listening to me (I shook my finger like my father) if you want to see a Republican in the White House, keep offering the same old planks in the platform. Planks like what money standard the country should have, or whether the tariffs should be lowered or raised, does not matter to the common voter. We must not offer them someone who has already lost an election. Americans love a winner and will not tolerate a loser. (The hall was deadly quiet.)

Remember who we are, why are here and what we can do if we stay united and focused upon the good of the country. Few presidential nominees have a clear vision of the future or a sincere desire to put the country before their self interests. Our nominee should never mention anything the common voter can not understand. Our nominee should be a national hero and I place Admiral George Dewey's name in nomination."

The only bright spot that I could see about the election was that my uncle might be a heart beat away from being President and this is what my grandmother had worked so hard for in the fall. I finished reading the description of the democratic convention in my father's letters and asked the captain of the USS Delaware how much longer until he would launch my portable submarine, the USS Swordfish.

"One hour until sunset, Ensign Caldwell, you better go find the rest of your crew and get on board."

"Aye, aye, Sir." Our mission that night was to begin the mapping of the opening of the Bay of Cattaro in southern Herzegovina. The Department of the Navy was convinced that a war on the Balkan Peninsula was only a matter of time. This peninsula is the eastern most of the three great southern peninsulas of Europe, bounded by the Adriatic Sea, where we were located, on the west and the Black and Aegean seas on the east. Its northern boundary is generally considered to be the Danube, with its tributary, the Save. Thus defined, the peninsula comprises, within an area of 175,000 square miles, the countries of Turkey, Bulgaria, Rumelia, Servia, Montenegro, Bosina and Herzegovina, Novibazar and Greece. Servia, Rumelia and Novibazar had no coast line, thank God. Greece alone contained over 300 separate islands, all with sea ports of some kind or another. The Captain of the Delaware estimated that if the Department of the Navy wanted all the sea ports from the Adriatic to the Black Sea mapped, it would take us about 10,000 man years of effort. He was then told to limit his efforts to one year with the ships and submarines at his disposal. He decided to start with all the major harbors and bays which might see action during a war between these countries. The captain hoisted the Swordfish off his deck and lowered it into the Adriatic.

"See you in the morning, Captain Caldwell." I liked being called a captain, even though the surveying party was only four men and a mass of equipment.

"Aye, aye, Sir." I clamped the hatch on the conning tower, stepped off the ladder and slid to the deck of the Swordfish. "Get us underway, Mr. Fisher. The Delaware and the others will be launching immediately after us." I was speaking through a tube to the engine hold at the rear of the sub. I put the tube to my ear and heard, "Aye, aye, Captain, engine turning over, engine started, drive engaged, moving forward."

"Keep us on the surface tonight, Mr. Jamison, there will be no moon." I did not need a speaking tube, the navigator was at my elbow.

"Aye, aye, Captain, bearing to mapping point is N13oW."

"Which sector are we assigned, Mr. Jamison?"

" Northwestern area 10-3, Sir."

"Increase your speed to 17 knots and keep us on the surface. Ensign Godwin, what do you see through the periscope? The conning tower windows are blurred now."

"Surface is clear all the way ahead, Sir." My exec was a year older than me but had less time in rank. The periscope on our portable submarine was a form of camera obscura, consisting of a long vertical tube with a prism or inclined mirror at the upper and a reflecting surface or prism, below. The upper end is designed to project several feet above water when the boat is entirely submerged. The periscope is, however, practically useless at night or in rough weather. For these and other reasons, the conning towers of portable submarines are built very high, so that direct vision through the glass windows of the conning tower may be obtained without exposing the body of the boat to the observation or attack of the enemy. That is why I was in the conning tower and my exec was at the periscope. Thanks to my year of transfer to Goat Island, I had considerable experience in a small submarine used for mapping. It was almost like second nature to me now to deal with the conditions affecting the stability of an entirely submerged boat, compared with those while on the surface.

Since the sectional area of the immersed body remains unchanged at all angles of heel, the position of the center of buoyancy is constant; the righting moment, therefore, grows more slowly as the boat heels. By suitable ballasting or arrangement of weights, adequate transverse stability is not very difficult to attain. But longitudinal stability is quite another matter. Any possible assistance from ballasting or the arrangement of permanent weights is insignificant, and the change of trim due to the using of fuel and shifting of weights is a very serious matter. This tendency to "heel upwards" is counteracted by the use of horizontal rudders, or shape of the hull, vertical screws, or quickly shifting water ballast. If the boat has a slight surplus buoyancy, the tendency to rise to the surface can be counteracted by vanes or a shape of the head of the boat, which tends to make the boat descend so long as it is moving forward. But as the effect of hull shape or permanent vanes changes with the speed, while the buoyance effort is constant, horizontal rudders are a necessity. From this description, it follows that short, deep and broad boats are the most stable, but such a shape is incompatible with a portable sub designed to be carried on a surface vessel, so I was constantly giving orders to my crew.

Until I had many more years of experience as a captain of a submarine, I would remain with the portable submarine or surface torpedo boat. The

Holland Class and the newer, larger submarines had sea-going capacity and a wide radius of action. The scope of usefulness of the portable submarine seemed confined to harbor defense or mapping assignments like we were on tonight. The qualities of the new submarines made it possible for them to accompany a battle fleet. The tactics for these new submarines were yet to be developed and I was confined to this "death trap" as my instructor, WH Hornsby, used to call them. Only fools and Englishmen ever volunteer to get in a portable submarine, the life expectancy is 92 days of service. His statement was burned into my memory as we approached the opening to the Bay of Cattaro.

We never saw the torpedo boat net that stopped our forward motion and sent us all sprawling on the deck.

"Stop all engines." I screamed, I forgot that a portable only has one engine. "Radio, send a message to the Delaware. Torpedo boat nets in place, warn all others. Keep repeating it until you hear back from them."

"Aye, aye, Sir." Came through the speaking tube and from the cross-trained seaman near me. I needed to find out what type of net was in place. Most nets are made of heavy wire rings connected with one another by smaller steel rings, once ensnared, it was almost impossible to free oneself in a few hours. We had until sunrise. I needed to forget about mapping and get my divers in the water with lights to examine the damage. They were already in their gear and I explained to them that the typical net was made up in sections about 15 by 20 feet in size, and those sections join to make the total defense, which is divided into three parts called the "main defense", "bow defense" and "stern defense". Most harbor nets omit the bow and stern defense and use only a main defense. We had to find out what system we were facing. If I restarted my engine to back away and a stern defense was there, it would wrap around our propeller and we would be captured by the coast defenses in the morning.

I sent the divers out through the conning tower and into the water.

"In coming from the Delaware, Sir."

"Read it to me, Radio."

"Maintain radio silence and return to us. It was sent to all boats in the survey parties, Sir." My mind was reeling. If we are ensnared and we can not free ourselves then we are captured, by the order to maintain radio silence, the Delaware has written us off as the 92 day makers. It seemed like hours but it was only minutes and the divers were back.

"It's a Bullivant net, sir. Attached to two long booms, we must be directly under the ship which has deployed it, Sir."

"Then they heard our messages to the Delaware. They know we are here and will be closing the booms and trapping us like rats. I picked up the speaking tube and screamed, "Start engines." Again, a portable only has one engine, but you get the picture of how frightened I was. "Full speed astern, load torpedo tubes."

"Sir, we don't have any torpedoes on board."

"Throw what ever trash, including the survey equipment, you can find to fill them and close inner doors and crank open the outer doors, I want the captain of that ship above us to hear the sound of the outer doors opening, they make a racket."

"Aye, aye, Sir. Are we going to dump our garbage on them if they don't surrender?" Everyone around me began to laugh. Sometimes a lot of pressure does funny things to men trapped in a tin can called a submarine.

"Edwards, remind me to put you in for a promotion to boat comedian, if we are alive tomorrow morning and standing on the deck of the Delaware." The USS Swordfish began to pull away from the torpedo boat net as the booms began to slowly close. I wished I was a diver and in the water to see what the closure rate was and how narrow our escape might be. "Navigator, put us on the bottom. The ball is in his court now. Will he drop charges on an unknown submarine? Will he radio for assistance? Let's see what he will do. Silence in the boat!"

We sat there, waiting. I whispered to my radioman, "Any sound of a message?" He shook his head no. An explosion rocked us and I screamed, "Fire all tubes!" I picked up my speaking tube and said, "Engine stop, switch to battery power."

"Aye, aye, Sir."

"Navigator, get us off the bottom and head for the last location of the Delaware, I assume that it has moved since we launched but I have no idea where it is now. We will start with its last known location and begin a search pattern. Let's hope that all that garbage will make the captain above us think we are hit and he will stop dropping charges."

"Aye, aye, Sir." We all watched the clock face inside our boat. We knew that the next explosion would be soon. The surface garbage would not contain seaman's bodies and an oil slick. It was two minutes and we felt the second explosion. It rocked us just slightly as we pulled out of the charge's circle of death. We had cheated death this time, I need to get out of these portable boats or I may not be as lucky next time.

Task Force Recalled
Norfolk, Virginia

The Department of the Navy did not want any more 'incidents' after they read my after action report and we were recalled to Norfolk for additional training. It was January, 1901 and the weather was terrible. Marisa was in the final stages of her pregnancy and she felt miserable. President McKinley had accepted my father's resignation as director of Naval Intelligence and he was grumpy. So there I sat, with terrible weather, miserable wife and a grumpy father in Seneca Hill, Pennsylvania, who still wanted to be involved in Navy Counter Intelligence. Life is never what you expect, I realized that I was the happiest in command of a submarine sitting on the bottom of the Chesapeake.

Never wish for something you are never fully ready for, your wish may be granted. I got a hand written message delivered to our housing unit in Norfolk. It was from my grandfather, General Schneider, in Washington. He had managed to get permission from my commanding officer to form a rapid response unit like he used in Cuba. This force would strike from the largest of the submarines now in service, the larger the better. Marines always carried plenty of equipment and supplies into battle with them.

Commandant Marine Corps
8ᵗʰ and I Streets
Washington, D. C.

Dear James,

I have been meaning to write to you about a project that I have been working on. After my great grand son, that soon to be baby of yours, is here and you feel you can leave Marisa and the baby for a few days, please report to my office. I have an assignment I think you will be perfect for.

I have been given the USS Starfish, a transport submarine stationed in Norfolk. It will be moved to the Washington Naval Yard. I need a captain that I can trust with the lives of my marines. I need the best, young submarine commander in the Navy. Your commanding officer said, that would be you. He thinks a lot of you, James, and so do I! You are the third

415

member in your family to serve in the Navy and that speaks highly of your desire to serve.

Love and respect as always,
Grandpa Schneider

Trip to 8th and I Streets
Washington, D. C.

I could not avoid it any longer, my commanding officer sent the USS Starfish to the Washington Naval Yard, with me as its captain. I was officially attached to the United States Marine Corps until further notice. The new class submarine was very large, it was designed for troop transport or hauling cargo of a highly classified nature. It had six torpedo tubes instead of the two bow tubes I was used to. I did have two of my old crew with me, however, and this made me feel a little more comfortable. Fisher was my chief engineer and Jamison was the head navigator. The Starfish had two engines, so I really could say stop all engines if I wanted to. We docked at the Navy Yard and I caught a cab into 8th and I. I found the office of the Commandant and waited to see my grandfather. When he came bursting into his outer office from the hallway, he nearly ran over me.

"Hello, James, nice to see you again. How is your mother?"

"My parents are both fine, thanks for asking." I had known my Grandfather Schneider all of my life, but I never understood him.

"Come into my office, I am in the process of cleaning it out for the newly appointed Commandant of the Marine Corps. I will move over to a desk in the Army Navy Building. God, how I hate sitting behind a desk!"

"I feel the same way, Sir."

"You must. You volunteered for one of the most dangerous assignments in the Navy. I respect that, James. Without danger, there is no fulfillment in military life. I learned that from your grandfather and later from your father."

"My father had a dangerous assignment?"

"Are you kidding me? You grew up with him. You must have known how he was passed over for promotion and ridiculed for his unusual and rare abilities."

"What unusual and rare abilities?"

"He has a photographic memory. He can remember things from different periods of time sequences and place them together and draw accurate conclusions. Based on these conclusions he can predict happenings in the near and distant future. He says it is a curse, I say it is a gift and this country should be making use of it, not letting him sit in northwestern Pennsylvania running a huge company like CI."

"I don't understand, Grandpa?" It was the first time, I had ever called him grandpa, it was always, Sir or Grandfather. He didn't seem like a grandpa until now.

"Your father, had the same abilities as his father. They were not blood related, but your father soaked up his father's habits and abilities over time. In fact, your father was a better officer than your grandfather, did you know that? He is the one who should have had five stars on his shoulder. Did you know he predicted the blowing up of the Maine before it happened?"

"No, how do you know this?"

"I listened to him when the families were together, James. He told us that Cuba was the powder keg that would ignite the conflict. He said we were so casual about our ships of war in Havana Harbor that it was only a matter of time before our EOD divers would discover mines attached to the hulls of our ships. He wrote this in several memos, here, I have them as part of the items that I am highlighting for the next Commandant to read." He handed them to me to read. He continued, "He was a thorn in the high command's side and he was ignored and shuffled aside, they even stopped the EOD teams from working and inspecting foreign harbors. They said it would not happen." I handed the memos back.

"What else did he predict?"

"The lack of mapping using his new techniques would not be implemented because of costs. What a stupid thing for this county to do! The French have more accurate maps of the Chesapeake than we do, for God's sake. This country needs to wake up and listen to the seers among us, your grandfather was a seer. I worked by his side most of my early years until he promoted me and sent me to work in the Army Navy Building as his aide. In fact, that was one of the reasons I called you to meet with me today. I found a rough draft of a hand written letter, or probably the notes, from which a letter would later be typed and sent to your grandfather. It is from Admiral Benjamin Hagood. During the Civil War, Ben was the supreme commander of the eastern office of naval operations, while your grandfather was the same thing for the western office. They sent several letters back and forth describing the major naval battles of the war. Your grandfather was with Admiral Farragut in the gulf and Mississippi. His friend, Ben, witnessed the battles on the east coast. The typed letter is probably in the Naval Institute if you want to look it up, but this hand written version, I want you to keep for your family."

March 10, 1862

Jason, Ben here:

On the same day that Johnston's retreat from Manassas was made known to us in the White House, a sea encounter occurred at Hampton Roads, off Fort Monroe. What I saw was the future of naval warfare as you predicted a year ago. I am referring to the combat of the Monitor and the Merrimac. As you predicted, American inventive genius has been at work at the Tredegar works in Richmond. The Merrimac was not completely constructed when it was rescued by its captors when Gosport Navy Yard was burned. The CSS Merrimac has been converted into an ironclad with a wedge shaped prow of cast iron which projects about two feet in front of this vessel. The original wooden sloping roof has been covered with two iron plates of armor, inside and beneath this are ten cannons.

The only iron clad available to us was John Ericsson's design that did not pass its sea trials, as you remember, it was defective in even moderate seas, but in light draft and nimbleness it would fair well against the clumsier Merrimac. It must stay in shallow waters of a harbor or river, however. It was being towed to Norfolk from New York because it was unseaworthy. I was on the USS Minnesota when I first saw it, like a "cheese-box on a raft". The Monitor presented only a thin edge of surface above and below the water line. An iron turret revolved in the center of the "cheese-box" from which two large guns might be rapidly trained and fired.

I had three frigates at anchor under the guns of Fort Monroe, and two others near Newport News. On Saturday, March 8th, this reconstructed Merrimac plowed suddenly toward us from the mouth of the James River. It was part of an armed convoy sent by the rebels to clear the harbor and break the blockade. From the Minnesota, I ordered the three frigates forward to engage the convoy. I signaled the two frigates at Newport News and the forts to begin shelling the convoy. They concentrated their fire on this strange looking craft before them; but to our amazement, the iron hail bounced from the sloping back of the "half-submerged crocodile", like rubber balls. There was little room for the Minnesota and her two escorts to maneuver in the shallow waters at low tide and all three ran aground. I ordered the Cumberland and Congress from Newport to engage the Merrimac. On came the monster, and crashed her iron prow into the Cumberland, which sank in forty-five minutes, carrying down officers and crew. The Cumberland's colors still floated at her masthead as the Merrimac, hovering about her, sent shot into the defenseless hull and those men in the water trying to save themselves. I have never witnessed such an utter defeat of an American vessel and the killing of unarmed sailors in my life. It enraged me, but I could do nothing, stuck on a sand bar.

Next, turning upon the Congress, which had made for shore, the Merrimac took up a raking position and riddled her with hot shot and shells, until after fearful carnage, that vessel burned until midnight, when her magazines exploded and blew her apart. The Merrimac could have finished off the three of us aground but she returned with her convoy to the Norfolk side and anchored under the guns of Confederate batteries until morning.

I can only imagine what consternation that day's news carried to Washington. This strange and terrible engine of war, impervious to our heaviest shot, what irreparable damage might it not inflict? Two of my three frigates were floated free at high tide, but the Minnesota stuck fast. I was asked to transfer my flag, but I refused, thinking, I can not abandon my men to the same fate as those of the Cumberland, I will not watch them be slaughtered, I will die with them.

My deliverance was providentially at hand, neither summoned nor sent for. By the light of the burning Congress, the puny little Monitor from New York was towed into Hampton Roads late that very evening. The captain of the Monitor, Lieutenant John Worden, came aboard the Minnesota, and asked me what I wanted him to do. I replied, "Sink that monster across the water at dawn." He left me and returned to his ship and took up station near the stranded Minnesota. On Sunday morning the Merrimac approached like a Goliath, sure of the prey, but the pygmy Monitor, like David, advanced to meet her. A single battle of three hours ensued. It began as a duel of the invulnerables and ended with no obvious impression made on either adversary. The Merrimac was twice the size of the Monitor and carried five times as many guns. Her great draft compelled her to maneuver in deeper water, while the Ericsson designed craft, drew only ten feet and it could run where it pleased and bring her guns to bear upon the iron target far broader than her own. The Merrimac began leaking and there was danger of penetrating the joints of her armor; she rushed in vain to sink the agile foe, having lost her iron prow the day before in the Cumberland. Unable to ram the Monitor, the Merrimac retreated back up the James River.

At the next high tide, the Minnesota was towed towards shore and I pray and hope that when the Merrimac returns after her repairs that Captain Worden can control her again. I need to

"The letter is not finished." I said to my grandpa.

"I know, that is what makes it so important to you. Your Grandfather Caldwell is gone, God rest his soul, I loved that man. You can not talk to him about it. But you can visit the Naval Institute the next time you are in Annapolis, or better yet, visit Admiral Hagood the next time you are in Savannah."

"Admiral Hagood is still alive? He must be how old?"

"He was the same age as your grandfather, they attended West Point together. They were born in 1817, that was 83 years ago. If you want to know about your family naval history, talk to him."

"I will. Thank you. What was the official reason that I was to report to you?"

"Ah, yes, I was born in 1835 and I will be 65 my next birthday, I do not remember things anymore, either. I do remember why I sent for you, though." He was smiling. "The Navy has asked me to retire on my next birthday and it is time to go and turn my chair over to the younger breed like you and your brother."

"My brother is at William and Mary, he wants to be a lawyer. Why do you think he would care anything about the military?"

"He has been writing to me. He knows that I went to Georgetown as an adult and he asked me what I thought of the law school there. I wrote back and told him that I finished my undergraduate degree and then applied to law school. I was not accepted, but if I had been, I would have graduated and finished my time in the Navy at the Judge Advocate General's Corps."

"Then the Marine Corps would not have its first two star general and one of the finest Commandants in recent history."

"Who told you that? I have butted heads with many people on my way into this office and I will be glad to be rid of it!"

"My Grandfather Caldwell told me there will never be another as good as you, Grandpa. I think, he doth protest too much."

"Ah, you know your Shakespeare. Have you heard this one? 'That one may smile, and smile, and be a villain.'"

"Hamlet?"

"Yes, but my favorite is: I love to look upon a woman when her eye beams with the radiant light of charity; I love to look upon a woman when her face glows with religion's pure and perfect grace: Oh, then to her the loveliness is given, which thrills the heart of man like dreams of heaven."

"That is lovely, I do not recognize it."

"Like I said, my memory plays tricks on me, but I think of your Marisa every time I do recall it."

"Why Marisa?"

"She loves you, like my Elizabeth loves me. We are very lucky to have them, James. I want to make one of my last assignments as Commandant of the Marine Corps a stepping stone for you. The rapid response unit of the Marine Corps is a fact and it will not disappear. The new Commandant will use your submarines to respond to things as far away as Haiti, for instance, in a matter of days, if not hours."

"That is the reason you called me here today?"

"Yes, Lieutenant Caldwell, I have a copy of your promotion here on my desk. I wanted to be the one to tell you the good news, Son."

"I had no idea I was being considered for LT-JG, Grandpa."

"You are not, starting today, you are a Lieutenant in the United States Navy, on assignment in the Rapid Response Unit of the Marine Corps. In two to four years, there will be an Atlantic submarine fleet stationed in

Norfolk and I expect you to be a Commander and in command of that fleet, James."

"You expect a lot, Grandpa."

"James, you and Louis understand what this country is facing. My own son, your Uncle Tom, hasn't a clue. He can not get over the fact that I was a warrior and helped keep this country free. He hates the military and wants nothing to do with it or me. I can not reach him, he has shut me out and lives his own life separate from mine and your grandmother's. That is his choice, but I will not give up on my two grandsons. Both of you are special to me and your grandmother, she loves you both very dearly. After I am retired and out of this puzzle palace, come and see us in our home in Georgetown, you and Marisa and that tiny great grand daughter, Star, are always welcome.